WE SHOULDN'T

To certify that the work
We Shouldn't
Was registered with UK Copyright Service on
16 May 2023
And that copyright is listed as belonging to
Holly Guy
It shall remain on record as evidence of copyright
Until the registration expiry date of
16 May 2028

CONTENTS

Content warning:
Dedication
Blurb
Chapter One
Chapter Two
Chapter Three
Chapter Four
Chapter Five
Chapter Six
Chapter Seven
Chapter Eight
Chapter Nine
Chapter Ten
Chapter Eleven
Chapter Twelve
Chapter Thirteen
Chapter Fourteen
Chapter Fifteen
Chapter Sixteen
Chapter Seventeen
Chapter Eighteen
Chapter Nineteen
Chapter Twenty
Chapter Twenty-One

Chapter Twenty-Two
Chapter Twenty-Three
Chapter Twenty-Four
Chapter Twenty-Five
Chapter Twenty-Six
Chapter Twenty- Seven
Chapter twenty- Eight
Chapter Twenty- Nine
Chapter Thirty
Chapter Thirty-One
Chapter Thirty-Two
Chapter Thirty-Three
Chapter Thirty-Four
Chapter Thirty-Five
Chapter Thirty-Six
Chapter Thirty-Seven
Chapter Thirty-Eight
Chapter Thirty-Nine
Chapter Forty
Chapter Forty-One
Chapter Forty-Two
Chapter Forty-Three
Chapter Forty-Four
Chapter Forty-Five
Chapter Forty-Six
Chapter Forty-Seven
Chapter Forty-Eight
Chapter Forty-Nine
Chapter Fifty
Chapter Fifty-One

Chapter Fifty-Two
Chapter Fifty-Three
Chapter Fifty-Four
Chapter Fifty-Five
Epilogue

CONTENT WARNING:

The female main character is a victim of domestic violence, and whilst I do not describe it in detail, it is heavily implied. The chapters where this is mentioned or even implied are:

Please read these with caution if this is something troubling to you. Books should make you feel engaged, not trauma.

Always remember to reach out to the appropriate resources if you're feeling heavily affected by the topics discussed in this book.

DEDICATION

To my university housemates who have suffered three long years with me. Thank you for eagerly and respectfully listening to the most fucked up sex scene planning over breakfast. Coffee and smut are the perfect way to start the day.

- ❖ Charlie Caldicott.
- ❖ Dylan Macdonald.
- ❖ Ebraima Jeng.
- ❖ Grace Smith
- ❖ And of course, my beloved: Ben Hounsfield.

BLURB

A dark, erotic reverse Harem romance novel.

Rebecca:

I just needed to be alone and write my new romance novel— two simple, achievable tasks— until my dad's hot best friend, Brandon, shows up in my life again. Promising to help me research for my new book, he introduces me to his sex club, but that's where I meet his two irresistible brothers: Dags and Vixen. I soon realise that Dags is an insane murderer and Vixen is my obsessive stalker and yet I can't help but spread my legs for them whenever they command it.

And then the pact is made: *play with each brother for a week, and by the end of it, I must decide which brother gets to fuck me first.*

Sounds simple enough on paper but a death sentence for sinful desires. *Must I really choose just one brother, or can I have them all?*

CHAPTER ONE

Vixen

She is so fucking beautiful it hurts.

The way her raven-coloured hair falls past her shoulders, to her hips, and sways whenever she moves her head to check on the dog that lays at her feet... My fingers itch to touch it— to *pull* it. I want to see how hard I need to yank on it before her lips fall open and release a breathy gasp. Her milky skin would look so pretty with the colourful bruises I want to paint onto her, too. Even the thought of my fingers touching her makes me groan. I want to see a small trail of blood smeared across her pale skin— across her cheeks too, painting a rosy blush. Blood will blend in with the tinge of her dark lips, I *know* it will. I want to draw it on her like lipstick and then lick it all off. I'm too far away to see her eyes normally, but I know their colour. Dark as sin. Just like mine. They shine back at me through the lens of my binoculars. She also has naturally long lashes that caress her cheek when she blinks *and* when she sleeps. Her eyes are my favourite part about her— *and that's a hard decision because she seems so fucking perfect.*

My morbid fascination with her started three weeks ago. She pulled up in that massive red truck, with a dog and cat in the boot, and barely any moving-in boxes. She built her house right in the middle of my running track. I watched the progression from bricks, to plaster, to painted walls— and now she is here. Who the fuck moves this far into the country? Who builds a house in the middle of nowhere? What is she hiding from? Or is it a *whom*? I want to know everything inside that pretty little head of hers. One day, I will get my answers, but for now, I'm content watching her every minute I have to spare.

Her house is really fucking weird too. *She* seems to be hiding from something, but with a single glance at her house, you'd think differently. A huge bungalow, nearly completely open plan, with *huge*— and I mean huge— windows that lead out into her garden. The windows stretch from ceiling to floor, wall to wall. I can see *everything*. Her kitchen, office, living room, *her bedroom— imagine my joy when I found that room out.*

I was intrigued by the housing plan beforehand, but when I first saw my little dove in her home, it was like an instant switch. I have what you'd call an addictive personality. My brothers mock me for it all the time— I'm a sweetheart and a romantic, but not in the stereotypical sense. I am an obsessive romantic. When I see something that I want, I go for it, and I *always* get it. And right now, I want her so fucking bad.

I shouldn't be here, hiding behind the tree in her garden, watching her through the windows. I shouldn't be stalking her as often as I do— hell, I shouldn't stalk her at all— especially in my line of work, but I can't sleep without seeing her face. She is like a cure for my insomnia. She calms me in a way I didn't think was possible; she puts all the stress of my job into a box and throws it out of the window— the same window that I constantly watch her through.

It's true: *I am fucking obsessed.*

I watch as she swirls on her chair which spins in circles. She's been like this, twirling around in her chair, placed in front of her laptop for about three hours now without a break; It's incredibly dull, yet I'm hooked. I can't remember the last time that I blinked. I must soak up every single thing she does. Every now and then she will lean forward to type something, before holding down the delete button and removing everything she's written. It makes me smile. *So indecisive.* I want to train that out of her. Soon enough she will learn not to doubt herself, and not to put so much pressure on her beautiful little brain. Her head falls back, and I can imagine her groaning in frustration. She dangles her arms over her face, and I can almost see the cogs turning in her head. After a beat, she suddenly pushes forward and starts typing again. The only difference now is that she has a confident look on her face. Her tongue sticks out of her lips as she concentrates. *I want to bite it.*

Expectantly, I stare down at the word document on my phone which is linked to her google drive. I fucking love the fact I can see everything she writes. I get the raw, unedited version of her thoughts —her stories. It takes a moment to appear but then I see it, her new novel in its beginning edits.

"Get on your knees." He demands with unwavering darkness in his eyes. I feel myself tremble when he brings his large hand to my head and pushes. Collapsing on the floor at his feet, I wait for my next instruction. I know that I'll get more instructions, so, I wait. He loves bossing me around. He wants me to be submissive and always waiting, and nothing turns me on more.

Slowly, he stalks around me, casting me bored looks every now and then; he even checks the watch on his wrist as if he could be anywhere else right now. Doing anything —or anyone— else. Then, he snarls as if I've offended him. "Pull your top down you dirty whore."

I almost jump at the opportunity to peel the clothes from my body. My fingers jump to the bottom of my tank top, but I'm suddenly stopped with a sharp thwack. My knuckles burn red as he pulls the long ruler away. Then, he slams it back down on my hand. This time, I can't help the hiss which falls from my lips.

"What was your instruction?" he barks. I almost stumble over my words as I try to please him.

"You told me to take my top off!"

Another thwack but this time it hits my bare arm. It stings and I cry out in shock. "Ow!"

My eyes fill with tears unwillingly. I want to push them away— I don't want to cry for him. Not yet anyways. That usually comes at the end of our session together. Today, I want to try and take as much pain and pleasure as he is willing to give me. Today, I'll be a good girl for him.

"You stupid whore!" He degrades me and it sends delicious shivers through my body. "I told you to pull it down. Do you know what the word 'pull' means? Huh? Do you? Probably not because you're so fucking thick! You dumb slut!"

My thighs press together as another flood of heat hits me. He knows exactly how to get me going.

"L-like this?" I whimper, pulling the material of my tank top down so that my breasts spring out of it. His eyes instantly soften. I want them to harden again.

"Good girl."

Fuck. My clit screams with desire as he praises me. Degradation and praise. It's the perfect mi—

My cock couldn't be harder as I read her words. She likes to be humiliated— *fuck*. That only makes me want her so much more. I wait for the next line, but it doesn't come. Pushing the binoculars back to my eyes, I wonder why she stopped writing.

My gaze immediately finds her as she rocks back in the chair, spreading her legs. The breath hitches in my throat. It feels as though time has slowed down; the cold wind doesn't bother me anymore. I'd freeze to death just to get another sight of her body.

I should look away— It's weird. But she never usually touches herself this blatantly. I often imagine her fingering herself in her bed, but the lights are off and my vision is limited. But here? Right now? Holy shit— you couldn't drag me away!

I've already crossed boundaries. I might as well continue. *Right?*

Her fingers toy with her nipples which spill over her tank top. Reaching forward slightly, she grabs the ruler on her desk. I watch in awe as she brings it up and then does something completely unexpected: *she spanks herself across her tits!* My cock jumps at the sight.

Her lips fall open and I curse the distance between us. *What I would do to hear that delicious sound.* She smacks herself against her perky nipples with the ruler before leaning forward and frantically typing at her laptop as if she'll forget the sensation and needs to quickly document it. I can't pull myself away from the sight to check what she's written.

Satisfied she has finished her sentence, she rocks back and runs the ruler between her breasts, before it falls, resting between her thighs. I am instantly jealous of the fucking thing. My dick twitches as she teases herself through the material of her leggings. Pulling her hand back, she smacks the ruler against her clit, sending a shockwave through her body which causes her mouth to fall open. The faintest noise ripples across the garden— her scream. I could have imagined it, but for the sake of my sanity— *or desperation* —I'll pretend that it's real.

She spanks her clit again, this time clenching her jaw as if not to let any noises leave her lips. Her nostrils flare with the pain; she continues connecting the ruler to her sex again, and again, and again. I've never moved so fast to fist my cock.

This is so wrong. I'm wanking over her as she causes herself pain, and I'm longing to be the one to make her cry out instead. I want her writhing below me, snot staining her upper lip, tears mingling with sweat. I want to lick up all the juices she gives me. *Cum. Tears. Snot. Blood.* Fuck— picking up the pace on my cock, I watch as she gives into temptation and slides her hand into her leggings. I can't see anything because of the fucking material but it doesn't matter. As she speeds up, her head falls backwards, and my breathing becomes heavy. She starts spanking her tits at the same time causing another cry to leave her lips— but I heard that one. I silently thank the open window as she spanks herself again, but it's too much, and she cries out in pleasure. I feel my orgasm approaching, hard and fast. I imagine fucking her— how tight her little cunt would be—how dirty she would be treated. How much she'd enjoy it. *I am a pleasure Dom after all.* I get off on her getting off... My orgasm creeps closer and closer and—

Suddenly, my phone rings, forcing a grunt to escape my throat as I reach for my phone rapidly before it can make another noise. *Shit!* Usually, it's completely off, but I must have forgotten when I saw how fucking fit she looked today. Declining the call does me no good as it vibrates again and again. I consider switching it off, but when I see the name, I know I must answer.

"There is a club I need you to visit." Brandon, my colleague, and my brother spits down the receiver as soon as the call connects. I release my cock and try to calm my erratic breathing as he continues. "It's just outside of Oxford. I want you to find three pimps for me. I'll text you the postcode."

"Right," I say through gritted teeth. Before I can say anything else, Brandon hangs up the call. As I take one last longing look at the beautiful girl through the windows, she bends over— panting breathlessly— as she comes down from her high. My cock twitches and the anger storms through me. *I missed it. I missed her orgasm. The first one I've had the pleasure of actually witnessing!*

With a growl, I buckle myself back up and fix my posture. I wish I knew her name; I wish I knew the woman who constantly causes my sleepless nights. It would be easy to find out— I am the researcher and stalker of my organisation after all. The best stalker in all of England— *fuck it, all the world—* and yet I don't want to find out. I want to hear her name on her lips when I am finally brave enough to make a move and ask.

I will be back tomorrow. I pray that tomorrow she touches herself again and I get to watch. But for now, there are some cunts in a nearby city who need to be found and dealt with.

CHAPTER TWO

Rebecca

The clock on the wall is going to be thrown across the room if it makes one more fucking ticking noise.

It's mocking me— I can tell. With each passing second, it taunts me that I haven't written anything new down on my word document. My brain is empty, no stories come to mind. *How do other authors make it look so easy?* I don't know how they can just sit down and pour their thoughts into a well-constructed novel when all I do is write the smut scenes first and then fill in the blanks later.

I guess that's why I'm so popular amongst romance readers. Everybody loves a bit of spice. I'm known as the queen of it. *Rebecca Jones- author of your darkest fantasies*—that's what they call me. And yet right now, I can't think of a single book idea to give the readers what they want. You'd think that after book nine, the stories would be flowing, but it's the opposite. I've already written about everything I want to read. What else could there be?

My phone flashes with another breaking news story, the same article that has been repeated for months. There is a serial killer on the loose. The police haven't been able to trace motives or any links to victims. I'm not following the story *that* closely; I hate horror stories because all they do is keep me awake at night, listening for any broken twigs outside, readying myself to be the next victim of a crazed serial killer. I drive myself sick with paranoia, so I try to avoid the news.

It doesn't help that I'm alone in this huge house, miles away from my closest neighbour. I could be attacked and killed, and nobody would know. Due to my mind constantly dwelling on this thought, I keep the breaking-news notifications on so that I stay up to date with the location of the kills.

I frown down at the story, as my eyes drag across the article; three more men have died inexplicably half an hour south of me. Police say that the murders were gruesome and bloody — the *work of an insane person*, they proclaim. I scoff. Well of course it would be. *What kind of normal person goes around smashing people to pieces?* Apparently, there seems to be no links between the victims yet. This makes the hairs on the back of my neck stand up. Rumours whisper the name: *The Dagger killer*. Finally, there is a name to the killings. But with no definitive profile of the victims of the Dagger Killer, nobody is safe. I switch my phone off before I can frighten myself any further.

A long whine from Fish, my golden cockapoo, drags my attention down to the curly mess at my feet. He nudges my leg with his nose before dropping the lead he had in his mouth on my foot.

"Not now, boy." I rub his head. The sound of his tail hitting the floor drowns out that god-awful ticking noise. "I need to write at least one chapter before we go for our walk."

He whines again. I shake my head. "Not now. I need to—"

He headbutts me in the leg again, much to my frustration. With a sigh, I march toward the huge patio doors that span the width of my house. I open the door and tap my foot up and down impatiently. Fish watches me like I'm crazy.

"Go on then. Go in the garden!"

Defiantly, he sits down. Since moving home, his behaviour has been inexplicably unlike him. He refuses to go to the toilet in the garden as if something has spooked him while being out there, and he feels unsafe. It's stupid— the garden is almost completely empty other than a couple of trees and bushes at the back. Perhaps a fox could hide in darkness, but I dug around to check any tracings of wild animals during our first week here. There were none. My conclusion is: my puppy is a scaredy cat. A sigh passes from my lips. "Okay fine, just a quick walk though. I really need to get this work done."

I lock the garden door behind me and as if Fish understands me, he goes wild, running around in circles. The idea of leaving the house always makes him crazy happy, and it brings a small smile to my lips. Then, on the other side of the room, *Shithead* saunters in. She struts in like she owns the place, one fluffy grey paw in front of the other. When her eyes meet mine, I stiffen. In all honesty, she terrifies me. She may be a small cat, but she packs a punch. I've learnt the hard way that if you breathe wrong around Shithead, she will attack you. Fish hides behind my feet. His head is low, and his tail is between his legs. His energy instantly depletes.

"Fuck you," I say to the cat before slowly picking up the dog lead. She stays by the exit door, smacking her tail challengingly against the wooden floor. I have a staring contest with her. "You need to move."

If she could talk, I'm pretty sure she would have called me a cunt. *She's just an asshole like that.*

"Shithead, move! Let us past." I creep closer to her, hoping that she will give us space to escape. She doesn't even blink. And I swear she smirked at our fear. I change tactics and head to her food bowl, grabbing a small piece of food before throwing it closer to her. It works. She leaps onto the food like it's a squirming mouse.

Fish bolts past me; *everyman for themselves*. I quickly follow him until I'm at a far enough distance that Shithead won't surprise attack me. I truly dislike that cat with every fibre of my being, but I also will never give up on her. My dad told me to leave her behind when I moved house— to rid me *and* Fish of that she-devil—but I couldn't do it. Those big sad eyes stared back at me, pleading with me not to give up on her—*that or she was daring me*. I have a theory that if I left her behind with my ex-boyfriend, she'd find a way to haunt me and continue making my life miserable. Besides, no living thing could ever tolerate living with my ex-boyfriend. Not even the she-demon cat herself. I reckon she'd find a way to escape, or worse, she'd wrap a rope around her fluffy little neck and jump off the cat tower. God knows I would have followed her if I stayed there one more day with him.

She's been with me for six miserable years and just won't *fucking* die. Even at thirteen years old, she struts around like a kitten. It's like she is taunting me with her existence. You'd think that with a dog, Fish would be the guard dog of the house, but no— it's Shithead. She flaunts her pride eagerly, not caring that Fish cowers in her presence— the roles are completely reversed between cat and dog.

"This way, Fish," I call out as I struggle to put my other shoe on. He leaps around and barks at me to hurry up. My body almost tips completely over as I struggle faster. "Not helpful!"

If anybody heard me talking to my dog and cat like this, they would think I'm insane. But I must talk to *somebody*, or I will go crazy. Fish is great company, though. He is happy about everything; he adores me. I am his queen and God. I can never do or say anything wrong to him. He never bothers me for book deadlines— bothers me for walks, sure—but the exercise is good for us both. It's my daily reminder to leave my desk.

I quickly shrug my coat on before snatching my keys and leaving my house, while Fish bolts out of the front door, down the path and turns left.

"No, this way!" I call out to him, trying to encourage him right. We've lived here three weeks now, and I haven't explored the path that leads into the forests, because Fish refuses to cross that boundary. No matter how many treats or cuddles I try to entice him with, he will not move an inch. And there is no way I'm going alone.

He stares at me unwaveringly and doesn't move.

"This way, Fish!" I smack my hand on my leg to signal him to come to me. He wags his tail excitedly at the attention but remains firmly glued to the floor. I sigh dramatically before sludging after him. When he realises that he's gotten his own way, he leaps up and sprints to the gate which leads us into the cornfield. I open it for him, and then he disappears. Every now and then I see his fluffy ears flop around as he jumps through the crops, trampling them. I should call him back. Somebody must harvest these. But I haven't seen a single person yet, and until I do, I'll let him continue mowing them down with his muddy little paws.

My phone rings and I answer it, to the shrill voice of my best friend, Sara. She screams into the receiver, and I flinch. "A little warning, thanks. I wouldn't be surprised if Fish heard you on the other side of the field."

"Sorry!" she squeaks. "I just have some fantastic news!"

I chuckle at her excitement. It's one of the many reasons why I adore her. Just like fish, she is always happy. I've known her since we were babies, and twenty-six years later, she is still just as excitable. Nothing can pull her mood down— it's something I love and loathe at the same time. Try telling sad news to someone who never stops smiling. "Go on. What's the *fantastic* news?"

"I got the job! You are talking to the newest member of Mworld!"

This time, I'm the one to squeal with happiness. "Oh, my goodness, Sara! That is amazing! Well done, I always knew you could do it!"

"I am thrilled, Becks! You can't even imagine! Everything is slowly falling into place! Soon, I will be the biggest and best marketer the world has ever seen."

I chuckle at her enthusiasm. "The world isn't ready for your abilities!"

I cast another look at Fish who hasn't slowed down racing around in the field. Every now and then, he will jump up to check that I'm still near him before he carries on his fun. "Speaking of, have you finished that article to promote my last book?"

"Oh shit—" she hisses. I can imagine her smacking her forehead in frustration. "—I completely forgot about that, Becks. Sorry! I'll do that as soon as I'm back at my desk."

I laugh loudly. "So much for the best marketer the world has ever seen when you forget to do the work people pay you for."

"Shove off!" she scoffs. "I have worked a lot of overtime recently. I deserve time off!"

Even though her words mean to be playful, I flinch. She has been doing damage control after my face was plastered all over social media, claiming some ridiculous rumour that I faked my abuse. I decided to pull out of the lawsuit after realising that I was never going to win over the jury. How could I convince them that Leo Rhineria—the hottest upcoming rockstar—beat me to a pulp? How could I convince them that I — a smutty author known for novels that sit dangerously on the edge of consent— didn't *enjoy* the abuse? I wouldn't have been able to.

But dropping the case has only unleashed a shit ton of backlash. According to rumours, I lied about the entire situation. Unfortunately for me, the truth is whatever they plaster online. Nobody bothers to actually research the case. My bruises, the lab reports, camera footage, the police statement— they are all available online. But nobody cares about that. All that matters is a controversial article that brings readers in. All at my expense.

"Ah, I'm sorry, Becks. I didn't mean to—"

"It's fine." I cut her off. "It's true, you have worked really hard lately. Thank you."

"I wish I could cut his dick off! That will teach him. The asshole is bathing in all the attention, you know. Just say the word and I will publish your side of the story to the media. Trust me, Becks. We can change the narrative!" She rambles on and even though she can't see me, I shake my head.

"It's fine, Sara. It's done now. It will all wash over soon enough."

"You could always follow through with court. You can get closure."

"You know I won't do that." a shiver takes hold of me at the thought of them scrutinising every word in each novel, reading out the dangerous and erotic scenes to a jury of disapproving and disgusted stares. They'd never understand.

Trying to distract myself, I call out for Fish and turn back toward the house. I cuddle further into my coat as the winter breeze floats towards me.

"I know, my love," Sara's voice is soft. "How is the new place going? I'll come down this weekend and we can have a proper catch-up."

"That'll be lovely." I release a sigh. Even though I love the seclusion here, it is incredibly lonely. My only companions are a dog who is currently bolting through some poor farmer's crops, and my asshole cat who likes to bully me. "I need some human interaction before I go insane."

"You're the one who decided to move an hour away from me!" she snorts. "I was very happy with my dream of living on the same road as my bestie. But no—you had to ruin that!"

"Shut up." I laugh. Fish races past me happily, leading the way, almost knocking me over as he goes. "I'm starting to regret it too. I haven't managed to write a single word of this new novel.

Where are you when I need you? Who else will force me to stay at my computer every day and work?"

She instantly switches into character. "Rebecca Emily Jones you better march your ass home and write that goddamn book, or so help me—"

"Ha!" I laugh at her weak attempt of being aggressive. "I think Shithead has a better chance of bullying me into writing than you do!"

Fish sits at the gate, wagging happily, and I let him through before closing the gate behind us.

"I just need to convince myself that—" I start but I'm cut off as something moves in the near distance. It was so fast, disappearing around the back of my house before I can fully set my eyes on it. I freeze. Fish notices it too, and he sprints back toward me, his tail between his legs. A long whine leaves his lips as he hides. *Fucking coward. Where's Shithead when you need her?*

I move my head to try and look around the back of my house, but I can't see anything. I try to calm my racing thoughts by pretending it was Shithead trying to frighten me, but I'm kidding myself. Shithead has small villages to terrorise rather than making me jump out of my skin whilst on a walk. And that *thing*— whatever it was—*was massive.*

"Convince yourself about what?" Sara's voice startles me. I creep closer to my house, keeping Fish at my side. My voice lowers to a whisper. "I think there is somebody in my garden."

"What?" Sara panics. "Who? Can you see them?"

"No. I just saw something rush past. Fish is acting funny too."

"Where are you now?"

Fish whines again and cuddles further into my leg. "I'm by the front door. What should I do?"

"Go inside and make sure everything is locked. You can see into the garden, can't you? Check if you can see anyone."

I quickly do as I'm told, racing to my bedroom. Moving the curtains slightly so anybody outside can't detect my movements, I frantically scan the garden for anything abnormal, but there is nothing there— just a large green space with a couple of small trees dotted around the large oak tree at the back. I wait to see any movement.

"Well? Do you see anything?"

Darting my eyes over the entire garden, I sigh when I see nothing. "No. There's nobody out there."

"You're probably just jumpy. I know I would be if I lived out there and alone! Especially with that Dagger killer just down the road!" Sara says quickly, the clear disapproval laced in her voice. She really didn't want me to make the move. She said it wasn't a good idea to isolate myself so quickly after the incident with Leo. I ignored her, of course. I wanted space— *needed* it.

"You're probably right," I whisper, but the uneasy feeling of being watched doesn't go. I don't tell her that though. I don't need to give her any more reasons to worry about me. "I will be fine, and I really need to go and write that chapter. I will call you if I see anything else. Deal?"

"Okay, darling. I'll swing by on Saturday. Give me a call if you need anything, kay?"

"Wait, Saturday?" I squeak. "I can't do Saturday. Dad's making me go to his for dinner."

"Awe, that's nice!"

"Well, no it's not." I bite back the anger. "He can't just pretend like noth—sorry, I won't go off on a rant about him. You've heard it enough times."

"At least he's trying?" She tries to offer me more positivity, but it doesn't work. I shout from the tallest rooftop that it's not fine. He did the worst possible thing that any man could do—he cheated on my dying mother. He had moved on before she even took her dying last breaths. How can I be near a man who did that? But I don't want to rant to Sara again. She's heard it all before and will only keep offering positive comments until I crack and pretend that she's right. I might as well skip the middleman. I sigh. "What about Monday?"

"Monday works!" she chirps merrily. "See you then. Byeee!"

After we finish saying our goodbyes and hanging up the phone, I take another look into my garden. I almost expect someone to jump out from behind the oak tree. I wait for the Dagger Killer to show up, screaming *'surprise'*, but nothing happens.

With a shaky breath, I force it out of my mind. I don't have time to procrastinate, and I definitely don't have time to scare myself. I need to write that bloody chapter and stay away from horrifying news articles.

CHAPTER THREE

Vixen

There is an art to torture, you see. It's nothing like the movies; It's not always pulling fingernails off and teeth right from their mouths— though these are *very* fucking effective methods. Physical pain gets results quickly but some of the cunts that I'm after don't deserve a quick punishment. If you ask Dagger, the killer amongst my brothers, he will thoroughly disagree with me. He is the messenger of death. He gets a hard-on for physical torture— but that cunt is fucking insane.

Me? I want to string the torture out for as long as I can hold out. It can be small things like a leaky tap that deprives them of sleep at night, misplacing things in their home to make them feel as though they are losing their mind or making them believe that everyone around them is out to get them. My favourite is throwing stones around to get them nervous and jittery; they make stupid mistakes when they're nervous. The mind is a wonderful thing, but it can also be your worst enemy. These people lose their minds before Dagger's knife kisses their skin.

Our *victims* — if you can even call the wankers that— are bad people, *very* bad people. They're human traffickers; these scum force vulnerable people into unspeakable situations. They use and abuse them, before eventually discarding them into a ditch when they get a new order of actual victims in. Most commonly, it's sex work. This comes in many different forms, which is something not many people are aware of. It's not always snatching someone from a street and selling them to the highest bidder, though this is sometimes the case. It is older men grooming young girls, making them feel special and loved, before pushing these vulnerable women into the sex industry. *Porn. Only fans. Stripping. Prostitution.*

In the worst circumstances, the abused woman doesn't realise that she's being trafficked. It's what the evil cunts rely on. *Who can she turn to if she doesn't believe anything bad is happening to her? How can she get help when she is completely oblivious to the need for it?* She doesn't and she can't. And this is exactly where my brothers and I step in.

I am not a murderer, unlike Dagger. I simply give karma a polite shove in the right direction. I drive them insane. They lose their humanity before they physically die. I am not *killing* anything— or anything that matters, at least— I am scrubbing a stain from the earth. And I am *very* fucking good at it.

Currently, I'm sitting in a purple booth opposite an old, fat man, with a cigar in his mouth. A young girl— no more than eighteen— clumsily dances on him. Her ribs and skinny bones pierce through her thin skin which is totally on display. She only wears a small skirt to cover her modesty, but from experience, I know that it will be removed very quickly.

Every now and then, her skittish gaze shoots over to the other man on the sofa— *her pimp.* His arms are stretched wide, and there is a glossy look in his eyes. He is off his fucking nut on drugs. He is supposed to make sure she stays relatively safe— or at least, that is what he tells her. In reality, he is here to make sure she does a good enough job to keep robbing the client of his money. *And* to ensure she doesn't run away if she is ever brave enough to try it.

With a small nod, he silently tells her she is doing a good job. She smiles at the acceptance while continuing to dance, running her bony fingers up the fat man's chest. He's old enough to be her grandfather. *It's fucking disgusting.* The old man surprises her as he roughly grips her hips, his chubby fingers digging into her skin, and her eyes bulge from her head as she looks back at her pimp.

"No touching," she says, but she's nervous and unsure. It always begins like this. The pimps promise the young girls it's just a meeting with an older man. Then it's just *one* dance which turns into a dance with no clothes. And then, the older men show their true colours— their perverse colours. The cycle repeats with each girl the pimp lures into these situations. Every time, the pimp chips at the young girl's boundaries until there is nothing left. She trusts her pimp— because why wouldn't she? *He* hasn't hit her, *he* hasn't raped her, *he* is here to save her from whatever vulnerable miserable life he '*saved*' — or should I say stole — her from. The best tool in this industry is indoctrination.

Her pimp dismisses her with a wave of his hand. She starts to tremble in fear but doesn't protest anymore. She keeps her eyes low, and I can almost hear her frightened thoughts racing around.

My teeth grind together, and my knuckles turn white. I count the seconds down in my head to stop myself from attacking and saving her. It's not my job—I am merely the stalker, the observer. I gather information for my brothers: Brandon (the brains) and Dagger (the brawns). Despite my large build and towering height, I am very fucking good at disappearing into the shadows. I am one with the night.

This week alone, I have brought the downfall of three pimps, saving over two dozen girls. I can tell that this man is very much aware of the downfall of his peers. His eyes constantly scan the surroundings, looking for me. He might not know who my brothers and I are by name or face, but he senses us. We are stripping his illegal organisation apart one fucker at a time. And he knows that he is next. It is why he is hopped up on drugs. He knows it will be painful— he's seen the way my brother leaves the bodies. Disembowelled, eyelids cut off so they're constantly awake and mutilated in ways I try not to imagine. Dagger is very fucking creative when it comes to these bastards. Not that I can blame him.

I check my watch for the third time in thirty seconds, knowing that in three minutes, the CCTV will cut out so I can sneak out of the building without anyone spotting me.

The old client grabs the young girl's ass violently. She hisses, but he doesn't let go.

"P-please," she whispers, still unsure of whether she has an option. "I don't like that—"

"Keep going," her pimp growls as his head limply falls back toward her, and he glares. It's a wicked look, one that would frighten anyone. She jumps in her skin, confusion spreading across her face. Then, her bottom lip starts to wobble. She slowly realises her mistake by coming here, but it's too late, the old man's hands are yanking her closer to him. She squirms, but he is far stronger. Not to mention there are two men against her.

This time, I act. *I can't bear to see her like this anymore.*

I quickly disappear behind the booth and into the toilets. In each sink, I shove multiple, balled-up toilet roll sheets down the plug hole before turning the taps on full blast. Hurrying out of the building through a small window, I hide in the alleyway, and yet again, I'm disguised by the shadows. I'm not *supposed* to act now—I should report back to Brandon, he'll come quickly and sort them out. I'm only supposed to find the information and report back, but I can't leave a helpless girl in a fucked-up situation like that. It's not right.

After a minute, I hear the squeals from inside, followed by a whole group of people charging out, running awkwardly as they try to shake the toilet water off their shoes. I count the women I see, and to my surprise, it's almost a full house under the pimp I'm stalking. They each cling to their half-naked bodies, freezing in the cold night. They dare not huddle together; the girls are torn apart from each other to keep them from understanding their combined plight. There are four or five perverse clients here too. Most of them are still buckling their pants back up. It makes me sick.

I check the time again. I have twenty-eight seconds left before the CCTV goes and I can leave.

A noise from behind me makes me leap for my knife. Within the shadows, my eyes zero in on a large figure stalking me. I smell the stench of whisky before I see him properly. I release a shaky breath. *Dagger*.

"Brother, what are you doing here?" I hiss, quickly turning my attention back to the crowd to check no-one can hear us. "*Leave!*"

"You came to have all the fun without me?" Even from within the shadows, I can see his wide grin. "You're not the only one who knows how to stalk. I found you pretty quickly."

I roll my eyes even though he can't see it. "Don't do anything stupid. I'm just here to follow."

"No fucking way. Brandon let me come!"

"Brandon wants him dead already?" I eye him up suspiciously.

Only Brandon gets to sign off on who dies and when. I hear the way Dagger holds his breath and tries to convince me that he's telling the truth— but I don't believe him. I need this pimp alive for a little longer. I *need* to see where they all head next.

When Brandon and I set up this organisation ten years back, we created strict job roles. I am to stalk and research our targets, Brandon is to rehome and shelter the victims in his club. Dagger joined us two years later. We saved him from pimps. Unfortunately, he is a loose fucking canon— we don't know the full story of his craziness, but it's not hard to guess the torture he went through whilst growing up in the same organisation we seek to destroy. His mum was one of the whores, and it wouldn't surprise me if he was hurt too. *Really badly fucking hurt.* You don't lose your fucking mind over nothing, and Dagger is as insane as they come. Red mist controls him, and he is constantly dangling by a thread. But he is fucking good at what he does — a liability, sure — but he is still my brother. Not biological— but duty binds us three together, as good as brothers. If anything, it's better. Throughout life, you learn pretty quickly that blood doesn't mean shit; family is who you choose it to be, and that loyalty prevails above all else.

"Scouts honour," he whispers for good measure, and I bite back a groan. There is no way Brandon permitted him to be here with me, but it's too late now. The crazy fucker is leering over, checking out the pimp, with a face like thunder. Then, he reaches back for his signature red-handled dagger with silver snakes engraved into the blade. I hear the way it wooshes as he spins it around in his fingers.

My eyes zero in on the pimp I've been stalking as he stumbles around the women, doing a headcount. He's nervous— I can tell in his skittish glances and jagged movements that he knows what's coming. He senses the monsters closing in.

Nervously, I check on Dagger who's lost in his own world, mumbling incoherent words under his breath. I wait to see if he recognises the pimp— it's his own personal mission within our organisation. He wants justice. He *needs* it. And he won't rest until every last pimp and fucker that hurt him and his family are dead, but he has the same usual crazed look in his eyes. It's a safe bet that, yet again, we haven't found the ringleader of the illegal sex work organisation, even after eight treacherous years of searching endlessly.

"Hush!" The pimp roars over the squeals and grumbles of the crowd around him. "Let me think! R-right, okay." He releases a shaky deep breath. "I'll get us some taxis— we will go to the other club. It'll be fine."

Much to Dagger's frustration, we wait patiently for the taxis to arrive. He wants to attack immediately, and I'm only just about able to reign in him with a hand against his chest. He shakes as if he's on vibrate mode, and low snarls start to fall out of his lips. The girls climb in first, followed by the pervert clients — they will all die later, but I'm not worried about them right now. My gaze lingers on the pimp attempting to enter the next taxi. Then, I look back to Dagger, drooling like a starved beast. My teeth sink into my lower lip. *Perhaps Brandon did send him here to kill the pimp? He permitted the other three deaths this week...*

Before the pimp can escape into the taxi, I scoop a pebble out of my pocket and chuck it at him. It smacks him in the back with a thud. Staggering forward, he almost buckles under the surprise attack, and Dagger seems to find humour in the situation. "Good shot."

I hold my hand up to silence him. The pimp twists and looks right at us in the shadows, completely oblivious to our presence. For weeks, I've been torturing him with stones. Every hour on the hour, I throw one in his direction. In the beginning, he would run away like the easily frightened bastard he is, his tail between his legs. *But now, he is pissed.* He is mad at being made a fool of, especially in front of three taxis worth of women and clients. I'm counting on this foolish rage to pull him close to me— to Dagger.

It works.

His ego and anger force him out of the taxi. He slams the door before patting the roof. "Drive on. I'll catch up."

Sure, you will.

Jutting his chin up and puffing out his chest, he marches toward us in the shadows. I can feel Dagger trembling with excitement. His heavy breaths give our position away, and the pimp's eyes home in on us. Keeping my hand firmly pressed into Dagger's chest, I hold him still until the last taxi pulls away. Then— and only then— do I release the monster.

CHAPTER FOUR

Brandon

My chest feels tight as I watch the CCTV monitors. The club is fucking packed tonight, dragging in every kinky person from miles around. They all gather to watch and participate in consensual and steamy sex acts. I hover my mouse over the camera which shows the stream of customers entering my premises. The hourly show is always a hit, bringing in regulars which I recognise and even newcomers who look skittish— as if they don't understand what it is they are about to witness.

I check my watch and then my phone to ensure the timing is right. Vixen was supposed to meet me here and take over the monitoring twenty minutes ago, but there has been no sign of him — or Dagger for that matter. *This* is what really unnerves me.

Just as I'm about to click the phone icon on my phone, it starts ringing. With a frown, I stare down at the unknown number. *Should I answer it? Who could it be?* Everybody I need to talk to has a contact already saved on my phone. Going against any reason that roams in my mind — and there are quite a few— I answer.

"Brandon?" A familiar voice rings through the receiver. I stiffen.

"Brandon? I know that you're there." My old best friend, Thomas, tries again, and it feels as though my heart is in my throat. I go to hang up the call, but he sounds desperate.

"Brandon, please answer me."

"What do you want?"

"Oh, my God!" He gasps. "It's really you! Brandon—oh, God! You're here! You're really here!"

"How did you get my number, Thomas?"

"I, er—" He is completely taken aback by my harsh tone, and I blink back the guilt. "I just— well, "

"Spit it out, Thomas."

"Join me for dinner this weekend." He says quickly. "Please. I don't know what happened between us all those years ago. But please. I miss you. And I *really* need to tell you something."

"What do you need to tell me?"

He sounds stressed, the way we linger in silence for a few seconds before he answers, only confirms it. "I'll only tell you in person!"

I bite back a hiss that is dying to escape. Thomas and I grew up together, and we were practically inseparable, like twins. Then, in the space of a week, everything changed. His wife died. I found Dagger. We both had huge life events, and I cut contact with him. Not to mention the fact I almost kissed his fucking teenage daughter. I swallow down the lump in my throat that has resurfaced. "No, Thomas."

But now he has located my new number— *the crafty bastard.*

"Please!" I flinch as he screams down the receiver. "Please, Brandon! I have some really exciting news! I want you to come for dinner. I need to tell you and Rebecca. I want to tell you both at the same time."

"What?" I almost choke when he mentions his daughter.

My ears prick up at the sound of his guilty tone. It's as if whatever he has to say is equal to an illegal activity that he has played a part in. "She's going to get mad at me when I tell her, so

I need back up."

"I will *not* protect you from your daughter!"

"Please— you're my best friend! You were like an uncle to her; she will listen to reason if you're there." He panics. *Like an uncle to her.* I feel sick.

"No." I grind out. As I'm about to hang up, I hear him speak frantically. "I know where you work and I'm not beyond coming to your job every day until you agree!"

I freeze. "How? How do you know?"

"I saw your face in Homebase, and I followed you back. You own the sex club near Southampton." He responds sheepishly. I bite back a hiss. *Curse buying ropes and duct tape for Dagger.*

"Please, Brandon. I need you, man. You're like a brother to me— whatever happened between us, we can fix it. I need you back, mate. Please. I want you back in my life." It hurts my heart to hear him beg. I cut him off cold so we would never have to do this again. Now I think about it, I should have started an argument with him, given him a reason to hate me. If he hated me, he wouldn't be searching for me after all these years. I unwillingly think about Vixen and Dagger— my new brothers, after Thomas. If one of them went missing, I don't think I'd ever give up searching for them, to make sure they are safe and happy. *Fuck,* I do it every day with Dagger— constantly checking on him. *Can I really blame Thomas for doing the same thing?*

"What do you say, Brandon?" His pleading voice breaks me. *Curse my soft heart.* "Fine. One hour."

I reason that I will start a fight with him and make him hate me during that hour. It's the only option that will force him to leave me behind— for good this time.

He roars with excitement. "Amazing, thank you so much! I really appreciate this, best mate. It's the same place I used to live at. Saturday, 7 pm. Got it?"

I hang up without answering. My heart feels like it's pounding one hundred miles an hour. I feel sick. *Why the fuck did I agree to that?*

There needs to be a distance between me and Thomas. I can't have anyone see me near him. What if one day my brothers and I are caught in our crimes? I can't risk Thomas being dragged down with us. I know he'd say stupid shit to try and defend me, even if that means incriminating himself too; that's what brothers do. My dear Thomas was too loyal— stupidly and blindly loyal.

And I wanted to kiss his eighteen-year-old daughter every fucking time I saw her. I have never had that intense feeling of lust before in my life, and I could barely control it around her. She knew the effect she had on me too. I *knew* she liked me back— short skirts, pouty lips, pushed-up breasts. *She* even tried to initiate an intimate moment between us one time, but I pushed her away and scolded her like a child. No matter how much I fucking wanted her, how *okay* it was— she was of age, and clearly consenting— I couldn't do it to Thomas. My best mate, my loyal brother. It was a huge part in why I had to cut myself off from them.

Fine— that was eight years ago. Things have changed. I was strong enough to walk away, something the cunts we're after aren't capable of. As far as I'm concerned, I beat my temptation, but it still makes me nauseous to think about seeing her again. She'll be twenty-six, much more mature, and hopefully ugly. I pray that she has a bad attitude and stinks. I pray that I am not tempted by her anymore. It would make my guilt much better. I hope that she tries to fight me too and sway her dad to hate me.

Suddenly, my phone rings again, forcing the bitter thoughts to a halt. *It's Vixen.* My heart leaps from my chest as I answer.

"It's Dagger," he cries out, horrified. "Fuck— Brandon— he's lost it *again*! Get down here— now!"

CHAPTER FIVE

Dagger

He's in front of me— the cunt is in front of me— I can almost taste his blood: the bitter metallic juice that I long to gulp down. I can almost hear his screams. Wait— *will he scream for me? Will he cry? Will he beg? Oh fuck,* it makes me hard in anticipation. My fists pulse around the dagger and I spin it around in my fingers one more time. It's a nervous tic I have before I attack. If I play with the weapon, it calms me down for a moment. It distracts the howling, ravenous beast inside. Vixen's hand is still firmly on my chest, a weak attempt to hold me back, but it does the job for now. I vibrate around it, and now pace between each foot. If I lunge forward, I could gut the pimp in one swipe. *Oh my god, I want it so fucking bad.*

Please let me go. Please let me go. Please let me go. I've never begged harder in my life.

Now that the last taxi pulls away with a squeak of the tires, Vixen releases me, "Go get them, boy."

Fuck yes!

Everything snaps and red completely takes over. My lips, as usual, are forced into a wide grin until it fucking hurts— not the painful sort of feeling, but the kind that hurts so damn good. The craziness within me escapes, and the monster howls. My fists lash out the way I've been dreaming of for *years*— or, at least, for minutes since laying eyes on the pimp. Clearly taking him by surprise, he snaps into a ball, protecting his head and vital organs. My fingers snake under his shitty guard, and I grab him by the material, fisting him into the air.

Come on, big guy. Fight back!

My fists pummel him over and over until it throbs. He's weaker than a sack of potatoes in my grip. *How fucking disappointing.*

"Come on!" I throw him to the ground and put space between us. "Get up! Get the fuck up and fight like a man!"

He cowers away and the complete lack of fight makes me fucking seethe. Driving my foot into his stomach, he cries out in agony, the noise like a sweet melody to my ears. Another punch, a knee to the ribs, a forceful throw of my head into his, causes my sight to become hazy and makes my wicked smile grow wider. The manic cackle in my head grows louder and louder— *too fucking loud*. It completely drowns out that weird ringing noise that lets me count time in my mind. I lose track of the minutes pretty fucking fast.

"F-Fight!" I shriek.

"Please let me go!" The pimp finally screams. I drive my knuckles into his nose, and a satisfying snap rings through the night; he finally begs—*I fucking love it when they beg!*

"Dagger don't play with your food," I hear Vixen's disapproving voice in the back of my head, but I'm having far too much fun with my pretty little prey.

"Fight back, Pimp!"

I stiffen when I realise that he's not even attempting to defend himself. *Why not? Does he think he's better than me? Is he purposely trying to mug me off? I am not a fucking bully— he needs to fight back. Fucking fight! Fight!*

It's all a blur as I beat his face into a pulp. Tears sting my eyes, and they swell in tune to the throbbing of my head. I feel like I'm blacking in and out of consciousness. Strange animalistic noises leave my lips. My heart beats one hundred miles an hour, and I think I might be sick. Flashes of memories burn my brain. *Five-year-old me. Twenty-year-old mum. Men— lots of fucking men.*

"Fucking fight!" The roar that leaves my throat doesn't even sound like me now.

Is this the man who hurt me? Maybe this was one of the cunts who killed my mum? Who ripped us apart until we had nothing left. Who stole fucking everything from us. Yes, it has to be! He has brown hair. No one else has brown hair, right? Sure— this must be him! It has to be! Eight years waiting, finally it's here— I'll fucking kill him!

My fist connects with his head repeatedly. A squelching noise jolts me slightly from my haze, followed by a gooey substance clinging to my fingers.

Then, I feel a hard hand on my shoulder. "Dagger! Dagger!" Vixen's faint voice penetrates past my ears. "Dagger! Stop— stop, mate. He's dead! We have to go. *Dagger*! Dagger, please!"

It sounds so far away but I don't stop. *Can't* stop. Hearing the faint wail of sirens doesn't deter me one bit either. My dagger joins the play and I slice the man's tender body until the blood squirts up my face, the bitter taste spurring me on. Everything happens so fast. One minute, I'm having the best time of my life; the next, I'm suddenly being dragged away. I flail my limbs around aggressively, striking out at anybody who comes near me.

"Get the fuck off!" I roar. "G-get the fuck off! Fight back pimp! *Fight*! Stop pretending to be dead! You worthless sack of shit!"

A blurry figure appears in front of my face, and I frantically blink back the tears— wherever the fuck they came from—and I see my older brother. His large, worried eyes stare intently at me. I now feel his hands cupping my face, and he holds me still. My long hair sticks to my sweaty face, and I'm now aware of how fucking hot I am. My mouth is dry, and I feel like I haven't had water in years.

"B-Brandon?" I squint at him. His lips are pulled into a straight line, and he scowls at me. I try to reach out to touch his face. I need to make sure it's him. It could be my mind playing tricks on me. It happens. Quite a bit. Too much nowadays— *the hallucinations just don't fucking stop.*

It's not him. It can't be. It's another pimp. They're out to hurt me again!

"It's me, Dags. It's okay. Calm down." Brandon's voice reassures me, before nodding at someone behind me. Suddenly, my arms are released from behind my back. I have no clue when they were snatched from me— everything is so hazy. So blurry. My fingers snap around Brandon's shirt, and I pull myself into him. I just need his touch— his embrace. My older brother. My saviour. The man who saved me from those men all those years ago.

"Fuck, Brandon." My throat hurts when I talk. "Fuck, man. Fuck!"

I feel his hand in my hair. "It's okay, Dags, deep breaths."

"Fucking hell, Dagger." Vixen releases a sharp hiss. I turn to look at whatever he's staring at, but I instantly regret it. The man on the floor— *if you can even call him that*— is completely unrecognisable. He is a puddle of guts and gore and mess, a sight that makes my entire body shake. *When the fuck did I try to hang him with his intestines? When did I slash his heart out? When did I cut his eyeballs out and place them in his mouth?*

"W-what?"

"It's okay." Brandon, as usual, takes control and pulls me away from the scene. The confusion haunts me. "Was that me?"

"Yes, mate, yes it was." His disapproving tone shows, but he's not disappointed in *me*. Brandon always looks out for me; he is never upset with my actions, no matter how much I test him. It's why I love him like no other— both of them, for that matter. They know my mind just doesn't *work*. It doesn't function like other people. Yet they haven't cast me away. They have been patient and tried so hard to get me to help: therapists, doctors, medication— *everything*. Tirelessly, they search for a cure for insanity, but sadly, nothing has worked. I've concluded that I am simply broken and there is no cure. Brandon refuses to accept my conclusion. Vixen never *truly* believed in a solution to begin with.

"I'm sorry, Br-Brandon." A sob makes me choke. When I wipe the snot dribbling under my nose, I smear the blood and shit across my face. The smell should make me gag, but I really like the warm sensation. It takes everything within me not to lick it away—it would only set me off again.

"You shouldn't have killed him." Brandon's lips press tightly together, and Vixen's head snaps in my direction. I begin to sweat. *Oh shit. Why did you have to go and say that, Brandon? Why couldn't you keep it a secret?*

"Dagger! You said you had permission!" Vixen cries out. His eyebrows shoot together, and the stress lines leap out at me. I long to push them back into place. Anything to make him look less— well, *pissed off*. Brandon grabs his head as if he has a migraine forming. "I said he could *join* you. I never said he could kill."

Sniffling up the tears, and offering my brothers an award-winning smile, I try to worm my way out of trouble. "I didn't lie to you though."

"No, but you *bullshitted* me, Dagger! You knew I would have interpreted that as—"

Police sirens wail louder.

"It doesn't matter now!" Brandon snaps as he casts another look at the barely recognisable body on the floor. I keep my gaze away from it. "No amount of cleaning will get rid of those stains. Leave the body behind. Let that be a message to the pimps in the area."

I swallow down the guilt, or at least, I'm pretending it's guilt. In reality, I want to give the body one last punch. *What's one more assault to the utter destruction?*

CHAPTER SIX

Rebecca

I can't shake the feeling that somebody's watching me since that *thing* flashed past me in the garden. But every time I look, there is nobody there. *It's so fucking strange.*

Fish is asleep, under my desk, cuddled away at my feet. His soft snores tickle my toes, but I don't pull away from him. This is the only way that he is comfortable, and I will give it to him. I turn my attention back to my screen— I have finished writing the first sex scene for this book. It only took a couple of red marks and stinging on my own body to get the scene perfect. It's a shame I have no definite characters or plot, that will come with time. *I hope.*

I turn my gaze out of the window, marvelling at how clear the sky is tonight. The stars are littered around the moon — the *earth's freckles*, as I call them. The wind beats at the trees, stealing their leaves away. I can hear the faint howls through my window and I'm thankful for being snuggled up in the warmth. I now realise my mistake of having a blanket wrapped around my body, it's far too hot in here. I always have the thermostat turned right the way up. It's counterproductive because I usually keep at least one window open. I like the fresh air, and a cold breeze to mix in with my sauna-like home.

My gaze wanders to the huge oak tree. All the leaves are gone, and the branches are spindly; it's surprising that the branches are still surviving in that awful wind. The enormous trunk keeps the tree sturdy. I wonder how long it has been there? I heard a rumour that you can count the lines inside a tree and that's how many years old it is, but I don't want to cut it down to find out. I just want to know. What stories does that tree have? Was there anybody here before me? Will there be people after me or will this house be knocked down, because after all, what crazy person would spend money to buy this place and be hopelessly lonely?

Suddenly, my eyes dart to the small area beside the tree as something moves with the wind. Casting only a dim light on it, the moon disguises the thing from me as quickly as it appeared. It's dark, but there is *definitely* something there. *I can feel it.* I freeze, waiting for it to move again, and my heart rate picks up in my chest. Never taking my eyes away from it, I slowly reach for the phone on my desk. I might not be able to call for help in time, but it could deter an attacker.

Something stalks around the tree. It blends into the black of night and could be mistaken for a shadow. Sensing my fear, Fish shoots up. I hush him back down, but he begins whining unhappily. He jumps up and scratches to be picked up, *to understand why I'm so frozen.* I take my eye off the shadow for a second to push Fish off, but it's gone— the creature has *disappeared.*

Suddenly alert, I jump to my feet, waiting for any other movement, but nothing comes. I hold my breath and I count down from three, plucking up the courage to call the police and potentially alert the threat to attack quicker before I can do such a devastating thing.

And then, I see it: *Shithead*, stalking around the tree. She wanders back toward the house, with that arrogant little strut, completely unfazed. I take a shaky breath as my heart rate starts to slow back down. Wide-eyed, I watch as she slips back in through the cat flap in the door which is left to this room. I hear her meow as she announces her arrival. *That little cat will be the death of me.*

Before I have the chance to calm down again, my phone rings, and I startle. After a couple of shaky breaths, I will myself stop being so on edge. *He's not here, Rebecca. Leo is not here. You don't need to be afraid.*

"Rebecca?" My dad's voice fills the receiver. I hadn't even realised I answered the call.

"Dad?"

"Hello, my dear. How are you?"

I eye up my garden suspiciously. "I'm good... why are you calling so late?"

Stumbling over his words as if I've accused him of something awful, he tries to get his words out faster. "O-oh, sorry, I'm just calling to let you know about a slight change in plans for Saturday."

I hold my breath and wait for him to cancel. It always happens. I'm actually surprised he's doing it with time in advance. Usually, it's ten minutes before the arranged plan.

"Do you remember Brandon? Brandon Powel?"

I stiffen when he mentions *that* name. "What about him?"

"Well, he'll be joining us for dinner."

"What?" I stop what I'm doing and pay attention to my dad. This is the man who broke his heart—literally and metaphorically. What kind of best friend leaves the country suddenly, when your wife dies? If Sara did that to me, I don't think I would ever be able to look at her again. Hell— she would be dead to me! So, why is he invited to dinner?

"Dad, I don't know about this. You were so hurt by him and—"

"Everybody makes mistakes, Rebecca!" He scolds me like I'm a child, and not twenty-six years old. "It doesn't matter about all that. He's back now, and hopefully for good!"

My heart rate quickens. *Brandon Powel* AKA the first person I

ever had a crush on. The first person I almost kissed too...
"Where is he staying? I mean, where does he live? I thought he sold his house when he disappeared—"

"Not sure, didn't ask him. I'll offer him to stay at mine."

I grind my teeth together, "Right."

"So, is that okay? I didn't have much chance to get your permission but if you don't want him there if you want just us, then I can always unin—"

"It's fine," I squeak a little too quickly.

How am I going to look the man in the eyes after what I tried to do all those years ago? For so long, I blamed myself for him leaving my dad— I mean, his best mate's daughter tried *so* hard to seduce him! Short shorts, flimsy tops, careless looks, not to mention the intentional, flirty smiles. And then when he gave me a lift home from a party, and I drunkenly leant over and tried to kiss him— and he *rejected* me! *How humiliating!* All that time I thought he was interested. I saw his longing glances... But no. I was wrong. I was naïve and immature. How could I really think my dad's best mate was interested in me? Hell— he is twenty years older than me! *Oh, what I would do to go back in time and slap eighteen-year-old me.*

"Okay, that's sorted. I get to have dinner with three people who are very important to me! My daughter, best friend and Cheryl!" My dad's excitement does not rub off on me. If anything, it makes my stomach twist more. I flinch when he mentions his girlfriend's name— my mum's immediate replacement all those years ago. Something I've never forgiven either of them for.

"I'm tired. I'll see you Saturday." I suddenly blurt out before hanging up the phone. I catch my reflection in the window, and my bright pink cheeks shine back at me. I pretend it's because I'm angry at the mention of Cheryl, but it has nothing to do with her, and everything to do with Brandon.

Why am I so humiliated? It happened eight years ago; he surely wouldn't even remember it. *Right?* I mean, he is agreeing to dinner with my dad *and* me. Surely, he is over it by now? *Fuck!*

I slam my curtains shut before sliding into bed; I pull the covers to my chin, but despite the warm cocoon of blankets, I am still trembling. Anticipation rocks through me. *What will I say to him? How should I act with him?*

This is ridiculous— for fuck sake! *I am Rebecca Jones, smut queen, and here I am, quaking over a potential kiss that happened years ago.* Yes, I have definitely lost it. I need to get laid. I reach for my phone and pull up tinder. What feels like hours go by, and after having swiped left on nearly all of them, I sigh and throw my phone down.

Nobody is as handsome as I remember Brandon being. I am simply not interested in anyone that isn't him.

I guess it's just me and my hand again tonight.

CHAPTER SEVEN

Rebecca

My heart is in my mouth as I knock on my dad's door. I have made a real effort to look good. Not for my dad, not for Cheryl, but for Brandon. I know my dad is going to hate the way I'm dressed up but the thought of that only encourages me more to go through with it fully. Anything to get a reaction out of him. I want him to be uncomfortable. Fuck knows he's made me uncomfortable throughout the years.

My tight, low-cut dress that reveals my breasts and stops at my thigh makes me look as if I'm on my way out to the club. It's scarlet coloured, my smokey eyes and red lipstick matching it perfectly. I smile brighter.

It is Cheryl who opens the door to greet me. Her bright smile falters when she sees my outfit, but she doesn't say anything. Instead, she pulls me in for a hug. Her vanilla smell tickles my nostrils. It is far too strong, and I almost gag. Her wiry hair covers my face, but I push past the urge to blow it away. She is wearing all white—but it's mismatched and looks odd.

"Hi, sweetie," she says, and I cringe at the name. Cheryl has never done anything wrong to me, she makes my dad happy and has always been pleasant. But I dislike her here in this house, in my mum's house. It's been years, and yet I still haven't gotten over the feeling that she is trying to replace my mum. Nobody will replace her— I won't allow it. She will always live on in my heart.

"Rebecca!" I hear my dad's voice and I pull back from Cheryl. He stares at my outfit before clasping his hands together happily. "You look beautiful! Like you've just stepped out of a movie premier!"

I suddenly feel ridiculous. That is *not* the reaction that I wanted. I now feel like a child playing dress up in heels and too much makeup. He embraces me, before gently leading me through the house by my arm. The décor is still outdated with browny-orange walls with pale trimmings, and every now and then there is a huge, misplaced piece of furniture that takes up way too much room. My heels sink into the dark carpet, and I struggle to keep myself upright.

"Were you filming content today?" my dad asks, attempting to make polite conversation. "I've seen some of those tiktoks you do to promote your work!"

My blush is dark and profuse. I start to shake my head but I'm winded when my eyes fall on the gorgeous man sitting at the dinner table— *Brandon Powel.* He is even more handsome than I remember, with his dark stubble kissing sharp cheekbones. His tanned skin perfectly matches the light brown hair and those almost orange-coloured eyes which now stare at me intensely. He has full, round lips that curve into a smile when he sees me. "Rebecca!"

My name on his lips makes me stiffen. He rises from the table, oozing confidence, before coming over to me, pulling me against his body — and even though he's probably already embraced my father and Cheryl, this feels different— far more sensual rather than polite. He smells of cigarettes and whisky but in the most delicious way. I almost feel drunk as I sniff him again before realising how weird it must come across. I go to move away, but those large arms trap me in an embrace, so I lift my hands and pretend to hug him back. Only then is he satisfied, and he lets me go. When I pull back, we are still too close, and with his ridiculous height, I must tip my head back to even make eye contact; it's only now I remember how much he towers over me.

I am far from short for a woman— being 5"7— but he towers over me. Even his build is huge— his muscles bulge out of that tight-fitting shirt and his tie sits on stony abs— or at least that's what I'm assuming is under there. He smirks and it's only then I realise I am silently eyeing up this man in front of everyone.

Startled, I put space between us and flash him my best smile to look normal.

"Hello," my voice is small and comes out more like a squeak. I mentally kick myself. The first humiliating thing of the night —*one of many I assume.*

"Would you like a drink?" Cheryl pulls me out of my trance, and I shake my head. "I can't. I'm driving."

"You can have one surely!"

"No, I really shouldn't—" I wave my hands around. Brandon gently pushes them down. "Nonsense. I'll pay for your cab home. Drink with us."

I stare down at our connecting bodies and blush wildly. *Why is he suggesting such a thing? What is his game? Why is he being so nice?* I can't even bring the words to my lips so instead I nod.

"Brilliant!" Cheryl clasps her hands together excitedly. "I'll get you a glass." she starts to leave the room before stopping. "Oh, Thomas, could you help me bring the plates in?"

My dad smiles lovingly at her. It makes me feel sick. "Of course, I can."

As soon as they both leave, I feel a ridiculous wave of nervousness. I turn my attention back to Brandon, and to my surprise, he is already looking at me. Though, now, he no longer wears that smile on his lips he had in front of the others. His eyes rake up and down my body. He looks starved. I long to cover myself with my arms to hide under his scrutinising stare.

"Rebecca. You look—" He begins. The hairs on my body shoot up under his gaze. "—*older*."

I stiffen and force my body not to respond to his words— the oh so delicious words pouring from his mouth— the same words laced with nothing but pure need. And his voice is *so* fucking velvety. I long for him to say my name again. I will definitely be touching myself to him tonight. *No—fuck sake, Rebecca— get your mind out of the gutter! That's your dad's best mate!*

He walks away from me and holds the chair out, gesturing for me to take a seat. I don't miss the way he's placed me next to him at the table, and I feel sick with nerves. He arches an eyebrow, and it kicks me back into reality. I quickly skitter to the chair before taking a seat. He moves me closer to the table with a ridiculous amount of ease. Then, he pats my shoulder before taking his own seat. His touch on my bare skin has me slamming my thighs together. I feel like a teenager again, drooling over him.

I scold myself again. *Get it together. Your twenty-six acting like you've never touched a man before!*

As discreetly as possible, I watch him out of the corner of my eye. He reaches for his glass and presses it to his lips. The whisky slips into his mouth but one drop escapes and drips down his full lip but his tongue darts out and he catches the drop. The movement is so erotic, but I have no idea why. When he turns to look at me, I almost melt. I pinch myself under the table to ground myself— It doesn't work. I want to throw myself at him. I want him to ravish me in so many different ways. The things I would do to that man if he gave me a chance. *What the fuck is wrong with me?*

He smirks as if he can hear my thoughts and my cheeks burn red, forcing me to tear my gaze away. Thankfully, my dad reappears, balancing a load of plates.

"Do you need any help?" I ask, mainly looking for a way to escape Brandon's hot gaze.

He chuckles and shakes his head. "Don't be silly. You're my guest!"

I almost slump in the chair as my dad waves me off. Cheryl returns with my glass of whisky, and I quickly gulp it down, realising the only way I'm going to get through this dinner is by getting very drunk.

CHAPTER EIGHT

Brandon

The last time I saw Rebecca she was eighteen. She has always been a fucking stunner, but now, at twenty-six, she is the definition of my wet dream. She has filled out her curves and has so much more confidence than that anxious little teenager she used to be. I haven't seen her for eight years. I thought that my addiction to her would have lessened over the years, but I was wrong. If anything, like a virus, it has grown— and I'm only just realising it. Before I arrived, I promised myself to keep my distance and keep my conversation to a minimum. Get in and get out. But how the fuck can I leave her when she looks like this? *Holy fucking shit—*

Now, she drains the whisky like its water. I make her nervous. She seems skittish around me; her eyes don't stay still, and she trembles ever so slightly. I want to reach out and touch her naked thigh where her dress has pulled up. It takes everything in me not to comfort her, and it takes even more, to stop me from making her even more nervous. I enjoy seeing her like this: squirming around— hot, bothered and hopefully turned on.

Fuck.

Now it's me who blushes as I readjust myself in my seat. I clear my throat to distract my wandering thoughts.

"So, what are you up to nowadays?" I ask her.

She stiffens before looking at me slowly. Her tongue darts out and she wets her lips before she responds. "I am an author."

"Really? What's your genre?"

Opposite us, Thomas and Cheryl are completely lost in conversation as they take their place at the table. I almost want them to fuck off so I can have my full attention plastered on the beautiful woman opposite me.

"Romance." Her voice is a whisper as she answers.

I jolt. "What kind?"

She clears her throat as if I've caught her off guard, her head turning to look at her father, almost as a silent plea for help. But sensing that he isn't going to answer for her, she shrugs off an answer. "A bit of everything."

"Don't be shy!" Thomas laughs, reminding me that he is here too. "Rebecca gets nervous talking about her genre in front of me, though I know exactly the kind of books she writes! The number of articles with quotes that I must avoid!" he chuckles. "Go on, Becs. Tell him!"

Thomas being Thomas, is completely oblivious to the dagger she sends him— the kind of look that could gut him. My stomach twists deliciously, and I almost long for her anger to turn on me instead. I just need to get her a little drunker and then that famous temper will escape. I will fight with her *and* Thomas, and then Thomas has his reason to never bother me again.

"I write erotica." she finally confesses, closely watching me for a reaction. Thank fuck she's watching my face— because my cock has just hardened. With all my might, I try to play a poker face. I want to end the conversation. This is fucking weird. I shouldn't be talking to her about this—especially when my cock is as hard as stone.

"She's writing her tenth novel now!" Thomas fills me in on the details. "Aren't you, Becks? How is it going?"

"Dad!" She squeals, her cheeks darkening with heat. Her dad is completely oblivious to her trying to kill the conversation. "Don't be shy. Tell him. Tell us about your new book!"

She hesitates, before sighing and giving in to her father's persistence. "Well, I'm struggling to start this new novel. I'm under a bit of pressure from my publisher, and it is just making my creativity die."

Want me to kill them? I itch to say.

"Ah, that sucks!" Thomas replies. *He is trying too hard.* Everybody can tell. He is desperately trying to involve himself in her life, trying to find something to talk to her about. The relationship is strained. He is trying to butter her up. I stay quiet and wait for whatever big reveal he is planning tonight.

"How weird is this, though? My daughter writes smut, and my best friend owns a sex club!" Thomas chortles. I startle— *not that kind of big reveal.*

Anyone else would find this conversation weird but not Thomas. He has always been very open about sexuality, just like me and my brothers— we take a very naturalistic viewpoint on it. Everybody has sex, most enjoy it— it's just like eating or breathing, sometimes comes even more naturally than those; Thomas doesn't make the exception of talking about it as if it's a walk in the park. Out of the corner of my eye, Rebecca's eyes pop out of her head. "You own a sex club?"

She's not disgusted or confused, it's more like an accusation as if she's asking me: *why didn't I know about this?*

"I own three," I offer slowly. She looks genuinely taken aback.

"What? Where? Not that I want to go, of course!" She squeaks, before staring at her dad awkwardly. He beams brighter, not bothered at all by the conversation. *I feel sick.*

"Nearest one is in Southampton."

I don't reveal the other place, very aware that Thomas is

listening. I don't need him tracking me down. He'll already know Southampton's place after stalking me there. Rebecca is still stunned, and I like that I've shocked her. I open my mouth to say something else, but suddenly, I'm silenced by the wail of a phone alarm. It startles everyone but Rebecca flinches wildly and throws her hands over her head. Her eyes slam shut, and her face contorts. She is in fucking agony— it's like her mind is screaming louder than the alarm. Her teeth grit together, and a hiss leaves her lips, causing my heart to pump wildly in my chest. It is only the typical iPhone melody. *Why is she reacting so badly? What the fuck is going on in her head? Why won't the fucking noise stop—*

"The beef is ready!" Cheryl smiles sheepishly before switching the alarm on her phone off.

"I'll give you a hand," Thomas says quickly, rising to his feet. He stares at his daughter nervously, darting his gaze around. "A- are you okay?"

"Yes!" She spits before he can finish the question. Her eyes are open now, but they are dark as if they're hiding in the shadows and trying to blend in with the blackness of her irises. *She's furious and has no problem showing it.*

"We will get the food," Cheryl looks incredibly guilty. Thomas bobs his head and escapes after her, like a puppy between its mother's legs. I hear him scolding her for the alarm, and I try to strain to hear more information, but it's useless. The noise disappears before I get any useful information. I feel her staring at me. *Tell me, little minx, why are you frightened of a phone alarm?*

"That club—" She distracts herself. "Where abouts is it in Southampton?"

"Depends," I hesitate. "Will you come?"

She visibly responds as if I've asked her to *cum* instead of *coming* to the club. It makes everything inside of me tense and twist, and that familiar ache makes my cock bob.

I am torn in two. I want her to say no— she needs to stay away from there— *away from me*. If she knows what is good for her, she'll go running for the hills after this encounter, but I desperately want her to say yes. I want to take her down there and introduce her to each of the rooms and teach her exactly what I've wanted to do to her after all these years. *Fuck the wasted time away.* Judging from her hungry eyes, and lip pulled between her teeth, I reckon she'd fucking love the club. My plan to anger her and never see them again slowly disappears as my cock does all the thinking.

"I'm looking for inspiration for my upcoming novel," she says in a low voice. I sink my teeth into my tongue.

"What's it called?" She arches a thinly plucked eyebrow.

I swallow down the gulp, "Spins."

"Spins," she repeats before pondering on a thought. "Which days do you work?"

The fuck?

"So, I don't show up when you're there— of course!" She squeaks quickly, mortified by how her statement could have been taken. "I just want to look around."

"You won't like it there," I lie quickly my heart racing erratically. *No, there is no fucking way she could go there.* I would follow her around like a lost puppy, or worse, Vixen or Dagger would catch sight of her. I mean look at the little minx—she is everything and more. They'd fuck her over and over until she couldn't stand straight, and no fucking way will I let someone else touch her. She's *not* mine— yet the word is on the end of my tongue.

She frowns. "How do you know?"

Fuck, Rebecca. Just accept my refusal.

"I just want to have a look around. Nothing weird—" She

presses before fumbling into silence. Then, her wide eyes meet mine. "—you could show me around? Again, nothing weird or whatever. I am very interested in those kinds of places. Maybe I could write a bestseller on your place? Who knows, just think about the publicity!"

My heart lurches itself out of my chest. "We don't need publicity."

She deflates and humiliation fills her. "You're right. Sorry, that was weird of me to ask."

"Yes." I jolt when the word falls from my lips.

She frowns at me and steals all the power away from me. "Yes, or no? Which is it?"

I almost choke on the air in my lungs. A metallic taste in my mouth draws my attention to my freshly bitten tongue. I don't know why I suddenly give in— call it being an obsessive horny cunt— but something changes. "Yes, I will give you a tour. Three rooms, that's it. Only the watching rooms."

"Watching rooms?"

"Yeah, where you watch others participate rather than joining in." I force the lump down in my throat. Images of her and me playing in the rooms spring to mind. Attempting to clear the images from my mind, I clear my throat. It doesn't fucking help.

"Amazing!" she squeals excitedly, clasping her hands together; she looks genuinely thrilled. I have to push myself further into the table to hide my straining cock.

"Just to let you know it's not a typical sex club. It's for the more... unusual kinks." I say nervously, waiting for some type of repulsed reaction. In the back of my mind, I hope this scares her off, I hope that she changes her mind, because being around her for however long it's been already is taking a rather large toll on my sanity—my ability to keep my hands off her is wearing rather thin to say the least...

Instead, it's the complete opposite. Her lip twitches into a smile. "Even better!"

Even better. Holy shit. Marry me right now.

"This new character is so difficult. I want her to have weird— well, you know— kinks, I guess. I need something that stands out to the reader, something that makes them remember my book." She gets lost in her thoughts as if she's the only one listening to her rambling. I am addicted to the way her face screws up and relaxes as she ponders longingly.

"Here we go," Cheryl's high pitch voice rings through the room as she starts serving up the food in the middle of the table. Thomas helps her, and before long, the table is packed with different types of food. My stomach growls appreciatively.

Thomas' eyes squint when he smiles, "Tuck in! There better not be any leftovers. My fiancée makes a mean roast dinner!"

"Fiancée?" Rebecca stiffens completely and my mouth drops open as I stare at my best mate and Cheryl.

"Ah, crap." Thomas chokes on his breath. "That is why I brought you both here today. Me and Cheryl—" He takes her hand lovingly in his and exchanges a warm look, "—we're getting married. I want you both there."

Out of the corner of my eye, I notice how stunned Rebecca is by this whole ordeal. She's deadly silent as her teeth angrily grind together, her knuckles turning white as she grips the glass, and I can almost hear her furious thoughts. Perversely, I enjoy the anger in her eyes.

"Don't be like that, sweetie. P-please say something." Thomas panics slightly, looking at me for help. I shake my head. I didn't think he'd fucking marry Cheryl! Then again it *has* been eight years— it's been a long time coming. But it's brave marrying the woman he had an affair with...

"Rebecca—" Cheryl starts to talk, but Rebecca cuts her off fiercely.

"Congratulations." The word is strained and ingenuine, to the point it probably would've been better off is she didn't say anything. She ticks angrily. I hide the smile on my lips in my drink of whisky.

"We can talk about this after dinner, my love," Thomas says slowly. Rebecca stares at him, blinded with rage, not even taking a single second to blink. He reaches for the Yorkshire puddings and puts some on his plate. With a nod to Cheryl, he silently reassures her. I feel bad for Cheryl; she looks devastated by the reaction. But then again, it was always going to happen like this. *What did she think was going to happen? That Rebecca would welcome her with open arms?*

"Would you like some beef?" Cheryl's voice is almost a whisper as she raises the plate to Rebecca who ignores her, turning her nose up at it as if repulsed by the beef and not the entire mess we're currently sitting in.

Again, I must hide the smile. The last time I saw Rebecca, she was a vegetarian. She would scream the roof down if meat even touched her plate. I remember her and her dad having a screaming match after he accidentally put chicken near her vegetables. She was a sensitive soul— rebellious and emotional. I don't blame her though. Losing your mother at a young age is difficult, especially if the situation is anything like this one. I unwillingly think back to Dagger and how he turned out without a mother, the man he's become is nothing how his mother would have raised him—that's a guarantee.

"No," Rebecca says firmly.

Thomas ignorantly deflates. "Don't be like that, Becks. We've been cooking it all day."

"I don't eat meat." Her lip curls when she responds. Thomas stiffens as he remembers, and then he smacks his hand on his head. Cheryl bristles. I have a hard time pitying them. Even I remembered that weird little fact about Rebecca. Her face is red. "Don't mind me, it's only been ten years since I last ate meat."

I sink my teeth into my lower lip. She sure still has that teenage rage even eight years later.

"Okay, Becks. It was a mistake!" Thomas says quickly. She is fast with her response. "Just like the marriage will be."

"Becks!" Thomas is seething now. "Get over yourself! You're being *so* rude!"

"Forgive me, father." She throws her hands together in a fake prayer. I jolt at the fire within my little minx's voice. The sarcasm drips through her.

"Drop the attitude!"

"No—"

"Rebecca, I mean it!" Thomas scolds, but it's an empty threat. His ears are bright red, and his jaw ticks angrily. I help myself to the food on the table, trying to distract myself from the brewing family drama, but, beside me, Rebecca doesn't even flinch. "Or what?"

"Rebecca!"

"It's okay dear—" Cheryl tries to defuse the situation. It's no use. That vein in Thomas' head has popped out, and he is trying to challenge the most stubborn woman I've ever met. Neither of them will back down. Rebecca's fingers tighten around her cutlery. For a moment, it's as if she is going to throw the knife at her father and *stepmother*. *Ew*— the word feels weird even to me.

"No! She will not talk to us like that." Thomas shakes his head and waves his hands around theatrically. Pretending to still be busy, I slowly cut up the food on my plate and dig in.

"*She?*" Rebecca scoffs. "You mean your daughter. Your only child— your only reminder of mum."

Dinner and a show— lucky me.

Thomas's face turns bright red. "I will not tolerate this amount of disrespect in my home!"

"Fine," she throws herself to her feet and a panic pulls through me. If she leaves, she will cut our encounter short. I don't know why the thought frightens me so much.

"Let's all take a breath," I say quickly. "Rebecca, sit down. Your father is right, you were rude—" *and it was fucking hot,* "—It is their house. This all came from nothing."

"Easy for you to say— *outsider*." When she spits that final word, it makes some primal ripple through me. I visibly jolt but not out of offence. I long to bend her over my knee and spank her until she is red in the face, apologising profusely for disobeying me— *for answering back*. Fuck I want to hurt her most deliciously. She might even plead for more punishment, and even the slightest though of her like that forces me to readjust myself in the chair to hide my bulging erection.

"Rebecca!" Thomas slams his hands on the table as he shoots to his feet. "I raised you better than this!"

"No, mum did," her forceful words make the room immediately uncomfortable. "But everyone seems to forget about that, don't they? Who bought this kitchen table? Who owned half of this fucking house? Mum! And yet we don't talk about her. We can't even say her name. Can we? Go on dad, say her name. Say, Emma Jones. *Yell it*— perhaps she will hear us from the dead! Invite her to your wedding, why don't you?"

She shakes with adrenaline and I long to wrap her up in my arms. Actually, that's bullshit. I long to throw more fumes on the fire. I almost want to push her to her absolute worst. Make her fuck up royally— I want her to turn on me, hit me, scream at me—*fuck*. I want to make her explode so I can punish her after. It's fucked up. But I don't care. I want what I want. I crave that anger to be turned on me. It would be so easy to cause an argument now that tensions are high.

"Out!" Thomas roars, and this time I stand up. I do the complete opposite of my original plan as the desperation sinks in. I wave my hands around. "I think everybody needs to calm down!"

Thomas explodes, "she is being a bitch!"

My eyes darken. "Don't say that, Thomas. Don't *ever* call her that." I don't give two fucking shits if that's his daughter. He will *never* disrespect what is mine, even if *he* doesn't know that she's mine. Even if *she* doesn't know that she's mine— *yet*. Because, after tonight, I've realised that is exactly what she fucking is. *Mine*.

He softens and drops his head low as he realises his slip up. I watch as Rebecca pushes the chair out from behind her and storms off. Nobody makes any move to go after her, so I do.

"She's had four whiskeys. She can't drive." I excuse myself hurriedly before racing to the front door. She has moved incredibly quickly and is already yanking at her car handle. The weather is fucking torrential, and as soon as I step outside, I'm soaked.

"Rebecca!" I yell after her. "Rebecca! *Stop!*"

She startles when she sees me. "What the fuck are you doing? Go back inside."

My stomach twists when she swears at me. One day I'll punish her for that. Not today though. I can't scare my little minx away yet.

"You've been drinking." I point out, stepping between her and her car, and her eyes widen as if she already knows my next move, "Get out of the way!"

"No." I cross my arms. "You're mad at your dad, fine, but come back inside and let me order you a cab."

"I can drive!"

"I won't let you— not in this state."

She pushes her finger into my chest and visibly jolts when she feels my abs underneath. Just as quickly as her amazement appeared, it disappears, and she plasters a displeased look on her face. "You're not my dad, fuck sake! You can't tell me what to do."

This time, my hand shoots out and I grip her arm. It's tight enough to show her I am serious, but not bad enough to cause any bruises. I bring my head down closer to her face. "You will not swear at me."

My words do something to her; she shivers and holy fuck I could ravish her right here, right now. She tries to look confident, but I don't miss the way her bottom lip wobbles. "*Move.*"

It's a weak attempt and I almost laugh in her face. "No."

"*Please*— just move!" When she is polite, it makes my jaw harden. Our conversation hasn't been longer than a couple of minutes, and she is already responding well to me. She's already learning her place— and oh, fuck does that mean she's going to be a fantastic sub. I smirk. *Wait.* I'm wrong. She won't be submissive; she is a brat. *My Rebecca is definitely a fucking brat.*

"No," I stand my ground. "Get back inside now. If you still want to leave in ten minutes, I will call a cab."

"It will be expensive. Let me drive."

"I am paying, Rebecca," I growl. "Inside— now!"

She stares at me defiantly for a few moments, before throwing her shoulder into my chest as she stomps past. It only hurts her, and she whimpers. Checking if I heard her, she casts a quick glance over her shoulder. I wink at her, only furthering her rage. But at least now she is inside.

Sheepishly, she heads back into the kitchen, and I follow her. She is drenched. Anybody else who has hair clinging to either side of their face, and makeup that is starting to run, would look fucking awful. But she looks like sin incarnate. Her mascara leaks a little under her eyes and I force myself not to groan. I can picture her on her knees, deep-throating my cock— gagging and spluttering as tears stream down her face. I want to ruin my pretty little thing. And that dress— fuck—with the rainwater, it's turning see-through. I can see the outline of her belly button, but there are a couple *of* really damp spots. She must still have that belly piercing she used to show off all the time as a teenager. There is a small panty line but it's thin—too thin. Almost like she is only wearing a tiny thong.

"I am sorry, Cheryl. That was rude of me." She apologises, and it takes the whole room by surprise. "This is your house now. I must accept that."

"Oh, darling," Cheryl springs to her feet and pulls Rebecca in for a hug. The Adam's apple in my throat bobs when Rebecca turns around. She has confirmed my suspicions that she is only wearing a thong.

"Please stay with us. I haven't even served dessert yet," Cheryl begs. Rebecca pulls away slowly before casting a guilty look at Thomas, but he's already smiling lovingly at her. He has always been a forgiving man. But I guess having a rebellious childlike means you must have the patience of a saint. She doesn't need to say anything to him— he understands her apology. It's his turn to make amends. "I spoke out of turn back there. If I demand respect, I must give out respect. I am sorry, Rebecca."

"It's okay, dad." She whispers before taking her spot back at the table. I go to sit next to her, but Thomas' hand shoots out.

"Thank you." He mouths. I stiffen under his touch. Then, I nod my head slowly and pull away. I can't verbally accept the gratitude. I didn't do it for him. I did it for my own selfish desires. I need her near me so I can assess how ready she is for me. I slot in beside Rebecca before gulping down the remainder of my whisky.

"So, is your cat still terrorising you?" Thomas creates conversation, and Rebecca snorts. "Every waking moment of the day."

"Oh, I heard about this!" Cheryl joins in. "What is his name?"

"*Her* name is Shithead."

I look at her to see if she's lying, but she just smiles happily. I frown. "You named your cat Shithead?"

"If you met her, you'd understand."

"*Fish*—" she turns to me and clarifies the name, "*my dog*, won't even go near her. Actually, he's been really weird since the move." She frowns in her dad's direction. "He won't go in the garden. I have to walk him twice a day at minimum."

"What's wrong with the garden?" He arches an eyebrow. She hesitates and casts her gaze around the room as she purses her lips tightly and shrugs. I hold my breath and wait for her reply.

"Anyway, dad, how is your job going? Last time we spoke, you said you were up for a promotion?" She swings the conversation around to Thomas, and soon the whole table is lost in the chatter. It feels like a quick conversation change and I long to press further, but she is clearly uncomfortable with the discussion.

Ten minutes past, followed by another hour of happy laughs and lots of drinking. Cheryl serves the cheesecake, and it doesn't take long until it's gone. For a bizarre moment, I find myself enjoying dinner. It feels like we are a part of one big happy family as we chatter about unimportant events.

We are onto our second bottle of whisky, and now that everyone is pleasantly drunk, I can openly gawp at Rebecca. She has dried off from the rain, but now her hair is frizzy. I want to stroke the loose tendrils down. Her eyes flutter open and shut and a lazy smile kisses her lips. Every time I looked at her, she was topping up her glass. She sways a bit and falls into me. A delicious giggle slips from her lips as she corrects herself. "Whoops! Sorry!"

My cock jumps and again my delusions run wild. *Did she do that on purpose?*

"It's getting late." Thomas wipes a tear away from where he was laughing so hard. I zoned out of the conversation, so I don't know what was said. But I plaster a fake smile on my face and pretend to chuckle along.

"I think I'm going to go to bed," he says, raising to his feet. He stumbles, chuckles, and stumbles again. Cheryl rolls her eyes playfully and helps him. "I think I'll go to bed too." she turns her gaze to me. "Spare room is down the hall on the left. Help yourself to towels, or whatever in the night. Our home is your home. You too, Rebecca. You can stay here too. "

"Thank you, Cheryl." I smile gratefully.

"Love you, bro! I'm glad you're home!" Thomas hollers as Cheryl leads him out of the room. The sound of a *thump* followed by an unruly laugh echoes out of the hallway. I can't help but feel happy for my best friend. He was truly devastated when Emma died. I made it worse by leaving. He then had to navigate an eighteen-year-old daughter and a shit ton of debt. Life wasn't easy for him. But now, as he jokes around with a new fiancée, stumbling around drunkenly and playfully, I can't help but feel happy that he's in a better place — even if he had to replace Rebecca's mum.

"I-I should g-get going too." she starts to get out of her seat but staggers and almost falls to the floor. Within seconds, my arms are wrapped around her, and she gasps in shock. Her head falls backwards and then forwards, and her eyes flutter open and shut. *She is truly wankered.*

"You're too drunk to get a cab," I tell her in a low voice. "Stay here. You can have the spare room— I mean, it was your room after all."

I'm almost frustrated that I don't get to have her room.

Something in my twisted fantasy enjoys the idea of lying in a bed where she used to be. But then again, I would do anything for her comfort.

"N-no way," she slurs her words. "I-I, I'm not staying h-here! My dog is all alone!"

I sober up quickly. "Well, you can't go back alone."

"Then you—" She thrusts her fingers into my chest. "—*you* take me home!"

I stiffen as her head falls against my chest, and I still haven't released her from my embrace yet— *she smells so sweet.* Even after ten years, she is still wearing the same sweet perfume, and it makes me smile. She owns that scent.

"Come on, big boy," she grins up at me. "Take me home!"

My teeth grind together. She doesn't understand the effect she has had on my body from that statement alone. If only she knew how *big* I could get for her- *Fuck.*

"I don't—"

"Oh, come on! Y-you can get a taxi back after," she protests, and I ponder on this thought for a second. She is far too drunk to go alone. I don't trust men in general, but with my little minx looking so delicious tonight, and now, so vulnerable... *who knows what could happen to her?*

"Fine." I hiss, before pulling my phone out and making the call.

Before long, the taxi is outside, and I slowly lead her out. She stumbles into me and breaks into a fit of giggles.

"Come on, Rebecca," I whisper, casting a look over my shoulder at the room where Thomas and Cheryl will hopefully be asleep. It doesn't sound right with me leading her drunkenly into a cab. I'll explain it all in the morning, but for now, it sounds a bit fucking odd. She digs her heels into the floor, and I accidentally walk straight into her. Her ass pushes up against my cock and my face contorts.

"Rebecca," I growl, snatching her by her arm. "Work with me!"

I finally manage to get her to climb into the taxi. She seductively bends over to crawl in and forces me to control any urge I have to look away. I try so fucking hard to be respectful. But out of the corner of my eye, I see how far the dress rides up, bunching under her perfectly round ass, and I have to bite down on my tongue to control my body's reaction, *again*, drawing blood until the metallic taste swirls around in my mouth.

The taxi driver watches her from the rear-view mirror with an appreciative smile, before drifting his eyes over to me, giving me a thumbs up as if congratulating me. I slide into the car and push myself forward so only he can hear. "If you want to keep those eyes, I suggest you stop fucking looking at what is mine — *drive*."

I recall a conversation we had earlier in the night when she revealed where she lived and tell the driver. He looks confused for a moment, clearly never driving down that country road, but eventually starts driving.

Rebecca fumbles with her seat belt, and I turn my attention back to her.

"Here," I whisper, reaching out to help her. She slaps my hand away and it takes me by surprise. "I can do it myself! I-I'm a big girl!"

She clearly can't. After a minute of struggling, she leans back and groans.

"How's it going, big girl?" I grin, and she shoots daggers at me. "Well, g-go on then."

I reach over and pull the seatbelt across her. Even though I try really hard, I can't help but stare at her breasts spilling over her dress which now strains against the seatbelt. It should be illegal to constrain such beautiful things. My tongue darts out hungrily and I wet my lips. Just as quickly as the perverse thoughts hit me, I will them away. *I can't do this.* To her. To Thomas... no, I can't. I *won't*.

"So, when-when are you taking me to this club?" She wiggles her eyebrows at me. She takes my disbelieving stare as confusion. "You know," she lowers her voice. "The s-e-x club."

When she spells out the word, I laugh, and her face screws up together. "Why are you l-laughing at me?"

"You're just funny like this."

"Am not."

Even whilst pissed, she is still stubborn. I roll my eyes and look out of the window. We have a thirty-something-minute drive ahead of us. This might become the longest thirty minutes of my life— or it could be the most painful as I must try and resist. I feel a finger press into my cheek. I startle and stare at her. She peers up, grinning. "W-whatcha thinking about?"

Fucking your brains out.

"Nothing."

She scowls. "Nothing?"

"What are *you* thinking about?" I twist the question back to her. She sighs happily. Then, her head falls onto my arm. I stiffen as she cuddles into me. This is *not* how this should be going. In my perverse thoughts, we have no romance. We are animals: we fuck like animals, and we fight like animals. Pure sexual deviants. Nothing more, nothing less. And she's ruining the plan by laying on me, running her fingers across my hands. I want to pull away from her, but I'm frozen in place.

"Lots of things." She whispers.

"Like?"

"C-can't tell you."

"What do you mean?" I frown. "Why won't you tell me?"

"My thoughts are f-forbidden."

My stomach flips in my chest. *Forbidden.* Oh, fuck, Rebecca. *You don't make this easy for me, do you?*

"I can't wait to see t-this club," she whispers, her tiny fingers toying with my much larger ones. I curl them into a fist, trying to deter her. It doesn't. She runs a gentle touch around each of my knuckles. I can't help but think of me playing with her clit — the image flashes into my mind before I can stop it, and now, I'm shuffling uncomfortably. I put distance between us, much to her disappointment, she juts out her bottom lip, and I tear my gaze away.

"Have you c-changed your mind about taking me?"

"What? No. Of course not. You're just..."

"I'm not drunk," she hisses.

"Yes, you are."

"Take me. Tomorrow."

Take me. Fuck. Shit. Bollocks. More erotic images of me fucking her brains out fill my mind, causing a groan to slip from my lips.

"Say it," she presses. "Say you-you'll take me tomorrow."

Shut the fuck up you, beautiful woman.

"Brandon!"

I relent. "Fine! Fine, okay. I'll take you tomorrow."

Her eyes flash wildly, and it takes everything in me not to bend down and kiss those soft lips. They've plagued my thoughts for the past eight years at a minimum. I've often kicked myself over not just doing it. For depriving myself of such sweetness. If I was going to run away after anyways, I might have run away over something— rather than just dirty thoughts. I want to ravish her. I want to ruin her for everybody else. And by the way, she smirks up at me knowingly, I don't think she would be opposed to it at-fucking-all. She might even beg for it on her knees.

HOLLY GUY

That is the dangerous part.

CHAPTER NINE

Vixen

Dagger is on edge— *more so than usual.* He's rocking back and forth in his seat, muttering inaudible things under his breath, completely lost in his own world. In one hand, he clutches his glass of whisky like if he drops it, he might explode and die. His eyes skitter across the room as if he is following a mouse running around on the carpet, under the tables and chairs. He cracks a smile as if the mouse has told him a joke— *it's so fucking unnerving.*

"Dags?" Brandon pulls him out of his trance for a split second. "Did you hear what I said?"

"Huh?"

"I asked if you recognised that man the other night. Vixen couldn't find his real name, only his pimp's name. I need to know if you recognised him from—" he trails off, and nobody makes any effort to finish his sentence. There is an unspoken rule to not talk about what Dagger went through in that organisation. His fragile mindset is too weak to be unbalanced with questions.

I gulp down the remainder of my coca-cola, the cold fizz burning my throat, but I welcome the odd feeling. *I wish I had alcohol*; that would make the pain disappear into numbness. I long for the bitter taste of vodka and lime— the more sour and stronger, the better. A humming sensation pulls through my chest, and my lips become dry. *The familiar pull of addiction.* It takes everything I have not to give in and pour myself a glass. The bottle is right *there*, next to Dagger, one simple arm stretch away. If I reach forward, I can—

"Well, did you?" Brandon snaps me out of my wicked thoughts unknowingly. I sink into my chair guiltily, pinching my thigh to distract myself from the loud thump of my heartbeat in my ears.

The room is tense. Dagger killed my target before I got any information out of him. I *needed* to see where those other taxis went, but by the time we calmed Dagger down, and got him away from the crime scene, they'd disappeared. We lost thirty women. They might be free for a week or two as the organisation finds them a new pimp, but then they are back in the same fucked up situation as before.

Dagger shakes his head slowly. "No."

I watch him to see if he's lying, but he is completely lost in his own world, again staring at the imaginary mice racing back and forth on the floor. He tips his drink back and finishes it, never taking his eyes off the floor. I watch the liquid slip from his lips and run into his stubbly beard. A sudden ridiculous urge to lean forward and lick it off pulls through me. His head suddenly cocks to the side like a monster hearing something in the distance and it's followed by an unnerving chuckle to something only he heard. Brandon and I exchange a nervous look. An unravelling Dagger is always a bad thing, but it's been especially bad in the past few months.

None of the help we find seems to work, and as each day goes by, he becomes more volatile and unpredictable. His hallucinations control him, and my worst fear is that he will accidentally take it out on one of the women, believing they're a pimp. The other night was a clear example of him believing he was under attack when he was perfectly safe with his brothers.

"Fine. Back to the drawing board then." Brandon sighs,

running a hand through his hair.

I look back at him. "Have you got enough space at the club to house these women when we get them?"

He nods slowly. "Yes, we are building a couple of extra rooms to accommodate them."

My stomach twists, I really don't like the idea of bringing the women from one club and putting them into Brandon's. It feels like we are not truly helping them, just switching their captor.

"Stop it. I know that disapproving look," he growls. "You know the deal. The women under twenty-one go over to the professionals and the council to help them back on their feet. The others who are too ingrained in this way of life, who have committed unspeakable acts themselves, who need our protection... they need another club to work at or they will just go running back to their abusive bosses. Or worse, they'll go straight to prison. You know the system doesn't take their vulnerability and trauma into as much account as they fucking should." Brandon spits out the truth I know deep down, but my heart refuses to accept.

I cast my gaze back at Dagger who laughs manically to himself. Whatever the organisation did to him, they've fucked him up royally. *How many of the girls we have working in this club have the same fragile mindset? Are there any working in our club? Have any been pushed to Dagger's extreme?* Yes, but they don't live to tell the tale.

Suicide is another major concern among these victims. I have often wondered if Dagger would ever pull the trigger on himself— and something deep-down thinks that he wouldn't, *not consciously* anyways.

When he is having an episode, it is a real fear of mine, to watch him slice himself up. He goes fucking mental for hurting himself too whilst attacking the pimps. It's like he must beat himself up too for being a part of the organisation. He never hurt a woman whilst he was captured there— I *know* he wouldn't have— but it doesn't mean it couldn't have stopped someone getting hurt. Whilst his mum was alive, Dagger was only focused on getting her out. It was dog eat dog. You'd turn on fellow victims if it meant getting a leg up for yourself. Dagger blames himself for a lot of the abuse others went through. And it was all for nothing. His mum died three days before Brandon and I stormed the place.

"We will just need to keep an eye out." Brandon sighs heavily. "Be alert for any new pimps that might pop up."

I nod my head at him but stay silent. Dagger falls to the floor next to me and raises his arms to the sky as if he's seeing God himself come down. He is stupidly drunk and it's not even eleven o'clock yet. I tend to ignore him when he's like this— it's the best way to help the situation— who knows what he would do if I attempted to intervene… who knows what *I* would do if I snatched the bottle of alcohol from him.

"He's been having this hallucination since lunch," I say slowly to Brandon who just watches him. It hurts him to see Dagger like this, but I feel numb to the craziness by now. "I tried to call you earlier. Where were you?"

Brandon stiffens, and he refuses to meet my gaze. "*Out*."

"Out for five hours?"

"Seeing an old friend."

I cock an eyebrow up. "Who?"

"None of your fucking business, Vixen," he suddenly explodes. I watch with intrigue as Brandon almost falls apart in front of me. He thrusts an accusing finger in my direction, and it shakes with adrenaline. "Are you going to tell me where *you* disappear to every night?"

It's my turn to freeze. "What?"

"You think I don't notice how you're untraceable the minute

WE SHOULDN'T

your shift finishes, or on your days off. You never used to be like that. You wanna tell me what's changed?" he wags his eyebrows as the accusing tone slaps me in the face— *rightfully so*. I shake my head quickly. I love Brandon—I trust that man with my life. Sometimes it feels like us against the world— us against Dagger— but how can I tell him that I'm stalking a woman who doesn't know I exist? Hell, our entire job revolves around protecting women from creeps who do similar things, yet I'm fucking hooked by the mystery brunette. My nails sink into my trousers to distract myself from her face.

"See, we both keep secrets," Brandon says through gritted teeth, rocking back in his seat. I almost choke on my breath. We used to agree secrets were the worst possible thing that could happen in our line of business, but now, we both understand that secrets and privacy keep people sane. I cast my gaze at the clock. In two minutes, my shift ends, and I can run away to my little dove in the open house.

"Go on," Brandon cocks his head to the side dismissively. "I'll watch the club and Dagger. Disappear wherever it is you go."

I stiffen, his words replaying in my mind on a loop. *Is this a trick?* Brandon doesn't trick people, and yet it feels like it. He returns his gaze to me and smiles. "I mean it, Vix. Enjoy your night off. In return, work the morning shift tomorrow. I will take the night again."

"You'll take my night shift?" I flinch. "Why?"

"Don't worry about it. Just go."

I don't ask any more questions. He's granted me an early leave to go and stalk the woman who plagues my wet dreams.

Within forty-two minutes, I am camped up outside her house, hiding in the bushes. To my disappointment, the house is dark. She hasn't drawn her bedroom curtains, and there is a soft glow of the light next to her. She is fast asleep in her bed. I frown. It's early- *why is she already in bed?*

I feel cheated out of my opportunity to stalk her. And yet, I don't move an inch, or miss a single twitch from her. *Anything is better than nothing.*

CHAPTER TEN

Rebecca

My fucking head is killing me. It pounds as I'm awoken by Fish licking my face. He whines and sobs as I sleepily ruffle his head, calming him down a little bit. Pieces of yesterday start to filter back to me. The argument with my dad. The dinner. The laughter. Everyone made up. I remember the nearly full bottle of whisky I drank to myself. *How the fuck did I get home?*

Suddenly, I shoot up out of bed.

Brandon.

I tear through my house, desperately searching for that wicked man. *Did he stay the night? Did we kiss? Shag?* Oh fuck! I grab my head and whimper. I remember staring up at him— his lips— I almost begged him to take me. *Fuck, fuck, fuck!* How pathetic of me! How desperate! *What did I say to him? How badly did I humiliate myself this time?*

I stare down at my clothes but I'm still in the dress from last night. So, at least he didn't undress me. Fish barks and I clutch my head in agony.

"Shush! Quiet!" I whisper yell to him.

He charges into the kitchen, and I find myself stumbling after him. "What is it, boy?"

Then, I see it: on the kitchen counter, a flask sits there, accompanied by 2 paracetamol, and a note. My heart lurches in my chest. I almost *don't* want to approach it. I don't want to read it. I want to completely forget how I acted last night, but I know I have to face up to the truth. The smell of coffee from the flask helps ease my nerves as I pick up the note with shaky hands.

Rebecca,

I hope your hangover isn't too bad this morning. Remember our date tonight; you made me promise 'to take you'. I'll pick you up at 9 pm sharp. Be ready to go.

Best, B.

At the bottom, his phone number is perfectly scribbled.

The bile rises at the back of my throat, and before I know it, I'm sprinting to the toilet. My entire body snaps in half as I throw up every piece of food, I ate at dinner last night. My strangled chokes fill my ears, and I shiver.

What the fuck is happening? What date? What did I agree to— a date? What the fuck! Why are we going on a date? And those three fucking words… *to take you.*

My legs slam shut as a dull ache begins. I groan in humiliation. The questions torment me and I long to drown them out. However, now that I've thrown up, I feel *less* like death. My stomach stops churning a little, and now there is no more threat of feeling like I might explode with sickness.

Weakly, I wipe my mouth with a bit of tissue before forcing myself to my feet. I am shaky, but I am strong enough to shower. The cold-water trickles down on my back, slowing working its way down my chest and legs, waking me up a bit more. I grab my razor and shave *everywhere*. I don't know why I shave down *there*— it's not like he is going to fuck me— and yet, I really want him too.

I rationalise it to myself that if he sees it, at least I look like I've made an effort. If he doesn't, then he'll never know. Freshly shaved and showered, I brush my teeth twice to get rid of that awful taste in the back of my throat, before changing into some clean clothes.

Outside the bathroom, Fish waits, wagging slowly, staring up at me. When he notices my attention is on him, he barks once, then again.

"Yes, yes I know," I groan, lugging myself out to the kitchen. I take the paracetamol and grab my coffee before sliding into my coat. With a huff, I slide my wellies on and push the front door open. Fish sprints past me, down his usual path, but I don't bother running to keep up with him. Instead, I walk slowly behind, sipping at my coffee. It tastes disgusting because of my freshly brushed teeth, but I know I need to drink it for energy. Especially if I'm going to figure out where the *fuck* we are going tonight. *What did I make him promise me?*

Fish leaps through the fields happily. As usual, I only see his floppy little ears flashing above the crops, before he disappears again. While he's completely carefree, I focus on not slipping over and dying. It rained pretty heavily last night apparently— the floor is soaked with wet slimy mud.

After the long walk, I bathe fish, much to his anger. He gets me drenched and I silently thank my brain for not taking the coat off prior. He now sprints around the house excitedly, rubbing his clean body up against all the furniture. He even barks as he sprints around Shithead who meows angrily. I roll my eyes and disappear back into my office. My laptop is still open from my previous writing session, and I settle in the chair in front of my desk before reading the final line.

Of course, it's a sex scene. The ruler on the desk taunts me about my last writing session. I got myself so fucking hot and bothered— I never thought to use a ruler before as a form of spanking, but I know that I've opened a door with this type of erotica.

I click the 'enter bar' on my keyboard a couple of times and start planning the next chapter, but everything is so shallow.

My characters have no depth yet, nor is the plot line going in the way I want it to. My creativity juices are almost completely gone. After half an hour of staring at a blank screen, I rock back and sigh. My eyes trail around the room until I see the note Brandon left me, scrunched up on the sofa. I think about his words *'to take you'*, over and over again. He obviously meant it in a non-sexual way, but of course, I'm going to interpret it that way. Then, suddenly, more memories flood back to me.

"*My daughter writes smut, and my best friend owns a sex club!*" My father had exclaimed. I stiffen. *Fuck- is that where we're going tonight? Is he taking me to his sex club?* I grab my head in frustration and pull at my hair.

Fuck. Fuck. Fuck.

I am a horny little freak for him as it is; how am I going to last in a sex club, next to that fucking God? *No, not God* — he doesn't want to be worshipped like something celestial. Brandon is Satan himself, dragging out your wildest sins and making them a reality; he will push and break and punish you until you're nothing more but a whimpering, writhing mess. And *fuck* do I want my sins to be brought out.

CHAPTER ELEVEN

Brandon

It's 8:59 pm, and I'm waiting outside her house. On cue, her front door opens, and she steps out. She is wearing a long fluffy coat which hides her outfit, but it stops at her thighs, and then it's all leg— so whatever she is wearing, *it's going to be short*.

I bite my tongue when she approaches. She has done her hair *beautifully*. It is long and curly but pinned up by a large silver clip on the left side. She wears stunningly long earrings, and her makeup is fucking perfection. Similar to last night, she has smokey eye makeup which darkens the natural blackness of her pupils, but this time, she's paired it with a light shade of pink lipstick rather than red. I didn't think I could be so turned on by my makeup— but she does it beautifully.

Before she can reach for my car door, I exit the car and race around to open the door for her. As she slides in, she blinks back her surprise and then blushes profusely. "Thank you."

I shut it behind her before returning to my side. Only now, can I see her outfit poking through her coat. She wears a tight-fitting black dress. It's a halter neck but has a key-hole appearance for where her breasts burst out— images of her perky tits tightly pressed together after I pull them through the hole, spring to mind. It gets worse because she isn't wearing tights, and her pale skin mocks me. I want to bite it, leave red marks— evidence that I've been here— *fuck!* I clear my throat and tear my gaze away before starting the car and pulling out of her driveway.

"I-I didn't know what to wear," she whispers sheepishly.

There is a strained element to my voice. "That's perfect. You look perfect."

Out of the corner of my eye, her cheeks darken wildly. I start the engine and pull the car out of her drive. She puts her seatbelt on, and my mind flashes back to last night unintentionally. "You were very drunk last night."

"I know," she flinches. "I am sorry. I'm assuming you ordered me a taxi? Thank you so much for making sure I got home safely. Did we—" she cuts herself off and shakes her head. She doesn't dare ask the question we both know she's thinking about, but I don't give her any solace. I almost want her to torment herself over the questions. I want her to panic and wonder what happened. I don't know why I enjoy her discomfort so much— *but it's fucking addictive.* I quite like her humiliation, because it might bring on her bratty side. Yes, that's it. *Fucking hell.*

"I am a little nervous about tonight," she confesses, taking me by surprise. "I mean, I've never been to a club before— well, sex club, I've of course been to a club, and—"

A wicked grin appears on my face as she rambles on, and I place a hand on her thigh to give her a reassuring pat, but the minute we touch, I regret my decision. Her softness shoots straight to my now-growing-erection, and I clear my throat to distract myself. I pull my hand away so fast it seems as though she's burnt me.

"You'll be fine." I instantly regret agreeing to take her to this place. How will I keep my hands to myself? How will I *not* check for her reaction every two seconds? I'm still figuring out how I can hide her from Vixen and Dagger. When I left, Dagger was asleep on the sofa in the office, and I let Vixen go early, *purposely*, to keep my Rebecca hidden from him.

"You told me it's quite a... well, a kinky place. Right?" she turns to watch me. "What did you mean by that? Like—how bad are the kinks? Nothing illegal right?"

"Christ, Rebecca," I startle. "Who do you think I am? Of course, there is nothing illegal!"

"No! I didn't mean it like that. Well, I guess— okay, fine, I did. That's all I wanted to know!" She seems to visibly relax but I am still stiff. I know I'm fucked up. I'm obsessive, controlling, fucked in the head. *But does she think what I do is illegal?* All my life I've fought against those institutions; it's hurtful that she'd assume—

"How does it work? I'm sorry, I really am quite nervous," she squeaks. I cast a look at her, and she peers at me with large, frightened eyes. I sink my teeth into my tongue. For someone so nervous, she still seems incredibly engaged and willing to go. Her happiness to put herself through unknown situations only excites me further.

"Each room has a different kink. Spanking, orgies, role play— you name it, we have it. We will be in the viewing areas so we can watch the performers."

"What about playing?" She takes me by surprise.

My head snaps toward her. "What?"

She blushes madly. "I mean, like, if I wanted to— never mind." She's embarrassed, and I really want to comfort her and tell her she can do what she likes; that's the whole point of this club. To watch *or* play. But the idea of her playing with other people —no, fuck that. I will cut off every fucking hand that touches her—that touches what is *mine*. But at the same time, I will not touch her either. I *can't*.

"You are not allowed to play." I hear my jealous voice snap and I quickly try to cover up. "It's not, *well*, not right of me. You're my best mate's daughter. I shouldn't see you, well... playing."

"Will we be going to the same rooms?"

Abso-fucking-lutely.

"You want to go to the rooms alone?" I arch an eyebrow at her.

"No!" she startles. "Well, I mean, I'd prefer not to. But if it's awkward for you, then I will."

"Why would it be awkward for me? I told you that I would take you. If we are just watching, it's fine. We aren't crossing any lines."

She ponders on this thought and pulls her bottom lip into her teeth. I groan at how delicious she looks right now. And the fact she wants to play— *fucking hell*. She will be the death of me.

"What about you?" she asks.

"What?"

"Do you go to play often?"

Her confidence takes me by surprise, and I have to force my cock to stay down in my pants. I would love to pull the car to the side and fuck her ruthlessly. I want to show her how much I play. I want to teach her all the fucked-up things I taught the performers there. *The only person who runs a club like this is another sick fucker with more kinks than hobbies.* It is just a bonus that I get to help the women escape dangerous places and work at a place full of safety and security.

"Sometimes," I say with a small smile. Her eyes widen in shock, but I'm unsure why. Running a place like this, she would at least assume that I'd join in from time to time, *right*? Then, her lips pull upward into a smile, and she stares down at her fingers in her lap. *What's going through that little head of yours, little minx?*

Finally, we're pulling up to the club, and I turn off the engine.

"What's our safe word?" I ask her, twisting to face her.

"Safe word?" she leers. "Why would we need a safe word? I thought you said we are not joining in!"

"Safe words aren't always for physical sex, Rebecca." I scold her like a child, and she visibly flinches. "We need one in case you are uncomfortable by anything you see. There are some kinks in there that really push the limits. I don't want you to be exposed to anything you're not—" *ready for* "—willing to see."

"Okay." She nods her head slowly. "The safe word can be *meat*."

"Meat?"

"I don't eat meat and I won't be joining in with the sex," she amuses herself. I'm stiff— *both my back and my cock.*

"Brandon?" she calls for me. I quickly meet her gaze again. I give her a grunt to let her know I'm listening, but I can't speak.

"Our safe word is meat, yeah?" she tries again. *Our safe word.* Holy shit. She makes it sound so fucking erotic. If only she knew the kind of things that she could get herself into with that word...

"Yes. Let's go." I climb out of the car and sprint around the other side to help her out. She takes my hand and elegantly slips out, it allows the direct flashing image of her crawling into the taxi last night with her perfectly shaped ass in the air, as if she was knowingly teasing me, and that it wasn't the countless drinks she downed speaking. *Fuck—stop thinking about that.*

We climb the long staircase up to the main entrance, and I suddenly feel very nervous. I keep checking the cameras around the room. I know that my brothers won't be here, but it doesn't stop the anxiety. They could be watching us right now, planning how they are going to steal my Rebecca from me. I love them, but we are each as hungry as the next. And a brat like Rebecca— so angry, willing, *sexy*— I'd have a hard time fighting them off.

I slip my coat off before helping her with hers, and she blushes before nodding her head as a silent *thank you*. Then, I turn and pass the coats to the receptionist who is taking other customers' tickets. Her blue eyes light up when she sees me. "Sir!"

I almost roll my eyes. I recognise her as Jamie, a woman I used to play with. She is very pretty, but not really my type. Her thick plastic lashes clump together and touch halfway down her cheek, and her overlined clown-like lips are the most noticeable thing anybody would see or focus on at first glance. As I pass the coats over the counter, she attempts to touch my hand in a more than friendly way— everything about her is more than friendly— but I quickly pull back from her and turn to Rebecca. "Is your phone in your coat pocket?"

She nods.

"Good," I tell her. "No phones are allowed in this place, to protect my customers' privacy."

"Okay."

Without another look at Jamie, I pull Rebecca through the red velvet fabric that separates the reception from the main floor. Jamie calls after me, but I ignore her.

"Who was that?" Rebecca whispers, but I don't answer. Silently, she mouths "oh" as she understands my refusal to answer. I wait for some type of expression from her— I want her to be jealous, but, if anything, she turns and gives Jamie the kindest smile. *Fuck sake. Why do you have to be so lovely now?* I want you to rip those blonde extensions from her head and choke me with them. *Be crazy!* I know you have the potential to be obsessive—*just like me.*

"Which room do you want to go in first?" I distract my thoughts as we come to a huge set of stairs. "This whole place is made up of seven floors, each floor ranging in kinkiness — the bottom being everything vanilla, and the highest being the most boundary-pushing sexual acts you could imagine. We have *a* lot of choices."

Her eyes widen. She almost runs to the huge board that has all the room information on it. I hold my breath and wait for her answer. Like a kid in a candy shop, her entire face lights up, and it's at this moment I realise how perfect she is for me, even if she doesn't know it yet.

"Let's work our way up. I want to start with floor one, room six," she smirks, twisting back to me. My heart leaps out of my chest when she chews on her lower lip. I scan her face quickly and she is ridiculously excited. "Come on!"

She pulls me to the room she wants, and I don't need to check the board to know *exactly* which room she's taken me to. It's just fucking weird that this is the first room I ever chose to go in, too. *Wax and fire.*

I watch her silently as she takes a shaky breath to calm her nerves. I push the door open. She slips in front of me before hesitating. It's dark for a minute as you choose which door you want to go into. *The playroom, or the watching room.* I quickly push her into the watching room, and I can sense her disappointment— she oozes it— but she doesn't say anything.

The watching stand consists of five rows of seats, like in a cinema, that sits opposite a huge window. There are about six people already in here, watching eagerly. I move Rebecca down to the front so she can get front-row seats to the action. She sits down quickly and turns her attention to the show in front of us, her eyes widening each second that passes as she tries to take everything in, her blinks limited to ensure she doesn't miss anything.

Behind the glass, there is a naked female performer— *or customer, I can't really tell*— strapped to a bed. Her body is tilted, her head near the floor so that all the blood rushes to her head. Two men stand proudly on either side. One holds a lit candle, allowing the wax to drip all over her, while the other holds a long lighter firmly in his hand as he trails it slowly across her room. Her breathless moans ripple around the room.

"I've never seen this done before," Rebecca whispers, in awe. "Can they see us?"

I stiffen with her confession. What I would do to take her into every fucking room and introduce her to my world of deviant kinks and fetishes, she would fit perfectly in this place.

"Yes, they can see us. Sometimes the performers can invite you in, from the watching room. Usually, if they fancy you." I tell her. She gawps at me, but not for long, before her attention returns to the show. *Nobody will be requesting you, though, my little minx. Boss' orders.* I don't tell her this. She will be frightened by my possessiveness. I have to ease her into my world little by little.

The woman's moans grow louder and louder as the wax is poured over her nipples. Her head tosses back and forth, and her mouth falls open in bliss. I'm not watching the show, though. I'm too busy studying Rebecca's reaction. She soaks up every single moment before casting a look over her shoulder towards the other people in the room, blushing as they all hold the same intrigued, *turned-on,* reaction as her. I feel her gaze settle on my face.

"What do guys do if they get an erection? Is it frowned upon?" her small voice rings out. I startle. She is no longer looking at me, instead, she casts her eyes around at the three men on the opposite side of the room to us. One of them with his hands in his pants, and the other two covering their erections with their grubby fat hands. I glare at them before pulling my phone out and typing frantically away.

"You have your phone!" her eyes are wide with fear.

"I'm the boss." I spit. "Anyways, there is a separate room if you want to touch yourself or—" I clear my throat. "—*anyone else.* They need to go to the playroom if they want to wank. They can't be doing that here when there are other people in the room."

"But it's normal for the show to cause erections?"

"Of course, Rebecca. It's a sex club. It's the same for women, right? I don't tell women they can't get wet whilst watching, so I can't do it for men." Before I can finish my sentence, two security guards come and tug at the men's arms. They look between each other, gob-smacked, before stumbling after the guards into the right room. I turn back to her, my mind full of delicious questions. *Are you wet, my little minx? Are you rubbing your thighs together right now, desperate for friction against your clit? Is that why you asked about men?*

Rebecca stares at me, mortified. "You snitched on them."

"There are rules in place to protect every client," I tell her slowly. "You shouldn't be exposed to their cocks in this room."

She crosses her arms defiantly. "What if I don't mind?"

I itch to grab her by the throat and choke the stubbornness out of her. Instead, I grind my teeth together. "You should mind. If you want to see old fat men wanking themselves off, you can watch them. They will be in that corner over there." My head flicks towards where the men now stand, continuing their previous actions.

"But you can't really see around there."

"Do you really want to see them? Or are you just trying to defy my wishes?" I don't know why I blurt the question. I expect her to rile back, hit me, or spit some insult at me. But, instead, she just smiles and stares at me with those fucking delicious eyes. She cocks her head to the side and frantically scans my face, causing butterflies to erupt in my stomach.

I rise to my feet, and she quickly follows. *We are too fucking close.* She rises to higher on her tip toes, and even like this, she's far too short.

Her voice is low, sultry, and fucking delicious. "You don't control me."

"It's my club." I bite back, my jaw ticking with building frustration— a frustration that some would view as sexual, but to me, it's *animal* tendencies— something *worse* than mere sexual attraction. I want to ravish her repeatedly until our throats are raw from howling our release.

"I'm a client. What happened to the customer is always right?" She challenges me. She fucking challenges me— *here, now!* My hands jump to her back, and I slam her up against me. She jolts and a look of fear flashes through her as I steal all the power back. I shouldn't be doing this. I need to put distance between us before I do something I regret. And yet, this is the only way a brat will learn her place.

"*Fuck* the customer," I spit out each word slowly. Her cheeks flash bright red and she doesn't miss the sexual undertones. Her tongue darts out to wet her bottom lip and my eyes greedily catch it.

For a split second, I almost kiss her. It wouldn't be slow or romantic— *fuck that*. I would kiss her like I'm ruthlessly fucking her. I'd force her lips open with my tongue and suck all the oxygen from her until she was trembling and moaning. Then, I would take her into a room where there are no prying eyes and pound her relentlessly. As if she can hear my thoughts, she takes a sharp intake of breath. "Let's go to the next room."

I release her immediately, and she scampers away from me, leading the way back out of the room. As soon as we get to the staircase, the breath starts to flood my lungs again. My body feels hot, and I've had to readjust my cock to sit in the waistline of my jeans so that she doesn't see my huge tent for her.

"Where to next?" I tell her. She scans the board before pointing at floor three, room 12: *degradation and humiliation.*

I can't help but tease her. "Jumping to floor three, are we?"

"It's for my book." she insists, but I saw the way her eyes

flashed deliciously when she spotted the room's description.

CHAPTER TWELVE

Rebecca

"It's for my book," I throw my hands to my hips and dare him to argue back with me, but he doesn't and instead, he gestures me toward the stairs. A disappointing sensation floods through me at the lack of fight. I physically resist the urge to take them in steps of twos and threes, so desperate to reach the next room. However, I do take pleasure in swaying my hips side to side as I walk ahead of Brandon. He mutters something under his breath, but I don't hear what he's saying. It makes me grin, nevertheless. I want him so fucking bad, even if I know we shouldn't, but I want to test the limits. *How far can we go before we snap?* It's fucked up of me, but I've always loved the forbidden shit.

We eventually slip into the viewing gallery and take our seats. There are fewer people in this room. Only two individuals sitting at the back. Again, Brandon leads me to the front, so we are less than two metres away from the action. This room is more my style. In the playroom, a woman sits on her knees, and she is completely naked, apart from a dog collar around her neck. The fully dressed man opposite holds the lead and tugs her forward so she must crawl to him. His cock is out, and proud, and the woman eyes it up greedily.

"You stupid fucking bitch," he spits at her. "You've made a mess all over my floor."

He gestures to the wet patch from where she must have just squirted. The juices still drip down her thigh, and I'm instantly turned on, imagining myself in that situation.

"Lick it up," the man demands. The woman stiffens and peers up at her owner. He is not joking or teasing. "Lick it up like the good little slut you are. If you make the mess, you will clean the mess with your tongue."

The woman whimpers and scurries back to her mess. Without hesitation, she lowers her head, and her ass sticks up in the air before lapping up her juices.

"Oh, my god," I whisper, bringing my hand to my face. Shocked, I stare at Brandon to gauge his reaction but he's already looking at me.

"Do you enjoy things like this?" I expect him to be disgusted when he asks me, but he isn't. He is actually curious. My breathing suddenly becomes irregular, and instead of talking, all I can do is nod my head. He blinks rapidly and tears his gaze away from me. He is so fucking good-looking right now. He sits back in his chair and dangles his arms around the back of the seat. His arm almost touches me, but he makes sure to put distance between us. I don't know if I'm grateful or furious that he's not touching me. I am in a delicate position right now— I couldn't be more turned on if I tried. I sneak a gaze at his trousers, searching for a tent or something. Every man I've seen has been rock solid, but not Brandon. He is calm and collected. It's as if he's watching just any old film, and it's only when his eyes turn back on me, that the hunger reveals itself.

"Which is your favourite room?" I ask curiously. His jaw ticks as he stares at me and it's as if he's counting back from ten, trying to collect his thoughts. "I'll show you one day."

"Not today?" I raise an eyebrow.

"Not today. It's the kind of thing you need to be eased into."

Eased into— fuck—the way he says it is so fucking erotic. He instantly notices the effect of his words. I wait for him to say something—do something, *anything* — but instead, he just stares at me, soaking up every flicker of emotion.

"You dirty little cunt," the man in the show insults the woman, and soon, I hear a whipping noise. This snatches my attention. He holds a metre-long ruler and strikes it down on her bare ass. The lady screams in pleasure and pain, and I can't help but lean forward. A red mark appears, and it's quickly joined by two, three, *four!* Whack. Whack. Whack.

"Shit," I hiss under my breath. Suddenly, Brandon pulls his arms to his side and slides further away from me. He is tense. *Really fucking tense.* And I can see him watching me out of the corner of my eye. If only he knew the kind of things I was doing to myself a couple of nights ago with a ruler. How much I wish I was that woman there, and how I would love for him to be the man...

"You like that?" Brandon's voice is dark and low, and I almost jump from my skin with how powerful he sounds.

"Yes," I whisper, but it comes out more like a whimper. I press my thighs together, his eyes darting down at the movement, and I'm immediately aware of how high my dress has bunched up. I watch his Adam's apple bob when he gulps. "You have enough research for your book?"

"Not yet."

He rises to his feet and helps me up. I almost don't want to leave this room, but there are so many rooms to be explored. His eyes shoot to the chair I was sitting on, and he growls. When I turn to look, I stiffen as my eyes immediately fall to the small wet patch where I was sitting. I'm embarrassed *and* turned on. I wait for him to spit something degrading, to humiliate me—to point it out to everyone here. Fuck, *I would enjoy that so badly.* And yet, he doesn't.

"Lick it up," the man in the show yells at the woman who has caused another mess with her cum. I've been too distracted by Brandon to see her squirt, but it's clearly happened again.

And yet the words he yells at her feel like they've been taken directly from Brandon's lips. He looks at me, at the chair, and back at me, his eyes darkening more each millisecond.

"Let's go," he says, and it's strained. I almost want to drop to my knees and taste my wetness. I want to show him how much of a good girl I can be. My cheeks burn and instead of doing what my dirty fantasies are begging me to do, I quickly leave the room. We both stumble out, slightly dazed.

"I think that's enough for today," Brandon says, looking *through* me. I frown at his unusual behaviour, but just as I go to turn and look at what he's looking at, he drags me down the stairs quickly. His jaw ticks, and he is stiff. The mood changes drastically, and I'm left wondering what I've done wrong.

"What?" I gawp when I realise that he is taking me to the exit. "*No*, there are so many other rooms I want to do!"

"You'll have to come back then."

"Are you inviting me back?" a small smile kisses my lips.

"Watch it, Rebecca."

Perhaps it's my horniness talking, or perhaps everything feels so surreal that I forget about what the consequences are, but for some reason or other, I fold my arms and jut my chin out. "Or what?"

"*Don't.*"

"Don't what?"

A fierce growl leaves his lips and I jolt. My traitorous arms jump out of their folded position, and I wince at how easy it was for him to control me then. *Why must my body respond so well to him?*

"I'm taking you home," he barks. Without another look, he marches ahead, every muscle in his back tenses, and it makes me smile. I like winding him up; he is fun to piss off. He was fun ten years ago, and he is even more fun to piss off now.

I quickly catch up with him. *How far can I push him? Will he punish me like the people in the performance?*

"Coats." He spits rudely to the receptionist lady, and she gawps. "Going so soon? I finish my shift in five minutes, we could—"

"I said—" his voice drops a couple of tones. "—coats," he thrusts his hand out impatiently and she springs into action. "Yes, Sir."

I can't help wondering whether that was their relationship. Did they have a dom and sub relationship? She calls him Sir a lot, but then he *is* the boss. Is this purely business or was there pleasure? Fuck, how can I tell when his business *is* pleasure?

She scurries around the desk and to the cloakroom. Now that we are alone, I take a step closer to him. "You're being rude."

"I don't care."

"Well, I do."

"Don't see me again." He spits, and for a moment, I'm taken aback by his rudeness. It's like a slap to the face and I'm fucking shocked. But the stubborn bitch in me doesn't let him see it.

"Wasn't going to," I say in retaliation, but a small piece of me hopes he knows I want to more than anything.

"You weren't?" he cocks an eyebrow up at me.

"Nope."

"Why not?"

"You're no fun," I blurt out the first lie that comes to my mind. His lip twitches up in a crude smirk and it absolutely fucking floors me.

"What more fun could you possibly ask for?"

"I want to join in." I almost stomp my foot against the floor like a child, but I resist, knowing he will only point it out, and patronise me. I like being degraded, but being made to feel silly? Immature? No. That's not fun. That's not sexy. It reminds me too much of Leo—

"Knock yourself out." He cocks his head, daring me to return to the rooms. I hesitate. On the one hand, I would fucking love to run away from him and join in on the playing. On the other, what fun is it if he isn't the one doing it with me? My cheeks burn again at the thought. Then, I can't help wondering if he would even let me return. He is so hot and cold with the decision. He must *want* me; I've seen the desperation on his face. Sure, he told me *'we shouldn't'* because of my dad. But are we really going to tell my dad that he took me to his club? *Fuck no* —he'd be mortified. *What's one shag from that lie?*

Suddenly, the lady returns, carrying both our coats. She passes them to Brandon before scurrying back behind her desk. He puts his on but refuses to give me mine. "Are you staying here or coming with me?"

"I want to go with you." I hear myself say and I flinch at how desperate it sounds. A smile tugs at his lips. He pulls me out of the building, without even giving me my coat. As soon as the doors open, the freezing chill hits me. I shiver and throw my hands over my chest. "Brandon! My coat!"

He ignores me and stalks closer to the car, forcing me to chase after him desperately. The sound of my heels on the gravel makes me wince, and I stumble pathetically until I bump into his back. Suddenly, he spins around and grabs me by my arms. It's a strong, possessive touch and he forces me still. His scrutinising gaze rakes down my body until they land on my breasts. I don't need to look to know my nipples are hard as rocks, completely revealing my bare chest. I didn't think wearing a bra was sex club etiquette. And I had anticipated taking my clothes off as soon as we got there, but now, I feel silly.

Hunger crosses his face, and he throws his head back. His Adam's apple juts out and I want to press my lips to it. Just as quickly as the thought appears, I force it away. As soon as he collects himself, he glares back down at me. We stand in silence as he takes my coat and dangles it over my shoulders to warm me up. I nuzzle into the thick fur but when I try to pull it across my chest, he stops me.

"No," It's a full sentence, and he doesn't elaborate— *he doesn't need to.* He wants to see my hard nipples, and fuck, is that the hottest thing ever. My legs press together, and I sink my teeth into my lower lip again. It must be pulled apart with how much I've bitten it tonight.

"Get in the car." He growls before throwing the door open, and I scramble in. However, just as I bend down, a pain shoots through my ass. I hiss as the stinging sensation remains for a couple of seconds, and then is instantly changed into pleasure as a wave of wetness pools between my thighs.

The fucker just spanked me!

My mortified gasp is only greeted by his low chuckle before the door is slammed shut. In my chest, my heart races faster and louder. We are dangerously blurring the lines. I have never wanted anything more than this. *I want him so fucking bad.* He has more restraint than me, but, clearly, it's slipping.

When he slides in beside me, he doesn't even give me another look before throwing the car into drive. My legs remain tightly shut as if, if I part them, he might smell my sex. That will definitely throw him over the edge; I really fucking want him to slip off the edge and ravish me, but the small voice of reason tells me to keep my thighs tightly pressed together and my lips sealed— *both sets.*

CHAPTER THIRTEEN

Brandon

I shouldn't have done that. *Fuck*. Everything was going so well. I managed to pull us out of that place before I did anything I would regret. *Before Dagger saw her*. He appeared out of nowhere, with his flavour of woman of the night, clinging to him, seductively. *He almost fucking saw us!*

And then she *had* to back chat. All I wanted to do was to humiliate her by taking her coat. I enjoyed the idea of her chasing after me, in those stupid little heels, stumbling and staggering, in the freezing cold, trying to catch up to my long strides. I didn't fucking think! What a pleasant surprise when her little rose buds were straining out of the material as they were trying to touch me. I wanted to sink my teeth into them.

And then my hand smacked her ass. I wanted to do it much, *much* harder but I know not to scare her off. Even though she hissed and squirmed away, I saw the lust in her eyes when I slid into the seat next to her. She tried to look angry. But I know that If I were to dip my fingers between her legs, she would be soaked.

"Are you staying at my dad's?" she surprises me with conversation. The way she says the question is as if she is going to offer me to stay with her.

"No."

"Well, where are you staying?" She frowns. "Have you found a place already?"

I ignore her and spin the car out onto the main road. I don't want to tell her I live at the club; either it's a shame that my work and private place are combined in one, or it's because I can't have her knowing where I live in case she shows up and I do something I regret.

She clutches her seatbelt and readjusts herself on the seat. I silently wonder whether this turns her on. I'm sure a naughty girl like her gets off on the pain, knowing it will be quickly replaced with pleasure. Perhaps tonight she will touch herself to it.

"Are you staying in a hotel or something whilst you're back in town?" She offers me a perfect lie.

"Yes."

"How long will you stay there for? I mean, how long are you back in town for? Is this a permanent thing, or will you disappear again?"

Fucking hell, she's incessant with the questions. *Why can't she be quiet and let me fantasise about her?* I refuse her an answer.

"You can stay at mine? I know it's not hotel quality and whatever. But it's warm and free." She looks nervous as she offers me. I stare at her in disbelief. I've just spanked her and humiliated her, and she's being nice? Or is she desperate for that greedy little pussy to be touched? *Fuck.*

"No." I refuse.

She reels at my rudeness. "I was just trying to be polite."

"Well, don't." I'm being mean, I know I am. And I'm sure she secretly enjoys the fight if she's honest with herself. Animals like me and her thrive off our natural instincts. We fight. We fuck. We fight again. I want the raw primal feeling from her. And she will learn to crave my rage, but I can't push her away too hard.

"I will take you back to the club Tuesday night," I state,

mentally checking the rota. It's just me working that night. It should be safe to bring her back.

Her eyes widen. "Really?"

I nod my head slowly. "If it helps you with your book and gets your crappy publisher off your back, then sure, why not?"

Of course, it's a lie; I want her with me. I want her turned on and needy. I shouldn't want her this bad, or even let us dance in the forbidden desires, but I can't help it. I *need* her near me.

"Okay," she agrees. "Can I join in this time?"

"No."

"But—"

"Just, *no*," I bark.

She glares at the side of my face, and strops. "I will just go without you then."

"You can try. I will ban you from going alone."

"What!" she almost screams. "So, I'm not allowed to play with or without you?"

My cock stiffens. "Exactly."

"That's not fair." she pouts.

I shrug. "It's my club."

Unwillingly, the dampness on the chair flashes to mind. *Lick it up,* the words were on the tip of my tongue. Literally, the only thing that stopped me from forcing her to taste her sweetness, was the two other people in the room. I don't want them to see her like that. I don't want anyone to *ever* see her on her knees for them again. She is mine whether she likes it or not.

We drive in silence for the remainder of the journey, and I'm almost thankful. She doesn't know what's best for her and keeps pushing. She will push herself away if she's not careful. I don't want to hurt her— but if she tests me, I will bend her over and spank the attitude out of her. *Fuck sake that's an image that will haunt my wet dreams tonight.*

"Thank you for taking me." She is suddenly, weirdly, grateful. I squint at her, trying to figure out what her aim is. "You're welcome."

"I'll see you Tuesday."

I nod at her slowly and she climbs out of my car. Only this time, I don't get out to help her, nor do I strike her on the ass, no matter how much I fucking want to. I wait for her to enter her house before driving off.

I'm still on the fucking clock. Instead of patrolling, I will go to the office and fuck myself over her reactions to me tonight.

CHAPTER FOURTEEN

Vixen

It was eleven o clock, and I started to drift off, but a light switch inside her house startles me awake. *Fucking finally— she's back.*

I have no idea where she has been— maybe walking her dog or seeing a friend— who fucking knows. All that matters is that she's back in my sight. As soon as she enters the house, my eyes almost pop out of my fucking face. The dress that she's wearing — holy fucking shit. I have *never* seen such a beautiful body wear such sexy clothes. I'm instantly hard. She hurries in and goes straight to her desk, her chest rising and falling almost breathlessly. I watch her yank the laptop closer and she starts frantically typing away.

I stare down at my phone, checking what she's written. She has now carved out rough characters. A dark-haired man, and a dark-haired girl. I instantly feel jealous— I want her to see my blonde hair and piercing eyes. I want her to describe *me* in her book. If I can't fuck her in real life, I want to at least imagine myself with her through a story.

She stops writing and I stare up at her expectantly. She reaches down and slips her heels off before throwing them away from her like they've offended her. Then, she gets up and disappears for a moment. Panic flashes in my chest when I don't see her in another room. There must be one other room that is north facing. Every other room, I can see straight through. *All except one*: next to her bedroom. Soon, she returns, holding a box. I watch in curiosity as she places it down and sinks to her knees.

Slowly, she pulls things out. I pull out my binoculars to get a better image. And holy fuck, my heart almost stops.

It's a box *full* of lingerie and toys. She pulls each set-out, holds it against her body, and admires it, before moving onto the next one. My cock springs to attention when she starts playing with the toys. There are cuffs, whips, gags… fucking *everything* that makes up my wet dreams.

I want to be jealous about why she owns this stuff. *Who has she been playing with?* But I can't bring myself to feel anything other than hunger. She lays them all out, and drags her fingers across them, before settling on a crop. Still on her knees, and still in that beautiful fucking dress, she runs the crop over her body. My mouth is permanently hanging open now as she runs the end over her nipples until they stand to attention. Her head falls back in pleasure. Then, she pulls it back and thwacks it on her nipple, her entire body shuddering with impact. I have to physically stop myself from bursting into that house and fucking her dirty. She smacks the other nipple, followed by spanking her ass a couple of times.

Then, she reaches for her phone and sets it up on the counter, and the breath is snatched from me. She clicks play and starts to play with herself. I could click a couple of buttons and watch her from my phone, but I decide to watch her in person— *it's far sexier*. She takes it in turn, playing with the whips and toys, inflicting pain on herself. Then, she reaches down and pulls her dress free. I fist the binoculars tighter, desperate to keep a grip on reality. Her large tits spring free and I bite back a growl. She twists to the window, and for a second, she almost sees me. I lurch back behind the tree and count down from ten before I can't resist looking out again.

She is wearing her little black thong and nothing else, legs spread apart, giving me the *perfect* view. I choke on a breath. She has repositioned her phone in front of the window. But now it's as if she is performing just for me.

I fist my cock and fuck myself as she brings a small vibrator to her clit. She remains on her knees— as if she's been perfectly trained. My good girl knows she is to cum on her knees for me. I imagine leering over her, smacking my cock on her face. She will ride her toys and suck my cock at the same time before I make her cum and she turns her attention to me and my cock, choking on the cum that she forces out of me. *Fuck.*

Her window is open, and I hear the faint, breathless moans slip from her. It almost throws me over the edge. I wonder what she's thinking of. Is she imagining that it's me between her legs, bringing her closer to the edge? She doesn't know me and yet I fucking better be in her fantasy.

A low growl hits me, and I chase my high, but when she clicks something on her phone, I freeze at the realisation. *Who the fuck is she going to send this to?* I'm a jealous asshole. I know I am, but I can't have her going any further, without knowing who she is sending this to. Before I can stop myself, I dial her number. I'm obsessive, jealous and possessive— perhaps I *am* crazier than Dagger in that regard.

I watch as she startles and stops playing with herself. She stares at her ringing phone but doesn't answer. I call her again, and again until she finally picks up.

"Hello?" That sweet, innocent voice rings through. So *that's* what you sound like, little minx.

Now I have her on the other end, and I freeze. *Who do I say I am? Her stalker? What do I say to her? Do I tell her to keep fucking herself?*

I keep my voice low, trying to disguise myself. "What are you thinking about?"

She is like a deer in headlights. "What?"

"You're touching yourself. What are you thinking about?"

"H-how?" She stumbles into silence before rising to her feet, fear slowly sinking into her. She tears her gaze around and tries to hide her modesty.

"Back on your knees." I bark, and she falls back to the floor. She tries to cover herself up with her arm, and I tell her off about this too. "Bare all to me, baby."

"Who is this?"

"Does it matter? You're on your knees like a good girl. We both know you enjoy being humiliated. Being used." I take a guess and get it right.

"Shit," she hisses. "P-please— who is this? Where are you?"

I watch as she squints her eyes, trying to spot me, but I push myself backwards further into the bushes next to my stalking tree.

"Turn the vibrator back on," I demand.

She shakes her head. "I'm going to call the police."

"Do it. I'll punish you before they get here."

I hear her gulp on the other side, and I could cum on the spot. She is so fucking hot, the way she obeyed me just then was hotter than I imagined it would be, and even though I never wanted her to know about me this way, the thought of her sending another man what is *mine* angered me. She's so willing to be degraded, but just as I remember her previous actions, jealous flickers over me. *Would she do this for anyone who knows her kinks? How many people has she been a brat for? Fuck. Has another man trained her?*

"I promise that you will not want me to repeat myself."

She jumps into action and turns the vibrator back on. A little whimper falls from her lips, and I eat it up. "That's it. Good girl."

"P-please!" She doesn't know what she's begging for. She is scared and turned on. I *knew* she got off on humiliation. "Are you going to hurt me?"

"I would never hurt you," I flinch. "Without your consent."

She visibly shivers. It makes my smile drop and my hunger grows worse. "Put the phone on speaker and place it in front of you."

She does as she's told, much to my delight.

"Now pick up that purple dildo and tease your hole," My eyes are wide, *frantic*, I can't miss a second of this.

"W-what?"

"Do it!"

She leaps for the dildo before pushing her thong to the side. She raises up on her knees before bringing it to her hole. My binoculars catch how fucking soaked the dildo is already on the tip.

"Don't let the vibrator fall from your clit." I fuck myself faster at the sight. "Okay, good. Now, slowly slide in."

"All the way?" She whimpers, causing a wicked grin to fill my face. It's about seven inches and thick enough for her to be full —but I need to see her do this. If she can't do this, she will never be able to take me. "All the way."

Her eyes are wide, and she's still trying to find me in her garden, but she is also very responsive. Slowly, I watch as her tight pussy swallows the toy. A pained look flickers across her face, and her mouth falls open as she rocks her hips to the pleasure that hits her. It's the most delicious fucking sight ever.

"I said all the way in!"

"I can't!" she exclaims. "P-please. I've never done this before."

"The dildo or phone sex?"

"Both!"

Her answer sends shivers down my spine— *how delicious.* "You're going to learn both today, then, aren't you?"

She bites her lower lip and sinks lower on the dildo. Her head falls back in bliss, and she starts bouncing. She doesn't even need to be told—she instinctively knows exactly what I want from her. I hear the faint buzz of the vibrator, mixed with her breathless pants. They get more intense until I know she's close.

"Stay on your knees and sink as low to the ground as you can," I order her, but she panics and raises higher until I tut. At the sound, she almost throws herself back to the ground. A scream leaves her lips as the toy sinks all the way inside of her. *Bliss is an understatement for us both.*

"Close your legs now," I order her, imagining how fucking full she is going to feel. Shakily, she readjusts herself, and her clit gets trapped around the toy— I can tell from the way she trembles and moans.

"You can release the dildo; that's not going anywhere. Your greedy pussy is going to cling to it. With your spare hand, reach for that crop." I am so fucking hungry as I openly stare at the scene in front of me. I've been around kinky clubs my entire adult life. I know exactly how to please a woman, how to move a woman, how to get them cumming hard and fast. But with her, I almost want to drag her pleasure out. A sadistic part of me wants to deny her orgasm together. I want to tell her she can't touch herself at all. I want to push her to her limits and then offer myself to give her that sweet release she is desperate for. But that would be punishing myself too, and I'm far too gone to have any restraint.

She picks up her crop and waits for her next instruction, like a good girl. "Spank yourself."

"Where?"

I groan at her breathless question. It shows exactly how delicious my good girl is for me. She doesn't stray away from knowing her place. I am in charge, and she fucking knows it. She is simply my sex doll to do as I please. It's like she doesn't need an explanation, like she *knows* that I am her pleasure dom, and she, my sub.

"Your ass. Right on the crack. I want it close to your asshole. Got it? Do that ten times, getting harder each time."

"Ten!" her eyes bulge out of her head. "I don't think I can. P-please, mister. I am really close."

"Already?" I grin. "You're such a whore."

She shivers and the way her body moves under the toys, makes her fall closer to the edge.

"Spank yourself— *now*! You are not allowed to cum until the ten are up!" My voice is strangled with pleasure. I'm right on edge as she shoots into action, knowing how close she is. The first one is soft. *Too soft.*

"Harder," I hiss.

"Yes, mister!" She squeals excitedly before delivering a harder blow. The most delicious scream falls from her lips. She spanks herself again and again, and as instructed, it gets harder and louder. I can hear the spanking from the window now as well as the phone. I have to stop wanking myself off as I get dangerously close to the edge. "Count the last three out loud. I want them as hard as you can."

"One!" she cries out. Her head rocks forward. She shakes like she's crying, but my little whore, fixes her position and spanks herself again. She can't resist following instructions.

"Two!" she folds in half again as she takes deep breaths. She desperately steadies herself and the pain, trying to avoid cumming all at once. Delivering the final blow to her body, she screams, "Three!"

At the same time, her orgasm shoots through her, and as soon as she starts cumming, I fist my cock violently and shoot my load everywhere too.

"Ohhh fuck!" she screams. "Fuck, fuck, fuck!"

The sound spurs me on more and I cum more than I ever have

before in my life. I wait for regret or guilt or post-nut clarity to hit me as soon as I calm down. But I can't bring myself to promise to never do that again.

Not now that I know my little plaything loves to—well— *play.*

CHAPTER FIFTEEN

Rebecca

Last night feels like a fever dream now— I have never been so fucking turned on. First, the club then my stalker made me cum so hard. *I fucking knew there was someone watching me.*

My blinds are down today to hide as I get ready. For all I know, my stalker is still out there right now., waiting for me to show some skin, to show the bruises that are slowly forming on my ass. I can't believe I did such a slutty thing! *Who even was that man? What if he took a picture? What if I've spurred him on enough to hurt me? Fuck! What was I even thinking? And worse— why do I want him to come back tonight?*

Yesterday was the first day I've felt alive in years. It's fucking stupid, at the humiliation and degradation of Brandon and my stalker, I felt more in control than I did in any of my encounters with Leo. Both men were in complete control yesterday, and yet I felt as though I was the powerful one. It's crazy. I barely know them— they're strangers—and yet I felt safe. *It's such a weird fucking thing.*

I hear Sara's car pull up onto my drive, and I force my blush down.

"Come on, Fish," I call out before throwing my coat and wellies on. When I open the door, she throws herself into my arms. "Oh, it's been so long! I miss you so much!"

"Hey, my dear," I chuckle into her hair. She doesn't release me, and I make no effort to pull away. We are inseparable, my best friend and I, but I broke that by moving an hour away from her. After a couple of minutes, she releases me.

"I thought we could take Fish for a quick walk. I'll show you around the fields and then we can grab a coffee back at mine after?" I tell her the plan and she nods excitedly. Fish runs out between my legs and jumps up at her excitedly, and scratches at her legs as if attempting to scale her body to hug her.

"Oh, my goodness! Hello, beautiful!" she squeals, pulling him close to her. I laugh and hurry them out of the house before locking up.

"Which way?" Sara asks as we get to the end of the path. I nervously cast my gaze right towards the end of my garden, and my cheeks flash red about last night's memories. I can't tell her this though, and it's hard— I've never kept a secret from her before, but if I try telling her that I not only answered a no-caller id number after having a psycho ex but also fucked myself whilst this stranger watched—*demanded*— she'd slap the shit out of me.

"Left," I say quickly. Fish is way ahead already, leaping down the path and into his familiar favourite crops and we trail after him.

"So, how was dinner with daddy?" Sara smiles before pulling my arm into hers. "Was the food magical?"

I chew on my lower lip. "Sure."

"Just sure? What's up? What are you not telling me?" she eyes me up suspiciously.

"Dad's engaged."

"Holy shit!" she exclaims. "To that Cheryl woman?"

"Yup." I feel sick thinking about it. "And there is something else… Well, do you remember Brandon?"

"Hot dad's best friend Brandon. The one you tried to kiss, and he pied you off? Sure, how could I forget!" she mocks me, and I groan at her playfulness.

"That's the one," I answer quickly. "Well, he was there too."

"What!" She stops walking.

"Yeah, my dad invited him." I suddenly feel shy about the whole situation. She cocks an eyebrow up at me and gestures for me to keep talking.

"Well, dinner was lovely and everything. Well—not amazing— you know how it is between me and my dad. But, anyways, we — I mean, *I* got very drunk, so I couldn't drive home."

"I like where this is going." she grins like a Cheshire cat. I playfully push her.

"Brandon called me a taxi, and, well, he took me all the way home in the cab. He didn't stay, or anything. But I was so drunk, Sara. Like—"

"Oh great, this is what I want to hear. My best mate decided to move twenty-something miles away from me just to get herself into dangerous situations that I can't help her out of!" She scolds me and I stumble to a halt in my sentence. *If only you knew exactly the kind of shit I've been getting up to here out here.*

"Why do I feel like that's not the end of this conversation?" she sighs dramatically. I give her a sheepish smile before telling her about the sex club. *That* I won't keep from her. I explain about the different rooms, the different kinks, and how it helped me with my next chapter. I tell her all of the surface details, but I resist describing how I felt, how *he* made me feel. How he degraded me and made my nipples hard, how he slapped my ass and bossed me about—*no*, I can't tell her about all of that. Not yet at least— she is already judging me as it is.

"What does your dad think about that? That's pretty weird, Becks." She frowns. I give her a pointed look. "I am twenty-six years old. I can go to a sex club if I want to! I mean look at my books—"

"You and I both know that's not the weird part."

"Sara! Stop, okay. I know it is wrong. I know that it's forbidden. We shouldn't, of course, I know that. Which is why we didn't—" I ramble on.

She cuts me off. "So that's the end of that story then, right?"

I stay quiet.

"Becks!"

"Fine! We are going back tomorrow night."

"Are you fucking kidding me?" She gawps. "He is like twenty years older than you! Not to mention your dad's best mate. Imagine, Becks. I would be fuming if you fucked my kid."

"Don't say it like that!"

"That's *exactly* what it's like though!" she bites back, and I suddenly feel really guilty. My shoulders slump. "You're right. I know it's bad. I really shouldn't entertain it, but I promise you, the sex club really did help my novel."

"I bet it did. But it's not good for your head. You can't fool around with older guys. They just use and abuse you, my love."

"Brandon is not Leo." I hiss.

Leo enjoyed hurting me, over and over— he enjoyed making me feel worthless and used both mentally and physically. He didn't do it because he thought I'd like it. He did it because it gave him power. Brandon isn't like that. I get the vibe that he would hurt me because I'd *beg* him to. Leo would stab me and leave me to die. Brandon would sacrifice me at the altar and lick my wounds clean straight after. He gave me a safe word, for Christ's sake!

Perhaps that's the difference between the men. One is sin— and I crave so much of it— the other is pure violence.

"I know. I am sorry. Maybe I'm not being sensitive enough." Sara lowers her voice. She rubs my arms up and down reassuringly. "I just really don't want you getting hurt again, Becks."

"I know. I know, but Brandon is different. I promise you. Not everyone can find their one true love the first time they meet a boy, like you, Sara. How is Andrew, anyways?"

She purses her lips and arches an eyebrow but drops it quickly. She starts walking again and I follow after her, her silence making me nervous. "Sara?"

"I need to tell you something."

It takes me by surprise. My usually wild and happy best friend looks tired. She is pale and looks exhausted.

"What is it?"

"I may or may not—" she pauses, collects herself, and then spits it out. "—I'm pregnant."

It's like time has stopped. The squeal which leaves my lips is like no other. I throw my whole body up and down excitedly. "Oh, my goodness! That is amazing news! Yes!" I stumble to a halt when she doesn't smile. "What's up? Aren't you happy? You've been trying for such a long time! Isn't this what you want?"

"Yes, it is." Her voice sounds strangled. I arch an eyebrow up at her. "What is it, Sara? Why aren't you happy? You can talk to me."

"I guess I'm just a little startled. It never felt real before but now it does. Like, I'm carrying a *child*, Becks. I am responsible for this baby. *Is that something I can do?* You know Andrew. He's always away with work. I don't know—" She sighs sadly. "—am I ready? Can I be a good mum?"

"Sara, stop it! You will make the best fucking mum ever, okay? Who else makes the sun shine on a rainy day? Who else will tell me *exactly* how something is? Only you, my love. You will be the most perfect mum. I can't think of anyone else who is better suited to becoming a parent." I ramble on about how amazing my best friend is because it's true. She is my rock. She has always been there for me when no one else was. She is only one year older than me, but she has played more of a motherly role than Cheryl in the last ten years. Sure, I didn't accept Cheryl with open arms. But my Sara was always there for me, to pick me up, dust me off, and push my head high, even on the days that I didn't want her, or anybody else, around. *That* is what makes a fantastic mum.

"Trust me." I stroke her arm gently. "You will be perfect."

Hope drifts back onto her face. "You think?"

"I *know*."

"Thank you, Becks. I really needed to hear that!" A wide smile slowly appears on her face and I blink back the tears threatening to spill over.

"Can't believe I'm going to be a teen mum!" She snorts.

"You're twenty-seven."

"See?" she says, exasperated. "*Teen* mum— *how ever will I cope?*"

CHAPTER SIXTEEN

Rebecca

My heart rate picks up as we pull into the car park of the sex club. I don't know why I feel so nervous. *Perhaps it's because of what happened last time I was here with Brandon.* He degraded me, spanked me, and I fucking loved it, but then I went home and came for another man. The memory causes my heart to overfill with guilt.

"You ready?" Brandon's low voice pulls me back to him. I give him my best smile before nodding. As usual, he races out and gets the door for me. I take his hand and step out of the seat, brushing off my dress. I'm wearing a very similar dress to the last time I was here. It's another tight halter neck with a keyhole part that my breasts burst out of, but this one is dark blue and has silver jewels tumbling where my naked thigh is. I didn't wear a bra today either; I hope Brandon realises this. I wouldn't mind a repeat of last time.

"You look stunning, by the way," he whispers before leading me up the steps. I grin at him and try to hide the blush that stains my cheeks. "Thank you."

We make our way through the entrance again before he stops me at the board.

"Choose a room."

I almost pounce closer to read all the words. My finger touches the board and I run down each of the lists. I find myself being pulled to floor four where all my main interests are.

"That one," I say shyly. He leans over me to read better, and I'm instantly wrapped up in that delicious oaky scent. I want to keep him this close to me forever; I never want to go sober from his scent.

"The weapon fetish room," he startles. I nod slowly and think of an excuse to hide my humiliation for liking this kink. "For my book character, of course."

"I'll take you to whichever room you want." He sees through my lies. Then, he holds his arm out. I stare at it suspiciously, before letting desire lead the way. I grip his bicep, and we start to climb the stairs, but with these ridiculous little heels that I'm wearing, it's going to take all day. As if he can read my mind, Brandon slows down, however, he doesn't wait for me to take another step and catch up with him. Instead, he scoops me up into his arms. I gasp and my hands shoot around his neck to keep myself stable.

"Brandon!" I cry out his name in shock, but it makes him turn rigid. Heat floods through me as I realise what his name on my lips has done to him.

"I want to get to the room already. I'm not doing four floors of you walking like a new-born deer." He grumbles and it sends a shiver through me. He is so authoritative, *so fucking sexy.*

"Whatever you say." I smile innocently. I am not going to complain about being so close to him, am I now?

Eventually, we make it up the stairs and he stops us outside the room before finally putting me down. I slither down at him, feeling our bodies rub against one another. I jolt as my clit hums in approval.

"Are we going to play?" I tell him with round eyes.

He glares at me. "No."

"Why not?"

He doesn't answer me and instead leads the way into the

WE SHOULDN'T

viewing area. I stumble after him, and to my surprise, the viewing room is empty.

"Just us?" I speak my shock out loud.

"I booked out the entire place just for us."

"What?" I gawp at him. "Why would you do that?"

"So, we can watch in peace."

"We watched in peace last time!"

He shakes his head. "*You* watched in peace. All I could focus on is the stares on the back of your head from other men."

"Really?" *I'm actually very shocked about this.* "I didn't notice anything."

"You were too busy gawping at the show."

"You mean like what I'm supposed to be doing?" I raise an eyebrow at him. It feels like an attack, and I become defensive.

He nods his head and grins. "Exactly. At least now we don't need to worry about potential distractions, eh?"

It doesn't make much sense to me, but I bat it off and turn my attention to the screen. I am instantly hot by the sight. A woman stands with her legs chained apart, her hands tied above her head, while she wears a blind fold. She whimpers when the sound of a door unlocking rings around. I watch, wide-eyed, as a man enters the room. He wheels in a tray behind him, and I gawp at all the weapons. *Knives, bats, whips, a gun.*

"Is that real?" I whisper in shock. Brandon watches me like I'm the funniest creature he's ever seen. But he doesn't answer me.

"Brandon? Is that real?"

He shrugs, but his lack of answer tells me what I need to know already. My heart leaps out of my chest and I lean closer to the window. The woman moans when the whip meets her naked body. The sound shoots to my clit, and I cross my legs to hide how horny I already am. *This* is my kind of fantasy. I've always felt like there is something wrong with me. I thoroughly enjoy pain during sex. The more it hurts, the harder I cum. It's fucked up. My fear, my anger, my pain— I can't help but be turned on by the thought of someone I trust doing this to me.

"What's he doing?" I whisper mainly to myself as the man strikes her one more time before picking something out of the tray. I can't quite make out what it is until he brings it to her body. Then, he flicks each of her nipples and attaches the chain to each one. My hands shoot up to my breasts and I subconsciously cup them, anticipating the pain. Brandon hisses beside me and I quickly lower my hands, but it's too late he caught me groping myself. My nipples stand proudly out of my dress, and he stares at them hungrily.

"Have you ever tried nipple clamps?" he licks his lips. I shake my head slowly, and it seems to only add to his desire. He curses under his breath and tears his gaze away. But I'm so fucking hot and horny for his gaze back on me. Just like my stalker who ordered me cum, Brandon oozes the same type of obsession for me, even if he refuses to admit it. I drop my hand to my thigh, and I draw circles on it. I sense his gaze back on me again, but I pretend not to notice, and stare into the window. The lady moans and writhes in pain as she buckles against the chains. My thighs part ever so slightly before I press them back together and pull them apart again. He must know I'm doing this to get some pleasure out of it, though he doesn't stop me.

"What are you most looking forward to?" he asks me in a dark voice. I stare at the table of weapons, and no matter how many times I try to drag my gaze elsewhere, it somehow always drags back to the gun. Curiosity takes hold of me. *What is the man going to do with it?* My tongue wets my lips greedily.

"Answer me," I jump when he barks an order.

"The gun!"

"Good girl," he says so quickly I almost mishear it. "What do you think it feels like?"

I gawp at him in shock. My mouth opens and closes like a fish out of water. "I-I don't know. What is he going to do with it?"

"Use that pretty little head of yours. What do you *think* he's going to do?"

I am completely taken aback by his words and so fucking turned on.

"Brandon," I say warningly. If he keeps teasing me like this, I don't want him to pull away. I don't want him to leave me panting, breathless, edged. I desperately long for a release. I want him to give it to me.

"You can touch yourself if you'd like," he tells me slowly, his eyes scanning me for any form of reaction.

"I thought we were not allowed to play. That it's crossing boundaries between us," I whisper. He shrugs his shoulders and forces himself back in the chair. He tries to look relaxed, but that hungry look never leaves his face. "I'm not going to touch you. You're not going to touch me."

"What if I want you to touch me? What if I want to touch you?" The words leave my lips before I can stop them. His nostrils flare and that wild look in his eyes eats me up. "I'm not going to touch you today."

"Today?" I raise an eyebrow. "But you want to touch me?"

I love how he readjusts himself to my words. He might be in complete control of my body, but fuck, it goes both ways. I have some power here too; he just has to look past his own limits. My eyes drag down and immediately, I spot his already hard length outlined perfectly in his trousers. The way it sits within them can't be comfortable— especially by the size— *fuck*. He must be like nine inches— it is fucking massive!

"Don't look so frightened. You want to touch me, remember?" he mocks me and snatches that power straight back.

I nod my head slowly. "I want to touch you *and* taste you."

He snarls. "Shut up and watch the show."

He switches on me so quickly it gives me a headache, but I do as I'm told and return to the screen. The man has picked up the gun and twiddles it in his fingers.

"Any guesses what he's going to do with it?" Brandon talks to me again but rises to his feet. I stiffen as he walks behind me.

"Eyes on the screen," he orders. I shiver excitedly, praying he breaks his rules. My body begs for him to touch me. "She might suck it."

On cue, the man thrusts the pistol into the woman's lips. Her tongue darts out and she tastes the metal hungrily, her excited moans filling the atmosphere.

"What does it taste like?" Brandon keeps teasing me.

"It's going to be cold, metallic and hard."

"Good girl," he praises me in his velvety voice before placing his hands on mine. He picks them up and controls my limbs. It takes my breath away when I hear his breathless grunts in my ear. Then, he brings both our hands to my breasts before he squeezes.

"Fuck, Brandon!" I hiss, but he scolds me.

"No, this is all you, Rebecca. You are touching yourself, got it? I'm just giving your greedy pussy a helping hand."

I want to complain and demand that he touches me instead, but I know it'll just make him stop. And like fuck do I want him to stop. So instead, I squeeze my tits hard and rub my palm against my nipples. The man in the performance pulls on the chain on the girl's tits as she sucks on the pistol. On cue, Brandon readjusts my fingers around my nipples before he sharply presses them together, trapping my nipple.

"*Oh fuck,*" I cry out in pleasure and pain, but Brandon doesn't relent. He pushes harder until I'm panting and dizzy, and only then does he stop squeezing. He makes me palm my tits to remove the pain before squeezing them again. He repeats this a couple of times until I'm squirming.

"I bet if you stand up the chair is going to be soaked," he growls into my ear. His hot breath on my skin makes my clit swell desperately.

"Remember to keep your eyes on the show," he demands, before gently pulling my hands down my body. I part my thighs expectantly. He is in complete control of me— I have no fucking clue how he manages to do this, without ever once touching me with his actual fingers. He pushes down on my knuckles and my fingers curl, until my nails are raking up my inner thigh.

"Shit," I hiss. It's humiliating how I haven't even touched myself on my clit, and I'm so ready to cum. The minute he stood behind me, I was panting and desperate for him. In the show, the gun is pulled from her lips before suddenly pressed against her pussy. The gun is swirled around her clit, and at the same time, Brandon forces my fingers under my thong, to touch my clit. I arch my back with a gasp.

"You play with yourself so beautifully," he tells me, running my fingers through my folds. I am so fucking wet. I couldn't be more soaked if I tried. And he feels how easily I run through myself, earning a low growl. Then, we circle my clit a couple more times, in line with the gun on the woman's pussy. The woman in the show gasps, but I'm full-on moaning and squirming around.

"Maybe we need to tie you down too," Brandon tells me with a dark chuckle. I almost scream 'yes please', but it doesn't matter what I want, because he is in control here, and I wouldn't have it any other way. My eyes are wide as the gun is lined up with her entrance. On cue, Brandon forces two of my fingers together and lines me at my entrance. A long mewl escapes my lips in anticipation of what is going to happen. Then, before

I can sneak another breath in, the gun is plunged into the woman's pussy, and my fingers are slammed into me.

"Oh shit!" I scream out in bliss. Brandon fucks me with my own hand, hard and fast, and fucking relentlessly. He grabs my other hand and forces it on my clit, and before long, I'm on the edge, begging to cum.

"Please! *Please*! Brandon, I want to cum!" I cry out.

He tuts in my ear. "Has the woman on set cum yet?"

I shake my head. "No, but—"

"Then you don't cum either."

I've never known a man to take control of my body before. The words 'your stalker' comes to mind but it's suddenly fucked from my brain as Brandon picks up the pace. I buck my hips against our hands. On set, the man throws a dog collar around the woman's throat and pulls. I pull my hand up to bring it to my throat, but suddenly, I'm choking and spluttering. Brandon's fingers cut off my airways in the most delicious way.

"Keep playing with your clit," he growls, and I shoot back down. My fingers work tirelessly inside of me until my head falls back, and I'm panting. "P-please, I can't hold off much longer!"

"Don't you dare cum," he barks, but it has the complete opposite effect. That dark voice, followed by the heat of the situation, his hand around my throat... *I cum so fucking hard.*

"Fuck! Oh my God! Oh fuck!" A string of curse words falls from my lips as I ride my high out. However, as soon as I break the rules, Brandon releases his touch on me. He is in front of me in seconds, holding his hands up to show me he isn't touching me, but at the same time, he watches me without ever blinking. He punishes me by not giving me my orgasm and leaves me to do it myself.

As soon as I come down, I peer up at him guiltily. What I do not expect, however, is that dark, challenging look that glares down at me.

"You disobeyed me."

I gulp. Something tells me I'm about to be *really* punished.

CHAPTER SEVENTEEN

Brandon

"You disobeyed me." I can't help the flash of anger; it's coupled with hunger and excitement. She knows it too. She sinks to her knees, as if in understanding. I stare at the wet patch on the chair, and I lick my lips. I really want to fucking taste her — *everything inside of me is begging for that.*

"Get up and follow me," I spit before twisting my heel and marching out of the room. As soon as the door closes behind us, I hear the woman in the performance roar with her orgasm. I smile. My dirty little minx was never going to last another couple of minutes. I played dirty. I knew my words would make her cum. I knew my fingers around her neck would send her overboard. Everything I did, I did with reason. And clearly, it worked.

"Where are we going?" She asks nervously, struggling to keep up. I march her down the end of the corridor before standing outside an empty room. Her heels click on the floor behind me.

"In," I tell her, pushing the door open. She looks at me sheepishly, before sliding past. I smack her ass and she hisses in pain, reaching back to rub it. I smile, relishing the sting on my fingers.

"Go to the middle of the room and get on your knees," I order her. She quickly does as she's told, and even puts her hands behind her back. I don't know if she does it on purpose or if it's an instinctual move— but holy shit does it make my cock strain. She is so well trained; she just doesn't know it yet.

I approach her and yank my tie from around my neck. I make sure to stand with my cock inches from her lips. She swallows hard, her eyes never leaving the huge bulge. And then, I bring the tie around her face, to remove her sight. She shivers.

"Remind me again. What is our safe word?" I tell her, not because I've forgotten, but because I need to make sure she remembers.

"Meat," she whispers apprehensively. I nod slowly.

"Good girl. Now close your eyes."

"What are you going to do with me?"

"If I tell you, that will just ruin the fun." I chuckle before heading over to the curtain on the far side of the room. I pull it back, revealing all my toys. My cock strains as I run my fingers over the different whips and paddles. I grab three before bringing them back before her. I drop them just next to her legs, and she jumps in shock as the noise echoes around the room.

"Reach out and feel them. Then you will choose which one you want to be punished with." I order.

She is hesitant at first but then eventually feels around on the floor in front of her. I am glued to the scene, the way her lips round, or when they pull up into a smile. I wait for any sign of discomfort. I anticipate any signs for me to stop.

Contrary to what many people think, a safe word isn't something to seek after. I don't *want* her to be pushed to ridiculous limits. I don't want her to have to use her safe word — that isn't the fun of rough and kinky sex. That is just a fucked-up power trip. No. I want her to feel scared but safe, pain *and* pleasure. If she uses her safe word, then I know that I've broken that trust, that I pushed her too far. That's no fun for anyone. Having said that, I will also keep my little minx being tested. I know she longs for all the fucked up things I can give her. I see the way her body reacts to me, to my words, to my abilities. She longs for the good and the ugly.

"This one," she says breathlessly, holding up the long thin ruler and I grin. The last time I took her to the club, she almost drooled at the sight of it. It's only right that I bring it back out for her punishment.

"Bend over and arch your back. I want your ass in the air, and your face pushed into the ground." I order her about, and she quickly pushes herself into the position I want. A hiss slips through me with how fucking perfectly she arranges herself. Most first-timers don't arch their back as deliciously as this. Her breasts and face are firmly touching the ground and yet her ass is high up.

"Well done," I whisper, stalking around her. "How many times do you think you deserve to be spanked?"

She hesitates.

"Come on, Rebecca. I don't usually give out this option. Pick a fair number." I tut.

"Five!"

I smirk and continue walking around. My eyes widen at the red marks on her behind. I run my fingers across it, and she shivers.

"How did you get these marks?"

"I, er-"

"Don't lie to me," I warn her, but I really fucking hope she lies to me. I'll be able to tell.

"I spanked myself."

"Why?"

"It turns me on," she answers quickly. I want to push further. I want to ask her in what circumstances, what with— I want to keep pushing her until she either lies to be or confesses the truth. Then I want to punish her for it each way. Instead, I cup her round ass and heat it up under my hot touch. I keep her grounded in the moment with me.

"You think five is a fair number for disobeying me?"

"Yes!"

"You're kinder than I am, but I will allow it for now. Five it is." I pull my hand away and test my whip on my own palm. The sting pulls through me, and I can't help the grin that spread across my face. "You will count each one and thank me for it."

The way her head is snapped to the side means I can see her lips open in shock. She then sinks her teeth into her lower lip and nods quickly.

"Use your words, baby." I scold her.

"Yes, yes, okay!"

Satisfied she understands what to do, I press the ruler to her ass before pulling it away and striking her. I make sure to hit her exactly on the red marks for maximal reaction.

"Ah, fuck," she cries out. I quickly hold the place where I spanked her to relieve some pain. "Are you forgetting something, sweet Rebecca?"

"One! Thank you, Brandon!"

Oh shit. Usually, my playthings call me 'Sir', but how the fuck can I deny my name on her tongue each time?

"Good. Again." I bring the ruler back down, hitting another part of her ass. She is ready for the pain this time and hisses instead of crying out. Then, she remembers her line, without prompts. "Two! Thank you, Brandon!"

I strike a third down before she has a chance to collect her thoughts. She jumps out of position and grabs her ass with a long mewl. I push her hands away and cup them with my own. The pain subsides slowly, and she grits her teeth together. I frown down at her.

"We can stop," I say, trying to hide my disappointment.

"No!" she eagerly says to my surprise. I stiffen and wait for her to say something else.

"Thank you for the third, Brandon. Please give me my last two." She gets back into position. I fist my cock to give myself some relief. She is so fucking hot that it hurts.

I readjust myself so that I'm standing directly behind her. Her asshole stares up at me and I almost cum at how tight and unused it looks. From this position, I see her pussy glisten with her juices. Before I can stop myself, I gently press the ruler to her lips and rub it slowly. Her ass wiggles as she grinds against the ruler.

"I bet you're getting off on this," I tell her, shocked. She moans in pleasure and then a sharp gasp leaves her lips. I realise what's happening. I thought she was in pain, but it was far from it. The little whore was going to cum! Without permission- *again*!

"You want to cum again?"

"Yes, please!" she answers without hesitation. I strike the ruler down on her ass again and she whimpers breathlessly. "Number four. Thank you, Brandon!"

I stare down at her in complete awe and wonder. I've never met anyone so responsive to pain before, so willing to be degraded and used. "I bet you could cum without being touched."

"Y-yes, Brandon!"

I am shocked by her answer. I've seen men cum without being touched before. But hardly ever a woman. They cum quickly with me—*very fucking quick*— but never without some type of clitoral stimulation. And then there is kinky Rebecca Jones, who is getting off to being spanked by a ruler.

"You ready for your final one?"

"Yes, oh, yes! W-wait, can I cum please?"

"Are you think you deserve an orgasm after disobeying me?" I smack the ruler gently against her clit and her thighs slam shut around it. The noise that leaves her lips has me fisting my cock faster.

"I'll do anything!" She cries out. "I am desperate."

I tut. "You are a desperate little whore, aren't you? Have you no shame? Grinding on a fucking ruler. Begging to be punished."

"Oh, my god," she whimpers.

"Fine." I stare down at the delicious mess before me. "You may cum with your final spank. Don't forget to thank me though, Rebecca."

She nods frantically. I take a couple of steps back and line up the ruler with the underside of her ass, where I know it will sting like fucking crazy *and* ripple across her pussy too. Then, I count down from eight so that she is dripping for it, unable to guess when it will hit her. Finally, I pull back and I swat it down on her ass so fucking hard, the vibrations shoot back up my arm. On cue, she screams out "Five" followed by "Thank you, Brandon!", before her entire body convulses from her orgasm. She rides wave after wave until she is a trembling, whimpering mess on the floor.

Just the way I fucking want her.

CHAPTER EIGHTEEN

Rebecca

He completely and utterly humiliated me in the most delicious ways possible. I knew I liked pain—but cumming from just being spanked? It's the kind of thing you only read about in smutty books. And fuck, I loved it. The ruler, the degrading words, *him*— holy shit. *Who would have thought I'd enjoy the punishment so much?*

I roll over in bed and feel that familiar ache in my ass. It's dull and throbbing yet sends sparks straight to my clit which is also bruised from the ruler. I reach for my phone and see three missed calls from an unknown number. My stomach immediately flips. *What if my stalker was trying to get hold of me again? Should I be scared that he has my number? Why am I so turned on by the thought of interacting with him again?*

However, my thoughts are instantly silenced when I see something green and long on my bedside. I shoot up in bed.

"What the fuck?" I shriek the words and scramble away from the piece of corn. It feels like my heart is going to pop out of my fucking chest as I stare at it. *How the fuck did it get there? Who put it there?* No fuck that, I know *exactly* who put it there. My stalker. *But how did he get in?*

Frightened, I stare my gaze around to Fish who has shot up in his bed from my screaming. He cocks his head to the side and stares at me with those sad, round eyes.

I scramble to my feet to check all the doors— *locked*. Rushing to the windows, I check those too, but yet again, they are locked. I feel sick as I embrace myself, desperate for some reassurance. Maybe my stalker isn't as harmless as I first thought when I spread my legs for him.

Fuck —how could I be so stupid? This isn't some type of book I'd write about—no, this is real life, where there are real consequences!

Scrolling through my phone, I stare down at all the missed calls by an unknown number which only brings more worries to my mind, and shivers down my spine. *What should I do? Who do I tell? My dad?* No fucking way. *Sara?* I can't! They will both ask questions. *And what if my stalker spills the truth about me? About my fucked up kinks?* I have enough about me in the news as it is. I don't need any more sexual fantasies of mine going worldwide, I'm having a hard enough time as it is convincing people about my ex's awful actions. This would only support his claim that I *enjoyed* the assault—*fuck*!

Fisting my hands in my hair as I pace back and forth, I have an idea, one that makes my heart skip multiple beats. With a shaky breath, I scroll through my contacts before finding Brandon's name with the number he left me the other night. Before I have the chance to change my mind, I click *ring* and anticipate the repercussions.

It rings once, then twice, and, on the third ring, he finally answers.

"Brandon?" I say breathlessly.

"Rebecca?" he sounds confused. "Are you okay?"

My heart beats more frantically in my chest, but I'm frozen. *What do I tell him? That I was spreading my legs for another man? That I'm nothing more than a little whore who has an overwhelming attraction to both my stalker and my dad's best friend? What kind of image does that send out?*

"Rebecca? Talk to me."

"Oh, hi, yes!" I squeak in panic.

"Are you okay? Why are you calling?"

I hesitate before I spin my lie out quickly. "Sorry, wrong number!"

Before he can ask any questions, I hang up the phone and chuck it to the other side of the room. My feet march me back and forth in frustration again. A strangled cry leaves my lips. *Why do I always get myself into these fucked up situations?* I need to stop living in my fucked-up fantasy world that everything is safe and fun when it comes to those two men!

Suddenly, my phone rings again. I quickly grab it, but my heart almost skips a beat when the unknown caller flashes to the screen. I chew my bottom lip so hard that it bleeds. Do I answer it? I can give him a piece of my mind and threaten the police. He'll leave me alone then, right? I will only have one fucked up desire then. My finger slides to answer the call and I press it to my ear. My heart skips a beat as I wait.

"Rebecca?" It's a female voice and it startles me. "Rebecca? It's me, Grace, your publisher. Sorry, I'm calling from this number. I had a call with someone previously and I didn't want them to have the office number. You know how these people are!"

I feel like I could kiss her out of gratitude but stab her in frustration. In the light of day, and with adrenaline pumping through me, I felt strong enough to take on my stalker.

"Hello?" She calls out again.

"Yes, I'm here!"

"Okay, good. We need to run through a couple of things." She says before sighing heavily. "Firstly, how is the book coming along?"

"I, er—" I hesitate. "—well, I have the characters sorted out and a couple of chapters finished."

I can imagine her lifting a thinly plucked eyebrow. "How many chapters?"

"Three."

"Three!" She squeaks in shock. "Rebecca, the deadline for your editor is in two weeks!"

"I know! I'll get it done, I promise, Grace!"

"You must! You know that your readers are slowly losing patience with the constant push backs. How many times can we delay a piece? We need to be in their good books, especially recently!" she sighs dramatically. "You need to get on that, okay? Anyways, let's change the subject real quick. We need to talk about Leo."

I feel sick and my heart drops in my chest. Shakily, I drop to the sofa and pull my legs to my chest. "What about him?"

"He wants to talk to you. He said he wants to reach an agreement."

"An agreement?" This takes me by surprise. My voice is shrill when I speak again. "Why would he want an agreement when he is denying it ever happened!"

"I know, I know, my dear. He wants you to sign a non-disclosure agreement."

It feels like the world around me is spinning. "Why would I do that?"

"He says that you're ruining his career. He will sue you for defamation if you don't sign it."

The scream that rips from me is unlike anything I've ever heard before. "Then I'll counter-sue for fucking domestic abuse, Grace!"

"You know you can't. The jury will have a bias, and—"

"I don't give a fucking shit!" I explode. The world becomes hazy as my eyes fill with tears. I can hear my heartbeat in my ears and the bile rises quickly in the back of my throat. I want to yell again, but my voice cracks into something weak. "I will not sign anything."

There is a short pause on the other end. "I know, my dear. I am so sorry that this is happening to you. I tried to negotiate with his manager, but they are refusing any other options."

"I-I can't." I sob. "I won't!"

"I will keep trying, okay? I won't make you do anything that you don't want." Grace's voice is a whisper. She knows exactly how hard this entire situation has been for me. I lost over ten thousand followers within two days when he claimed I was lying about the situation. The numbers have been plummeting ever since. Everything I worked so hard to build is quickly falling down.

"Ah, crap—" She hisses. "Right, another number is calling. I am so sorry to leave you like this, Rebecca. You've got this, okay? I'll call you right back, my dear!"

She hurries it along before ending the call. I am frozen in the chair, rocking back and forth. The snot dribbles down my nose and my face contorts into an ugly, painful scowl. My entire chest aches. Awful sounds escape my body— noises I didn't think were possible. It happened three months ago, and yet it hasn't gotten any easier. It feels like the whole world is against me. The lump in my throat grows bigger and bigger until I'm almost choking on it. My jaw hurts too, and now my entire body throbs awfully.

My phone rings again. Without checking the number, I answer it. Frustrated blubbers escape my lips. "No, I won't do it, Grace. P-please don't make me!"

"Rebecca?"

I stiffen. *That's* not Grace's voice.

"Rebecca? Are you crying? What's up?" Brandon panics. It feels like my chest just empties when I hear him. I force myself to be strong and I try to sniffle up the snot without him hearing. My eyes squeeze shut to force out any tears, to make my vision less blurry.

"Rebecca, answer me, god damn it!" he barks. "Don't make me come over there!"

"I'm here!" I startle. "I'm fine, Brandon!"

"You're not fucking fine. Do not lie to me, Rebecca."

My heart aches. I rock myself back and forth slowly and drop my head to my knees. "O-okay, I'm not fine."

"I'm coming over," he snaps, but I refuse. I don't want him to see me like this. I don't want him wasting his time on me. I am supposed to be the cool and sexy plaything, not the snotty, dribbling mess. "No, no. Please don't. I just need to be alone right now."

"I'll be ten minutes. Stay where you are." He doesn't give me any time to protest before he hangs the phone up. I hear the sound of car keys before it ends.

Wiping my tears and snot on the back of my pyjama top, I have no clue how he'll get here in ten minutes when I'm in the middle of nowhere, but a part of me— *scrap that—my entire being* doesn't care. It feels as though Brandon will be the only person who'll understand me right now. He doesn't need to tell me. I recognise another broken soul when I see one.

True to his word, after ten minutes, I hear the sound of a car pulling up. He bangs on the door, and I weakly open it. I'm suddenly wrapped up in his strong arms. That delicious smell fills my lungs, and it relieves me almost instantly.

"Are you okay?" he asks, his tone is nothing but concern for me. I feel him press his lips to the top of my head and my heart throbs. I need to push him away; I need to restate our boundaries. We can only touch whilst we are in the sex club. That is our place to be foolish. To make bad decisions. To be other people— not my dad's daughter and best friend. But I can't push him away. *How can I?* He holds me close to him and doesn't relent.

For a second, I consider lying to him but then shake the thought away. "Honestly? No, I'm not."

"Talk to me." He pulls away, but he seems reluctant. Then he gently takes me into the sitting room, as if he knows the layout of my house like the back of his hand. As we pass my bedroom, I see him, out of the corner of my eye, scan the room. His eyes fall on something, but I don't see his reaction before he hurries me to the sofa. Mentally exhausted, I collapse onto it, pulling my legs to my chest.

"It's my ex-boyfriend."

"What about him? Did he hurt you?" It takes me by surprise the way his jaw ticks angrily.

"N-no." I lie to him, and he slams his eyes shut tightly, before snapping them open again. When those stunning eyes fall on me, I shiver. They are as black as the night, like a hunter who has located his prey.

"Don't fucking lie to me." His voice is just as cold as his expression.

"I-I'm not lying."

It feels like I *must* lie. There are so many reasons keeping me from telling him the truth. For one, those eyes are telling me everything I need to know about the thoughts rattling around his head; he looks intent on killing Leo. His knuckles flash white from how tight he is balling them into fists and that vein in the side of his head jumps out menacingly. His teeth grind together aggressively. Secondly, should I be practising for the NDA? Eventually, Leo and his shitty managing team will coerce me into signing it, so I might as well get used to the pain and hiding. I know that when I tell Brandon, everything will change. He oozes power. Rage. I don't think for one minute he will let me walk away from this without having a serious plan in place to hurt Leo. Or at least, he won't let me walk away without convincing me to stand my ground. But should I listen to people fuel my stubborn fantasies? I gulp.

"Rebecca," he calls me back to him. The way he says my name almost unravels every ounce of strength I have left in me. "Did. He. Hurt. You?"

"Y-yes," my bottom lip wobbles.

"How?"

"Brandon, I don't want-"

"Tell me," He is stressed. It's like hearing the words out loud will send him into a full-blown attack.

"I-I can't!"

"Yes, baby, yes you can," he reaches forward and takes my hand in his. His touch is warm and comforting. It's like he removes all my stress and fear. But he is still just a man; Leo is a God. He has managers, security, and lawyers… he has everything that makes him untouchable. There is nothing we can do.

CHAPTER NINETEEN

Brandon

I comfort her in the only way I know how— I touch her. But this is unlike our other touches. No, this one is softer, gentle, kind. I wait for it to feel odd, or to have that urge to pull away, as I do with nearly every other woman, but it doesn't come. I mean, even when I walked through that door, and saw her tear-stricken face— I *had* to embrace her. Hold her still, give her strength when my little minx lacked it. When I heard her sobs at the end of the phone. *Fuck.* I've never felt my heart twist so weirdly.

I only called her back out of curiosity about why she hung up on me. I don't know why I feel so strongly about her sadness. I want to believe it's because she is only allowed to shed tears for me, and yet something much stronger pulls through me. I've known her for her whole life; I just want her to be happy.

"You can trust me," I tell her, shuffling closer. Those wide, sad eyes examine me quickly. She pauses, takes a shaky breath, and starts. "He was a-abusive."

A sharp hiss leaves my lips, and I must physically slam my mouth shut to stop the curse words.

"I tried to leave, multiple times. I promise I did, but he threatened my career, my life. I only finally managed to escape when I realised that I could buy a new place hidden away. H-he can't find me here. Surely."

She says it slowly, examining my reaction. But she's holding things back. I don't know what to say. All I want to do is comfort her and then find the cunt and kill him. But I keep the violent thoughts to myself. All she needs now is a shoulder to cry on; I never thought I'd be able to offer that, but, I will try. A sudden wave of guilt hits me. *The sex club. The kinky rooms. Humiliation.* Have I pushed her too far? How fucking stupid of me to involve her in fetishes, without knowing her limits? Without knowing her triggers?

"Rebecca—"

"What we did was different," she suddenly snaps. Her hands grab mine and she pulls me close. "You hurt me because *I* want to be hurt. He did it because it brought him joy. You are so different. We have a safe word. He refused me one."

"Shit, Rebecca—"

"I'm not crying about that. That was months ago. I just f-found out—" she pauses to collect herself as a sob escapes her lips. "—he is going to make me sign a non-disclosure agreement so that I stop talking about it, or else, he will sue me for defamation. And I can't counter-sue! I can't afford a case either! And just look at my books, what I'm into—"

I pull her into my arms for the second time today. She fits so well in my grasp. I just wish we learnt about this under different circumstances. My shirt grows damp with her tears, and it makes me tense. "We will sort this out."

"We?" she suddenly pulls away. "There is no we, Brandon. This is my problem."

"Not anymore."

"W-what do you mean? You have to promise me that you won't do anything with this information. Let me sort this out alone!" Her large eyes plead for a reason. I shake my head.

"No."

"Brandon, please!"

"You will not suffer alone. I won't let you," I growl out the words, and she shivers. I instantly feel guilty; I'm scaring her, making her feel worse, but I can't fucking unclench my fists. All the ways I could torture him come to mind. He will fucking pay for hurting her.

"Y-you're not going to kill him right?" She looks petrified.

"Christ, Rebecca. No, of course, I won't."

A lie.

"No," she is stubborn. "You won't do anything. Let me handle this, please." The way her eyes shimmer with tears does something to my heart. I sink my teeth into my tongue. I really don't want to agree to her terms. All I want to do is to set my psychotic brother on Leo and see how long he lasts. She thrusts her pinkie finger out at me.

"Pinkie promise me, Brandon."

I blink back the confusion. "What?"

"Pinkie promise me that you won't do anything to Leo and you will let me handle this."

I'm reluctant, but how can I say no to someone like her? With a deep sigh, I bring her hand to my face and kiss her pinkie. I know that's not what I'm supposed to do, but it's what feels right in the situation. "Fine. But if he tries anything again, I'll take over."

"B-but-"

"Now you pinkie promise me that you'll tell me if anything else happens," I thrust my pinkie out at her, and she blinks at it a couple of times, shocked. Then she brings her lips to my pinkie and kisses it. I know it shouldn't but something delicious twists in my stomach. I almost want to slip the digit into her mouth and make her suck it. The wild thoughts claim me before I can stop them.

"Why are you helping me?" She takes me by surprise.

I frown. "What do you mean? Of course, I am going to help you."

"Why?" She forces me to say the words, but I won't. I'd rather choke than confess whatever the fuck is growing between us. That's the shit that makes you weak. It's too soon to have a description for it. Just wild, mad lust.

"As a matter of fact." She pulls back. "Why are you with me at all? What changed, Brandon? Why have you suddenly reappeared, and you all of a sudden have an interest in me? You didn't like me before you left, so why now?"

"What?"

"You know *exactly* what I'm talking about. The kiss! You didn't even want to kiss me then but now you're taking me to sex clubs, making me do sinful things with my body. Making me feel things I have never felt before."

I'm mortified. "Christ, Rebecca. Are you still upset over that kiss?"

"Yes!"

"*Fuck sake.* You were eighteen. My best mate's daughter—"

"I am still his daughter," she hisses. I watch as the sadness transforms into anger. Her fingers curl into fists and I have to bite down the excitement that grows within me. *Will she fight me? Will she hit me? Does she think that she can actually hurt me?*

"I wanted you to be my first kiss. I trusted you; I liked you. And you pushed me away, I felt stupid, immature—" She rambles on, and even though I try really hard to focus on her words, all I can do is watch her eyebrows pinch together, the rage flickering in her eyes, her tight lips. Fuck, she looks so good right now.

"Who was your first kiss?" I'm a cunt for asking selfish questions at a time like this, but I don't care. "Who took your virginity?"

I shouldn't torture myself with the information, but I *must* know. *Who the fuck took my place? Who do I need to hurt?* She doesn't answer me and instead purses her lips.

"Your abusive ex? He was your first?" My eyes bulge out of my face. Then, the information sinks in more. "You were a virgin at eighteen? You hadn't kissed anyone at eighteen?"

Her cheeks flash a dark red, and the hunger only grows within me. Hunger *and* anger. I gave that up. I could have taken her, just like I wanted back then. But no— I left. When she wanted me most, *needed* me. Her mum died; her dad moved on—*fuck*.

"Have there been any others?" My voice is a whisper. The jealous part of me roars for her to say no. The reason within me begs for her to say yes. Please tell me that Leo didn't get to own you completely.

"No," she says. "I lost my virginity at twenty-three. I was waiting."

"Waiting for what?"

"I, er—" she stiffens.

"A name. Give me a name, Rebecca." I grind out.

"*You*" she whispers. "I was waiting for you, but you were gone."

Another sharp hiss slips from my lips, and I have to physically look away to hide the snarl on my lips. I count slowly down from five until my heart doesn't feel like it's going to explode.

"It's ironic, isn't it? I am a near virgin, and yet I write the most deranged, fucked up scenes."

"It's only deranged if you don't understand it." I bite back. "But you understand it. Don't you? You love that shit."

I turn back to see her cheeks darker than they've ever been before. Something primal in me wants to lean forward and bite the rosy apples. Her squeal would be just as sweet as her skin.

"I do." She confesses, eyes full of lust.

I gulp down my anger. "It should have been me. I should have been your first."

"You should have."

"But we shouldn't be doing this." I gesture between us slowly. "It's not right. Your dad is my best friend. He'd never forgive us. W-we shouldn't do this."

She agrees. "We shouldn't."

Something within me snaps. Suddenly, I feel my body lurch for her, grabbing her cheeks with my fingers. I hold her still before slamming my lips to hers. A long-time fucking coming, and yet completely forbidden. She gasps, and it gives me space to deepen the kiss. My hands jump to her hips, and I bring her onto my lap. She straddles me instantly, and it takes everything within me not to fuck her right now.

My hard cock strains against the material of my jeans—against her little pyjama shorts. It would be so easy to move them to the side and touch her. I bet she's already soaked. A slight moan slips past her when my fingers dig into her thighs. I kiss her with everything inside of me. I want to replace all those times she sought the touch of Leo when I *know* she wanted it to be me. She is so fucking sweet against my lips. I could get lost in her taste. Her touch. Her smell— *everything*. I want to drown in Rebecca Jones for good. And yet I must stay afloat.

Slowly, I pull back and it's the hardest fucking thing I've ever had to do. She whimpers from the lack of touch and fists my shirt. My cock strains: I will it to go the fuck down. I will not be having sex with her today. Not for a while. Not if I can help it. I must hold out. Reason screams that it shouldn't happen at all. But my heart screams that I will give it to her as soon as she learns to beg for it.

There are so many reasons to *not* do what I'm doing. And yet my fingers won't unclench from her thighs. I want it so fucking bad.

"Wow," she whispers breathlessly. The corners of her lips tip up into a smile. "That was worth the eight-year wait."

I groan. I really want to show her *how* much she'll miss me. But I resist the urge. "You cannot tell your dad about this."

Her eyes grow wide. "*That's* what you're thinking of right now? You couldn't give it a couple of seconds!"

"I'm thinking of that *and* fucking you raw and hard."

She gasps at my crude words. Then her eyes darken hungrily, and she licks her lips. I gently push her away from me to put distance between us. If my fingers are on her naked thigh much longer, I will not have the restraint to leave.

"Please." It is the hottest fucking sound. I shake my head.

"Trust me, little minx. One day, I'll fuck you. I'll fuck you so hard that you won't know which way is up and which way is down. I'll bring all your filthy little fantasies to life, and I'll ruin you for any other man. On that day, you will be completely and utterly mine. Got it? Tell me you understand."

Her chest rises and falls quickly. My words have a huge impact on her. She slams her legs together, and I have to clench my fists together to avoid spreading her thighs and seeing my impact on her. "I understand, Brandon."

There it is again. My name on her beautiful lips. I rise to my feet quickly. I must leave. It's too dangerous to be in a room with her when she is this riled up. When I'm too close to snapping.

"When can I come back to the club?" She calls out when I turn to leave. I stiffen and ponder the thought. *When are Dagger and Vixen not working?*

"I saw an article that there is a themed night on Thursdays." She tries again. I twist to face her, amused. "Are you stalking me? My clubs?"

Please say yes. Oh, please for the love of fucking God, say that you're stalking me. I don't know why I find it so hot.

"Perhaps." She whispers. I cock an eyebrow up. "And do you know what the theme is tomorrow night?"

She sinks her teeth into her lower lip. *So, she does know.*

"Go on. Say what the theme is. Tell me what you're desperate to go to." I flash a cocky smile. She gulps and casts her eyes around nervously. Then, she finds confidence and holds her head high. But I see the way she trembles and almost tipped her chin downward. "It's the dom and sub night."

"Good, girl."

Her face lights up in excitement. "So, are we going?"

"No way."

Her smile vanishes quickly. "What? Why?"

"I'm not going to let others see you with a collar and skimpy clothing." I force myself to gulp and remove the images from my mind. By my side, my knuckles whiten. *Others such as Vixen and Dagger.*

"Why not?"

"Did you not hear what I just said, little minx? Go on, repeat my words."

"That I'm yours. Completely and utterly yours," she whispers.

"Exactly."

"Are you going?" She arches an eyebrow. I hesitate.

"That's a yes," she spits bitterly, finally breaking eye contact. She stares down at her fingers in her lap angrily.

"I'm working," I tell her tightly. "It's my club. Do you know what that means? I have to be there to manage the new events. Dom and sub night included."

"Will you invite that receptionist to be your sub?"

I am startled by her jealousy, and yet furiously turned on. I grab her chin and force it upward, so she has to maintain eye contact with me.

I don't know why the words fall out of my lips so quickly. "You are completely and utterly mine. And I am completely and utterly yours. I don't want any other woman, okay? Nobody even compares to you, little minx. My cock grows hard for you. Only you. Understand?"

She nods quickly. I see the satisfaction on her face. "Good."

Reluctantly, I look at my watch. My shift starts soon. "I need to go now. But I will see you in the week."

"When?"

I press one last kiss on her forehead. "Soon."

Really fucking soon.

CHAPTER TWENTY

Vixen

I discovered the name of this club: *Shark city.*

A stupid name for a stupid club.

When I pull up outside, I'm instantly on edge, despite the sharp blade in my back pocket. I never leave the house without a weapon. I guess I'm just as bad as Dagger there. The club is down a dark alleyway and it's the early hours of a Sunday. Nothing scares me— not truly, anyways. But something in my chest screams that something is wrong. It's too quiet out here for this time in the morning, especially if the reports of this new club are correct— it should be buzzing.

I take a quick scan of the area to look for entrances, but it looks as though the front doors have been boarded up. Even the windows are covered. Down the side of the alleyway, two guards are hovering outside a red door. They're big fuckers and bald as eggs. Even though I don't doubt my fighting skills, I also don't want to attract much attention to myself. I need to keep a low profile to hide my brothers and me from the pimp's attention, to keep them in one place, so we can bring them down swiftly.

"You open to new clients?" I try, needing a way in.

The bouncers cast each other a look before one of them scoffs at me. "What's it to you?"

"I'm looking to become a member of a strip club. I'm new to the area. Paul recommended me this place." I make sure to drop the name of the last pimp we found and retrieved information out of. The larger bouncer trails his eyes up and down me. I give him my best smile.

"Get lost," he spits and my face falls.

"We aint lookin for new clients," the other adds for good measure. They don't give me a second to back away and reach for something in their back pockets. I unconsciously reach for my own knife too, ready to fight, but just as they start to pull something out, they stiffen. I hear a bark in the earpiece they are wearing. someone shouting orders at them. They look at one another and gulp. I wait patiently for them to turn back to me, but they don't. Instead, they open the door behind them and disappear inside, the heavy door slamming in my face.

I take a step backwards and scan the building. There is an open window above a couple of large bins. I sigh, realising what I have to do. With one final look to see if anyone is watching, I head over to the bins and climb up. It's wobbly but I finally get my balance before reaching up to the window, but I'm far off. It takes everything in me not to mutter under my breath the bitterness.

I jump and grab the window ledge. My fingers throb under my weight, and I slowly raise up to see if anyone is in the room. Satisfied that I'm in the clear, I throw my arm over, and quickly tumble through the window, trying to make my landing as soft as possible. My jeans get caught on the window and they rip and I grumble bitterly. Why does this have to be me? Where are Brandon and Dagger climbing through windows?

Just get in. Get the numbers. Get out. The voice of reason calls out in the back of my mind.

I rise to my feet and quickly scan my surroundings. I'm in a dressing room, and there are dozens and dozens of outfits. I make a mental note of the rough number. I listen out to the hallway, before sneaking out. Down the corridor, I can hear soft whimpering. My heart breaks as I sneak closer and closer.

There are a couple of voices in that room, and from the slightly ajar door, I can see at least eight women, sitting on the floor, cuddling their legs to their chests. Two pimps walk back and forth, hissing things into the women's faces.

I bite back a growl and resist the urge to attack and defend. It would be so easy to slip into the room and stab the pimps to death, but the trauma that the women would experience as a result— I can't. Dagger will take their life tonight without harming the women. I am just the observer.

I can't make out what they are saying, and I don't take the risk to go closer. I don't want to cast a shadow and bring attention to myself. All that I need to do is get a count of victims. I slip away from that room and stalk down the corridor, listening out for sounds.

A scream downstairs captures my attention, and I charge to the end of the hall, practically flying down the stairs. My protector senses tingle, and I can no longer stand and not help. Another cry for help from the very end of the building ripples, and my gut clenches. I slip against the shadows of the wall in case anybody goes to investigate, but nobody comes. I keep pressing forward but I can't see because the door is shut. I hear a smack followed by a female whimper. Then, begging for mercy follows. My heart is in my throat, and I do something I shouldn't— I knock on the door.

Then, I slip backwards against the wall again to hide. After a short pause, the door flies open.

"What? What is it?" A fat man with his trousers by his ankles stumbles out. He tears his gaze left and right down the dark hallway. "What the fuck? Where are you? Why are you knocking?"

I twiddle with my knife in my fingers, all the ways I could kill him spring to mind. It would be so easy to slit his throat and escape before anyone would realise. Even the victim wouldn't see it. So why am I hesitating? He goes to re-enter the room again, so I pull a pebble out of my pocket, and I throw it around the corner. The pimp snarls and charges after it like a Pitbull after a tennis ball. I slip into the room quickly and lock the door behind us.

A thin little creature is curled up on the floor. When she peers up at me, I have to bite my tongue to hide the hiss. She is black and blue with bruises, and the only other colour is crimson blood staining the wounds.

"Who are you?" she gawps and scrambles away. I try to make myself as least threatening as possible, but her eyes home in on the knife, and a fear whimper escapes her. I quickly slot it in my back pocket. "No, no! I'm here to help you! Don't fear me—"

"That's what *they* said!"

I freeze when I hear the door handle rattling. It's followed by a banging, and then the man starts yelling. "Princess, let me in! Open the door right now! What do you think you're doing?"

Mortified, she stiffens. Her gaze tears towards me and the door. "You're going to get me punished!"

Quickly, I punch a hole through the cardboard covering the window and check the surroundings. We are completely alone, and free to escape.

"Come on," I tell her, holding my hand out. She resists and I grow more frantic. "Trust me. I will take you to the police station. You will be safe!"

She shakes her head violently, and my heart pounds in my chest and I feel sick. The pimp begins calling for help. I can't be around much longer without getting caught. "I'm leaving, Princess. You don't have to come with me, but you must run. Do you hear me? Escape this hell hole. There are organisations which will help you. Don't stay here."

Tears brim in her eyes as she stares up at me. "You might be like them!"

She makes no effort to move. I go to grab her and force her to safety. I want to force her to live, to choose life, but it doesn't work. Instead, she screams and lurches away. *Fuck. I've frightened her.*

"No, I'm sorry! I don't want to hurt you-"

"Princess? Princess? What's happening!" The pimp roars. "Let me in, sweetie. What's happening?"

I want to force her to safety, but I don't. I *can't*. She has to make the decision for herself. All I'm doing is scaring her. I leap out of the window when the door starts to be pounded against harder. She glares at me with an indescribable hatred. She's been so indoctrinated that I will always be the bad person in her mind.

I give her one final nod, before disappearing into the dark. The only thoughts on my mind are to pray to whichever cruel fucking God out there that permits this kind of twisted stuff.

I pray for him to save her soul.

CHAPTER TWENTY-ONE

Rebecca

What the fuck am I doing?

I'm sitting here, working tirelessly. My legs ache from how long I've been cramped up in this chair, and a dull ache vibrates around my head from looking at the screen for hours on end. My eyes flicker to the piece of corn and I can't help but reach out for it, feeling the bumpy ridges. It's fucked up that I kept it, and *it's fucked up that I brought it into my office*, but something makes my body twist in the most delicious way possible. It's a reminder of my stalker and the power he has, how he makes me feel, and the dirty things I *need* him to do to me.

I tried to find him in my garden tonight, but he was not there. Perhaps this is the first time that he's not here; *not watching*. I feel strangely light, but heavy at the same time, like I'm unprotected when my stalker isn't stalking, it's as if he frightens all the other monsters away. Sadly, tonight, I'm completely and utterly alone, and I fucking hate it.

I fist the corn in my hand tighter. *What the hell am I doing?* I shouldn't be here. I should be at the club with Brandon. He gets to have all the fun tonight *alone*. I wonder if he's looking at any other women, *touching* them? Does he enjoy them the way I enjoy him *and* my stalker? I feel a wave of guilt. How can I dictate who he can and can't sleep with when I am desperate to see my stalker tonight, to spread my legs for him, to make him make me cum. *Is it fair that I want both men, whilst wanting them to both only want me?* No, of course not. *Will I change my desires?* Never.

The box of lingerie and toys is still on the floor under my desk from the other night. I eye up some of the sexy leather outfits and dog collars that lay on the top and my stomach twists. It would be so easy to show up, disguised, and play at the club. How will Brandon know it is me if I wear a mask? He would never find out. *Right?* I could just go for an hour... Maybe two max. Just to get some notes for the book—

I tingle with excitement, and just like that, my mind is made up. Quickly, I change into a long leather skirt and black lingerie bra that has flowery lace wrapping around me in strips of material, and I grab the matching lace mask, eagerly fixing it to my face. It stops just above my lips but hides everything else. I put on the brightest red lipstick I can find, before scooping my dark hair back into a ponytail. Then, I pick the dog collar up and slot it around my neck, and the tight feeling makes my stomach twist deliciously. When I catch myself in the mirror, I can't help the smile which stretches across my face. I look stunning if I do say so myself. And yet, something is missing. I run my fingers over my outfit as if that will help me figure it out. Then, I grab the piece of corn and pull off a green leaf. It almost looks plastic and fake with how perfectly shaped it is. It makes me wonder if my stalker spent hours searching for the perfect corn for me. I then take my hole puncher to make a small hole, before I slot a necklace chain through it. I don't know why I'm so attracted to wearing this leaf. It feels like I'm owned when I wear it like I'm marking myself as my stalker's property which is fucking insane since I'm about to go and seduce Brandon hopefully. It only turns me on more.

As I walk up to the front doors of the club, nervousness seeps through me. I wipe my clammy hands on my skirt and resist the urge to chew on my lower lip in case I smudge my lipstick. Maybe I shouldn't have done this. *What if I do get caught?* Brandon will be fucking fuming. And yet I want his punishment. I don't want anybody else in that place. I just want to watch and play with him. *Is that so wrong of me?*

"Have you got your ticket?" The receptionist shoots her hand out expectantly.

I freeze. "A ticket?"

"It's invite only. You would have been sent an invite by post."

"Ah, I forgot it," I lie quickly. "Is there any way I could just buy a new one now?"

She pulls a disgusted face. "Did you not hear me? It's invite only. Besides, where is your Dom?"

"He's in there already."

Her lips pull into a tight line, and she stares at me hesitantly. The panic rises in my chest, and I suddenly feel silly. Brandon's clubs are exclusive; *why did I think I would make it past reception?*

"What is your name?" The lady asks. "I can try to search for you on the system?"

I should probably lie so I don't get caught, but I tell her the truth and pray Brandon has put me on the system. "Rebecca Jones."

She arches a thinly plucked eyebrow. "Rebecca?"

My heart stops in my chest when she starts typing on her computer. I wait for Brandon to come out from behind the curtain and escort me off his property. I can almost feel his hot breath breathing on my neck as he works himself up, thinking how I'm purposely disobeying him. *That sharp slap on my ass as my punishment starts...* I squeeze my legs together to suppress the dull ache.

"Who is this beauty?" a deep voice takes me by surprise. I startle and look at a *huge* man with muscles bigger than I've ever seen before. His dark hair falls below his chin, clearly unbrushed. I mean, everything about him seems untamed. Those dark eyes, stubbly beard, sinister smile. *Fuck.* Something in my stomach twists deliciously. He wears a dark mark on the right side of his face, covering his eye and halfway down his cheek. There are thin lines of flowers dancing around on the mask to make him look less intimidating but if I'm honest, it doesn't work. My fingers itch to remove the mask and see what's underneath. What is he hiding? Something screams *danger* about this man, and I'm instinctively hooked. It's stupid but desire always did get me into stupid situations.

"Sir, her name is Rebecca." The lady at the reception offers my name to him. "She claims her Dom is inside, but she doesn't have a ticket either."

Sir.

Boss or sex name? I gulp and anticipate getting swiftly kicked out before I can even spot Brandon. How humiliating! The man in front of me grins— *actually fucking grins*, like a lion whose found the most vulnerable prey—and for some reason, unbeknownst to me, it melts me. He runs his tongue across his top teeth.

"Rebecca," my name vibrates from his lips. Instantly, my legs slam together, a wave of heat pulls through me, and my traitorous cheeks light up like it's Christmas. The man is *so* fucking good-looking. Taking me by surprise, he snaps his arms out and pulls me flush against his chest.

"I'm her Dom now," he says, oozing control.

Yes, fucking, please! I hear the words begging on the tip of my tongue.

"Oh?" The receptionist pulls back, flustered. "Yes, Sir. I'll mark her in on the register and write her down as yours for future references."

As yours.

My heart lurches. *Oh, shit.* I start to protest because I can't have

Brandon seeing my name written under another's, but the untamed beast in front of me, quickly pulls me away, forcing me to slam my lips shut as nervousness seeps through me.

"So, Rebecca." The man grins devilishly. "Which room do you normally go to?"

My heart skips a beat. I know that I should refuse him now that I'm in and run to find Brandon, but I'm fixed to the floor. He leers over me, and his towering height only spurs me on more. Suddenly, he snatches me and throws me over his shoulder. Everything happens so quickly that I don't have time to protest, and a gasp escapes me. He carries me as if I weigh nothing, and places a hand under my ass, where the material of my dress has ridden up. For a moment, his touch lingers there as if he's going to pull the material free and expose my bare ass to the world. But, to my eternal gratitude, he simply hides my ass from the sight of two men who are slipping past us on the stairs. As my *man-handler* takes the steps in threes, a breathless moan escapes me from the jagged ride where his shoulder juts into my stomach.

"Careful, princess. If you keep making those noises, I won't make it to the playroom before fucking you senseless," he growls, causing my heart to leap from my chest. I feel dizzy upside down, but I don't complain. My entire body is on fire in the most delicious way possible.

"Is that a promise?" I hear my breathless flirt.

"Fuck—" He hisses before putting me down in front of him. It's violent and clumsy, but it suits the man *very* well. He inspects me intensely. "You're new. I haven't seen you here before."

"I haven't seen you either." I counter quickly. The corner of his lip quips up into an amused smile as those sinful eyes drag up and down me, and it makes me gush again.

"I'm the boss."

"You are?" I'm breathless.

He nods slowly and a devilish smile spreads across his face. "One of them." Then, he barks an order— *"Come"* — before leading the way.

I follow lamely after him, and my heart almost stops when he takes me straight to the playroom instead of the viewing area. *I'm finally doing it— I'm finally going to play, fuck yes!*

As much as I wish it was Brandon in front of me, my sinful body is alight with desire for the other boss. I wonder if he will bring me as much pleasure as Brandon? When I stumble into the room, it feels as though all eyes are on me and the man. He glares around, and growls, and as if a switch has been flipped, everyone looks away. Even I find myself lowering my gaze to the floor out of respect for the predator who now commands the room's respect.

The man turns back around to me. "Come here, Rebecca."

I almost jump out of my skin. He frightens me with his deep, daring voice— yet I'm fucking drenched. "W-what's your name?" I dare myself to ask him.

His eyes light up in amusement. "Call me Dags."

"Dags?" *What a strange name. It almost reminds me of—*

"Oh yes, baby, say my name." He is instantly on me, lips attacking my neck. My head snaps backwards and a breathless moan escapes me. *Holy fucking shit* this is hot. His large hands grab my ass, and he squeezes. It hurts— *a lot*—but only spurs me on further. I throw my arms around his neck. Instantly, I feel drunk under his touch, and his grunts and heavy breathing make my legs snap together, but he pries them open. Suddenly, he throws me in the air as if I weigh nothing. He forces my thighs around his waist, and I instantly feel his huge fucking erection against my heat.

"Oh, God!"

He pulls away for such a short moment. "There is no God in this place, my little freak. There are only unsalvageable souls looking for more reasons to be punished."

"Little freak?" I say breathlessly.

His fingers curl into my soft skin. "Yes, my beautiful little freak, because I have a feeling you are going to like all the devious shit I plan to do with your body. We can be freaks together— only freaks crave this kind of unredeemable sin."

CHAPTER TWENTY-TWO

Brandon

"I found the new club where the girls have been transported to," Vixen sighs, kicking back into the chair. He puts his feet up next to the keyboard and rocks back. I eye him up suspiciously. "Go on."

"A place not far from here, actually. We can do the raid tomorrow morning as everything is in place. Quite a few girls are there, too. I will sneak back out tonight to confirm numbers and targets."

I give him a sharp nod. "Okay, good."

The familiar buzz ricochets through me. It's the best feeling in the world when you realise that a mission is slowly ending and we've rescued more people. My head thumps— this past month has been particularly difficult. The girls would have already been saved by now if it wasn't for Dagger's explosive outburst; it only makes everything so much more tense. I stiffen and push forward on my desk. *Speaking of the fucker*— "Where is Dagger?"

"Last I saw, he was patrolling the rooms." Vixen sighs. "Probably looking for some fresh Sub pussy to steal off another Dom. You know he loves to fight for it."

I roll my eyes and pull up the CCTV monitors in search of my explosive little brother. It takes me a while, but I finally catch him in the reception area. He is chatting with a woman who has her back to me. She stands with confidence in her tall heels and keeps her head high. I can see the way a band slips around her ponytail, so she must be wearing a mask. Her hair is long, curled and falls down her back. I appreciatively take in her curvy figure. She looks tiny opposite Dagger, but she doesn't tremble under his intense gaze. *I can't tell if she's brave or stupid.*

"Poor woman," Vixen scoffs. "She doesn't know what she's going to get herself into."

"It's none of our business," I release a shaky breath. Despite my words, I make no effort to stop watching. Dagger pulls her by her arm, eager to get her to a playroom— not that I can blame him. Her body is fucking stunning, it reminds me almost of my little minx. Suddenly, he throws her over his shoulder and his hands slam against his back in a short protest. I stiffen.

"Go save her," I tell Vixen quickly. "He's slipping too much lately to be trusted."

It fucking sucks that my brother is just as unpredictable and deadly as the men we hunt. It's fucked up because my brothers and I are into some *extra* kinky shit, hence why we pushed the floors up to severity seven.

Vixen and I know the limits—we are good at reading body signals when women are unable to use their words, but Dagger? He craves pain but it's mainly *his* pain. Women find it frightening when he asks them to bite, scratch, and *stab* him. If they don't give him pain, he gets frustrated and ends the scene early, or will *act out* and hurt himself in front of them. If that's not your kink, I can imagine it's fucking terrifying. Not a single woman has ever complained—*and I've asked them multiple times out of fear my brother was too rough with them.* But I also don't want my brother to push it too far, *especially* now that he is slipping away from reality.

"On it," Vixen dips his head before slipping from the room. I click on a new camera to see if I can get a better look at the woman. *Who will I have to pay to silence if my brother goes crazy?* He marches her to the fourth floor before putting her down. Again, her back is to the camera.

Turn around.

I will for the woman to look at the camera, but she doesn't.

Turn around. Turn around, damn it!

He pulls her against him, and she almost melts in his chest. Then, she looks right and then left, which takes my curiosity. *What, or who, are you looking for, little devil?*

I lean closer to the camera and catch a flash of red on her lipstick which peeks out under her dark mask. My cock hardens. That will be smudged all down her face by the time she leaves tonight, if not by Dagger, then most definitely by someone else because she is far too hot to walk out unfucked— and she seems to know it too by that cocky, confident sway of her hips, and flirty touches.

I wait for Vixen to appear on camera, but the two lovers disappear into a room before he arrives. I frown and message Vixen an update on where they've disappeared to. I can't see them anymore because we don't allow cameras in the actual playrooms for the security and safety of everyone. I'm almost disappointed I don't get to see the woman in action which is very fucking rare of me. My little minx comes to mind, and soon, I forget about the woman's seductive power and only worry for her safety in Dagger's gip. Impatiently, I twiddle my thumbs and count the seconds down for Vixen's arrival. *It would probably be fucking quicker to go down there myself*, but I shouldn't have to keep babysitting Dagger. Vixen can handle this one, I've done the last eight or so years.

Speak of the devil— he appears on camera before slipping into the room. A couple of seconds pass by before he marches out, the woman stumbling behind him. He drags her by the arm, and I wince. I didn't want him to be *that* rough with her. She stumbles to a halt, looking all dishevelled and breathless. As if she can sense me through the camera, she turns and looks directly into the lens. Her lips pull up into a smug smile, and it completely catches me by surprise. *I recognise that devilish smile anywhere.*

Fuck— *fuck*! I've never run so fucking fast in my life to get her. By the time I catch up to them, I'm seeing red. My teeth grind together, and I feel my own sanity slipping as my knuckles pop into their familiar white colour when I clench them. *She fucking disobeyed me.* She refused a command— *and now look at her*! Dagger *and* Vixen have their dirty fucking hands on what is mine.

When she sees me, her eyes under the mask go wide, as if she didn't expect me to appear so quickly.

"Rebecca," I growl, and she shivers when I say her name, and she has every fucking right to be nervous. Even I find myself second guessing the noise— it sounds nothing like me, possessive, jealous, promising *so* much punishment.

"Brandon." Her voice is small, and she plays the innocent, happy-to-see-me card. She slips out of the other's grip and stumbles toward me, where my hands snatch her hips and her chin. She winces but I struggle to care.

"What the *fuck* are you doing here?"

"I-I came to find you." I rip the mask from her face, so I can judge her apology better. I expect to see that bratty attitude that gets her in trouble usually, but instead, her wide-eyes and pouty lips greet me. Gulping down the desire, I force myself to be strong in my anger.

"You disobeyed me."

"What the fuck?" Dagger startles and we both turn our attention back to the other two. I hold my breath and wait for them to mock me or do something that they will fucking regret. Dagger looks upon us with a ridiculous amount of lust. The tent in his pants is huge and I roll my eyes. *Of course, he'd get off on this.* He has always wanted us to share a girl— it's been a dream of his for *years*. I always refused because there is no girl in the *world* who would be able to handle my brothers *and* me; we are too rough, possessive, horny. When I look at Rebecca, a pounding in my heart screams that she would be able to, but this time it's different because I am far too fucking possessive and jealous of this one to share. Yet, she was more than fucking happy to be thrown around by Dagger.

It is Vixen's reaction that shocks me: he looks numb almost. Those icy eyes are cold, and he glares at Rebecca as if she has torn his heart out. She feels the tension and unknowingly takes a step closer to me. *Wrong move.* She backs straight into my erection and gasps, and I can no longer think about my brothers— I'm hard in anticipation of her punishment. When she peers up at me, I recognise that look in her eyes. She is desperate— hungry— *ravenous.*

I have to make a scene. It's the only way I can assert dominance over her. *How can I claim her for myself in front of Vixen and Dagger?*

"On your knees," I bark. I feel the way she shivers under my touch.

"B-Brandon?"

"Don't make me repeat myself."

Instantly, she falls to her knees and hisses. The floor is cold and hard, and she will most likely bruise. I keep my hands on her shoulders so she can't get up again. She faces the other two men; their gazes are locked on her. Nobody breathes, and everybody waits for my next move.

"Why are you here?" I growl, grabbing her hair. The most delicious gasp escapes her. It makes Dagger's eyes light up with desire, and it makes me nervous. I need to make it *clearer* that she's mine. "Tell them who you are."

"I-I'm Rebecca."

"No, what are you to me?"

She hesitates, racking her brain for the answer I want to hear. "You own me."

Holy fucking shit. I was going for dad's best friend to show them how off-limits and forbidden she is to all of us— *but that works even better.* My cock jumps in my trousers again.

"You disobeyed me, Rebecca," I tell her sternly. I need to make a scene out of everyone. Teach everyone here that she's mine. *Only* mine. "You came here without permission, snuck in, came into the play area. You could have been hurt."

"B-but!"

"Did you kiss her?" My vicious gaze is back on Dagger who is startled. He looks lost— *miles away,* like an animal ready to switch to hunting. He starts to shake his head no but then stops lying. "*I* kissed her."

Fuck sake. I grit my teeth together. The anger is all-consuming. "Where?"

He points to his neck and then his chest, and this time, I growl. Viciously, I pull my lead out from my back pocket before bringing it to her neck and clipping it into her dog collar. She gasps and her hands jump to pull at it, but I quickly smack her protests away. "If you're going to act like a horny bitch, I'll treat you like one."

I yank on the lead, enough to pull her onto all fours, but not hard enough to cause any real pain. As much as it fucking kills me to let others see her in this compromising position, I have to do *something* to assert my dominance over her. *My ownership.* She is on her knees for *me*, and nobody else. I bare my teeth at the prying eyes, and they startle. When my attention returns to Rebecca in the crawling position, I am stiff as a fucking rock. Her perfectly round ass sticks in the air and she arches her back as if on instinct. She knows exactly how to keep me hooked.

"Then again, I reckon you are fucking loving this." I roll my eyes. "Reach between your legs. Push your knickers to the side, I want you to feel how wet you are for me."

She stiffens.

I squint at the thin material which is now being stretched across her ass, which also has *no* knicker line.

"You're not wearing knickers, are you?" I turn my nose up at her.

"No, Brandon."

Holy fucking shit, my name on her lips will be the death of me. *Yes, that's it, my dirty girl, say my name over and over, remind the others who you belong to.*

"Why not?"

"B-because…" She trails into silence.

"Because you are a whore."

"Because I am a whore." She is excited at the opportunity to degrade herself. A slight tremble takes hold of her, and I don't miss the way her thighs press together. She desperately tries to gain some friction.

"Who are you wet for?" I bark.

She answers almost immediately. "You, Brandon!"

Well, fucking trained. I can't resist teasing her— tormenting my brothers. I want them to know that she's off limits, but I also want to show them how well she responds to *me* and only *me*.

"Show us how wet you are."

She hesitates, but with a pull of the lead around her neck, she snaps back into reality. Quickly, she reaches up her skirt and almost falls at an awkward angle. I yank the lead to keep her neck held high and to balance herself. Then, she slowly removes her fingers and holds them up to me. *Fucking hell.* A sharp hiss falls from my lips, and it takes everything in me to calm down my racing thoughts. A clear liquid covers her fingers, stringing from them. I fist her hand, resisting the urge to lick it all off because I know I won't be able to resist going for seconds, and then thirds. When I taste her for the first time, I want it to be direct from the sweet source.

So, I settle for second best. *Humiliating her in the most delicious way possible.* "Taste yourself."

Her eyes widen and I use my thumb to part her lips before bringing her fingers to her lips. Obediently, her tongue sticks out of her mouth, and she tips her head back. I slide her fingers between her lips, and she flicks her tongue over her wetness, those delicious fuck-me-eyes never leaving my face. A soft moan slips from her mouth and her eyes flutter shut. I fucking snap. *She shouldn't be enjoying this as much as she is. I want her to be blushing, humiliated, not hot and ready. Not putting on a show for the others.*

"Come." I bark, before charging out of the room, my grip tight around the leash. She yelps and scrambles after me, remaining on her knees. It is the fucking hottest thing I've ever seen.

"You want something to suck?" I growl as soon as I lead her into a private room. Then, I twist to face her and yank at my belt. She stiffens, but her eyes light up with desire, and she nods frantically. I quickly free my cock from my jeans and pants.

"Fuck, Brandon!" She gasps, eyes full of lust.

"Mouth open." I bark.

"Y-you're huge," She is startled but does as she's told anyways. I fist her hair and pull her closer, and as if she's been trained perfectly, her tongue sticks out submissively and she tilts her head back to keep eye contact with me. *Holy fucking shit.* She hasn't even touched me yet and I could cum all over that pretty little face. I really didn't want to fuck her face yet, I wanted to hold off. I wanted to see how far I could push her delicious fantasies. But I've lost all sense of my mission, and I need her pretty little lips wrapped around me, almost as though I might die if I don't get it.

"Suck."

She pushes forwards onto her knees and comes face-to-face with my cock. She licks her lips before pressing a kiss to the tip. A groan tears through me at the softness.

"Wait." I groan, putting distance between us. "This is too easy for you."

Her eyes widen with concern, and she starts to protest but I quickly disappear. She knows better than to move without permission, and when I return, she is in the exact same position I left her.

"Close your eyes," I tell her. "And spread your legs wide."

She does as she's told quickly. I put the machine between her legs before gently pressing on her thighs to push her down. I push the vibrating seat against her clit, before taking a step back and admiring my work. She shakes with anticipation. I pull on her leash and her eyes shoot open again. Her tongue remains out of her mouth, waiting for my cock again. I push the tip between her lips, and she moans happily.

"The last time you were here, you came without permission," I tell her with a grunt. I feel her tongue lick at my hardness, and I watch as her cheeks hollow out as she sucks. She looks fucking amazing taking my cock to the back of her throat. She gags slightly, before pulling out and concentrating on the tip. Then, I pull the remote control out of my pocket and click on it. The sound of soft vibrating fills the room, followed by her squeal. She shoots upward but I quickly push her back down with a tut. "Oh no, my little minx. You're going to show me how much of a good girl you are, aren't you?"

Her eyes are wide. She sucks my throbbing fat cock so beautifully, keeping her arms by her side, never once using them to give her mouth a break. She is so painfully well-trained without much effort. It's fucking amazing.

"Feel the vibrations against your clit, getting faster and more intense, pushing you closer to your orgasm," I grunt, fucking her face quicker. She responds so well and lets me use her. "But you are not going to cum, are you? Oh, no, my little minx. Your orgasm is mine, your body is mine— and you definitely don't get to cum without my permission."

My words make her eyes squeeze shut and I watch as she desperately tries to control her impending high. I turn the machine up slightly, and she jolts upward. My hand gently takes her cheeks and I hold them as I fuck her mouth. A tear slips out of her eyes as she gags again.

"Good girl. Remember the safe word. I will never be disappointed in you for using it. Okay? I might have control over your body, but you have control over the situation. You have just as much power as me, got it?"

She reopens her eyes and there is a hunger I've never seen before in them. A gasp leaves her lips when I change the speed again on her vibrator. It's followed by a cry of pleasure. Now, her hands shoot forward, and she grips my thighs. She doesn't realise it, but the pain makes my cock harder if that's even possible. Her nails sink into the material of my trousers, and I hiss. "Fuck yes, baby. Suck that cock."

I fuck her face faster until I feel my release nearby. "I am going to cum into your pretty little mouth. Swallow it all down, baby."

Before I can stop myself, my release storms through me. It feels like I'm falling over the edge as I snap in half, emptying my load. The pleasure hits me over and over again in waves until my head feels dizzy. She cries out in pleasure as I push the switch up higher until the noise echoes around the room. "Cum for me as you swallow my cum!"

She responds quickly and soon she is screaming around my cock as her orgasm slams through her. She sinks her nails further into my thighs, and I revel in the pain. I watch as she gulps my cum down and slumps forward once her pleasure stops hitting her. I reduce the vibrations, but I do not stop them altogether. I zip my trousers back up, and grin.

Wide-eyed, she stares up at me and starts to raise from the machine. It feels like I've fucking snapped at the sight of her. *So beautiful, so willingly punished.*

"Where do you think you're going? Your punishment isn't over yet."

CHAPTER TWENTY-THREE

Rebecca

His growl is so fucking hot. *"Where do you think you're going? Your punishment isn't over yet."*

My stomach flips and every hair stands on the edge— it's the hottest fucking thing he could have ever said. The vibrations ripple along my sensitive clit, and it takes everything in me to keep my moans to a minimum. Then, he raises the vibrations, and a squeal leaves my lips. "Fuck!"

"You're going to keep cumming until I'm satisfied you've learnt your lesson."

"Brandon, p-pl—"

"It's too late for begging." He grins, and just with that lopsided smile, I feel my release close again. My eyes slam shut, and I try to focus on not cumming, but then I feel his fingers around my neck. They fist the make-shift-corn-leaf-necklace and then he pulls at it, breaking it. My mind screams at me to grab it from him, but I don't because just as his fingers stop scraping past my skin, my orgasm rocks through me, wave after wave. "Fuck! Fuck!"

"You're such a good girl." I hear him coo, as he cups my cheek. I'm sweaty, and I'm sure mascara is dripping down my face, but I know that's exactly how he likes me. I raise slightly from the board, waiting for him to push me back down again, but he mercifully gives me a small break. I feel how swollen and soaked I am, and what's worse, I *know* I could cum for him multiple more times. All he has to do is ask, and I would do it for him.

"What have you learnt from this lesson?" He cocks an eyebrow.

"Never disobey you."

"Good girl." He smiles proudly, and it oddly makes my heart pull in the most delicious way. "One more and then we are even."

My eyes widen, but I don't protest. I don't truly want to protest. I want him to give me everything and more until he breaks me. Because I know that he will kiss the broken cracks once he's done.

"Sink back down on it. Press your clit to the vibrator."

The vibrations attack my sex, and my head falls back as a long string of moans tumbles from my lips. I can still taste his salty cum, and it only spurs me on more. How forbidden and wrong the whole situation is... How I want everything he can give me. *And more.*

"Brandon!" I squeal, and my hands shoot out involuntarily. They curl around his hard biceps. He growls and turns the machine up higher. "That's it, my little minx, cum all over the machine. You take your punishment so fucking well."

His words push me over the edge. Suddenly, the high smacks through me. Wave after wave of pleasure attacks me repeatedly until my head feels dizzy. It feels as though I'm going to fall, but his large hands hold me still. My entire body feels alive and tingly. I breathe in his familiar scent, getting drunk off him.

"Atta girl," he whispers into my hair, before pressing a kiss to the side of my head. "Let me take you home. You must be tired."

I nod slowly, but the world around me feels heavy. The sudden exhaustion takes hold of me. He scoops me up in his arms, and I can't help but snuggle closer into him. I don't even care that everyone is watching him carry me out; I don't seem to be humiliated by anything he does to me. If anything, I welcome his hate *and* his love. *It just works.*

True to his word, he drives me home in my car. I'm grateful for him taking care of me or else I'd have to figure out a way to get it back tomorrow. When he pulls up, he quickly hurries out and gets the door for me, like a true gentleman. Only now I see how handsome he looks in his dark suit which clings to all his muscles. In the club it was dark, and my entire body was alive with lust. Lust will never die around Brandon, but at least now, I can think straight. He takes the keys from me and unlocks the door, leading the way into my home. He navigates himself into my kitchen and sticks the kettle on, to my surprise. He acts so much like he's at home, it makes my stomach twist deliciously. I haven't lived with anyone else since Leo, and I must admit that it's been weird not to have a man in the home, or hell, any person in the house other than two animals.

"How do you take your tea?" He calls out to me. I bristle at his question and blink back the confusion. "I, er—"

"Milk and two sugars?"

"H-how—" I stumble into silence as he pokes his head around the door. A knowing smile pulls at his lips. "You always liked sweet tea growing up. Didn't you?"

A little dumbfounded, I nod slowly. The fact he remembers that means weirdly a lot to me. I always felt like an immature child around him, like I wasn't really a *human*. The conversations he'd make with me were to be polite, and always in front of my dad. They never seemed to be made out of genuine interest, but clearly, he remembered. That must count for something. He disappears to make the tea and I sink into my sofa, pulling the fluffy blanket to my chest. Fish comes bounding in excitedly. He jumps around, licking my face and wagging so fast, it looks as though his spine is snapping left and right repeatedly. "Okay, boy! Calm down! Calm—"

Fish only seems to get more and more excited as I ruffle his ears around. He sits on me, *like actually on me*, so that I'm pinned to the sofa. His large head buts me over and over in the chin, begging for head kisses like I always give. I make the kissy sound, which makes his tail wag faster and louder against my legs. "Good boy! O-okay, down now."

He hesitates as if to decide whether he'll listen to me or not, but with a stern look, he gets off the sofa. Instead of retreating to his bed on the other side of the room, he flops in a ball on the floor below me. When Brandon re-enters, Fish's tail starts wagging against the floor, but he doesn't move from his position.

"Here you go," he says, handing me the cup.

"Thanks."

Instead of sitting next to me, he heads over to my desk where my open laptop is. I startle, remembering exactly what scene is open on my laptop. "Wait—"

"What's this then?" He arches a smug eyebrow at me. My heart leaps in my chest as he reaches for the laptop. I hold my breath and wait for the humiliation to sink in. However, at the last moment, he brushes over the laptop and picks up the corn. I stiffen. *Even worse.*

"A piece of corn? Like the one you were wearing earlier?" He stares intently at me as if he's anticipating my lie. Like a fish out of water, my mouth opens and closes and I stumble on the words.

"Did you pick yourself corn?" Brandon chuckles before dropping it back down.

"Yes!" I quickly take his lie. Before I can stop myself, I do another scan of my garden to search for my stalker, and I hold my breath. *What if he's out there right now, watching me with another man in my home? What will he think of me? Will he punish me like Brandon punished me?* Oh, I fucking hope so!

I bring the hot tea to my lips to distract myself. The heat doesn't help my burning cheeks.

"How is the book getting on?" He switches subjects before taking a seat on the sofa next to me. I kick the blanket out at him to give him some too. He stiffens as if he's deciding whether he should accept, and makes no move to snuggle under it, but he also doesn't push it off. *Small wins.*

"Eh, it's coming along. I have a couple of chapters now, I guess." I sigh dramatically.

"What's it about?" His eye contact is intense as he watches me squirm under his gaze. I grip tighter onto the tea. "I've decided it's going to be about a professor and a student."

Lie. The main character is the exact replica of Brandon *and* the female main character's stalker. It's almost like I'm writing a book about Brandon and my stalker in one— *the perfect man for me*— but, of course, I don't tell him this though. For one, what if he is startled that I'm using him as a love interest? Secondly, how do I explain the stalker fantasy without admitting to having one myself?

"Oh, really? Why's that?" he arches an eyebrow. For a moment, it's like he doesn't believe me. I shrug and play it off. "Just a common romance trope, I guess."

"Sure." I try to read into what he means by the word, but nothing really comes to mind. He casts his gaze out of the garden, before looking back to me. "I can't wait to read the book."

I almost choke on my breath. "You'll read it?"

"Yes, of course, I will. I want to read the novel that my sex club has inspired." he sends me a cheeky wink, one that makes me feel weak in the knees. If only he knew how much the book is inspired by him. *Would he go running for the hills? Would he think I'm weird? We've only been—wait, what even is this? It's just sex. Right?* There are no feelings attached, just primal urges. That's how it should be. It's almost like getting *romantic* is crossing the line, he is still my dad's best friend after all. Still twenty-something years older than me! It's wrong. It's forbidden. *We shouldn't.* And yet, it's exactly what I crave.

"I should return to the club," he sighs before draining his tea. I have no clue how he managed to drink it so quickly whilst it's so hot. "What? Already?"

"I only took you home to make sure you were safe, Rebecca. I'm still on the clock."

My cheeks flash a dark shade, humiliation hitting me. I snuck into his club, snatched his attention away from work, and then let him drive me home. I just completely undermined his job.

"You're too pretty for doubtful thoughts. Don't let the voice in your head dictate your desires." He whispers, and his words take me in shock. He rises from the sofa before coming over and pressing his lips to my forehead. My entire body melts under his kiss. Reluctantly, he pulls away. "I am going to take you for dinner Thursday night."

Another surprise. "You are?"

"Yes."

"Why?"

He doesn't even bat an eyelid at my shock. "Because I want to know your mind as well as your body."

Hot, holy shit. I'm dumbfounded by his confidence. "O-okay."

The smile he sends me could make me melt into a puddle. He brings his hand up to my cheek, and I want to nuzzle into it, but I resist. The way he stares down at me is unlike any look I've ever seen before— a cross between desire, happiness and disbelief. Then, he turns and leaves, with one final comment. "Good night, my Rebecca. Dream of me."

CHAPTER TWENTY-FOUR

Dagger

I am obsessed— fucking obsessed— like a hungry dog who has seen a bone for the first time. I want her. *Need* her. What the fuck is wrong with me? When I saw her for the first time, I knew that she'd be fun. How she enjoyed being thrown over my shoulder—moaning into me when I squeezed her ass. Her skin tasted so fucking sweet, like pomegranates and honey, as I ran my tongue up and down her neck, and toward those breasts which jumped out to greet me in her tight sexy outfit. *Shit.*

My mind keeps running back to her dropping to her knees for Brandon— *oh, lord.* I know he told me that she's his— *only his.* But I don't want to leave her alone. I *can't* leave her alone. She's on my mind all minutes of the day. Since I saw her last night, and *tasted* her soft skin, the beast in me is roaring to be released. She showed me how much of a bad girl she could be, and I long to claim her.

Even now, as I hide in the bathroom stall, swinging my legs happily as I perch on the toilet seat, I'm thinking of her. I'm waiting for Brandon and Vixen's signal and then I can come out and do my bit of the mission. My silver dagger nips the edge of my fingers like I always do to calm myself down, but there is too much scar tissue that I don't feel the pain anymore. I run my tongue over my teeth and try to slice my tongue for the pain instead. The sensation is sharp, followed by a metallic taste.

Then, I hear the familiar shriek of a pimp. I leap from my position and stalk out of the bathroom to the main lounge. Brandon and Vixen tower over a chubby man with more tattoos than skin. He is large, but he's already on the floor, holding his hands up to protect himself from Brandon's lethal punch. The pimp's head snaps left and blood flies out of his mouth. Something inside of me jump starts at the sight.

"You good, mate?" Vixen is very wary of me as I stalk out of the shadows. I twist my dagger around in my fingers and smirk. "Couldn't be better."

I can see him watching me out of the corner of my eye. He is worried and nervous that I might let *it* slip again, but I promised him I wouldn't. I gave him my word. *Then again, the monster inside doesn't deal with words, he deals with action.*

"Who the fuck is that?" The pimp howls when I step forward into the light. His eyes snap to my scarred face, and he jolts. I know *exactly* what he's frightened of. The skin pulls in above my eyebrow, curves through my eye—*leaving only blackness behind*—and slices down my cheek. It's wiggly and raw and ugly. It's the first thing people notice when I approach, and it's the last thing they see before they die.

"This is Dagger," Brandon thrusts a thumb at me. The pimp's eyes widen in shock and horror. It only makes me grin. "That's right, my lovely. *The Dagger killer.*"

I twirl the blade around and close in. His sweaty fearful stench drifts up my nose and it feels like another threat snaps on the rope I'm desperately trying to hold onto. His bottom lip wobbles and a horrified shriek echoes around the room. My head snaps to the side and my eyes start to burn from where I haven't blinked in a while, but I can't miss a single second of this. I fucking love the way they shiver and cry for me. It's one step closer to my sweet revenge for my mum.

"Where are the women?" Brandon asks tightly. My eyebrow arches as I look at Vixen, his stone-cold expression and tightly pressed lips prove to me that he's completely, and utterly numb. What do they mean by 'where are the women'? *Are they not in the back like usual?*

The pimp spits more blood out from his mouth, and it lands right in front of my shoe. My beady eyes soak up the drops. It feels as though they have blackened, and I choke on the breath in my lungs. Another thread is pulled away from my handle on the rope of sanity. I feel Vixen's hand reach out and he holds my shoulder to reassure me. It barely dents my emotions.

"Must my brother repeat the question?" The noise comes from me, but it doesn't sound like me. Even though the three of us are huge, muscular and ooze power, the pimp's eyes are firmly locked on me. *Can he read my mind? Does he know I'm crazy?*

My Adam's apple bobs as I gulp down the emotion.

"I-I don't know," he splutters.

"Don't lie to us." Brandon brings his face closer to the pimp. I watch as he easily intimidates people with one look. I *fucking* love brutal Brandon. I love it when my brothers switch their monsters on. I don't understand why we can't remain on the evil side of us; people would be safer and much fucking faster if my brothers joined me in my terror campaign. *We'd be fucking uncontrollable!*

"I p-promise! Just let me go," he begs, and my cock twitches. *Fuck yes. Beg for us.* "I don't know where the women are! They just left about three hours ago!"

"Why?" Brandon spits.

"We thought someone was hunting us!" The pimp roars. Brandon's head snaps in Vixen's direction who gulps, and only now do I see how far away he seems. This isn't like my observant older brother. He is usually like a camera, scanning everything with those crystal-coloured eyes— eyes which catch *everything*.

The pimp stays quiet. Brandon whacks him around the face so hard that I hear the snap echo around my head a couple of more times. *Pain! Pain! Pain!*

I lick my lips. "Can I have a go?"

Vixen is the one to answer me. "Not yet, Dagger."

Damn, it.

Brandon fists the pimp's shirt. Then, he nods over at me. "You better start talking mate, or else Dagger is going to have a go. And trust me, you don't want to be tortured by him. You might have seen his work on your friends."

His eyes go wide, and he stares at me in horror. I send him a cheeky wave and my best smile. *That's it, pussy. Keep your secrets. Come to daddy. I'll make you squeal like a pig.*

"I swear—" He lies. Vixen removes his hand from my shoulder and nods. I pounce. The red mist chokes me in my lungs and fills my head until the dizziness is all-consuming. I swipe my blade across the man's face, mimicking the scar I have. He howls in agony, my cock bobs again. *That's it, my dear. Squeal for me!*

"Tell us, you fucking cunt," the anger bubbles up in my throat. Another swipe, and then a near-fatal punch.

"Alright, Dagger." Vixen tries to step in, but I put my arm out to keep him away. *No. It's my turn. They had their chance to get the information.* I thrust my knife in and out of the pimp's leg multiple times, making sure to twist it each time for maximal pain. Like a frightened pig, the man squirms and shrieks.

Brandon's clipped voice rings through the pounding of my heart. "Dags, stop it."

Keep going!

"Dagger, slow down," Vixen tries to grab my arm but with a

swift elbow upwards, I disarm him. He grabs his nose and staggers backwards. I don't bother checking if he's okay. The pimp howls and shrieks for help. Suddenly, everything around me fades out. I am completely and utterly alone with my squealing prey. Instincts take over.

Wrong move, cunt. Where was your mercy when you were raping my mother? Me? Stabbing us? Torturing? Multiple—

"That's enough, damn it," someone's arm swoops around my neck, cutting off my oxygen supply. I feel my eyes instantly roll to the back of my head. It doesn't prevent me from bucking my whole body back and forth, trying to shake off my attacker. *Fuck, Fuck— Dagger! Fight back. Kill them. They're attacking you! They want you dead! The pimps are after you. Kill them!*

Panic fills me. I throw myself around violently, lashing out as much as I can. But my attackers know my moves before I do. Suddenly, they lower me to the ground and use their weight to hold me to the cold floor, and it burns my hot skin. *What the fuck is happening? Who are these pimps? Where is my dagger?*

My vision starts to come back and now I can see the pool of blood inches from my face. *Lick it.*

"Calm down, Dags." A harsh voice is strained. "Do your number exercises."

The blood is so close to us. Just get a taste. Just a little one.

"Count, fuck sake, Dagger!" Another person is struggling to keep my lower half down. The red mist keeps rising and falling like someone is throwing a red blanket in front of my eyes. My eyebrows pull together. *What the fuck do they mean count?*

"Come on, together! Ten, nine, eight—"

"Seven, six—" The other voice joins in. Their voices are oddly soothing. It feels like a lullaby. The adrenaline stops pumping out into my veins, and the familiar dizziness of exhaustion takes me. My lips move to say the next numbers, but I feel too tired to make the noise. The cold hard floor sinks into my face and it stings worse. My surroundings start to reappear, and I hold my breath. I recognise the voices around me— *my brothers. My family. I'm safe.*

"Three, two, one." I finally find the sound to finish the countdown. My muscles ache and I stop resisting. Only then, do I feel Brandon's hand on my back, patting me. "Good lad."

Fuck. What happened?

Slowly, they release me, and I shakily raise to my knees.

"Don't look, Dagger." Vixen shields my eyes from the pimp. A trembling breath escapes from me, and for a second, it sounds like a sob. My head drops low. The guilt and shame consume me. "It happened again— *didn't it?*"

"Yes, mate. It did."

"Fuck." I blink back the disappointment. I promised them I wouldn't react, I promised them I wouldn't kill without instructions. I let them down—I let my brother down. *Again.* "W-well did we get any information?"

Brandon's eyes are soft, but he doesn't answer me. He doesn't need to. I understand my mistake again.

"I'm sorry Bran, Vix. I-I don't know—" I choke on the sob. "What's happening to me?"

"You're fucking insane, is what you are," Vixen's cold words sting. Like a fish out of water, my mouth opens and closes, breathing almost impossible to accomplish. He shakes with rage, and spit flies from his lips, smacking me directly on the nose. It's not a funny situation— I don't want to make my brother angry— but I can see the small bubble on the end of my nose. It takes everything within me not to go cross-eyed and stare at it.

"You are crazy, Dagger. D'ya, hear me, mate? You're a fucking lunatic!" He roars.

"Knock it off!" Brandon growls.

Any ounce of funny vanishes, and my bottom lip begins to wobble, and it brings back bad memories of being told off by the nasty men where I grew up. My jaw grinds together and I beg the tears not to fall. I try to repeat the phrase my mum taught me when I was being scolded by the pimps: *I am strong, I am fearless, I am—*

"Fucking look at him," Vixen is fucking seething. "He can't keep a lid on it anymore, Brandon. He can't come anymore. I won't fucking have it! You are a fucking nutter, Dags!"

Vixen is upset with me; I've hurt my brother. He clutches his nose and only now do I see the slow stream of blood leaking into his mouth. It feels like someone has punched me in the stomach. *Did I do that?*

Brandon remains silent, and I look at him desperately, with big sorry eyes. "I promise, it won't happen ag—"

"You already broke your promise," Vixen cries out, throwing his arms around angrily. "You can't keep promises Dags, you're too fucking insane to! Look around you, mate— fucking do it!" I sheepishly stare around at the pile of dead pimps and a singular dead girl in the corner— *but she was dead before I showed up.* A lump in my throat is the only thing keeping the sick down.

"This was you! *All* you! If you didn't fuck everything up, *she'd* still be alive," he points at the purple-faced girl who has foam around her lips. "And we'd have all the other girls by now!"

My bottom lip wobbles faster and my vision becomes blurred as the tears prick my eyes "How can I make it up?"

"Leave!"

"Leave?" the shocked whisper falls from my lips. Surely, he doesn't mean—

"Get out of here, Dagger. Just *fuck off*!" Vixen strikes in my direction, and even though I know he won't hit me, I flinch and drop to the ground to avoid a connection. I don't know what

I'd do if my brother hurt me— family doesn't hurt one another. *Right?*

My body rocks me back and forth instinctively, desperately trying to calm the sobs down, but my breathing is erratic and it's near impossible to draw in a successful breath. Distraught, I peer up at Brandon. *Stand up for me, big brother, tell Vixen he is just being mean, that he is just upset. Remind him that he still loves me, and we will all laugh about this tomorrow.*

But Brandon doesn't utter a single word. Instead, he just lowers his head into a nod.

He's dismissed me.

I can't look at them anymore, but it doesn't matter if I could. The world becomes hazy with tears. The lump in my throat doubles, and I sniff up the snot in my nose. "Okay."

Sluggishly, I push myself onto my knees. I don't even rise to my feet— *it feels like a crawling mood.* Desperately, I try one last thing to salvage the mood. "I'll see you guys tomorrow?"

"Leave, Dagger!" Vixen is much more furious than before. I visibly jump out of my skin before scattering away as though he might chase after me. Words can't describe the distress that rocks through my body. *My brothers hate me, they want me to leave.* They are the only family I have left, and I keep hurting them.

How many more times do I need to screw up before they need me gone for good? How many more times can the crazy man be excused before becoming a permanent liability?

CHAPTER TWENTY-FIVE

Vixen

"That was harsh." Brandon scolds me as soon as Dagger scrambles away, his sobs still audible for a couple of more seconds. I heave another body part into the bin bags. "Are you fucking kidding me right now?"

"He can't help it."

"Doesn't change the facts." I spit back. It smells so bad in here, and it doesn't help my foul mood. And all I can do is stare at the dead girl in the corner of the room—*Princess*. She didn't escape; she stayed. Ultimately, she was strangled to death by her pimp, and God failed yet another woman. "What are we going to do about him, Brandon? He's too dangerous to not be watched, and we don't have time to be babysitters."

"He'll be fine."

"You're kidding yourself—" I pull the plastic gloves up to my elbows after they slip down. "He needs serious fucking help. Like professional help."

"He *needs* his brothers." Brandon refuses to see the truth.

"He needs to be on medication and locked up."

Suddenly, Brandon lurches for me. His fingers curl into my shirt and he yanks me closer to him. We are similar in size and build, but he packs a much harder punch than I do. Mental violence is more my thing.

"Take that back," he growls, searching my eyes. "We will not give up on him. He is our brother. I don't care how fucked up he is, he remains by our side. Got it?"

"He needs help."

"He needs us," He shoots back viciously.

A disbelieving scoff falls past my lips. "Somebody is going to get seriously hurt one day—an innocent person. You watch, Brandon. Dagger will hurt the wrong person, and it won't be him facing the consequences. The fucker is too mad to understand the repercussions—*but me and you?* We are fucked. And the poor fucking victim that gets on the wrong side of Dagger. You watch this space, he will kill an innocent woman one day. Mark my fucking words. *Hey*—" I pull him back around to face me when he turns to move, "Do ya hear me? Their blood is on your hands. This is all on you."

"Deal." Brandon hisses without another thought. *Stupid fucking man.* We size each other up for a moment longer, neither of us backing away. My breath is shallow, and I tremble with anticipation. I don't want Dagger to be taken away just as much as Brandon, but he is far too fucking dangerous to be unguarded. My brother has had far too many chances, and truly, my only motivation is the safety of the women.

"I'll figure something out." Brandon's calm quickly replaces his angry one. He takes a step backwards, "Leave it with me."

I crack a small smile to lighten the mood. "Was going to anyway."

"Apologise to him tomorrow. You know how he gets when he thinks we are mad at him. Poor fucker is probably crying himself to sleep as we speak," he rolls his eyes before spraying the floor with more bleach. Then, he drops to his knees and starts scrubbing the gore away, rinsing the sponge into the bucket every now and then.

I chew on my lower lip guiltily. "I know. I will."

"What's the time? Ten, is it? Your shift ended an hour ago. Go home and get some sleep. It's been a long day for everyone." Brandon sighs.

"You sure you got this?"

He nods. "Used to it by now. Go on, scram. I'll see you at the club tomorrow."

I almost jump for joy to escape this place. "Kay."

But I don't go home. *Why would I?* I now know exactly who the little dove is that haunts my fucking dreams. *Rebecca Jones.* I feel cheated that she didn't get to tell me her name and that precious moment was stolen from me. When I saw her in Dagger's tight grip, and then on her knees for Brandon—*fuck*, I was fuming. It felt like everything I've ever wanted was ripped from me. This realisation probably contributed to my outburst with Dagger too, and this makes me feel even worse for the way I reacted.

Before long, I am in my usual hideout by the oak tree. She sits on her bed, dressed in skimpy nightwear, as she stares deeply into her phone screen as if fixated on whatever she sees. She looks so peaceful as she scrolls through something. Her tongue pokes out of the corner of her lips as she concentrates. Then, she sits up and reaches for her laptop which is next to her on the bed. She types something on there, before turning back to her phone. She does this a couple of times before her head hits her pillow dramatically. Then, she turns over and stares directly out of the window.

My heart lurches in my chest. *All it would take is one step forward and I could reveal myself to her.* I could give her the introduction I wanted a couple of nights ago. She scans the garden as if she's looking for me and frowns. I don't move. Brandon made it very fucking clear that she was his. It destroys me inside that he gets to have such the perfect woman.

WE SHOULDN'T

Submissive, obedient, horny. She would be the best pet to keep and use, and she'd fucking love it too. She is so perfect it hurts.

I need to get over this obsession, this weird crush. That is why tonight is the last night I will be visiting my little dove. It hurts too much to picture her with anyone else when she doesn't know I exist. I'm not opposed to sharing, but the way she ground on Dagger— how she looked up so submissively at Brandon whilst on her knees, the way she screamed *and* creamed for Brandon in that separate room during her punishment which took everything in me not to burst in and watch... I'm not so sure how much of her I can share. My only lasting hope is that I made her fuck herself before she was with Brandon. It's sick, possessive and jealous but I don't fucking care.

I turn my gaze back to her. She bends over and puts her laptop on the floor but does it in such a sensual way my cock instantly springs to attention. Her tiny shorts ride up, so her entire ass is on show, and she arches her back so beautifully— *oh lord, Rebecca. You will be the death of me.*

Then, she turns back around and stares out of the garden again. It's like she is waiting for me to make a move. My heart pounds violently in my chest. *Does she want me to come in? Is she trying to lure me closer?* My cock bounces in my pants.

She lowers herself onto her knees and faces directly toward me. Then, her dainty fingers play with the hem of her nightdress shirt. She teases me, lifting it up and then dropping it down. She trails her taunting touch across her naked thighs, caressing her curves, squeezing her breasts together— *Fuck, she's not wearing a bra.* In the binoculars, I can see her pebbled nipples shooting out. They're begging me to taste them; I'm *so* sure of it.

Slowly and sensually, she lifts her top off her body and throws it to the side. Those huge tits bounce, and a low growl slips from me. I'd love to tie her up, to put a clamp on each nipple with a chain between it. Knowing her, she'd fucking love the pain and pleasure that I could give her.

"That's it, baby." I hear myself guide her on even though she won't be able to hear me. She twists her nipples, and her mouth drops open in a breathless moan. Her back arches and her head lulls backwards. She keeps playing with herself in front of me before I can't take it anymore. I pull my hard cock free and start fisting it— she can sense me, as though she's watching me, watching her, and it's the fucking hottest thing I've ever seen.

Who am I kidding? I could never let this one go. She might be Brandon's to touch, Daggers to look at, but she is most definitely mine to play with from afar.

CHAPTER TWENTY-SIX

Rebecca

I've had this stalker for about a month now. Well, at least, that is how long I've noticed him. He could have been watching me for longer. This thought should fill me with terror or fear, or even rage, but it's oddly comforting. When I feel his scrutinising gaze on me, I know that I'm safe. It's definitely fucked up that he gives me a sense of protection, but I feel it deep in my bones that if I were to run into trouble, my stalker would finally reveal himself, and save me. Or maybe that's the fairy tale my fucked-up brain has come up with. I should really call the police—hell, I should tell my dad, or my best friend, that I have a strange man watching me nearly all hours of the night. Somebody ought to know what is happening in case my mystery man hurts me. They'd kill me if they knew I was keeping this from them! And yet I enjoy having this little secret. Every other aspect of my life is scrutinised and judged, so my little stalker gives me a sense of privacy. *Is that fucked up to say?* Probably. *Do I care?* Not really.

There have been times when I thought I'd almost catch a glance at his face but he is always hiding in the shadows. I don't need to see him to know he's there; I can *feel* his presence.

I spend sleepless nights thinking about what he could possibly be looking at. *Why me? Is he a fan perhaps? Did he watch me at my previous place? Why start now?* Perhaps it's because I'm in the middle of nowhere so if he did want to attack me, I have nowhere to go for help. What if he is that serial killer running around? He could hurt me in *so* many ways. And yet, he hasn't, but he could be pushing boundaries, testing the waters on how far he can shove me before ultimately stealing my life.

Again, I should be terrified. *So, why is my hand dropping down between my legs? Why am I putting on a display for my stalker?* It's a dance that I seem to keep repeating for him.

It's like I'm addicted to the danger that he could bring. I spur him on— *encourage* him to attack. I don't want to be hurt — truly I don't. And yet I spread my thighs further apart, hoping he is out there tonight. I often imagine that he is touching himself because of my action. *Maybe he's doing it now?* Perhaps he is fisting his cock, imagining me, whilst I fantasise about him.

Fuck— why am I so turned on by that thought? I need therapy. I must talk to someone about this strange addiction I have with my stalker. I never used to be this desperate and touch deprived. He's corrupted me. I haven't even seen his face or said a single word to him, but I'm pretty sure he's corrupted me just as much as Brandon has, but I fucking love him for it.

It's so wrong, Brandon made it clear that I'm only his, but something in my heart tells me that I have far more love to give. I've never been monogamous; I always knew that I had a wandering eye—I never cheated, but I often fantasised about being in a polygamous relationship. *Fuck* would I love to get into one with Brandon, my stalker and that hot crazy mess the other night- *Dags*. Even the other guy who came to find us was fucking hot as sin, with fluffy blonde hair, and piercing eyes. When my mask was ripped off, I could feel the hunger ripple from him. Holy shit do I want *all* of them at once. A dream made true.

My top is gone now, and I play with my nipples. It feels so fucking good, and I imagine it is those men. I pray that they are pleasure Doms- it's my favourite thing to imagine. I want to be used over and over. I welcome as much pain as they are willing to give me because I know the pleasure will be just as intense.

My high comes quickly— it's all too much, too soon— and my legs slam shut. I trail my hand down between my breasts, past my stomach and I slip them into my shorts. I fucking hope he is enjoying the display tonight. I want to tease him. I want him to imagine what I'm doing, without showing. I trail around my clit and it's so fucking sensitive already.

My phone rings, causing me to jump and pick it up immediately. An unknown number appears on my screen, and I quickly answer it, knowing exactly who it must be.

"Take those shorts off." He gets straight to the point. It's *so* fucking hot I could cum without even touching myself. He oozes dominance and control. I want him so badly. And yet, I try to take back control.

"What will you do for me?"

"Be a good girl, Rebecca. Don't make me come in there."

"How do you know my name?" I startle.

He laughs, and it's a throaty chuckle. *It is so fucking hot.* "I'm in control here. Got it?"

"Yes, Sir." I cringe. *Why would I say 'sir'?* I've never called someone sir in my life, and yet it fell from my lips so fucking easily!

"Don't make me repeat myself."

I almost jump out of my skin at the opportunity to strip for him. I put the phone on speaker and put it to the side before slipping my shorts off. I'm not wearing any underwear. I know that he'll love that.

"You're such a dirty whore for your stalker, aren't you?"

Fucking hell. Another gush of heat hits me.

"Go grab your toy box," he barks, and I do exactly as I'm told. When I return to my bed, I lay all of them on the bed in front of me and await my next instructions.

"You got my corn then?" He growls and I stare at the corn which I put in there the other day. My heart skips a beat. *So, it was him!*

"Run it over your nipples."

I pick it up in my shaky hands and obey his commands. The bumpy edges catch my nipples, and I can't help the breathless moan that escapes me.

"Spank them."

Fucking marry me. I pull the corn away before slapping myself on my tits over and over until they are red and stinging, causing a hiss to escape my lips.

"Oh, that's it," he growls. "You're so fucking hot."

I pluck up the courage. "P-please can I see you?"

"No."

"Please, Sir!"

He hesitates on the other end. I stare out into the garden. Suddenly, there is a flash, and I startle. And then, my phone *dings*. I grab it quickly and open the text message that has come through.

"Holy fucking shit," I whisper under my breath. His cock is fucking *huge*. At least eight inches and as thick as my wrist. The dark veins stand out proud and I want to run my tongue up and down them. On cue, my mouth waters. It also curves upwards, and I can only imagine the pleasure that would come with riding it. I bet it hits all the right spots.

"You like that baby?" his voice is low and dangerous.

"I want to taste it."

"Soon," he tells me and it fills me with a ridiculous amount of joy. "Now, listen very closely to what I'm about to tell you."

I gulp and tremble in anticipation.

"Hold that purple vibrator to your clit and pull your shorts back up." I startle. *Does he mean the remote control one?*

"But only I can contr—"

"Did I fucking stutter, Rebecca?" he bites back. The authority in his tone has me snapping into action. I do exactly as I'm told, looking out to the garden with lust-filled eyes. Then, suddenly, I feel the vibrations start. I learn forward and a hiss escapes my lips. The rumbles of pleasure hit me over and over again. "H-how are you doing that?"

"My secret."

He turns up the intensity and I scream. "Oh, fuck!"

"That's it, darling. Ride the pleasure I'm giving you. Now, grab the dog collar there and put it on as tightly as you can."

My head feels dizzy when I secure it, and it only increases the pleasure more. My fingers desperately grab the bedsheets as if they will ground me. But it's too late and I'm instantly falling over the edge of my high before I can stop it. A scream leaves my lips as the waves lap up around me but he doesn't stop the vibrations.

"*Again.*"

"What!" My eyes pop out of my head.

"You heard me, beautiful. We are going to cum together this time. Got it?"

I nod frantically. The whole situation is so fucking hot, I could explode instantly. My overly sensitive clit screams at me. He increases it, and it suddenly hits the right spot. I fall onto my back and my legs start shaking wildly. "Fuck, fuck!"

"That's it," he grunts. I can hear him breathless on the phone and it only pushes me closer faster. He continues teasing me for a couple of more minutes, and his low grunts on the other end have been ready to explode instantly.

"Now. Cum now!" He orders. Before he can even finish the demand, my orgasm smashes with a sharp scream. It feels like I'm fucking drowning in pleasure as it rocks through my body over and over again. My fingers fist the sheets tightly until it feels as though my knuckles are going to pop, and my pants are breathless and shallow. It feels like I'm being swallowed up by the bed. Eventually, he turns the vibrator off, and it's like the breath is shot back into my lungs.

"Atta girl," he tells me. "You are going to wear this from now on. Got it?"

"What?"

"Whenever you leave the house, wear it."

"Everywhere?" I gawp in disbelief.

"*Everywhere*." He confirms. "Now, get some sleep, beautiful. I will see you tomorrow night."

My heart flips in my chest. It is fucking insane. Everything I've just done— cumming for my stalker *again*— and yet I really can't wait for him to reappear tomorrow.

CHAPTER TWENTY-SEVEN

Dagger

Is it weird that I am hard right now? She is sleeping and I am watching. Her breasts rise and fall with each soft snore so maybe that's the reason why? *No*—I think it's because she is so vulnerable right now. She doesn't even know that I'm here, standing over her, cock in my hand, while she sleeps soundly on top of her covers.

It was very fucking easy finding where she lived. All I had to do was hide and wait for Vixen to lead the way. I *knew* something was up with him when he saw her the other night, in my arms. He looked like he could rip my throat out. So, I followed him tonight straight to her house. What I was not expecting, however, is the *nature* of their relationship. She came so fucking hard for him. *Twice.* I have no clue how Vixen didn't hear me in the bush opposite him. My head still thumps from where I held my breath for most of it, out of desperation to not get caught. I heard everything. *Every. Fucking. Word.*

And now I'm rock solid, leering over her, like a creep. She is still wearing the vibrator in her shorts, clearly falling asleep as soon as she was finished with Vixen. As soon as he left, I made my move. It's not fair— both Brandon and Vixen have had fun with her. I want it to be my turn. I reckon she'd bathe in all my fucked-up glory. I don't have my mask on right now, but she's asleep and I won't wake her, so she doesn't see my face. It gives me the restraint I need because I really want to wait until she is begging for me rather than giving it up easily.

A wet patch remains between her legs— on the covers too— and it makes my cock jump even higher to attention. It takes everything with me not to bend down and taste her through the knickers. A soft moan slips past her lips as she turns around in her sleep. Now, she is so fucking close to my cock, I might explode all over her. It takes everything within me to take a step backwards. All I want to do is unzip my trousers and put my cock between those soft lips. My kinky little freak would probably cream her knickers when she realises what is happening. She seems to enjoy being used and pleasured.

She stirs a little but doesn't wake up, which makes it that much hotter. I sink my teeth into my lower lip harder, desperately trying to contain my groans. Her beautiful little face scrunches up as she rolls over again. I really want to cum all over her milky skin. I want her to wake up and *know* that I've been here, but I don't. As much as I can take a good bloody guess about what she wants, I still need to hear her say it. I want her to *beg* for the monster to be unleashed.

I lean over a new piece of corn that has been left on her floor. *Vixen's work*. I almost want to throw it away and give her something of my own. I don't know why but a flash of me leaving a lock of my long hair on her bedside table rings around my brain. Fuck it would be so hot to see the fear flash around her. I leave it alone and walk over to her laptop which is open on the floor on the other side of her bed. I stare at it. I lean down to move the parser, allowing the screen to activate from being left alone for too long, and a word document pops up. Paragraphs of her writing draw my attention— *I really wish I knew how to fucking read.* I would love to see the kind of thing she has written.

Brandon tried to teach me to read and write in the beginning. He was very fond of the opinion that I should learn, but after much-failed practice, and my patience slipping, I gave up. I don't need to fucking read or write to murder. We all have things we are good at, and I don't plan on changing my skills. Well, not really, at least. I wouldn't mind *her* teaching me though. Perhaps she could suck my cock every time I get the answer right? *Oh lord.*

I take a couple of steps backward and steady my breathing. I need to figure out a way to get her back to the club when I'm there. That's the only time I'll be able to approach her without scaring her, but then Vixen and Brandon are there.

Wait —did she even know who Vixen was the other night?

I noticed he didn't go any further than the tree line and the shadows, and he didn't show her his face. That makes it a little easier for me, I guess. At least that means that I am only *really* competing against Brandon for her affection. I know I really shouldn't— this will be the thing that gets be banished from the group— but how can I resist her sweet sinful temptation? She was made for my brothers and me, she just doesn't know it yet. I'll just have to prove it to her, and then she'll convince the others. *Yes. That's what I'll do.*

Thank fuck I'm great at ruining things. I will just have to figure out how to distract Brandon to get her alone before I make my move. *Only then will my little dove be mine to dirty.*

CHAPTER TWENTY-EIGHT

Rebecca

He looks so delicious in that suit, standing at my taxi door, clutching a rose. I take a step out, careful not to trip in my thin silver heels. My long, black sparkly dress restricts some of my movements too, but with the slit that shoots up my thigh, I can just about walk. It doesn't help that I'm wearing the vibrator in my knickers too as per my instructions. I know I shouldn't do it — it's disrespectful to Brandon. But I've learnt my lesson about disobeying powerful men, and I will not push my stalker to his limits. *Who knows what he has in store for me?*

He takes my arm and gently helps me out, he gulps harshly as he breathes in my perfume and dress. My breasts burst out from the top, and my loose silver necklace brings attention to the way they swell.

"You look fucking fantastic."

"Thank you." A blush passes my cheeks. "You too."

He is in complete awe, even his mouth is slightly parted. I cock my head to the side and suck up all the attention. To have such a handsome, powerful man drooling over me is a sight I wish I could see more of. He gently leads me to the restaurant, and we slip through. The thin waiter beams when he sees us.

"Mr Powel," he exclaims. "It's so nice to see you again."

Brandon nods his head politely. "I reserved a table."

"Of course, sir. It's all ready for you."

He leads the way, and we follow behind. My heart is already pounding loudly. The restaurant around us is busy, and filled with riches I can only dream of touching. The light is low and flattering, and every single person is dripping head to toe in money. I am *so* grateful Brandon gave me a hint of what to wear so I didn't humiliate myself, but I still can't help feeling like I stand out like a sore thumb.

Eventually, we get to our table, and I am stunned. A small round table with a snow-coloured cloth and a small candle burning in the middle. Silver plates, expensive cutlery and napkins moulded into flowers, the table sits on a balcony which overlooks the whole city. Dazzling lights shine back at us, competing with the stars littered around in the sky. I am utterly breath taken.

The waiter places the menus on the table. "What can I get you to drink?"

Brandon pulls my chair out for me, and I slide in. Then, he tucks me in before taking his seat opposite.

"House white, please." he quickly casts a look at me before adding. "Is that okay?"

I blush like a mad man. "It's perfect, thank you."

The waiter dips his head before leaving us. I turn my gaze back to Brandon, but he's already staring at me. "You truly are stunning, Rebecca. Such a beauty."

I hide my face. "You're going to make me go all red!"

"Good. I like it when you blush," he grins, and it melts me. Then, he gently takes my hand in his and sighs happily. "I am very happy I can finally do this."

"Do what?" I frown.

"Spoil you the way I've always wanted to."

It feels like everything around me blurs into a low hum. My cheeks burn from how much I'm smiling. "You're such a romantic."

"For you, I'd be anything you wanted."

The waiter returns and tops up our glasses before disappearing again. Brandon pulls one hand away from mine and lifts his glass. I copy him.

"To our first date." He beams. I sink my teeth into my lower lip to try and contain the huge smile. I *tink* my glass against his before taking a sip. My eyes flutter shut as the gorgeous taste fills me up, it's unlike anything I've ever tasted before—light, sweet, and tastes like summer if that's even possible. A moan of approval slips out and when I reopen my eyes, Brandon is watching me with that hungry look.

"Problem?" I say innocently.

His jaw tightens. "Don't make me bend you over and fuck you in front of all these people."

My thighs press together. *Fuck, I really hope you do.*

"Not yet anyways," he visibly relaxes. "I want to get to know your mind tonight."

"What do you want to know?"

He doesn't even take a second before asking, "What got you into writing?"

I stiffen and stare into my glass. Then, I bring it to my lips, and I take a gulp. I don't want to lie to him, but I also don't want to ruin the mood. He squeezes my hand and pulls me back into the moment with him.

"It was a great form of escapism from life."

"And now? Is it still a form of escapism?" he arches an eyebrow and watches me intently. He scans me for every reaction, and I resist the urge to squirm under his intense gaze. I think back to the sex club, my relationship with him and my stalker. "I have other means of escapism. Writing is now just a job."

His Adam's apple jumps when he realises what I mean. His jaw is stiff, and he looks away. "The other night—" he hesitates. "— with Dags…"

"I'm sorry, Brandon," I cut him off. "I came looking for you, I promise. And then, he started kissing me and—"

"Did you enjoy it?"

I startle. "What?"

"Did you enjoy Dags kissing you— *touching you?* And don't lie to me. I'll know if you're not telling the truth."

"Brandon," I start before hesitating. *Of course, I fucking did.* Dags oozed a sense of recklessness and danger that I'd never felt before. He was delicious, and he touched me in all the right places. He knew exactly how to get me going, and if that man hadn't shown up and dragged us out— I know full well I would not have stopped Dags from fucking me like an animal. I squeeze my legs together and avert my eyes.

"You did, didn't you?" when I peer at Brandon, I expect to see anger or jealousy. Instead, he is ravenous. "Go on, tell me."

"I did," my voice is barely above a whisper. "How does that make you feel?"

"Many things," He confesses slowly. "Possessive, frustration, desire, confused."

The air rips from my lungs. "Do you know him? Dags, I mean."

"Yes, he works with me, Vixen too. The other man that was there."

"They work at the club?" My eyes are wide. I've never seen either of them before. I *know* that I would remember them if I had. Brandon gives me a slow nod. "Something like that."

I want to press further and ask what he means. I want to dig around in his gorgeous head. But the stony look that passed through his eyes tells me that I shouldn't pry on that subject. My hands shake when I take another sip of my drink. "Have you ever— *wait*, never mind."

"Ask your question, Rebecca," he demands. I swallow down the fear and pluck up the courage. "Have you ever played with them before? Like at the club?"

Brandon smirks, and it almost melts me. "What exactly do you mean by that, Rebecca?"

I suddenly feel stupid and immature. My cheeks burn. I sink my teeth down on my tongue and pray for that courage I had a couple of seconds ago to return. "W-well, if you said they work *with* you, not for you. So, they are like bosses too, right? So, they must play in the playrooms too. And—"

"Spit it out."

I take the risk and ask the thought that is haunting my dirty thoughts. "Have you ever shared a girl with them?"

"There it is," he smirks. I wait patiently for him to answer my question. "No, I haven't shared a girl with my brothers."

Brothers! I almost lurch out of my seat, spluttering on a gulp of wine that has gone down the wrong way.

"Though, I'm sure Dags has fucked many girls that Vixen and I have been with, just so he can imagine us sharing." He rolls his eyes and shakes his hand dismissively. This makes my ears prick, and an odd sense of hope feels my chest.

"But I will not be sharing you if that's what you're thinking about," he says, watching me intently for a reaction. Disappointment consumes me. "Why not?"

"You don't know them. They are possessive and obsessive."

I raise an eyebrow. "And you're not?"

"Watch it." His low growl has me almost jumping out of my seat. "What I mean is Dags is crazy, Rebecca. He is my brother and I love him, but it's a fact. He isn't just a little bit crazy; he is clinically insane. It's hard to control him—" he is pained as he talks about him and I feel guilty for bringing him up, "He is extreme, rough, and painful."

I don't mind that, the thought in my head pops up. "What about the other one? Vixen."

He ponders on that thought, and it is almost impossible to read his facial expressions. I silently pray that there is no good reason. I haven't properly met Vixen, but his face is burnt into the back of my mind. Hot as sin with pale feathery hair. When he looked at me the first time I met him, it felt like he didn't just *look* at me, he *observed* me, as if he stared straight through me, my mind, my clothes— *I'm hot just remembering it!*

"I don't want to share you," he finally confesses. I open my mouth to protest, but, suddenly, his phone rings.

That fucking sound.

Before I can stop it, Leo's evil face flashes to mind— that ugly, twisted smile glaring down at me as he bends me over and...

"Fuck." I hiss. My heart races one hundred miles an hour, and suddenly, my hands smack over my ears, and the breath races from my lungs— trying to get as far away from the noise as possible. It feels as though thirty rubber bands are constricting around my heart and I splutter for oxygen. Everything starts to get small and my heart beats through my vision until everything is hazy, that familiar pumping noise in my head drowns out the sound of my gasps, which only makes me panic more.

"Fuck, Rebecca," Brandon cries out, racing to my side. He has already switched the noise off but it's haunting me, ringing over and over. *I can't stop fucking hearing it.* It burns into my brain until I can't take it anymore, and my only solace is the large glass of wine in front of me that I quickly drain. Only then, do the bands around my heart start to snap. I reach for the bottle and fill up the glass again before gulping it down too.

"Rebecca, it's okay," I hear Brandon cooing to me. I feel his hand on my thigh and it's weird but the breath sneaks back into my lungs. I grab his shoulders and use him to ground myself. My eyes are still wide, and I'm waiting for Leo to stroll into the room any minute now, playing that fucking noise— the noise he'd torture me with if I misbehaved. It was always the same fucking song, the typical beeping alarm on an iPhone, and he would thoroughly enjoy my panic in public if it went off on a stranger's phone, sending me into a weeping, apologetic mess —

"I'm here. You're safe," Brandon reassures repeatedly. The phone on the table starts vibrating but the noise doesn't come again after he switched it off. I glare at it and fight the urge to throw it over the fucking balcony, to get rid of it for good. Pissed off, he snatches it and answers it before giving me an apologetic look, never removing his calming hand from my body.

"What is it?" he spits knives before pausing and then starting again. "No, no fucking way. I'm busy."

Another pause.

"Get Vixen to handle it." his face contorts angrily. "Fuck sake, Dags, if I have to come down there— *what?* Really? Okay, shit. *Hide.* I'm coming."

My entire body deflates. *He's leaving?* He ends the phone call before pulling me into a tight embrace, completely taking me by surprise.

"I am really sorry, Rebecca. I have to go."

"What is it? What's come up?" I sound miserable.

"It's work." He hisses, full of regret, pulling me back slowly. "I would never do this normally, but it's just— well, it's an emergency."

"Oh." I can't hide the disappointment in my voice.

WE SHOULDN'T

"I know, I'm really sorry. I can't leave it. I have to go."

"Well, can I come?" I perk up. The thought of the club makes my thighs press together. He stiffens.

"Please, I won't get in the way at all. I promise!" I try again. "We can resume where we left off after?" I squeeze his thigh seductively and bat my eyelashes.

It works. He melts instantly. "Okay, fine."

Excitement fills me as he helps me up, and it feels as though the last five minutes never happened. I would believe it too if it wasn't for the thin layer of sweat that now coats my body. Brandon pulls out his wallet and leaves a one-hundred-pound note on the table, making my eyes bulge before quickly guiding me out of the building and into the nearest cab.

Before long, we arrive at the club. There is a queue of people waiting to enter the premises, but Brandon pushes us to the front. I struggle to keep up in the heels, but he keeps me from falling with one large arm wrapped around my waist.

"Where are they?" Brandon hisses as we bump into Dags. He leans on the door frame, waiting for us. When he sees me, his smirk pulls up, and my heart leaps out of my chest. It's so devilish and sinful. I quickly avert my gaze, remembering what Brandon said to me. *He is clinically insane.* As much as I would fucking love this man to ruin me, I saw the frightened look in Brandon's eyes, and if Brandon is nervous about him, I should most definitely be too.

"Back there." Dags cast a lazy point over his shoulder. Brandon hisses and looks between us.

"Go ahead," I tell him a little weakly. "I'll wait here."

"I'll take good care of her," Dags slurs seductively. If looks could kill, he'd be dead right now, the way Brandon is glaring at him. He steps threateningly close to Dags. "If you fucking touch her, I will hurt you."

I hear every word and my heart flips around in my chest repeatedly. Dags holds his hand up in the air and grins. "Scouts honour."

"I mean it, Dags," he says before turning back around to me. He yanks me flush against him and kisses me as if his life depends on it. It's so fucking hot and steamy, I'm momentarily dazed. I feel the way he gropes me up and down, and how his tongue completely overpowers mine. I am fucking stunned and wildly horny, desperate for more, to the point I almost drop to my knees and beg him to stay. Reluctantly, he pulls back, causing a disappointing moan to slip out from my lips.

"I'll be back soon." He promises, and after one more evil look at Dags, he disappears beyond the curtain. I look at the madman nervously who is already staring at me intensely.

Then, his lips curve into a devilish smile. "We are going to have *so* much fun together."

CHAPTER TWENTY- NINE

Vixen

"Yes, I know, I am really sorry officer," I try to reassure the policeman who sits in the office. "I can assure you it won't happen again."

"It better not," he grimaces, trying to look tough as he puffs out his chest. I stifle a laugh. He is much smaller than me, and clings to his stab proof vest as if I can't remove it with a couple of buttons. It looks like a boy dressing up in his father's clothes.

"What's going on?" Brandon bursts into the office and my heart lurches as I turn to face him. He looks like he could kill as he storms in. Quickly, he assesses the situation, raking his eyes over the three policemen opposite me.

I quickly take control. "There was a fight outside the club earlier, but it's all been sorted now. Hasn't it, lads?"

"Between whom?" Brandon glares. I send him a look as if to say *you know who*.

"We will get a testimonial from the victim tomorrow morning. He's pretty badly beaten up and is in hospital at the moment. I believe—" the skinny policeman takes charge, but looks to the nervous woman with the high pitch voice for reassurance, "He's in surgery right now?"

"Yes, there were a couple of broken bones," she agrees timidly while scanning the office again as if the madman is about to jump out and get her too.

"Please do let us know if the victim can identify the attacker. We run a zero-patience policy for violence here," I say quickly, already planning exactly how we will cover our tracks. If the man in the hospital knows what's good for him, he will never speak a word of the event again. I look at Brandon who is lost in thought, distress written all over his face. *Good.* I hope my words from last night are repeating in his mind. *Someone is going to get hurt. We will face the repercussions. Blood is on your hands.*

"Do we know what the fight was over?" he says, but he sounds far away and lost. When he looks up, a shallow look flickers across his face.

"Unfortunately, not. The CCTV didn't capture the fight leading up to or after. We've checked," the most confident policeman sighs unhappily. I shake my head and put on my best poker face. "I can't believe it, either. We will get the filming company back in to get a camera for the blind spot around the back. It's unbelievable that they missed it!"

Yes, pass the blame along. Nobody needs to know about your quick thinking and hacking skills.

"These things happen—" The policeman shakes his head, before rising to his feet. "Well, we've taken up enough of this gentleman's time—" I almost laugh at the name, if only they knew exactly the kind of guy I am, the kind of things I want to do to Rebecca; I am *nowhere* near a gentleman. "—we have got your report, and we will keep looking for witnesses. We will be in touch."

The police slowly file out of the room, but I dislike the way they examine the place as they leave, casting their gaze over different files and sealed letters that only require one peak in them to reveal all our plans. I slide them from view and gesture for the door, much to the female police officer's nervous side

WE SHOULDN'T

glance.

"We will see ourselves out." She says slowly, and I give her my most award-winning smile, which makes that professional mask crack slightly. She blushes, bobs her head, and hurries out after her male co-workers.

As soon as they are gone, I drop the preppy smile from my face and slam the office door behind them.

"What the fuck?" Brandon hisses. "Who was the victim?"

"Some loser. Dagger said that he slapped a woman who didn't want it— I don't know, Brandon. He could be lying," I sigh dramatically.

"Did you not watch the footage beforehand?"

I stare at him in disbelief. "Was I to look at it during or after the police visit? I didn't fucking know about it until I get a call from reception."

"It's bad. We can't have the police around here. You know most of the performers won't— *hell*, even the clients won't want them snooping around," he runs his hands through his hair angrily.

"Where is Dagger now? Did you see him on the way in? He's probably hiding with his tail between his legs." I scowl at the floor.

Brandon stiffens. "Shit. No, he's with Rebecca."

My heart lurches from my chest. *Rebecca. She's here?*

"We were on a date, and then I got the call, so— it doesn't matter. I'll go save her from the madman—" Brandon rambles on before flying back out of the door. I can't help but follow after him. It feels like all of the troubles have instantly vanished now that I realise that she is close. The timing is very fucking odd, and I wouldn't put it past Dagger to do something to lure her close, but that's not the thing that swarms around my brain. The only thing I'm interested in is whether she has

HOLLY GUY

followed instructions...

CHAPTER THIRTY

Rebecca

My heart drops in my chest when Dags takes another step toward me.

"Brandon said don't touch me." I don't know why I say this, perhaps out of fear, but is it fear for my safety or fear of what Brandon will do to him if he disobeys him?

"Brandon loves me. He would never hurt me." Dags responds and It's oddly comforting and sweet. It's also very odd coming from this six-foot-six man whose shoulders stick out so much he could hug two of me and still have space for more. He is wearing that mask again on his face, and now I can see it more clearly in the light. It's a black plastic cup with white roses on it. There is a hole for his eye, but the eye is *so* dark, that it looks almost hollow. He is quite terrifying this close.

"Go on. *Ask*," he purrs.

I pretend to be naïve. "Ask what?"

"The mask."

I gulp.

"Go on, little kitten. Don't be scared of me. I haven't hurt you. *Yet*." He whispers. The words wrap around my head repeatedly. I squeeze my thighs together. *Maybe I'm the mad one?* He's threatening me, and all my body can do is respond deliciously to him.

I gulp. "W-Will you hurt me?"

He ponders on this thought before sending me a lob-sided grin. "Do you want to be hurt by me?"

Fuck yes! My entire body shakes like it never has before. Fear and arousal shoot through me. His malicious grin only grows. "That's what I thought."

Then, he takes another step toward me. I feel my back smack against the wall, and my chest rises and falls in fear. *Is he going to hurt me now? Will he dare do it with Brandon in the same building? How much pain could he give me before we are stopped? And why the fuck is my thighs clenching at the thought?*

"Ask your question about my mask." He distracts my racing thoughts. The breath is snatched from me. It takes everything I have to pluck up the courage. "Why do you wear a mask?"

He answers quickly. "To hide my scar."

The question is on the tip of my tongue. I really want to ask him where he got the scar from, but suddenly his eyes aren't on me anymore. He stares up at the camera as if he can see through it. He's like a wild animal on a hunt, as though he's recognised a threat in the near distance. He bares his teeth as if he's going to go and fight, but then his eyes shift back to mine — *black as night.*

"Want to go to a playroom?"

"Brandon says—"

"Are you always this boring with him too?" he hisses.

I visibly recoil in shock. "Excuse me?"

"Well, all I'm saying is I thought you'd be a little more rebellious, perhaps. Or did my brother punish you well enough the other night to knock that pretty little head into subservience?"

I am completely and utterly speechless. He continues, eyes never leaving my face, constantly scanning me for emotion. "It sounded like an amazing punishment. But, If you were mine,

WE SHOULDN'T

I don't think I would have let you get off the machine. Three orgasms aren't enough. I bet that greedy pussy could take more."

"H-how did—"

"I like it when my women are loud. You'd be so fucking perfect for me. I could hear your moans all the way down the hallway. I wonder, how loud will you scream for me?" he purrs, and my pussy is soaked within seconds. His words are so fucking forbidden and scandalous. He really shouldn't be saying this to me. I try to think of a reason to get him to stop. *Could I threaten him with Brandon again?* That'll only result in him calling me boring— and I'm by no means boring. *I am fucking Rebecca Emma Jones!*

As if he can hear my thoughts, he grins wider. "Let's go to a playroom."

"Which room?" I fold my arms defiantly. Without another word, he twists on his feet and marches up the stairs. I follow him like a lost puppy, losing count of which floor we are on after number four. The nerves sweep through me because Brandon always reminded me how the severity and uniqueness of the kink or fetish would go up each floor. When I'm with him, I get to choose the room. Something tells me that Dags won't be as lenient and caring, he'll take me to the room *he* wants. The control makes my knees weak.

"Here we are," he smirks at me and leads me to a red door.

My heart hammers in my chest. "What's in there?"

"Secret. Why, have you changed your mind?"

"No!"

He keeps pushing me. "You a chicken?"

My cheeks turn bright red. "No, I'm not a chicken!" I push past him and lead the way. He gently leads me to the playroom rather than the viewing area, and it makes my pussy throb greedily. He is so fucking delicious.

As soon as we walk in, the moans of a woman echo around the room. When my eyes fix on her, I am utterly speechless. There are three men around her— one has his cock down her throat, another is below her, fucking her pussy, and the final one is about to push his cock into her ass. It feels as though the world around me has exploded. This is the hottest fucking room ever.

"Oh!" I gasp, throwing my hands to my face. I am suddenly very aware of him standing behind me. His heavy breathing only spurs me on further. I want to push back into him, to feel him against me. I want to see how hard and ready he is.

"You like that?" he growls. I can feel his hot breath on my cheek, and I stiffen. I push my thighs together and I get a little bit of friction on the vibrator. A breathless gasp leaves my lips. Fuck— if only my stalker was here. If only he knew the kind of dirty shit I'm up to. I almost want to check my watch because we usually play around ten o'clock, and I'm hoping he will turn the machine on and imagine where I am, and what kind of naughty places I'm getting off in. *Oh, please do!*

"Answer me," Dags demands, and I jump. "Yes! I like that!"

I'm hooked on the scene. The large man slowly eases his cock into her ass, and she squeals around the dick in her mouth. Her face is full of pleasure with her eyes rolling back, and the smile pulling at her lips making it hard for her to suck. She moans and writhes around, and now, they all work together to plough her. *I'm so fucking jealous.* I would *love* to be in that position. Brandon, my stalker, Dags, even Vixen! *Fuck*— I'd do anything!

"Does it turn you on?" Dags' breathing is erratic now. I nod quickly, much to his amusement.

"Maybe you're jealous of that woman."

"I-I am."

"Shit, little dove. You are meant for this place." he hisses. I see his hands snake around my waist, but he doesn't touch me. It takes everything in me not to push back into him. He follows Brandon's commands and yet disobeys them at the same time. A ridiculous urge to tease him and make him snap pulls through me.

"I wonder how it feels," I hear myself whisper. A low growl ripples past my ear, and I instantly realise I'm playing with fire. His fingers curl into fists and he shakes— actually *shakes*— like he's fighting off demons. His voice is strained. "Did you want to touch yourself? Make yourself cum over the scene?"

I'm trembling too. He is so sinful; he will get me in so much fucking trouble it's unreal.

"Go on." He goads. "Touch yourself. I won't tell anyone."

I really fucking want to.

"Give yourself that release. You know that greedy pussy is throbbing for all those cocks. I bet you've soaked your panties. Don't deny yourself the pleasure. I reckon you could cum before my brother is finished with his meeting. He'll never know." It's like the devil himself is tempting me. I can't help it anymore. My shaking fingers find my breasts and I give them a squeeze, scraping my nipples in the most delicious way. My teeth grind together, and I catch a hiss on the edge of my tongue. He still doesn't touch me, and I'm almost mad at him for showing restraint. I want him to be the one to make me cum, I want his mouth on mine, and his fingers so deep inside of me that I'm screaming my release within seconds.

"That's it. Good girl," he coos. I drag my fingers down from my breasts, and they curve around my hips. Just as I go to lift my skirt up, the door slams open. My head snaps in that direction. Suddenly, the room feels much *much* colder. Brandon storms in, face like thunder, and Vixen is close behind.

"I fucking knew you'd take her here," Brandon growls. His voice is challenging and malicious. It makes me choke on the air in my lungs and I quickly drop my skirt and put distance between me and Dags. Behind us, the performers are almost reaching their orgasms— not pausing for one second to check the drama unfolding next to them. The lady's screams of pleasure rattle around my brain. I feel faint; like this is a fever dream, all of the blood in my body rushing between my legs.

"How comes?" Dags throws his hands in the air innocently. "I didn't touch her once, Brandon. Just like you told me."

Brandon is shaking with rage. "Don't bullshit me!"

"He is telling the truth," I quickly defend him. The rush of adrenaline flows through me. "He didn't—" suddenly, the vibrations start against my clit. I take a sharp intake of breath. *Fuck sake, stalker. Not now— Not now!*

"Didn't what?" Brandon glowers. "Tell me. Say the words, Rebecca."

I'm fucking trying!

The vibrations go faster, and I try as hard as I can to keep my face level. My clit screams with pleasure, and my legs start to feel wobbly. I'm just really fucking thankful the vibrator is deadly silent. My gaze tears around the room. *Is he here? Does my stalker know where I am? Is he watching me right now?* All eyes are on the performance in the middle of the room. And there are no phones allowed in here—*boss' orders.* Surely, a phone is the only way my stalker can control the remote-control device. Then a shaky feeling fills me: *what if it's one of the bosses?*

Brandon is glaring at me viciously, waiting for an answer. His jaw is hard, eyes cold. Vixen is staring at the performance on stage, he doesn't give me another look. And then there is Dags, who is standing there, grinning like a madman. His eyes scream sin— it could well be him. *He could be my stalker?* Hell — he's obsessive and crazy enough, but he seems almost too unhinged to think of something so fantastic. What's more, he would have started the vibrations as soon as we were alone, a man like that doesn't have such self-control. I have a feeling he'd want to make me cum repeatedly, rather than just torture me now.

Brandon stamps his foot on the floor impatiently. "I'm waiting."

I swallow down the lump in my throat. "He didn't touch me!"

"Bet she wanted me to, though," Dags offers unhelpfully. I send him an evil look, but he simply smiles innocently. Behind me, the woman roars her release, followed by the grunts of all the men around her. My teeth grind together, and I focus on anything but how fucking turned on I am. I try to take deep breaths, but it's futile. I'm panting and desperate.

"I need—" I start to push past them. *If I can go to the bathroom, I can take it out.* Vixen's arm shoots out; he moves so fucking fast I almost didn't see him. When his eyes meet mine, I'm stunned. The most magnetising blue I've ever seen. He searches me for answers. "You dare walk away from your owner?"

My stomach flips. *Your owner.* I know he means Brandon, but fucking hell, the way he says it is so possessive, so full of ownership. I almost doubt who my owner *is* here. They all tower over me, making me feel so helpless—so fucking desperate for them. I yank my arm away, to his amusement. He cocks an eyebrow up, and a small smile follows. Then he drops them both. I feel the vibrations grow, and now my breathing is shaky. *I'm being too fucking obvious.*

"Toilet," I force the single word out and race out of the room. I run as fast as I can to the end of the corridor to the toilet— but it's too late. The way I run only rubs the vibrator against my clit in the most delicious way. I stumble to the floor as my orgasm rips through me. A squeal of pleasure escapes, and I slam my hands over my face. My eyes squeeze shut, and I ride through the wave after wave of immense please, my legs trembling wildly. The fucking vibrator won't stop—only pushing me higher and higher through the waves.

"What do we have here then?" Vixen is standing opposite. His eyes are hard and unforgiving as he watches me writhe on the floor. *Fuck!*

"I, er—" I stumble over my words, the lie isn't coming to my mind quick enough. The vibrations slowly subside, and now I can grasp the breaths easier. "W-where is Brandon?"

He looks hurt for a second but masks it very quickly. "He's with Dags. They're having a—er, well, a conversation." He bares his teeth into a smile, but it doesn't reach his eyes.

My head falls against the wall. I've finally got the rise and fall of my chest under control, but my legs still feel weak.

"Did you just cum?" he asks, emotionlessly.

My eyes snap at him. "What?"

"It looked pretty intense," he stares at me, *through* me. *There is no fucking way he saw that. Shit!* A sudden nervousness pulls through me. I stare at him with a clenched jaw. *What the fuck is he playing at?*

He holds his hand out at me. "Our secret."

I go against better judgement and shakily take his hand, and he yanks me to my feet. However, he pulls me too hard, and I stumble into his chest. Those arms snap around me and he holds me stiff against him, and the breath vanishes from my lungs before he suddenly puts distance between us like he's remembered exact *who* I belong to.

I can't stop the fucking words rattling around my head. *Did you just cum?* It's so full of fucking emotions. Did he pick up on my behaviour or is he my—

"You should clean yourself up before finding Brandon," he interrupts my thoughts before twisting on his foot. "He might be able to smell your sweet cum and start asking questions."

Then, he disappears down the hallway, leaving me in a trembling wet, desperate mess.

CHAPTER THIRTY-ONE

Dagger

"Are you out of your fucking mind?" Brandon shoves me in the chest as soon as the other two disappear. I wasn't prepared for the way it snatches the breath from me. I was too busy watching Rebecca almost cum in her panties— *my dirty little dove.* Having the information means it was very obvious that she was about to cum. *Wicked Vixen, tormenting the poor girl in front of Brandon.*

"You brought the police here, Dags," he roars before clipping me around the back of the head. I duck away from him. "Ouch!"

"Why? Why did you do it?"

I stay quiet. *The fight, or take his girl to this room?*

"He's in hospital you know," Brandon growls. He marches away from me, so I quickly follow him.

"I promise he deserved it. He got rough-handed with one of the —"

"Are you lying to me?" he cuts me off abruptly. I startle before shaking my head slowly, slightly taken aback. "No, Brandon, I wouldn't—"

He groped the dancer inappropriately *and* I knew that Rebecca was with Brandon. All I had to do is start a fight and kill two birds with one stone. Justice, and bring my dirty dove closer to me.

"Then you take her to *this* room?" His eyes turn black. "What are you trying to do? Steal my girl?"

I almost scoff in his face. If only he knew how much *his* girl has been playing with his brothers.

"You need to back off, Dags," he tries again, thrusting a finger into my chest. "She's mine."

"Have you asked her what she wants?"

"What?" he startles.

"She's polyamorous."

Fucking hell if looks could kill, I'd be dead. Brandon invades my personal space. "And how do *you* know that?"

I shrug and put distance between us. *I should stop— I should stop provoking the only man who loves me truly and wholly for who I am, but I can't. I've seen that pretty bird in action and I fucking need her too.* "I just do."

Anger crosses his face. He storms out of the playroom and heads towards the woman's bathroom. He throws the door open and disappears. Before long, he returns, empty handed, and it makes me smile. She is making him go crazy, too. *Join the club, brother!*

"Now where is she?" He growls under his breath. I follow after him happily and resist the urge to skip. It takes everything in me not to laugh at the situation. *Vixen* went after her. He went to watch the consequences of his actions— I can't blame him. If I had a choice, I'd also watch her cum in her panties unwillingly in front of everyone. My cock jolts with the image.

"She's very pretty," I say absentmindedly.

Brandon is stiff. "I know."

"I think she is a very lovely woman, and she is—"

"There is no what *you* think, Dagger." He spins around and

shoves me into the chest. "She's mine."

For now. Hiding my true feelings, I throw my hands in the air and smile innocently. "Of course, brother. She's yours."

He searches my face. Eventually, he grows bored of my wide, preppy smile, and he turns to continue his search. We get back to the office, and I'm assuming we are going to check the cameras to find her. To my surprise, Vixen is here *alone*.

"Where is Rebecca?" Brandon is tense. Vixen doesn't look up at us. Instead, he points to the camera as he watches her climb into a taxi. My heart drops. *No, I wanted her to stay. I wanted to play with her a bit more.*

"Fuck," Brandon hisses under his breath. He goes to move after her, but Vixen reaches out. "Stop, brother. Let her be."

His nostrils flare. I stiffen, and wait for the fight to kick off, but, instead, he visibly relaxes. *What?*

"You're right." Brandon eventually sighs before falling into the chair. I watch him, wide-eyed, trying to figure out what's changed. His head falls back limply. "If she knows what's good for her, she'll leave and never return. We will only hurt her with our possessiveness."

I stiffen. I *really* did not want him to say that. I can't believe I'm saying this, but I would rather have her on *his* arm, and present in my life, than not with any of us, and completely gone from my life.

CHAPTER THIRTY-TWO

Rebecca

I feel so dirty and guilty. *Why must my body betray me like this?* I wanted Brandon so bad tonight, and then we went to the club, and then there was Dags, and then Vixen. Oh, fuck. *Vixen is so hot.*

I *know* that he finds me attractive. The way he looked at me was like he could eat me for breakfast, lunch and dinner. He spoke to me in such riddles— something inside of me *longs* for him to be my stalker, they have the same smooth talk, powerful essence, ridiculous sexual energy. Maybe it is Vixen just using a different voice? But I don't get that vibe from him. He had the opportunity back at the club to flirt some more, but he didn't, and my stalker wouldn't have been able to resist me squirming on the floor, below his feet, post-orgasm. No, it can't be him.

And then there is Brandon— I feel *so* guilty. I am entertaining his brothers— lusting, challenging, begging for them. I want them all. *Why can't I just have them all, for fuck sake?* I had to get out of there quickly. I couldn't look at Brandon whilst my cum for someone else sits between my legs. For that reason, I'll never wear that fucking vibrator again outside the house. Stalker be damned!

So that brings me here, at home, Fish by my feet, Shithead probably terrorising the nearby village, and me staring at my laptop like it owes me money. Every now and then I lift my hands to write something else in the chapter, but the thoughts aren't coming clearly. I'm plagued by a polyamorous relationship in my book. I just *can't* write something monogamous now. Not now that I've tasted how delicious multiple partners can be.

Does it have to be a monogamous book though? I ponder on this thought a bit longer. Perhaps this is what I can do? I can change the book slightly—I can write about my desires. Like therapy in a way. Write all down my thoughts, feelings and desires. *Yes, that's what I'll do.*

My fingers move faster than the thoughts in my brain, and soon enough, I'm grinning ear to ear. The story seems to flow out of me like no other has. The characters, the plot, the smut— it's all there. Everything fits in perfectly. Time seems to fly by and before I know it, thirteen chapters have been completed. I stare at the first quarter of the book and smile happily. I have nine days until the book needs to be sent off. If I keep having writing sessions like this, I'll easily make the deadline!

My phone's buzzing startles me and even wakes Fish up. I answer it happily, without looking at the number. I feel on top of the world. *Bring on my stalker. Bring on my editor.*

"Rebecca?"

Fuck. The whole world comes crashing down on me.

"Baby, it's me," Leo's gruff voice pours down the phone. It feels as though my heart has popped in my chest. The words are snatched from my lips.

"Speak to me, god damnit," his sudden anger makes me jump in fright. "I swear to fucking God— sign the contract! Sign it, Rebecca, or I swear to God I'll come down there and—"

Plucking up all the courage in the world, I hang up the phone. It's all too much and everything hurts. My muscles feel heavy, my head pounds and my mouth is too dry. I choke on a breath, and lean over, heaving. The familiar pain of a panic attack rips through my body. I slip from the chair and curl up in the ball. The world becomes a blur of tears and mess.

Fuck. He has my new number. How the fuck did he get it? Who gave it to him?

Fish goes wild. He's licking desperately at my face, but I cower away from him. The sobs pull through me and I can't fucking breathe. I'm choking, suffocating, *dying*. Everything slips from between my fingers. *Why is he back? Why won't he just let me move on?*

The pain is blinding and achy all in one. It's never felt so fucking painful in my life. I shake so hard it makes me nauseous.

Desperately, I reach out for the phone. *I need him. I need Brandon. He'll make the pain stop.*

I ring him, and splutter on a sob when it goes straight to voicemail. I try again, and again, but then the feeling dawns on me — *he's purposely ignoring me!* The thought that he's busy rips through me, but it quickly vanishes. No, he is mad at me. I flirted with his brother, and then I acted strange and ran away from him. He must have thought *I* was mad at *him* rather than…

I am a bad fucking person for what I'm doing. I'm messing with three, at minimum, people's feelings. I'm stringing them along, making them play happy polyamorous lives, while all the time, most likely, hurting them in the meantime. Perhaps Leo is my punishment, maybe I deserve to suffer.

CHAPTER THIRTY-THREE

Vixen

Brandon's phone rings multiple times, but he ignores it every single time before switching it to silent. I don't see the name, but I don't need to. Something *tells* me that it's Rebecca. Maybe she is calling to check on him? I shouldn't have pushed them apart like that—I shouldn't have made her cum in front of me. Fuck— there are a *lot* of things I shouldn't have done. Would I take anything back? Fuck no. I wanted to make her cum repeatedly until she was begging, but I *can't*. I want her so fucking bad, but I refuse to take her until she knows exactly who I am. I want her to cum for me, her stalker, not her *owners* brother. Even describing Brandon as her owner pisses me off.

"Whatcha thinking about, handsome?" Dagger tries to lighten the mood. He is the only one not scowling. He has a huge fucking smile on his face, and this light in his eyes that tell me he's enjoying the situation way too fucking much. I glare at him and remain silent.

"And you?" he casts his gaze over to Brandon as he sulks in his chair, religiously watching the monitors, though I'm not sure why. She won't be coming back. I humiliated her too much; perhaps pushed her too far and she'll need time to recuperate. I would love to go see her tonight and push her limits there too, but I resist. She needs time to herself, to figure out what it is she wants.

"Okay, fine. If nobody wants to share with the class—" Dagger sighs dramatically. "I'll go first. I think that Rebecca is the most beautiful creature I've ever seen."

"Get her out of your head," Brandon growls. He doesn't look up from the screens and his grip on the mouse tightens until his knuckles turn white.

Dagger releases an exacerbated sigh. "I can't. I tried!"

"Try harder."

I smirk at Brandon's quick response. I should really second the opinion— I also can't get her out of my head. All I want is to take her hard, fast, and over and over again.

"When did you meet her?" I hear the words fall from my lips. Brandon turns to face me and arches an eyebrow. He debates whether he should tell me. Then, he sighs. "She's an old friend's daughter."

"Who?"

"Thomas." The pain flashes across his face as he says his name. I have never met Thomas, but I heard everything about him. Brandon loved Thomas like they were twins, inseparable by the hip. Then things got dangerous with the job, and he had to cut everyone off who might ask questions. Anyone who could be used as collateral if anybody ever caught us in our acts. Or at least, that's what I guessed. But now— his face twists in regret.

"You fucked your best mate's daughter?" Dagger's jaw drops in shock. Then, he smirks as the amusement sinks in. He lurches over the table and holds his hand in the air for a high five. Brandon glares at it. He's better than me, I might have punched Dagger in the face if he tried to high-five me over Rebecca.

"We haven't—" He starts. I jolt forward in my chair. He quickly catches onto my response; I try everything I can to calm down but it's too late. The room suddenly feels really fucking hot.

"You haven't had sex yet?" Dagger frowns. "Why?"

Brandon hesitates. "I was waiting."

Dagger loses himself in a fit of laughter. The madman has never looked madder as he throws his arms around and cackles loudly, smacking his hands together. I flinch every time.

"Waiting," he roars. "How do you wait around someone like *that?*"

Brandon flies from his chair. "Someone like what?"

Dagger should be frightened of the way he is being stared at right now, but he takes little to no notice. He smirks up at his older brother; he *loves* it when we get mad. He loves pushing us to the edge, trying to get us to snap and hurt people. He lives for the pain.

"Someone so willing," he says. Within a blink of an eye, Dagger goes lurching across the room. He smacks into the wall with a mighty crash. Then, he tumbles to the floor in a heap of bones. I wince at the impact. *That's going to fucking hurt.*

Brandon begins to stalk him, but I quickly slide in the way. "Calm down."

"Oh, now you're on his side?" He glares at me. "Get up, Dagger! Come on, big boy! You talk about my girl like that?"

My teeth snap together angrily. "Stop it. She's nobody's thing! You said so yourself— she needs to stay away!"

From the floor, Dagger sits upright. His eyes are dark and malicious, and a growing smile kisses his lips before he tears the mask off his face, revealing that twisted scar. I gulp.

"Are you blind, my dear brother?" he taunts Brandon, the insanity oozing out of him bit by bit. "She isn't *yours.*"

"Yes, she is!"

"She's everyone's," Dagger grins and it sends shivers to my bones. Brandon glares between me and Dagger. "What the fuck does that mean?"

Dagger chortles uncontrollably like he knows something we don't. Brandon and I exchange a worried look. *Has he fucking lost it for good?*

"Rebecca seems to have eyes for everyone in this room," Dagger slowly rises to his feet. He wipes the dirt off his body and rolls his shoulders. When he looks back at our confused faces, he bares his teeth. "Oh, come on, brothers. You two are the smart ones. Rebecca has Brandon, that much is sure, but she also wants to fuck me. She likes my crazy—" he pauses to point at me, "At least *someone* does." Then he consumes his mental fucking rant, "—And then there is Vixen. Oh, what can we say about Vixen?"

My heart sinks in my chest. *What does the fucker know?* My jaw ticks and I try to ground myself.

"Vixen has had an obsession for a while, wouldn't you say, brother?" Dagger sends me a lopsided smirk. "He visits his little obsession every night. We've all known there would have been someone, but how delightful for us to find out *who!*"

The cunt knows. But how? How the fuck does he know?

"Is this true?" Brandon is like ice. When he turns to face me, my eyes squint, trying to get a read on him. Everything I expected to see written across his face— anger, jealousy, fury— none of it is anywhere to be found, only numbness consumes him. He is slowly understanding that he doesn't have as much power over the little minx as he originally thought he did.

I take a shaky breath. "I didn't realise it was her until I saw her in the club."

"You've been stalking her?" his teeth bare together. The flicker in his eyes promise so much pain and misery. I put some distance between us. "Yes."

"Has she noticed?"

I gulp. "Yes."

"H-have you fucked her?" Brandon has never seemed so hurt. This makes my chest hurt and I take another trembling breath. I shake my head no.

"So, nobody has fucked the elusive and beautiful little creature?" Dagger finds humour in the situation. "In reality, nobody owns her then."

"Shut up, Dagger!" Brandon roars. He visibly struggles with the information, and now marches back and forth in the room. I hold my breath and wait for him to speak. For a long moment, there is an awful silence, that feels like it could suffocate all of us.

"It's clear we won't forget her, and knowing her, she won't forget us." Brandon finally hisses. "So, that leaves us with one choice. *She must choose.*"

He has a face like thunder when he turns to face us. "No-one fuck her pussy, but, we have until the end of the week to play with her however else you choose. Then, she will choose which brother she wants. The winner stays, losers walk away. No more sharing. Deal?"

"Deal!" Dagger throws himself in instantly. *What does he have to lose?* I remain silent.

"That includes no more stalking if you don't win." Brandon pushes. It feels like I'm going to be sick. *Can I really agree to such horrific terms?* I haven't been able to sleep without seeing her at least once a day. How will I cope if I lose? The grim thoughts suffocate my mind. *I can't fucking lose.* That's the only way forward.

"Fine. I'm in."

CHAPTER THIRTY-FOUR

Rebecca

I am awoken by my doorbell ringing an ungodly number of times. I feel fucking awful. It's as if somebody has hit me multiple times with a truck, and then set me on fire to make sure I remain dead. My throat throbs and my eyes still feel puffy as I throw my legs over the bed. Slowly, I make my way to the front door before peeking through the sight. On the other side, pacing around in distress is Sara. I throw the door open, and instantly, she embraces me.

"Oh, my God," she shrieks, hugging me tightly. Then, she pushes me away and scans my body repeatedly. "Are you okay? I'm *so* sorry that he contacted you, my love! I saw your message this morning. I can't believe I didn't hear the phone go off! You should have called me! Andrew! I would have come instantly you know I—"

"Sara." I release a shaky breath. "It's fine."

I feel so incredibly deflated. She hurries in and sticks the kettle on. I fall onto the sofa and curl into the blanket, feeling too weak to move. She makes us coffee before joining me on the sofa.

"Tell me, what did he say?" she asks worriedly. I take the hot cup in my hands, and let the heat consume my skin. It burns, but my brain doesn't let me move away from the pain. When I speak, my voice is hoarse. It's clear I spent the whole night in floods of tears. "He told me to sign the contract. Then, he tried to threaten me. I hung up before I heard it. He's blocked now."

"Good girl for hanging up," she squeezes my leg. "Have you told the police yet?"

"Why would I?"

"Rebecca!" She squeals. "Are you kidding me? He breached the conditions, he contacted you! He threatened you!"

"Conditions of what? I dropped the case!"

"No— stop it! This is so fucking serious." Her entire face is red. "He can't get away with this! You *must* reopen the case, my love. I know it hurts, trust me, I understand. But he won't stop until you sign the contract, and there is no fucking way you're going to sign away the right to speak the truth. Ya hear me? I won't let it. We need to bring the fucker down!"

It's all too much. The tears bunch up in my eyes again and my nose stings with that familiar sensation before you cry. I wipe my eyes with the back of my pyjama sleeve. "I don't know, Sara. I just—"

"Just nothing. I've got you, my love. Nothing bad will happen to you. Who cares what the people say? If the jury is fucking smart, they'd see through his bullshit lies!"

"They might be smart, but they also won't turn down a bribe." I sniffle. She purses her lips and sighs. It's deep and full of pain, and her eyes well up. "Oh, Becks. What are we going to do? How can I help you? Make this all go away?"

"It's fine, it will all go away eventually," I whisper. She squeezes my leg reassuringly before casting her eyes over the mess that is my home. In my fit of despair last night, I smashed anything and everything that I could lift. Looking back, it was an expensive temper tantrum.

"I tell you what," she starts. "Let's walk Fish, get you out of the house for a bit, and then we will clean up this mess up, together. Yeah?"

I'm so grateful, I could kiss her right now. The tears well up in my eyes again. "Sara, thank you so much."

"What are best friends for if it's not this, eh?"

True to her word, she gets me out and cleans the whole house. It took a while to convince her that I'm okay to stay alone at night. She insisted that she'd stay or that I go back to her house, but, I refused more times than I could count. It's fucked up but I almost want to stay in the house near my stalker. I know that nothing would ever happen to me whilst he's out there. No fucking way. He'd protect me better than Sara and Andrew could. I don't need her staying with me either. If she stays one night, she will want to move in permanently to make sure I'm okay. It's a sweet gesture, but I need to be alone. It's why I moved here, to begin with.

I managed to force another three chapters of my book before falling back in my chair and giving up. The words just aren't coming easily today, and it feels like I'm far too fragile to write anything of value. On cue, my phone dings. It takes me a while to steady my breathing. I almost expect to see Leo's name pop up on the screen, taunting, and threatening me, even though I know he's blocked.

Instead, it's a voice note. Shakily, I click play, holding my breath and waiting for the worst.

Dags's deep voice rings through the phone. "Come play with me?"

How *the fuck* did he get my number? Better yet—*am I annoyed him for having it?* No. *Should I be?* Probably. And yet, I'm in two minds. Half of me wants to slip into bed and sleep the night away, the other half knows that I can't live my life in fear and misery of the past. I've also missed five calls from Brandon. My finger hovers over the call-back button. *Maybe he isn't mad at me anymore? Perhaps he was just busy last night?* I click the button and on the first ring, I hear him.

"Rebecca?" he sounds panicked. "Where are you? Are you okay?"

I stumble over the onslaught of words. "Y-yes, I'm here. I'm good."

It's a lie but I don't want to tell him the truth. He told me he'd step in if anything else happens with Leo. I don't want to dirty him with my drama. I like him being the escape, not the solution.

"I'm on my way," he says, and I hear the car rev louder. "I only just saw my phone, I had it off all day. I am really sorry. Why were you calling las—"

"Can I come to the club instead?" I interrupt him. "I just want to get out of the house."

He hesitates and I hold my breath. "Are you sure? I can come to you. As I said, I'm already—"

"I want to get out," I say quickly. I don't know what my plan is. *Make up with him, and then play with Dags?* It feels sneaky and wrong, but I can't shake the longing for both.

"Okay. Well, I'll pick you up and bring you back anyways. I'll be fifteen minutes." He negotiates. I agree before hanging up and racing to get changed. Satisfied with my tight jeans and halter neck top, I slip some boots on before waiting patiently at the door. He shows up right on cue. As usual, he climbs out and helps me into the car before slipping in beside me.

"Are you sure that you're okay?" he asks me as he pulls off. I can see him out of the corner of my eyes staring at me. He knows something is up, but I plaster the best fake smile on my lips. "Of course, I just missed you last night, that's all."

He doesn't seem convinced. "Really?"

It was a stupid lie to say because otherwise I would have just stayed at the club to find him, but I've said it now so I need to stick at it.

"Of course." I turn to face him and place a hand on his thigh. My distraction works and he instantly becomes stiff. "I *really* missed you. I thought you could have come back to mine to continue where we left off. *Alone.*"

"Fuck, Rebecca," he hisses. His reaction spurs me on. The fake smile quickly turns into a real one. I bat my eyelashes a couple of times. "Can we play tonight?"

"Yes." He answers so quickly that it almost gets hidden under my question. My heart flutters in my chest and my pussy starts throbbing in anticipation. I don't know what the fuck has changed in his demeanour, but I love it.

I bite my bottom lip seductively. "Is it just you working tonight? Will I be distracting you from your job or will someone manage the place without you for a bit?"

AKA will your handsome brothers be around?

"Dags and Vixen will be there too, but they are monitoring CCTV and security."

My heart flips in my chest at their names. If I had it my way, we'd all play together, but I know that's asking too much. And after last night, I know that I can't do that, after the way Brandon reacted when I was *near* Dags.

"I was thinking," he says, taking me by surprise. "You don't always have to play with me."

"What?" My heart races quickly. *Is he going to drop me? Is he not interested anymore? Am I too hard work or not involved enough—*

"Stop it, not for any bad reason," he snaps as if he can sense my mind running wild. Then, he grips my naked thigh and squeezes, and the sensation rushes straight to my pussy. "If you want to play with Vixen or Dags, you can."

The air is snatched from my chest. "What?"

"Only if you want. There is no pressure."

"What changed?" I am speechless. Everything I've ever wanted is slowly revealing itself to me on a golden fucking platter. *How do I scream 'yes please' without looking desperate?*

"I know you fancy Dags, and Vixen is a good-looking lad, too. You can play with any of us if you choose."

I must be fucking dreaming. Pinch me.

"What do you say? You don't have to, Rebecca. It's only if you want to, of course." He rushes the last part, eyebrows furrowed together. He drinks up every reaction I have.

I blush madly. "O-okay."

If he's hurt by my answer, he doesn't show it. Instead, he squeezes my thigh tighter, leaving my sinful thoughts racing.

CHAPTER THIRTY-FIVE

Rebecca

As soon as we step through the fabric and onto the main floor, I see Dags. He stares at me hungrily and licks his lips, causing my stomach to flip in my chest as I look between the men. *How will this work? Is it a take turns kind of thing, or all together?*

"Hello, beautiful little freak," Dags whispers before he yanks me closer to him. I stumble, and then suddenly, his lips claim mine. It's so fucking rough and passionate and violent and... *perfect.* His tongue pushes straight past my lips and fights with mine for dominance. His hand curls into my hair and he directs me at the exact angle he wants me. I could melt on the spot under him. He nips at my bottom lip, and I taste the blood mixing in both of our salivae. It only spurs me on. For a long moment, I kiss back with just as much speed, forgetting about Brandon right behind us. His low growl forces me to remember. I stumble backwards, feeling lightheaded. He grabs my arms and keeps me upright.

Dags stares at me with a ridiculous amount of hunger. He licks his lips and my pussy throb at the sight.

"To be continued," he sends me a cheeky wink before brushing past us. He disappears up the stairs, and I'm left dazed. *What does he mean? Does he know that Brandon is letting me play around?*

Suddenly, Brandon pulls me close to him. He ravishes me with the same speed but with a ridiculous amount of passion. It's so different from Dags' kiss. Dags kissed me like he hated me, and Brandon kisses me like it's our first and last-ever kiss. My pussy is fucking soaked from one kiss alone, and I moan into it. I feel his hands wrap around my waist and he scoops me into his arms. Then, he pushes me into the wall. I gasp when it smacks against my back, and he takes the opportunity to claim my mouth with his tongue. I am so fucking drunk on his taste. Between my legs, I feel his hard member almost double in size. It presses through his jeans and into my barely-covered knickers. A moan escapes me. "Fuck, Brandon!"

He growls and grips me tighter.

"P-please," I'm begging but I don't know what for. He pulls away slowly, not before sucking on my cut lip and stopping the blood. He groans as if it's the most delicious thing he's ever tasted. "You taste so fucking good."

"You too," I respond breathlessly. He doesn't put me down and instead charges up the stairs.

"Where are we going?"

He ignores me. It's like he can't speak when he's this riled up. The mischievous thoughts run around my head, and soon, I can't resist them. I press my lips against his cheek. Then, I kiss down his chin and up his neck to the spot just behind his ear.

"Fuck, Rebecca," his voice is low and warning. "Stop that before I take you right here on the stairs."

Yes, please!

If anything, I up the antics. I pull the sensitive skin between my teeth and roll it, earning a sharp hiss from him. In response, he slams his hand down on my ass. I shriek as the pain flies through me. Quickly, he holds my red ass cheek and absorbs the pain, but it still stings with a reminder. I pull my lip between my teeth to stop myself from tormenting him any further.

Soon enough, we arrive at the location. He hurries me through the door and straight to the playroom. I don't know what to expect, every room is so fucking different and brings so much pleasure. I quickly recognise the room as the humiliation and degradation room.

"Do you remember what happened the last time you were here?" he asks sternly. I nod slowly. *I drenched that fucking chair.*

"This time, you're going to cum for me. I'm going to lick it all up, and you're going to taste yourself on my lips. Got it?"

"Yes, Brandon!" It's so fucking hot how he takes control. He consumes my mouth again, kissing me like my life fucking depends on it. I'm shaking, that's how much I need him right now. He slowly lowers me to the ground before hovering above me. I am in awe as I watch him lower himself between my legs, never removing his eyes from me. I push up onto my elbows to watch him. He nips at my thighs and my pussy hums greedily. Then, I feel him press a kiss through the material of my knickers. The gasp slips from my lips. He pushes the material to the side before admiring my wetness. I feel his finger glide through my folds, and he groans. "Holy shit, Rebecca. You're so fucking wet for me."

"P-please!"

"Play with your nipples," he demands. I quickly pull at my hard rosebuds, and the pleasure shoots straight down to my pussy. His finger trails around my clit a couple of times before sliding back down to my hole. Then, he pushes in. A long moan escapes me. I feel him push all the way to his knuckle before he removes it and sides in again. He does this a couple of times, getting me used to it. I'm a whimpering mess below him.

"That's it, my pretty girl. I love watching your greedy pussy take my finger." He growls. I feel his hot breath on my clit.

Then, he tastes me with one flat lick of his tongue. My back instantly arches off the floor and I almost scream in pleasure. He thrusts another finger inside of me and pounds me relentlessly until I'm a moaning mess. All the while, he picks up the assault on my clit. Within seconds, I'm close to the edge.

"Br-Brandon!" I cry out. He pulls away for a split second.

"Cum for me."

His teeth close around my clit, and the pain shoves me over the edge allowing the orgasm to rock through me. My legs snap around his face, and I hold him still as the pleasure forces its way through me repeatedly. My eyes slam shut, and I focus on the pleasure, trying to hold onto it for as long as I can. I'm trembling and whimpering.

He licks me up as if he's starved. As soon as I come down, he presses his lips against mine. I can taste how sweet I taste on him, and it makes me so fucking hot. The breath is still shaky in my lungs, and my head is dizzy, but I choose him over oxygen. His arms snake around my waist and he pulls me to his lap. I pull him close and kiss him like my life depends on it. It's not until I hear a low growl, that I pull away.

Startled, I stare up at Dags who glares down at me. *"My turn."*

CHAPTER THIRTY-SIX

Dagger

She is so fucking beautiful when she cums.

Brandon sends me the filthiest look as if to tell me to *fuck off*, but I bat it off. There is no fucking way I'm leaving— not after seeing her like this. No way in fucking hell am I leaving without my own taste of my dirty freak. Her jaw drops as she drinks in my huge erection for her. I fist it through the material of my jeans.

"You like sucking dick?" It's crude and I beg for her approval.

Her eyes flash with desire. "I love it."

"Get over here then." I undo my jeans and let my cock spring free. I see the panic flicker across her face. I'm really fucking thick- many women have complimented *and* complained about it before. I cock an eyebrow up at her and wait for her to do either. She slowly crawls over to me, not before giving Brandon a look of permission. He is very fucking reluctant. I clear my throat and it reminds him of the deal we had. He nods at her, and she lights up excitedly.

However, just as she crawls to the position in front of me, I scoop her up in my arms. She squeals as I spin her around so she's upside down. Her legs flail around, and I quickly fix them around my face. She screams as I tuck into her delicious pussy instantly, not giving her a second to warm up. She is so fucking tasty— that *fucking* sweet, intoxicating scent that is now all over my nose, lips and beard. I rub my face in it like a wild

WE SHOULDN'T

animal in mud— *I'm fucking addicted.*

My tongue darts out and I catch her clit. She shivers and clutches my thighs harshly, the pain only makes my cock bob. Then, I feel it. Her fucking lips wrap around the tip of my cock. It takes everything in me not to explode all over her pretty face already.

"Fuck, Rebecca," I hiss into her. She moans in approval and takes me deeper. I start thrusting my fingers inside of her. She gags and splutters— it only pushes me closer, much quicker. I wrap one arm around her to keep her secure. Then, I bring my spare hand to her pussy. I get one finger all covered in her juices before bringing it to her puckered asshole that stares straight at me. I can't help myself. It's *begging* to be touched. I circle it a couple of times and wait for her to say anything in protest. Instead, her whimpering gets louder and more desperate. Then, I push all the way down to my knuckle. She cries out around my cock. "Oh, fuck!"

The smug grin on my face is quickly lost when Brandon glares at us both like he could dig a grave tonight. "Want to join us, brother?"

He growls in my direction. I pull my finger out of her, much to her disappointed groan, before repositioning her. I hold her upside down so Brandon's cock is in front of her face. She gasps in delight and quickly unbuckles him. At first, he is stiff and reluctant, but as soon as her pretty little lips touch his tip, he is much more on board. He holds her hips still and secure and starts thrusting into her mouth. I dig back into my meal, licking at all her juices. I can't help how fucking crazed I am for this taste. It's at this moment that I realise: the end of the week be damned, I ain't giving this girl up. *No fucking way. They'll have to kill me.*

With that thought, I pull away and push a finger into her tight pussy. It swallows the whole thing. I pull out to the tip before lining another finger up with her ass. Slowly, I push both digits into each hole. She squeals in pleasure. My cock couldn't be any fucking harder. Then, I start thrusting my fingers in and out of her, and she squeezes tightly around me. Clumsily, she reaches her arm back and wraps her fingers around my cock. It's an awkward angle, and the grip is loose, but it doesn't fucking matter—the fact she's touched it has me ready to fucking blow.

"You want to cum soon? Show my brother how beautiful you are as you cream everywhere?" Brandon hisses. I wrap my other arm around her to make sure she's doubly secure. She tries to nod around his cock, but it starts slamming the back of her throat. I can't take it anymore. Her moans- her gags— *fuck*. My fingers plough in and out of her, and then suddenly, she's squeezing around me tighter than ever before. At the same time, she screams out her release.

I squirt everywhere. My orgasm pummels through me until my head goes dizzy. It doesn't take Brandon long to finish in her mouth too. I hold her still as he empties into her, and then, I gently lower her to the ground. She swallows the whole thing down, and my cock is instantly erect again.

I stare down at the dirty little thing, laying on the floor, dazed, red-faced, tears and makeup smudged everywhere, cum leaking down her thighs and my brother's cum across her lips... and the happiest fucking look on her face.

CHAPTER THIRTY-SEVEN

Vixen

I've heard the stories already— how they both had their way with her *together*. Dagger came bounding in as soon as Brandon left to take her home. He told me everything. *Every fucking detail.* My fists still haven't unclenched since he boasted about it. I was out of the door the next second. I didn't think they'd work that fast to pounce on her, but now it's my fucking turn. Especially since she hasn't worn the vibrator again since the other night. *Punishment is in order.*

I charge out of the car as soon as I park it in the nearby field. It only takes me a minute to run the rest of the way and slip into her garden. I make note that Brandon's car isn't here so hopefully he's on his way back to the club.

That's when I notice her door is open. My heart lurches in my chest. *Is that an invitation?* I creep closer, and now I hear the shower pouring down. My cock jumps up appreciatively and in anticipation of what is about to come. I slip into her home. Suddenly, the dog bounds into the room. He startles when he sees me and barks once, then twice.

"Shut up," I hiss, holding my hands out. He stares at me wearily and starts running round and round in circles. I race closer to him, and he runs away. Then, I shut the door behind him. He barks again. This time, the shower turns off. *Oh, fuck.*

I hide quickly behind a wall and listen for her. Before long, I catch her in the reflection, a towel wrapped tightly around her waist. Her long-wet hair sticks around her face. She is nervous and trembling ever so slightly.

"Hello?" she calls out. My cock strains at how beautiful she is like this. All it would take is one tug and she's naked in front of me. "Come out! Show yourself!"

If you say so.

I sneak up behind her and throw one hand over her eyes. She instantly fights back, and it makes me so fucking hot. She lurches left and right and screams loudly. My other arms stop the assault from meeting me.

"Calm down, my beautiful Rebecca," I purr into her ear. She instantly relaxes, and it's the fucking hottest thing ever. Her chest rises and falls dramatically, and she desperately tries to snatch the breath back into her lungs. "Atta girl."

"How did you—*shit*, did I leave the door unlocked?"

"Did you do it on purpose?" the smirk is evident in my voice. In the window's reflection, I can see her nibbling on her lower lip in anticipation. Then, she gives me a small nod. *Fucking hell, Rebecca. You're going to be the death of me.*

"I want to see what you look like," she whispers. She is pressed flush against my body and it's so fucking erotic; she readjusts herself, but it only grinds into my growing cock.

"Not yet." I plant a kiss on the side of her face. "Tonight, you will cum for me, but you will be blindfolded. Permit me, my love, tell me I can make you feel so fucking good."

She presses her thighs together, and a breathless moan slips out.

I nudge her gently. "Your words, baby, use your words. I need to hear you tell me I can."

"Yes! I want you to make me feel so fucking good."

The smirk on my lips is ridiculous. I've never felt so fucking proud and excited in my life. "Stay there. No peeking. I mean it. If I catch you, this all stops. Got it?"

"I promise I won't look,"

Fuck. My cock swells with how trusting she is with me. *A stranger. Her stalker.* I quickly march into her bedroom and find the box of toys before re-entering the room. She stands in the middle, eyes still firmly shut. She shivers slightly and holds onto her towel.

"So, fucking beautiful," I whisper. She pulls her lower lip between her teeth with my words and blushes profusely. I turn my attention back to the box and I tip it out on the floor. Then I see something, and I can't help but laugh. "You have a scream mask?"

She stiffens before hugging herself protectively. I quickly put the mask on before checking the sight in this thing. *Clear as fucking day.* Then, I strip my top off and slowly walk over to her. "Open your eyes."

She trembles and hesitates. I run a hand down her bare arm gently and she responds so well under my touch. She opens her eyes and stares at me, half-naked, in the scary mask. A whimper escapes her, and it takes everything in me not to attack. Her eyes dilate and she tilts her head lower. I can see the desire in her eyes.

"Drop the towel," I demand. She does as she's told, not wasting a second. Soon, the material pools around her feet, and I help her step out, and fuck is she stunning. I've always had a thing for thick thighs and hips, and she fills her curves out so fucking well. My fingers curl into the soft skin, I can't help but leave a red mark on her. A type of ownership. *Mine,* the world growls around my head.

Her fingers shake as she reaches out to me. I feel her soft touch on my hard abs, and I stiffen. I wait to see what she does next.

Still trembling, she leans in closer to me, and that honey smell almost knocks me out.

"How long have you been watching me for?" she whispers. The smirk smacks me across the face even if she can't see it. *So inquisitive.* "Do you really want to know the answer?"

"Y-you're my stalker."

I pull her dangerously close to my body. "I just like people-watching, darling." I pause and chuckle. "Well, I only like watching you. Nobody else compares to you. You respond so well to being scared and turned on."

"You're crazy," she whispers. "I should call the police."

"Do it. See what happens."

Her eyes widen. "Are you going to kill me?"

"And why would I do that? I'd lose all the fun I plan on having with you." My head cocks to the side, and she visibly recoils. But it's too late— I feel the switch turn. My hands are around her ass and pulling her around my waist within seconds. She gasps and pushes at my chest. It's weak and pathetic. She's not trying too hard to get rid of me, and now that my tongue is in her mouth, she melts so fucking beautifully around me. My mask pulls up slightly revealing my mouth but with her eyes shut, I'm not worried about revealing my identity. The hand which smacked me in the chest a couple of times now snakes around my head. She pulls me closer and increases the speed. A growl slips between us, and I feel my nails sink deeper into her soft flesh. She squeals; I snap.

Within a blink of an eye, I bend her over the sofa, so her ass is in the air and her hands are firmly behind her back. My cock is perfectly aligned with her pussy. Just one push forward and I could do it—I could fuck her relentlessly, make her cum so hard for me. She shivers and presses back. So, fucking willing for my cock to be buried deep inside of her.

My jaw clenches. I spin her around before I lose my sanity. Her legs wrap instantly around my waist, and yet again, she lines herself up with me. *So, fucking perfect*. It takes everything in me to not plunge into her and move her to the sofa. I push her legs apart and drop between her thighs. I lift the mask to reveal my mouth, but I never let her see my face. She gasps when I stick my tongue deep into her folds. Then, I lap at her as if I've been starved for months. Her fingers jump to my hair through the mask, and she pulls. The pain almost awakens me more and I become more frantic. She is so sweet, and her mewling only spurs me on. But I don't want her to cum like this. She's already cum like this from my brothers. I need to do something different. With one final kiss to her clit that has her moaning, I pull back. I grab the thick dildo from the box and run it through her folds, getting it nice and wet.

"Please, I want your cock!"

Holy fucking shit. I force the hunger to stay down. *The game. Remember the game.* But everything in me shivers to ravage her.

"You don't deserve it yet," I spit, before plunging the rubber cock inside her pussy. It's hard to push through as her tight walls clamp down. She screams and becomes wild. Her hands jump everywhere as she desperately tries to cling to something. I don't relent in my pounding and press my lips back to her clit. She is so fucking wet, and her juices spread all across my face.

"Oh, my God!" she shrieks. "Oh, fuck! Yes, right there!"

Fuck, and she's vocal. She couldn't be any more perfect for me! I push it downward so it will hit perfectly into her G-spot, and suddenly she sings louder than I've ever heard her before. Her legs flail around and her back arches. Then, I feel it. The way her pussy clamps around the rubber cock. *Holy crap*. She orgasms so beautifully underneath me, trembling and moaning loudly. I continue sucking her clit until her fingers find my head and she pushes me away. It takes everything within me to not push her hands away and make her cum again. After the day she's had, I *know* she needs rest, but the hunger within me doesn't want to listen. I reign it in quickly and pull away from her as if she's burnt me.

She lays there, breasts rising and falling quickly as she pants, legs still spread apart, juices all down her thighs— *fuck. She is a sight.* Then, never taking her eyes off me, she drops to her knees. She is so fucking pretty like this. I'm frozen to the ground as she crawls closer. Then, she wraps one hand around my cock; her hand looks so small wrapped around it. I can't look away. I'm completely frozen. Gently, she presses her lips to the tip of it and moans. My stomach drops in my chest at how fucking hot it is. She slowly wraps her mouth around it, bobbing in shallow thrusts. I feel like I'm going to lose my mind.

"Fuck, Rebecca," I hiss. She moans happily and her eyes flutter shut. Her cheeks hollow out as she sucks and takes my cock deeper into her mouth. Her hand reaches up and she cups my balls. Then, I snap. My fingers grip her hair and I thrust into her mouth quickly. She gags and splutters, eyes now wide and hungry. I am fucking hooked on the sight. A tear slips down her face and my balls tighten. She takes it so well, so fucking beautifully. Her tongue presses to the bottom of my cock. It makes it so fucking tight. "Rebecca, I'm going to cum. Swallow it all. Got it? Good girl."

She lets me fuck her throat until my seed shoots out. More tears pour from her as she deep throats all of me. My orgasm hits me, wave after wave. It feels like I'll never come down. She swallows my cum and licks her lips to make sure she catches it all.

"You taste delicious," she smiles innocently up at me. My cock bobs as it starts to rise again. It shocks her, and she looks between me and my growing erection before reaching out again. I slap her hand and yank her upwards and then over my shoulder. She squeals, and suddenly her fear is back. I can't help but smile under my mask.

"What are you doing? Where are we going?" she panics.

"I'm taking you to bed," I grumble. "You're too horny for your own good."

When I lower her onto her bed, I expect her to scramble away, to put as much distance as she can between us, but instead, she slips under the covers and pats the bit on the bed next to her.

I frown even though she can't see it. "What?"

"You can stay if you'd like. I can't imagine it's comfortable out there in the tree line watching me all night."

I startle. "You're inviting me into your bed so I can watch you comfortably?"

Please say yes, oh for the love of god please say yes.

"Exactly."

"I am your masked stalker. The man who watches you all night, who ravishes you repeatedly and you're inviting me into your bed to stalk you up close? Are you not scared?"

She pulls her bottom lip between her teeth. "You've given me no reason to be scared of you."

I tower over her. "Do I need to give you one?"

"Perhaps." She completely misjudges my threat to be something sexual, and it makes my cock harden. As much as I want to ravish her again, I know I can't. I shouldn't. I don't think I'd be able to resist fucking her and ruining the game. The thought of making her keep the secret has run through me repeatedly. But I can't. When I fuck her that first time, because there *will* be a time, she will be mine. *Wholly and utterly mine.*

With a huff, I slide into the bed next to her and twist her around, so her back is pressed up against me. I wrap my arms around her chest to stop her from wriggling around to face me again.

"Sleep, my dirty little dove," I grumble. She starts to protest but I slap her on the ass. "Sleep or I promise you I will give you a reason to fear me. I want you rested and ready for me when I do ruin your greedy little pussy. But keep testing me, and I'll take you here and now repeatedly until you hate me. Got it?"

She trembles in my arms, and it does nothing for my fully erect cock. However, she makes no more attempts to protest. I know I should leave now that she's in bed and understands the situation. I need to return to the club and rest myself. But now that her strawberry-scented shampoo drifts up my nose, and her sweet sweaty smell clings to me like it's home, I can't move. I don't *want* to move. So, I hold her until our breathing becomes light, and I feel sleep take hold of me.

CHAPTER THIRTY-EIGHT

Rebecca

He's gone.

My masked stalker slipped out of my bed and disappeared before I awoke. He fucked me with a dildo until I came hard and then cuddled me tight until soft snores echoed around the room. *And* he has given me a ridiculous number of ideas for my book.

After four hours of not moving an inch from my desk, and ten chapters later, I give myself a break. My entire body has been aching for the last couple of days so I run myself a bath. It's the least I deserve.

When the water is bubbling with beautiful strawberry scents and popping bubbles, I strip down and slide in. The water kisses my skin beautifully, and I can't help but melt into it.

A phone call has my eyes snapping open again. I reach out for it and answer, and my dad's voice fills the phone.

"Hey, my dear!"

"Hi, Dad?"

"How are you? Long time no talk." I can almost imagine him grinning as he holds the phone to my ear.

"I'm good thanks. Just doing the same old thing. Writing—" the blush shoots to my cheeks about the *other* things I've been up to. "—and just plodding along, I guess. How about you?"

"I'm wonderful! There's something I actually need to tell you."

"You going to marry someone else?" I can't resist the playful dig. My dad laughs down at the receiver. "Same woman, but it is the right topic. We have a date for the wedding, in one month—"

I almost lurch out of the water. "So soon?"

"Yes, well..." he is flustered, "Cheryl and I were thinking why wait? We've been saving it up for a while now, and there is an opening at the beautiful country house not far from here. We only want a small, personal reception anyways and—"

I zone out as he babbles on about his plans. I know I should pay more attention, but my brain whirls over his voice.

"Rebecca? You there?" He notices my silence. I swallow down the lump in my throat. "Yes, dad. That sounds great."

"I know it's hard for you, my dear. And I'm sorry. I really don't want you to feel sad or—"

"Dad, I'm happy for you." I hear the words leave my voice and ready myself to wince at the insincerity, but it doesn't come. Instead, a genuine happy feeling floods me— my mum died too long ago for my dad to be holding onto that marriage. I am the only thing that's holding him back from starting again; I am the only person preventing his happiness right now. I saw the other night how in love they were, so maybe it's time to put my differences to the side.

"I am excited about your wedding. Of course, I will be there, no matter when it is."

"Really?" he sounds shocked, and it just makes the guilt creep higher in my chest. How many times has the poor man had to fight me on these silly topics? No more. I refuse to be the person who drags my dad's happiness down.

"Brandon and Sara are going, oh and that husband of hers too.

But, if you can think of anyone else that you want there, feel free to invite them! As I said, it's only going to be small, but I want you to be comfortable and—"

"Dad, this is *your* day," I interrupt him again. I can hear the whirring of his anxieties and I want to help him. "Don't worry about me. You make sure it's perfect, okay?"

"I know," he sighs and it's as if he releases all the tension in his shoulders. "But the offer still stands. You can bring a date if you'd like."

Dags and *Vixen*. I don't know why my brain screams their names instantly and I quickly scramble to push them away. My cheeks blush. "Dad! I'm not dating!"

"You might in the next two weeks."

"Do you know something I don't?" I have to fire a joke in his direction or else my head might explode in awkwardness. He chuckles down the receiver and I can picture him shaking his head. "No, no, darling. It's just an idea!"

"Okay, dad, whatever you say!"

"You know me, my love, I just want you to be happy. Maybe it's time to start dating again? Who knows? Maybe the next one is your Mr.Right!"

If it's not plural, I don't want it. "Sure, dad. I'll keep an eye out for Cupid and his little bow and arrow."

He belly laughs down the phone and it fills me with joy. I can't help the smile which sticks to my lips. It feels so nice to talk to my dad again without that elephant in the room, it's as though we are finally on the same level, and as much as I hate to say it, I think Brandon really helped me see the right direction.

"What's that?" My dad calls to someone out of ear shot, "Yes, love. Okay, ye-yes, I'll do it now. " Then he directs his attention at me. "Garden needs mowing apparently. Duty calls!"

I chuckle. "Okay, dad. I will speak to you soon."

We say our goodbyes before hanging up. I sink into the bath more and sigh happily. My heart fills so fully. Before I know it, my thoughts drift off to the brothers and I try to imagine what they are doing now. *Do they miss me? Would they rather be with me than working? Will they come visit me tonight?*

My phone dings and I check the notification. Another hate message has slipped through the comment filters I set up. This one reads '*Kill yourself, lying bitch!*' it goes on to say other things, but I swipe off it before I can taunt myself anymore with the wicked words. I choke on the breath in my chest. It takes everything in me to ignore it, but it haunts me in the back of my mind.

Throwing my phone to the side, I sink lower into the bath until the scolding water covers my face. My eyes open under the water and I stare up at the ceiling. It burns my eyes, but I can't seem to stop. The message repeats over and over in my brain, growing louder and louder each time. I am used to the hate comments by now. Everybody has an opinion on the matter, and although I *know* I can't stop them from expressing their feelings, it is never easy when the messages are so direct. It's that awful reminder that nobody believes the victim, the awful reminder that anything I do is futile— I will never escape the abuse, because where there is an abuser, there is a circle of enablers.

My chest burns as I hold my breath for a little too long. It reminds me of what I used to do whilst living with Leo. I'd see how long I could stay under the water— I was never brave enough to fully commit to it, but I guess that's fitting. At the time, I wasn't brave enough to walk away, so I certainly wasn't brave enough to take my own life. A wicked thought enters my mind: *but you did walk away, you were brave enough to do that, so why don't you—*

With a strangled gasp, I throw myself out of the water, spluttering for air. That tightness yanks in my chest and my heart struggles to regulate itself as the adrenaline surges through me. It's been weeks since I last thought about *that* and now the thought is plaguing my mind. It's not that I want to die, I just want the shit to stop. Overcome with emotion, I pull my shaky legs to my chest and drop my head to my knees as a sob pulls through me. Crying is better than the alternative option.

CHAPTER THIRTY-NINE

Brandon

Another pimp lies limply on the floor in front of us. It only took Vixen a couple of hours to find a new trail. He's like a sniffer dog that one—*never misses a fucking thing.* It's terrifying and brilliant all in one.

Dagger is in the far corner and I'm keeping a close eye on him. He promised me that he wouldn't go near the pimp today, though I almost told him to 'go fuck himself' and banish him to the club, but then he gave me those puppy eyes, ones that scream his innocence. *How can I deny my brother the satisfaction of finding out the answers too?* After all, he is the one who needs revenge, we just need justice.

"Cut the crap and tell us where the others are." Vixen takes charge. He stalks around the man on the floor, never taking his eyes off him for a moment. The man squirms uncomfortably, much to my frustration. These pimps, despite being in such a high-level organisation, sure are fucking weak and pathetic. Every time we get our hands on them, they blubber and sob. *What happened to no mercy? To strength?*

As usual, the pimp doesn't reveal the truth right away. Vixen strikes him across the face and a singular tooth shoots out of the man's face and skids across the floor. Blood splatters follow closely behind. I stiffen and peer at Dagger who stares at the mess right in front of him like it's the most fascinating thing in the world. He looks lost in thought, and I hold my breath, waiting for him to attack— to break his promise, *again.* The room is *so* fucking tense, even the pimp is watching Dagger with wide, nervous eyes, as he grabs his jaw in agony. He cries out, and it makes me wince—the prey has made the distress call to the hunter. I countdown the seconds in my mind for Dagger's blade to go hurdling across the room. However, nothing comes. Dagger smiles up at me innocently. Currently, there isn't a *single* fucking thought behind those dark eyes.

"They are at Luna lo's!" The man shrieks the answer. We all turn our attention back to him; I can't shake the bad feeling I have. *Was it really that easy?* Vixen shoots me a knowing look before turning back to the victim. "You willing to bet your life on it?"

"Y-yes!"

"If we go there and it's a trap—" Vixen's voice is low and malicious. It promises so much hate and pain. The pimp shakes. "I promise you it's not!"

"Well, that was easy." Dagger jumps up from his seated position and almost skips over to us. I feel the urge to step in between him and the pimp. Dagger's eyes the man up suspiciously and then something flashes in those dark eyes. Stressed, I hold my breath. His head snaps to the side, and his lips part slightly, eyes homing in on the pimp's neck. Then licks his lips, like a beast who has found a floundering, injured deer.

"What the fuck!" the pimp screams when Dagger's ragged scar comes into view under the dim lighting of a flickering lamp. He starts squirming around and tries to put distance between them, but it's futile. Whimpers leave his mouth too, and I sigh and wait for the inevitable. *The prey has given the monster distress signals.* Opposite me, Vixen starts to close in, getting ready to stop our younger brother from losing his fucking mind again.

"What happened to you?" The pimp roars in fear.

"Don't—" I try, but it's too late. Dagger lurches. Everything happens so fucking fast. One minute he's next to me, smiling, the next, he is on top of the man, holding his hands above his head. Dagger snarls in his face and flashes his teeth. For a second, I fully anticipate him biting the poor fucker's nose off.

"Dagger!" Vixen spits, full of venom. It's useless, though, he won't be able to hear us if he's snapped. I begin to roll up my sleeves and ready myself for the inevitable dance of danger we are so used to, casting one last glance to the multiple bin bags which are ready to scoop up bits of pimp.

"That's not a nice thing to ask!" Dagger screams, voice cracking. It takes me by surprise. It's so full of disgust and pain, but not that deep growl which tells me the monsters are out. Then, he snatches the man by the neck. Again, I wait for some sick and twisted torture, but it doesn't come. Instead, Dagger grabs the chain around the man's neck. He pulls it into his hand and stares down at it, lost in thought. I take a slow step forward and peer at the dog collar. "You okay, Dags?"

When he looks up at me, his eyes are so full of sadness. "What does it say?"

Vixen is visibly nervous. He switches his weight between each foot and clicks his knuckles. "Is now the time to practise reading?"

The room is so fucking tense, and Dagger's emotions are only getting more and more heightened every second. "Yes. There is always a good time to practise reading!"

I place a reassuring hand on Dagger's shoulder and send Vixen a look to tell him to back down. The pimp whimpers when I come closer and leer over the dog tag. He is shaking like a leaf in the wind, and it brings me momentary happiness. I want to pull Dagger away and get him at a safe distance where he can't attack, but something in my gut twists. He is responding so normally— *normal for him*. It's so fucking bizarre.

I give him the options slowly. "Did you want me to spell it out or just tell you?"

"Spell it."

"Okay," I hesitate. "P-r-o-p-e-r-t-y."

"Slower!" Dagger hisses. His face scrunches up as he concentrates. I repeat the letters three times, as slowly as possible. The pimp's face turns white and then within seconds, he passes out. When his head smacks the cold floor, I'm sure it will set Dagger off, but instead, his tongue is sticking out of the corner of his mouth, and he is repeating the letters over and over.

"Give me a hint," he finally says exasperatedly before peering up at me. "I can do this. I know I can."

"I believe in you, Dags. So, it begins with *prop*. The last letters have an *er* and then a *ty*. What does that sound like?"

"Bran—" Vixen tries to interrupt; he doesn't have faith in him. Of course, he doesn't. There are only so many times Dagger can let us down. Yet, I can't help the suffocating hope in my chest. "Let him think! He can do this!"

Dagger glares at the floor and repeats my instructions multiple times. I don't know why my heart feels heavy, and my mind is thumping loudly. I've been trying to teach Dagger to read and write for about eight years now, but he always became physically violent and aggressive each time he got it wrong. He was not interested in learning something new— all he wanted to do was kill. One of the very first therapists that tried to help him, told me that if he could write, he might be able to write his feelings down, stopping him from bottling them up and then exploding. I held onto that thought every fucking day. And here he is, without pressure, trying it for himself. *There might be hope for my beautiful, insane brother after all.*

"Prop," he ponders out loud. "That last bit sounds like ay-ty."

"Erty." I correct him gently. Then, his eyes widen and it's like a kid at fucking Christmas. The joy spread across his face, and he springs to his face. "Property!"

"Fuck yes, Dags!" I can't help but celebrate. He throws himself into my arms, that strong grip winding me before I slide my arms under his to give myself some breathing space. He laughs maniacally and the sound is magical. When I look at Vixen, he is in disbelief— jaw dropped, eyes wide, and completely stunned. He hides it just as quickly, but I saw the hope echo around him too.

"Brilliant, Dagger. Well done." He still gives the compliment, but it's not as genuine as the emotion I *know* he's feeling.

"Property!" Dagger roars again, "I did it! I can read!"

I laugh. "One step at a time, big boy."

"First this, then I can read Rebecca's books!"

I stiffen. *There it is. The real reason he's trying again.*

"What?"

"Yeah, I want to read, Brandon. I want to be able to read her new book!" his eyes are so full of hope and excitement. It feels as though I'm going to be sick. Vixen slaps me on the back, and it snaps me from my thoughts.

"That's great, Dagger. Aim high!" I don't know what game Vixen is suddenly playing. Is he trying to wind me up, or is he genuinely happy about our brother's change of heart? Either way, I should be grateful —there is hope for the madman after all.

But I can't shake the bitterness in my heart. Dagger is having feelings—*real, normal feelings*— towards Rebecca. It's not just sex for him, it's not just untameable lust. I recognise the sinking feeling as jealousy. I want Rebecca romantically *and* sexually. When I made the bet with my brothers, I didn't fucking think they had any intentions of romance with her.

And yet, here we are, all staring at each other warily, plotting the ways we can dirty her to make her *ours.*

CHAPTER FORTY

Vixen

"What does property mean, though?" Brandon scowls. He rocks back in the chair and sighs. "Why would the pimp have that necklace on? Surely it would be for the women?"

"Do you think he's a—" I start before looking at Dagger warily to check if he's listening. He is fast asleep in the corner, slumped in his armchair. He snores softly, mouth hanging open and a bit of drool teasing the corner of his lips.

I look back at Brandon. "Do you think that guy was a prostitute instead of a pimp?"

"How can he be? You said you followed him, right? What did you see?"

I swallow down a lump. Ten years of this business and it still doesn't make the words any easier. "He was definitely grooming the girls."

"And yet he is property too."

"Maybe he could be wearing it to keep it safe or something?" I frown, before shaking my head. "No way. Those men and their egos—"

"We should visit Luna Lo's. Maybe we'll find out more?"

I look back at Dagger who readjusts himself in the chair, stirring slightly, before snoring louder than before. My heart throbs painfully when I look at how calm he is. If only he could be as peaceful in life as he is in sleep.

"He's improved today." Brandon follows my gaze. "There is hope for him."

I stay silent. Brandon has far more hope for him than I do. It's not that I don't want my brother to get better, but I think Brandon fools himself too much. The boy is clinically unwell, and we are not trained in keeping a lid on things. Besides, I truly believe one day he'll snap too far—and making someone who snapped, *snap* further is a recipe for disaster.

"Believe in him, Vixen." He tells me softly but I can't bring myself to discuss the topic further as the lump in my throat worsens. To distract myself, I shrug into my coat. "I'm going to go to Luna Lo's."

Brandon arches an eyebrow. "You sure? I can come too."

"You stay with him. I'm sure it's nothing down there anyways." I shrug. "I'll also keep tabs on that pimp. See, there are some positives to keeping them alive. They will eventually lead us to the source."

"But they also recognise our faces." Brandon scowls, much to my humour.

"Then I just won't get caught."

He gives me a half nod, but his face tells me how much he dislikes the idea of it. I usually check everything out alone anyways, but that pimp gave the location up far too easily. If it is a trap, I'll figure it out before Brandon will anyways— I have far more experience with the stalking and locating side of things. Plus, it's better if someone watches Dagger.

"I'll call you if I find anything."

"Be safe."

I grin. "Always am, brother."

It takes about half an hour to drive there, but when I finally arrive, I'm greeted by a rackety old warehouse. There is a huge sign with a woman on the front with her boobs out, censored by spirals. It's deadly fucking silent around the town tonight, and there isn't a single person for miles. The cold pulls through me as I park the car a couple of streets away to keep myself hidden. Then, I slip out into the dark and stalk around the building. It's completely boarded up at the windows by carboard, and the front door is locked. A bad feeling sinks through me, but I push on.

I find a window where the planks have a gap and peek through. An empty barren room with nothing but dust greets me. I continue down the dark alley way to the next window. Again, there is nothing when I peer through. I take another step down, but my stomach twists uncomfortably. The air suddenly feels much colder and easier to choke on. I risk one more window, before deciding it's too risky.

However, I hear them before I see them. The cracking of branches on the floor, bats being smacked into palms for a display of intimidation, and the sound of spitting on the floor. I feel a white-hot rage flow through me when I turn to face the five men, each stockier than the last. They stand in a line and block my escape exit out of the alley way. I cast a quick look over my shoulder, and hiss. *They've backed me into a corner.*

"Oi, Dagger cunt," One yells, gaining my attention. "Not so clever now, are you?"

To my surprise, the pimp from earlier isn't one of them. To my humour, every single one of them wears black work trousers and a tacky wife beater, and bandanas of different colours push the hair out of their sweaty, round faces. I can't help my amusement. "You gonna do a song and dance for me? Like, seriously, if you're going to be threatening, at least don't wear a shitty 80's music video get-up. And for your information, I'm not the Dagger Killer."

I can be worse.

"Keep laughing, cunt." The man in the middle steps forward. He has a big belly but even bigger arms, and this is a problem

WE SHOULDN'T

for me. The fat ones are harder to knock down because they can use their weight against me. However, they are also slower. He juts his chin out to feign confidence. "You're going to get hurt. *Very* hurt."

I crack my knuckles. "I'd like to see you try."

"There are five of us, and one of you," he points out smugly. They all chuckle amongst each other and it makes my blood boil. I sniff, roll my shoulders and hold my fists up, revealing the knuckle dusters I've just slipped on.

"I hope you don't mind if I don't fight fair either."

He's shocked but quickly masks it. "Worry about yourself."

"Take your own advice," I shoot back quickly.

He arches a thick, disgusting eyebrow before nodding at two men on the far right of the line. They are almost identical in looks, and both have disgusting moustaches stuck to their upper lip. They take a menacing step toward me at the same time. *I'm going to rip the moustaches off their fucking face,* I decide with a smile. I ready my stance. "Come on, big boys."

Simultaneously, they charge towards me, but I dodge them effortlessly, spinning around to meet them in the combat. I kick one of them in the back, sending him forward, before punching the other in the face. They recuperate quickly. One flies another punch at me, and I miss it minimally whilst trying to dodge the other's elbow to the nose. My body snaps up and down, left and right, as I work on dodging. They tire a little, and it gives me an opportunity to start giving the assault back. My fist meets a nose and a satisfying crunch echoes down the alleyway, I deliver the same blow to the other one who tries to shove me. I feel a foot against my back— the first successful attack—and I stumble forward. The dull ache instantly pulls through me, and I hiss. When I turn to face my attacker, I realise there are now four men in the fight. They start to close around me.

"Give up, mate. You're not going to get out of this," one snarls. My breath hitches in my throat when I realise two of them have knives the size of my forearm. For a brief moment, the fear sinks in. I swallow the lump down in my throat.

"Now you're fucked." I growl before lurching into an attack. My fist collides with the middle person's throat before I spin and throw my head as fast as I can into another person's face, forcing my knee into their stomach at the same time. I feel the sharp hiss of a wound opening on my shoulder from a light slash of a blade. Quickly, I turn and disarm the man, snatching his weapon before thrusting it straight into his stomach. The shrieks of the men ripple throughout the alley way around me. It makes for a delicious soundtrack. I channel my inner Dagger and go psycho on these cunts.

Everything happens so fast. With a blade in my hand, I'm faster, more accurate, less of a target. They now work on defending rather than attacking. The smile spreads across my face as I do the dance of death— one I watch so often. I much prefer torturing my victims mentally; I gave up fighting, alongside drinking because it was getting out of control, but maybe Dagger has a point— fighting *is* addictive and so fucking delicious. When the fourth man falls to the floor, roaring in agony, clutching their wound, I frown.

"Get up. We are not done here!"

For the first time in my life, I understand Dagger's disappointment when the fight is over. I twist back to the man who set the hounds on me. However, he is already running away. I drop the weapon and give chase. He is fast— *not fucking fast enough* —and soon, I'm on him and I'm pummelling him with punches until his face bruises and swells.

"Who do you work for?" I scream, grabbing him by the shirt. He trembles but resists with a good amount of effort. He spits blood back in my face, and I wipe it with the back of my arm before landing another punch on him. A bit lands in my mouth and I taste the bitter metallic taste. Something sinister swarms through me. Again, I sympathise for Dagger's addiction to the wicked thing. It truly is fantastic having the warmth of it on your skin.

"Don't make me repeat myself," I howl, lifting my hand again threateningly. The man shrieks and hides his face, crying out pathetically. The snot, tears and blood mix into one disgusting stream down his face. If I were Dagger, I'd lick it.

I change my line of interrogation. "The girls? Where are they?"

The man below me has a frightened look ripple through him, but that's not the thing that unnerves me— it's the smug one that quickly follows. Then, suddenly, I feel something sharp sink into my shoulder, before a roar of agony explodes from my lips.

CHAPTER FORTY-ONE

Rebecca

I tremble slightly as I step into the club. I clutch my phone tightly in my hand, and click the voice note from Dags's number. His deep, velvety voice rings through the receiver. "Come play with me, little freak. Floor three, room two."

How can I refuse such an inviting offer? I climb the stairs quickly but hesitate before I enter. *What will he have in store for me? What delicious things will he inflict on my body?*

When the door shuts behind me, I realise that I am completely engulfed in the darkness. My stomach flips and I take a shaky step forward. "Dags?"

Nothing.

"Dags? You here yet?"

Suddenly, something from behind grabs me. I flail around with desperate squeals, but it holds me firmly still. The hairs on the end of my body shoot upward and the panic floats through me. With all my might, I try to fight my attacker. I throw my elbows back, but it doesn't do any damage to him. If anything, it brings out the most delicious chuckle from him.

"Keep fighting me. I like it."

Dags.

And then I feel... *it.* It's huge and presses firmly against my

WE SHOULDN'T

back. A whimper escapes my lips as I thrash around again, but all I'm doing is rubbing against his hard cock. Frustrated, I cry out again but his hand jumps from over my mouth to my throat. He squeezes, and my head instantly feels hot.

"Scream for me," he growls. I desperately try to inhale but it's no use—he snatches all the air from my lungs as his other arm forces me still so I can't escape. Then, his large muscular hand travels lower and lower. It mortifies me how my body instantly responds to his touch. *Fuck. I knew I liked fucked up shit but this*—

Suddenly, a sharp pain stings my left nipple and then my right. "Fuck, Dags! That hurts! What is it?"

"A nipple clamp for those greedy nipples that crave pain."

"It hurts," I moan. My head falls back into his chest, and he holds me still, gently swaying us. I feel his lips the back of my neck and I shiver. Truthfully, it doesn't hurt that much. It actually feels really fucking good. *But how much can I reveal about my deviant sexual fantasies without looking mental?*

Then, I feel him pull on the chain which rests between them. Real pain hits me, and I hiss.

"You like this don't you? Whore."

"Fuck!" More heat rushes to me.

His breath is hot against my skin. "Let's play a game. If I touch your pussy and you're wet, you lose. And if you're dry? You win."

I'm fucked. "W-what do I win?"

"Your freedom."

I gulp. "And what do I lose?"

"The same thing."

Holy fucking shit. If I wasn't turned on before, I am now! My heart sinks and I push back against him. I feel his cock digging into my ass and I quickly lurch forward, but he traps me. "Nah ah ah. Where do you think you're going?"

"Dags, please—you *know* that I'm turned on. This isn't a fair game!"

"I never said it was going to be a fair game, did I?" I can hear the smirk in his voice. He pulls gently on the chains, and I respond with a whimper. Again, more heat rushes to my pussy. "Dags—"

He cuts me off. "Agree to my game. That's all you have to do, baby. And I promise to make you feel so fucking good."

"I agree, I agree!"

As soon as the words leave my lips, his finger is on my clit. He isn't gentle either and soon I'm panting like a dog. He runs it through my folds repeatedly and then a devious chuckle escapes him. "You're fucking drenched for me, baby."

I whimper and lean back further into him. He teases my hole with a finger and slowly slides in. All the while, his other hand starts to unbuckle his pants. I feel his cock spring against my ass, and I bite back a scream when he pushes my cheeks open.

"What—"

"Trust me," he bites my earlobe, sending another shiver down me. "You're going to enjoy this."

I want to scream. Nobody has ever fucked me in the ass before. I've heard it hurts, that it's *really* painful. Especially if the cock is big— and Dags' is huge!

Then, he runs his cock through my folds. I cry out in pleasure. He distracts my mind. I am so desperate for him to just fuck me. But instead, he gets himself all lubed up. I feel him position at my entrance. I push back onto him; my desperation to be fucked screams. He hesitates but then growls and moves his cock before it can slip into my wet pussy. I moan in disapproval, but the noise is stolen from me because suddenly

I feel him position himself at my ass.

"Breathe, baby. Remember to breathe," he nips at me again. Every fucking nerve is alert right now. He pushes the tip into my ass, and I squeal. He is so fucking big, it's like I'm being torn in two. The pain is blinding, and I want to push him away. I want to run away and never come back— It hurts so bad, he is *too* much. *Why did I think I could take him?* But his fingers snake around, and one jumps to my clit, and the other slides two fingers inside of me. I am suddenly breathless. The pleasure smacks into me so hard I almost pass out.

"Holy shit, holy fucking—" I can't help but swear. I'm like a crazed person as he starts slowly moving his cock in and out. The pain with pleasure is all too much. He thrusts into my ass a little deeper and gives me fast shallow pumps. That, coupled with the fingers deep in my pussy, force my body to lock up. The pleasure shakes through me. I hold my breath to try and control my body, but now I'm stuck. The lack of oxygen makes my head dizzy, and he slides deeper before realising something is wrong.

"Breathe— I said *breathe*, god damn it," he growls before slapping me on the tits. The air rushes back into me as I gasp in pain. The pleasure is all too much, my head doesn't stay up right, and before I know it, my orgasm slams through me. He holds me still and continues fucking hard and fast, catching each of my waves. A scream echoes around the room and it takes me a minute to realise it's mine. "Fuck! Dags! Dags! Dags!"

"That's it, baby, scream out my name," he roars his own release. I feel his hot cum shoot inside my ass. He holds onto me, making sure I receive every fucking bit of him. Our bodies are flush, stuck together by sweat, and it's hot in here— but neither one of us makes any effort to pull apart when he comes down from the high. My breathing is erratic; he puts his hands over my heart, and I melt into him.

"I knew you could take it, baby."

I whimper in response to him. He holds me gently and for a strange moment, I feel nothing but happiness in the moment. It's so sensual but not erotic— so fucking strange after how he just treated me.

Suddenly, the doors fly open. I almost jump out of my skin and hurry to redress myself. Brandon stands in the door, eyes like thunder. "Dags where the *fuck* have you been? Have you not been getting my calls?"

"Can't you tell?" Dags is amused. "I was busy."

Brandon looks at me, like *really* looks at me. Messy hair, red cheeks, half dressed. His nostrils flare and for a moment I can't tell whether he wants to kill me or fuck me.

I advance towards him. "What's wrong? Are you okay?"

He puts distance between us. The lines in his forehead jump out and the stress is evident. There is longing and anger in his eyes, and he completely overlooks me. "Dags, let's go. It's work."

"What about work?" Dags shoots back, not wanting to leave. Like a kid, he stomps his foot and folds his arms defiantly.

Brandon's eyes darken and his lip curls into a snarl. "*Your* work. A *meeting* has gone wrong."

Dags stiffens. Then, everything happens so fast. He chucks his clothes on, stumbling around and cursing under his breath. He gets lost in his own world monster— a seems to be ripping at his sanity and his lip curls violently.

I am in awe, confused, and humiliated. The way they both act as if I'm not standing here makes me feel silly.

"I'll go," I say quietly. Brandon looks at me but it's as if he looks *through* me. The Brandon I know doesn't seem present in this moment. Then, his eyes soften as if he senses my hurt. "I will come find you after work."

"Okay," I say slowly. I start to leave the room, but Dags grabs me, and kisses me violently. My head spins and I feel drunk on his kiss. It's so fucking tasty and it awakes the desire in me again.

"Dags! Go!" Brandon barks. I leap out of my skin. He has never sounded so fucking angry before. *What has crawled up his ass and died? What is stressing my beautiful man out?* I want to stop his stress from increasing; I want to kiss his frown— anything to make him feel better. Dags races past him without another look back at me.

"Drive home. *Stay there.* I will see you soon." Brandon hurries me out of the room. He doesn't even kiss me. There is nothing in his movements which echoes the usually soft and romantic man I crave, and it leaves me with a hole in my heart.

CHAPTER FORTY-TWO

Vixen

The pain is fucking excruciating. It rips through my shoulder and aches all the way down my arm. All my training goes out the window as soon as the pain hits me. I fall forward and the dagger is ripped out of my arm. Quickly, I roll over so I'm on my back. The hard floor against my wound makes me howl in pain.

One of the twins leers over me. His blood drips down his face and splatters on my white shirt. Towering over, he raises his weapon, but before he can plunge it back into me, I pull my knees back before kicking him as hard as I can in the stomach. He roars and staggers backwards, but quickly rights himself before attacking again. I move before the knife can smack my face. It nips my cheek and stings but nowhere near as much as my fucking shoulder. Throwing myself to my feet, I get back into the fighting pose, but with my punching arm disarmed, I'm royally fucked.

The guy I chased jumps to his feet and both the men back me against the wall. I could run, I could try and make it back to the car, but with my shoulder in the state, I'm too scared to even move it out of fear of causing more injury. It doesn't feel fatal, but it stings like a fucking bitch.

"You were saying about winning?" He smirks. He takes the weapon off his little bitch and lowers it. I raise my fist and ready myself to fight my way to the death. However, just as he raises the knife, he goes flying left. It's a fucking blur as he tumbles to the floor with a howl. A body forces him down and moves with a ridiculous speed. The punches are hard, fast, and vicious. The other man tears his gaze around in fear.

Perhaps it's delirium, but I smile wider than I ever have before, "I told you I wasn't the Dagger Killer, but you *are* going to meet him tonight."

Dagger leaps off the main leader now that he's firmly unconscious—or dead— I can't see his chest rising or falling anymore. Then, he prowls towards the other man. My brother's eyes are terrifying. His usual animal instincts take over, and he prances on the man as he tries to run. Only now as my brother rips the men limb from limb with his trusty dagger and that sinful laugh, I feel the air creep back into my lungs. When I look up, Brandon is running toward me. His eyes are wide as he stares at the blood staining my entire body.

"Shit, Vix," he hisses. "What the fuck happened?"

"It was a trap."

"I can see that!" He gently takes my working arm and leads me to the car that he pulled up in. I collapse in the seat and work on breathing through the pain. It's fucking blinding and rocks through me in waves.

"It's alright mate, we'll get you sorted out. You'll be fine." Brandon panics as he throws the car into gear. My head falls to the side, and I stare out the window at Dagger who has gone full on maniac on the bodies around the side. The last thing I see is him tearing someone's ear off with his teeth. I wince and look back to Brandon. "How did you know?"

"You didn't answer your messages. I knew something was up." His eyes are cold as he glares ahead of him. I feel the wind tearing over the top of the car as he hits record speeds. The nausea rises in my chest.

"Here," Brandon reaches for a bottle of vodka on the backseat. He passes it to me, but I try to refuse it. With a grunt, he forces it back into my hands. "I *know* you don't drink, but trust me, you're going to want to be drunk for the stitches. That shit hurts a ton."

My stomach twists and my head thumps. I haven't drunk in years. Sober nine years and forty-three days. Even the thought of getting that buzz which used to haunt my mornings makes me nervous. The littlest drop of alcohol used to send me into a rage— I'd fight everything and anything that came near me. In a way, I became Dagger for the night, every time I drank. People got hurt; *really fucking hurt.* I never want to do that again.

Pissed off, I glare at the bottle that used to rule me.

"It's all right, mate," Brandon calls me from my terrifying thoughts. "I won't let you get bad. I will watch you."

My mouth wets at the thought. I feel that familiar pull in my chest. *Just one night. Just enough to get me through the pain, the stitches.* Reason kicks in instantly. *No, fucking way. It's always 'just one' and then it's to the club to start a fight.*

As Brandon tears the car around the corner, I feel my shoulder rub against the seat, and I wince. It hurts so fucking bad. Without another thought, I twist the lid off and start necking the awful stuff like it's water. I feel Brandon assessing me out of the corner of his eye, trying to figure out where the worst of the blood is.

"Stabbed twice in my shoulder. Sliced my cheek." I grit my teeth as the awful after taste hits me. "Five of them, one of me."

"Well done, mate. They looked worse than you do."

"Doesn't fucking feel like it," I moan before gulping more down.

Time passes really fucking quickly, and before I know it, we've pulled up to the club. Brandon hurries out and helps me out, slinging my good arm around his shoulders and basically carrying me to the back entrance of the club. We slip through the door and down a flight of stairs until we get to our flat. My breathing feels erratic, and the pain is achy, but now the warm feeling in my stomach drowns out the worst of it. I swig more of the bottle, and then a bit more. Soon, I'm sitting in the bath, with my shoulder to Brandon. He kneels on the floor and lays out the medical kit in front of him, scanning the different tools. My vision feels foggy and my head thumps louder. I hold my head in pain before taking another large gulp. The room starts to spin.

"That's enough." Brandon hisses before taking the alcohol from me. I instinctively reach out to grab it back from him, but he keeps it behind him. I don't miss the shock which ripples through his face though when he sees how much I've finished. *I've finished three quarters of the litre bottle.* The bile rises in my chest, but I force it back down.

Brandon cuts my shirt off before assessing the wound. I feel him wipe it down and the dull ache reminds me it's still there. I cling to the numbness the alcohol gives me. "Do you think any of them will survive Dagger?"

He doesn't even hesitate. "Not a fucking chance."

"It's good— it's good you know." I'm starting to slur my words, really aware of the alcohol in my system now. It bubbles up in my chest and burns in the best way possible. "Killing people. Dagger has a point."

"Don't start with that shit," he hisses angrily. "You aren't Dagger. You're not a killer."

"I-I do—" *hiccup*, "—torture people though."

"Leave the physical violence to him. He's good at it."

A lazy smile crosses my face. "So am I, apparently. I've still got it."

"You got stabbed."

"I had it, though." I point out quickly. He doesn't answer me as he concentrates, and it takes everything in me not to fall forward as he picks up the needle and thread. For a couple of minutes, it's deadly silent. Thoughts and conversation starters ripple around my mind. Anything to get the silence out of here but the only thing that my mind floats to is my beautiful little dove. "Where is Rebecca?"

"She's gone home, mate."

I force my eyes to remain open. "She was here?"

"She was..." he begins before swallowing. "Playing."

"With you?"

"With Dagger."

"Oh." I hum happily. I try to look at the wound he's fixing but he gently pushes my head forward. I do as instructed and sigh. "Who do you think she'll choose?"

He ignores me.

"D-did" *hiccup*, "Did ya hear me?"

"I did," he grinds out. Then, he pulls back and rises to his feet. "There, you're done. Don't get it wet for forty-eight hours. And take these—" he hands me some little pills. "—they will help with the pain. You'll feel good as new in no time."

"I know, I know." I groan. I try to raise to my feet, but Brandon grabs me tightly. He's angry as he glares down at me. "Take it easy, Vixen. Don't pop the stitches."

"Try and stop me." The drunken humour makes me chuckle but Brandon finds little to no pleasure in it. As best as he can with me squirming around, he helps me out of the bath and towards my bedroom. However, as soon as he reaches for my bedroom door, the front door swings open.

Dagger stumbles in, drenched in blood and chunky bits of gore that I don't even want to imagine what part of the body they are from. Those wild, dark eyes are still dilated and show no signs of humanity. He doesn't talk to me. Instead, he watches me in silence, assessing me when I stumble a little. Brandon says something but I can't hear him.

Dagger gives a sharp nod before sliding past us and into his own room.

"H-hey, Dags?" I call out after him. He stops in the doorframe, turning to face me with an arched eyebrow.

"Are they all dead?" I ask.

Guilt crosses his face. He lowers his head and readies himself to be told off.

"Yes." It's little more than a whisper.

For the first time in months, there is no anger for his answer. Instead, I smile. "Good. Well done, brother."

CHAPTER FORTY-THREE

Rebecca

He didn't visit. Brandon promised he would come and find me, but he didn't. My stalker didn't show up either— which meant I spent the whole night alone. And for the first time in a while, it scared the fucking shit out of me. For the most part, I sat in bed, writing my book. I kept my blinds down too, as if the real monsters out there would sense my unease and attack. The only positive thing is that I'm past halfway now in my book; but, if I'm being honest, I would have preferred a night with either of them over my job.

This morning, I took Fish for a walk, and called my dad and Sara. I've tried everything I can to distract myself and make the time go quickly. I haven't heard from any of them— it's strange. Usually, I would have a voice note or an invite, or someone would show up. Today is the first day I've felt completely alone. Seven o clock comes around, and I'm bored and lonely. I try calling Brandon, but he doesn't answer. It makes my stomach twist. *What happened last night? What upset him so much that he couldn't come see me after?*

Eventually, I decide to go to the club and see him. However, as soon as I step outside my house, I'm greeted with the most disgusting present on my doorstep— a dead bird with its wings ripped off. My heart leaps from my chest. It feels as though time has slowed down as I stare at it. *What the fuck? Who left that? Why?!* Something inside me screams that it's not my stalker— he would never leave something so disgusting, and I can almost *sense* when he is outside, watching me. I also rule out Fish; he doesn't leave without me, and he most certainly did not bring that thing back when we returned from our walk. If I wasn't going to leave the house beforehand, I most definitely am now.

I hurry to my car and speed off. My breathing feels tense, and my mind is heavy. The terrifying question comes to mind. *Was it Leo? Is this another threat?* I try to reassure myself that he doesn't know where I live, but the anxiety shoots back that he didn't have my number until last week either. It all feels too much.

Before I know it, I'm at the club, and it feels like the anxiety and dread in my chest dissipates instantly, as though nothing will be able to hurt me when I'm here. I don't miss the irony over the fact that this is the place where I'm pushed to my limits and become vulnerable. As I climb the steps, I tell myself to forget the bird for one night— it can be my problem when I return home. For now, I need a stress reliever in the form of one of the brothers.

I approach the receptionist's desk, feeling silly when the blonde lady casts me a disgusted look, raking her eyes up and down my jeans and low-cut top— not the dress code.

"Erm, hi— I was wondering if you knew where Brandon was? Or Dags?" I start before quickly adding. "Or Vixen?"

"I'm not sure," she says unhelpfully. "Are you going in or what?"

I stiffen. "Yes, sure. I'll go in."

She gives me a half nod before holding her hand out impatiently for my coat. Snatching it out of my fingers, she dismisses me with a brisk nod of the head. I put her rudeness down to jealousy, recognising her as the lady who Brandon swiped off the first day I came to the club, and slip past the curtain to the main floor. Nervously, I look up the stairs which lead to the playrooms, but something tells me the brothers aren't playing— *not without me, at least.* So, instead, I creep towards the stairs which lead downwards. I've seen the brothers come up these a couple of times, so there must be an office somewhere. *Maybe it's down here?*

I feel myself moving before I can stop myself, and soon, I arrive at a narrow corridor. In front of me, there is a wooden door that must lead to the office. Behind me is a dirty-looking door which I imagine leads out to the car park, so I ignore this one and raise my hand to knock on the office door. However, I pause before it connects.

Should I be here? Will they find it weird? Am I being too clingy? What if they are purposely distancing themselves from me—

Suddenly, the door opens, forcing my anxious thoughts to stumble to a halt. Dags' wide smile greets me as he readjusts the mask to his face, hiding his scar. Before I have another second to take it in, he yanks me into his embrace, those tight arms squeezing me tightly.

"My beautiful freak!" he exclaims, before slowly— cautiously— pulling back from me with a small frown. "What are you doing here? Have you come to play with me?"

"I came to find you and Brandon. You guys left so quicky last night and—"

"Rebecca?" Vixen's voice rings around behind Dags. To my surprise, the door doesn't lead to an office but a huge living room— I barely glance around, my eyes fixed firmly on Vixen.

"What the fuck," I push past Dagger and clutch at Vixen's face, moving his chin around to get a better look at his sliced cheek. Holding my breath, I inspect the damage before raking my eyes down to his arm which is against his chest, in a sling. "What the hell happened to you? Your face? Your arm!"

He winces when I raise my voice, clutching his head as though he's hungover. My whole body hums with adrenaline as I look at the beautiful, hurt man— but then I stumble to a halt when I realise how obsessive I am being. *Why do I feel so strongly about this? What is wrong with me?*

"Don't worry about me," he sends me his best smile. "You should see the other guy."

"*Guys.*" Dags puts an emphasis on the plural.

My eyes almost pop out of my head. "What the fuck? What happened?"

"Bar fight." Dags offers an answer quickly. I wince and stare back at Vixen who glares daggers at his brother. His lip twitches and for a second, it looks as if he's going to protest, but he drops it quickly, much to my confusion.

"It's true." His voice is strained.

My eyes bulge out of my head. "How many were there against you?"

He hesitates. "Two."

"Don't be so modest, brother," Dags chuckles, smacking Vixen on the back, earning a low grunt from him. Dags swiftly ignores the reaction and continues boasting. "There were five of them, but my big mean brother—" He pulls him into a lopsided hug, missing his slinged arm minimally, "—fought them all off singlehandedly. What a man!"

"Dags," Vixen spits. Dags presses his mouth against Vixen's ears but makes no effort to lower his voice when he goes to whisper. "The ladies love a fighting man. Tell the truth!"

Vixen rolls his eyes and pushes his brother off him. He heads toward the couch in the middle of the room and only now he is sitting down, do I take a minute to look around. We are in a huge living room, with pictures of flowers on the cream walls, a large, red sofa and a wide television on the opposite side. A small wooden table rests next to the couch, but that's it—there is nothing else in here, and it feels empty. There are closed doors dotted around the room too and I long to explore.

"Welcome to our home," Dags takes me by surprise as he whispers into my ear. His hands hold my hips still and I shiver under his touch. Just the simple touch has my body responding to him within seconds, and I force myself to swallow to distract my wandering thoughts. "Where is Brandon?"

The brothers exchange a nervous glance. It's Vixen who answers. "He is in a meeting."

"Is it about the meeting that went wrong yesterday?" I ask timidly. Vixen stiffens and averts his eyes, looking lost in thought for a moment before he turns back to me. He pats the seat on the sofa next to me. "Join me?"

I blink back the confusion. My gut screams something is wrong, but nobody makes any effort to let me in on the secret. *Why? What are they hiding?*

"I'm going to watch a film. I don't want to be alone, *wait*—" Vixen stumbles over his words. "—unless you and Dags were going to go downstairs and play?"

I look back to Dags who waggles his eyebrows at me. There is a growing tent in his pants already just at the thought, but I ignore him and take a seat next to Vixen instead. I don't truthfully know why I turn down the opportunity of fantastic sex, but when I look at Vixen's pitiful face, I can't walk away from him. "What are we going to watch?"

"Your call," he hands me the remote. Casting a quick look over my shoulder, I try to involve Dags in the plan, suddenly nervous at the idea of being left alone in a room with Vixen. "You going to join us?"

"Why would I waste the evening staring at pixels on a square? I'll pass." It's the strangest fucking thing to come out of his mouth. He frowns at us before exiting the room through a door on the far side. Before he disappears, he turns around to face me one last time. "When you get bored of him, come find me."

My cheeks flush with humiliation, much to his amusement. Sending me a cheeky wink, slides behind the door and leaves me alone with his brother.

I feel my heart pound in my chest when I turn back to face Vixen. It's the first time I've been alone with him since the hallway incident, and there is something about him which makes me nervous. I think it's the way he is incredibly observant, catching everything with those intense crystal eyes — they are like cameras, constantly watching me, looking *through* me.

"Relax. I don't bite, my little dove." He smirks then adds, "Unless you ask nicely."

My cheeks burn. I switch the television on and flick through a couple of programs to distract my racing thoughts. Meanwhile, I can feel his gaze on me. He observes every inch of my face like he's never seen it before. My tongue darts out and wets my lips nervously.

"You're beautiful. You know that right?" He takes me by surprise.

"I am?"

He stares at me with an intensity I've never seen before. "The prettiest little thing I've ever seen. Fuck that—you're the most beautiful creature I could ever dream of, little dove. The devil himself really out did himself when he created you."

"The devil?"

"Yes, baby. Because God could never create such a filthy whore."

My cheeks burn. He is so sinful in the most delicious way. I can't help the question that's on the tip of my tongue, "Why do you keep calling me your dove?"

His face contorts. "Because you're the most beautiful and pure bird, but your wings have been clipped. I want to help you be free again."

"Why do you say that?"

His eyes rake up and down me, and I feel like I'm being scrutinised. "I recognise a broken soul when I see one."

"Vixen—" I'm breathless.

"Don't worry. I won't tell anyone. Every little dove needs a predator with sharp teeth to slice through the restraints wrapped around your beautiful wings."

My heart leaps from my chest. His words are breath-taking and send a delicious shiver through me.

"I wish my arm wasn't in a bandage. I want to bend you over and show you just how filthy you can be for me." His eyes flash with hunger which makes my pussy throbs hungrily. Then I do something completely unexpected and brave. Slowly, I raise from my position and straddle his lap. He stiffens underneath me, and his mouth moves as if he's going to protest, but no sound comes out. Maintaining eye contact, I grind against his growing erection; it presses against the thin material of my knickers under my skirt, and a small gasp escapes me.

"Let me make you feel good," I say breathlessly before pressing my lips to his neck. He is silent and still for a moment. My tongue darts out to lick the sensitive spot before pulling it between my lips and twiddling it. He growls and grabs my hips harshly, his resolve slowly slipping away.

My hands jump to his jeans zipper, and I undo it slowly before I slip between his legs. His huge size jumps out of its restraints, and I lick my lips hungrily. "You're so big."

"Fuck, my dirty little dove. You're going to be the death of me."

I press it against the material of my knickers and use it against my clit. My head falls back, and I can't help the whimpers that have already begun. His grip tightens against me, only spurring me on. I move my knickers to the side and run him through my wetness.

He hisses. "Holy shit, Rebecca. Look how ready that greedy little cunt is for me."

I line it up with my entrance, needing him to be inside of me. I can't wait any more— I want to ride him hard and fast, show him exactly how desperate I am for him. However, just as I ready myself to sink down, he stops me. His nostrils flare and his eyes are dark.

"Suck it," he says, but the longing in his voice is pleading for me to refuse. There is something in his facial expression that longs for me to protest and sink myself down on him. But the idea of tasting the precum has me trembling. Quickly, I slip off him and slide between his legs. His hand instantly grabs my hair, and he tugs. It hurts and feels so fucking good at the same time. I smile against the tip of his cock before placing a little kiss, the delicious and salty taste sits on my lips.

"Fuck, Rebecca," he growls. The sound shoots straight down to my clit and I can't hold off anymore. I wrap my lips around the tip and hollow out my cheeks. Slowly, I work my way down, getting him nice and wet. His grip is so tight on my hair, and it spurs me on. He controls the speed, the deepness— *he controls everything.* My thighs slam together.

"That's it, baby, suck your juices off my fat cock. If you're good, I'll even let you swallow it," he grunts, picking up the speed. His sinful words have me squirming below him. I take the part of him I can't fit in my mouth in my hand and pump him at the same time. My other hand cradles his balls and I play with them, rewarding me with a low growl of approval.

It doesn't take long before he moves me at a desperate speed. He is so close to his high. My head swims when I forget to breathe, too busy preferring his taste. The room is filled with my spluttering and gags— it's so fucking hot. Then, he pushes my head all the way down and it slams at the back of my throat.

"I'm going to cum, Rebecca. Oh, fuck—" and then I feel the hot ropes shooting down my throat. I've never been so turned on to gulp it all down. He watches me intently as I pull him out of my mouth and lick up any juices that escaped.

"Dirty bitch," he hisses as he slowly releases my hair. My heart swells with pride. It's so degrading but I can't help how fucking hot it is.

"You've recovered well," a voice startles me from behind. I jolt and twist around to spot a glaring Brandon. His arms are folded tightly across his chest, and he wears a disapproving look on his beautiful face. My cheeks burn bright red. I should feel humiliated that he caught me pleasing his brother, but only dirty thoughts rule my mind. I long for him to punish me like before.

"Thanks to my beautiful nurse," Vixen smirks. He pulls me up into his embrace and holds me tight as if he's scared that I'll leave now Brandon is here.

"Where were you?" I frown. Brandon crosses the room silently, stripping himself off that huge coat and his gloves. He throws it onto the opposite sofa before collapsing next to me on the sofa. His large hand squeezes my naked thigh. I am a panting dog within seconds.

"Work," he spits out a singular word. All the while, he never stops glaring at Vixen who still looks smug.

"I was expecting you last night," I say slowly.

"I was busy."

I jolt at his bluntness. "Are you okay? You seem mad at me."

"I'm fine," he runs his hands through his hair and sighs. Then, he reaches forward and pulls me into his lap. Vixen growls and tries to grab me back, but not before wincing at the pain in his shoulder. He slumps back into his seat miserably, giving me

WE SHOULDN'T

up to his brother. Brandon wraps me up and holds me close, breathing into my neck. His hot breath sends shivers down my back, and my pussy is soaking again.

"This is what I need after a long day of work," he whispers. I blush profusely and hold him tighter. He kisses my neck and traces patterns across my back— I can't make out what he's writing or drawing, but the feeling is soothing, and I melt into him.

"Bad day?"

"One of the worst," he grumbles. I pull back slightly and cup his face, watching the way his dark eyes melt a little.

"What happened?"

He stiffens before looking straight past me at Vixen. The look is grim on his face. Much to my disappointment, they have a telepathic conversation and ignore me. Eventually, Brandon turns back to me. "It doesn't matter, my dear. I don't want to bore you."

I feel a little restless. "You can bore me. I want to hear about your day!"

He brings my forehead to his lips and leaves a lingering kiss on me. Then he smiles wide. "Not today. Another day."

"Okay." I feel a little stupid. *Why won't he tell me? Does he think I'm not smart enough to understand or something? What could he possibly have done today that I am not capable of hearing?*

"Ah, here he is, my beautiful brother," Dags' voice echoes around the room. He opens his arms wide and embraces both me and Brandon. I'm instantly engulfed in that oaky scent of his that has my head spinning like I'm drunk. I don't miss the way his hand cups my ass and the heat rises. When he pulls away, his eyes are ravenous.

"What are our plans for the evening then?" he says to the whole room, but he never looks away from me. "Perhaps we could have a little fun?"

"Vixen might have beat us to that already," Brandon grumbles. I feel my cheeks darken significantly when Dags arches an eyebrow up at me. "The cripple made you cum?"

"Shut up, Dags." Vixen growls. "And no, I didn't get to do her because *someone*—" he glares at Brandon, "—interrupted us."

"That wouldn't have stopped me." Dags boasts.

"It's okay," I say, not being able to take much more. My entire body trembles with humiliation and hunger. Dags comes over to me and yanks me from Brandon's grip before chucking me over his shoulder as though I weigh nothing more than a doll. I hiss and smack him on the back. "Dags! Put me down!"

"Brothers, I think our greedy, little whore needs satisfying."

"Way ahead of you," Vixen agrees quickly.

My head feels hot and starts thumping from being held upside down. Dags carries me into a dark room that smells like vanilla. Slowly, he lowers me to my feet and removes his hands from my body. It's pitch black in the room, and I tremble, anticipating his next move. Then, the light from the living room pours in as Brandon and Vixen enter the room too. I get enough light to see Dags handing his brothers night vision goggles. They both grin and quickly put them on before the room becomes black again.

CHAPTER FORTY-FOUR

Rebecca

"Hello, my beautiful little freak." Dags is suddenly in front of me. His lips press against my cheek and my eyes flutter shut. My body trembles with excitement and memories of last time shoot to mind.

"What's happening?" I'm breathless and needy. I want their hands on me instantly, I want them to make me cum so hard, I've never wanted something so bad in my life. *All three of them, one of me.*

I feel him press a kiss to my forehead as his hands gently take my cheeks. Then, I feel another pair of hands snake around my waist. I stiffen. Lips press to my neck and I can't help but melt into the kiss. My mind whirls with all the possibilities of what is to come. Then, I feel something pull at my ponytail. It forces my head back, and now there is a person either side of my neck, licking, sucking and nibbling. Whimpers escape my lips. "Oh, my God!"

It's followed by a sharp slap on my ass.

"When you are with me and my brothers, there is no God. Only sin." Dags' voice ripples through the air.

"Remind me." I jump when I hear Brandon's voice in my ear. "What is our safe word?"

I blush and feel a little stupid over the name I chose all those weeks ago. Another slap to my ass has me squealing the answer. "Meat!"

He chuckles against my neck. "That's right. Now, remember that, okay? You can stop our game at any time."

"Game?"

"Yes, baby, a game," Vixen purrs. "We are going to touch you and taste you. You will guess which brother it is. Got it?"

"But you're hurt," I protest but it is futile as he slaps my ass. "Nothing, and I mean *nothing*, could stop me from making you cum. Got it?"

My pussy screams with joy. Then, three different pairs of hands start to grope my body. Every nerve is on the edge, desperately trying to soak up every brush. Already, I can just about make out Brandon on my left, Dags might be on my right, and I *think* Vixen is in front of me. If they speak throughout the whole thing, I might be able to win the game. *Seems easy enough.*

"Back to my game," Dags says. "If you get it wrong, you will be spanked."

Suddenly, the hands on my body disappear and I hear Dags' voice go from my left ear to my right. *Shit.*

"Do you agree?" I feel his hot breath against my right cheek before he presses a kiss there. I melt under him. "Yes. I agree."

"She's trembling." Brandon is behind me. I feel his huge cock press against my ass. I grind back into him, earning a delicious groan. His fingers sink into the softness of my curves, and a hiss falls from me. He doesn't relent. Then suddenly my hands are pulled together and held above my head. I hear a clipping sound. When I try to move my hands, they don't budge. *The fuckers have tied my hands up.* The same thing swiftly happens to my ankles.

"Shit," I hiss as someone's thigh presses between my legs,

spreading them wider. My thighs burn a little from the awkward position, but it only adds to the erotic nature of the game. The vulnerability for them only makes me so much hotter.

"The game begins now." Vixen nibbles my ear, and it sends a shiver through me. Then, I'm left alone, and nobody touches me. I count the seconds down in my mind. The anticipation has me hot and ready.

A sharp scratch sinks into my thigh as someone drags their nails down my skin. My head falls backwards as the pain shifts directly to pleasure. They rake up and down my left thigh, leaving a wake of stinging, before a tongue licks up the pain. It's so fucking sensual, mixed with pain— *it could be any of them.*

"Vixen?" I hazard a guess. It's quickly followed by a sharp slap on my ass. I buckle against my restraints and hiss as the pain vibrates through me. Someone chuckles but the tone of voice is drowned out by the racing of my heart. I try again. "Dags?"

Another slap only much harder. This time, I squeal. "Fuck! O-okay, it's Brandon!"

"Good girl." I hear his throaty chuckle in my ear. Those two words remove every memory of the pain on my skin. Then, he's gone, and different hands touch me.

They curl around my neck and squeeze. My head is instantly hot, and my tongue falls out of my mouth instinctively. A low growl from behind makes my guess easy. "Vixen."

"Fuck." He chuckles. "She's going to play dirty."

Pride swarms my stomach as I realise my game plan. *They can tease me, but I just have to tease them back to find out who it is.*

A soft slap across my tits has me jolting. Then, I feel warm lips close around each nipple. I cry out in pleasure. "That's cheating! There are two of you!"

Nobody responds to me, and instead, the people on either side of me continue tongue fucking my rosebuds. I feel sharp nails sink into my left ass cheek until I'm sure that it's left a bruise. *There is only one person who is madly obsessed with my ass.*

"Dags on my left," I say through gritted teeth, breathing through the pain. He growls, disappointed that he got caught so fast. The person on my right- either Brandon or Vixen— doesn't do anything to stand out. They circle my nipple a couple of times with their tongue and flick it. My back arches in response. I take a guess based on Dags being on the left, and Vixen being the person beforehand.

"It's Brand—" I start and then they sink their teeth down around my nipple. *I know that move.* "Wait, no; it's Vixen! You tricked me!"

"Well done, baby." He chuckles before kissing away the pain. Suddenly, hands sink into my hips.

"Fuck, this," Dags hisses, and suddenly I feel his cock against my ass. I squeal as I feel his hardness threatening to part my cheeks. "I have a new game. Let's see how quickly she can cum for each of us."

"Good idea." Vixen's amused voice rings through my head. "Do you think you can last two minutes with me, dirty little dove?"

No fucking way! "P-please, I don't think I can—"

Dags snaps. "You can take everything my brothers and I are going to give you and more. You wanna know why? Because you are one of us. You are just as sinful and perverse and dirty. I know for a fact that our greedy pussy is begging to be pushed to its limits."

"Fuck, Dags," I am breathless.

"Is that a yes?"

This time, I don't hesitate. I *can't* hesitate; he is so fucking right. "Yes! Yes please!"

"I'm going first," Brandon growls. "Since she was mine first."

My stomach flips in the most delicious way. He presses lips against mine in a passionate kiss. I hear the sound of a timer being set behind us but block it out. The only thing I want to focus on is his fingers which are twisting my nipples so deliciously. Then, his lips move down my cheek, to my neck. He sinks to his knees and positions himself between my legs before lifting me up, as far as the restraints will allow it. Then, I feel his tongue against my clit as he holds my thighs around his face and I hold the restraints above my head to keep me stable. He laps at me repeatedly before pulling my clit between his teeth. He twiddles it so fucking pleasurably, and then his finger pushes inside of me. I can't help it— my entire body is alight with desire. He doesn't give me even a second to take a breath before thrusting inside me at a ridiculous speed. It's all too much. Suddenly, I'm falling off the edge with a scream. The shakes devour my body. Brandon holds me still and helps me ride the high. He smiles into my sex when the waves stop hitting me. "Good girl."

"One minute thirteen seconds," Vixen says in amusement. My heart flips in my chest. *Is that it?* "My turn." And then, before I have a chance to recover from my first orgasm, Vixen plunges his finger inside of me. *Three* fingers in my pussy, over and over again. He flicks my clit so perfectly, and soon, I feel that familiar clench inside of me.

"Cum for me, my dirty little dove. Show my brothers who you respond so perfectly to," he growls in my ear, and it sends me over the edge instantly. My orgasm shakes through my entire body, and my head feels dizzy. It slumps forward before falling backward. Repeatedly, the waves shatter through me until I'm panting.

"One minute, five seconds," Brandon says through gritted

teeth. It feels as though I'm completely drained of everything. *There is no way I can give one more! My body might give up.*

"Oh, my beautiful little freak," I hear Dags' whistle. My traitorous body responds so fucking well for him. Instantly, I'm breathless and ready to go again. He wraps his hands around my neck, and I choke. "Let's show my brothers how much you love your ass being played with."

Fucking sin incarnate.

"Spit," he demands. I feel his hand below my lips. I do as I'm told. I hear him spit too and I imagine him choking his cock with our combined spit in his large hand. Then, he slips behind me and lines himself up. I flinch and ready myself for the pain. Suddenly, the lights snap on. Dags and Vixen howl in pain as they tear the machines from their faces.

"What? That's cheating!" Brandon nostrils flare. "No sex, Dags."

"I'm not fucking her pussy." He retorts quickly. Even though I can't see them, I can feel the anger pulsing through the room. It's fucked up that their anger only spurs me on, making that desire twist tighter in my stomach, but what the fuck do they mean by *no sex*? It only just hits me that none of them has fucked my pussy. *What the hell is going on—*

Dags pushes into my ass, and I squeal. The pain is awful and splits me in two. His hands hold my hips still. "Good little freak. Just like last time, remember? *Breathe.*"

Vixen snarls at his words and lurches forward but Brandon holds him back. Within two thrusts, the pain turns to blinding pleasure. My head falls back onto Dags' chest, and he picks up the pace. I'm panting and moaning and withering, but he holds me still and drills to me. Then his hand snakes around to my front, and as soon as he touches my clit, I'm tumbling over the edge with a scream. "Yes, yes! Please Dags—!"

It feels like I'm above the clouds. The pleasure consumes me and makes my head fuzzy. Every hair stands on edge, and that familiar washing sensation pulls through me. Soon, I'm a whimpering mess as he pulls out of me. He wraps those large arms around me and I sigh into his embrace. Someone unties my wrists and ankles, but my eyes are still shut, trying to come down from the high.

"What did she do it in?" Dags mumbles into my neck. It's Brandon who answers. It's stiff and angry. "Fifty-eight seconds."

Holy fucking shit.

The weakness instantly hits me, and I slump into somebody's arms. It's humiliating how pathetic I feel; all I want to do is slump into a ball on the floor and sleep. My eyes flutter shut, and my breathing becomes heavy. I'm so warm, wrapped up in a cuddle. They play with my hair and hold my head against their chest. I can't help it; the fatigue steals me away.

CHAPTER FORTY-FIVE

Vixen

As soon as I hear the faint snores of Rebecca as she sleeps in Brandon's bed, I spin around to Dags. My anger is blinding. "You fucked her ass?"

"Yeah why?"

"Why?" It feels as though something is snapping inside of me. "The rule was no sex!"

"No *vaginal* sex," Dags points out smugly. "It's not my fault that you two were too thick not to find the loopholes."

"I'll fucking kill you."

"Do it, cripple." He challenges me with a lopsided smirk. Then, he takes a threatening step forward. I crack my knuckles and push back the dull ache in my shoulder that began once I pushed myself too fast too quickly with Rebecca; I don't regret it though. Now, I should rest but something inside of me howls. *If he wants a fight I'll fucking fight him. How dare he! He has de-blossomed her, stolen her ass virginity from the winner. He knew exactly what he was doing.*

Brandon clips Dags behind the head. "Knock it off the pair of you! You'll wake her up."

"Are you not mad he fucked her ass?" I turn to him in disgust. Brandon herds us out the bedroom and shuts the door behind him. "Course I fucking am. But what good does it do now? It's done."

"He'll keep getting away with it!"

"I will," Dags nods his head smugly. My fingers curl into fists. *I want to knock the smile off his fucking face.*

He suddenly becomes animate. "I mean, what was I supposed to do? It was right there—!"

"Both times?" I growl.

He holds one hand on his chest and the other in the air. "Scouts honour."

"Scouts honour," I mumble angrily before lurching at him. He dodges me and laughs manically. I charge after him again, and again, but the fucker is too quick. He roars with amusement, jumping side to side. He keeps lunging toward me but before I can connect my fist with his body, he's gone again. The pain is blinding through my own body. He laughs at my slowness now that I'm injured.

"I swear to fucking God—" Brandon hisses, spinning around to both of us. "Next person to make a loud noise is going to get shot. She is sleeping!"

I shoot an evil look at Dags who smiles innocently back at me. For a moment, I seriously consider my odds with a bullet hole. "You're a disgrace."

"Don't be jealous, brother," he shoots back. "In three days, I'll fuck her pussy too."

Three days. Is that it? Fuck.

"She's so fucking tight, it'll be like choking my cock," he continues mocking me. I resist the urge to groan. I know how tight she is— she swallowed that dildo and clung to it like there was no tomorrow. It was near impossible thrusting it inside of her without breaking a sweat.

"May the best brother fuck her greedy pussy first," I growl out. Brandon remains silent, his eyes do all the talking though. He is nervous. He agreed to the conditions, but never once did he imagine the outcome could be this fucking close.

I distract everyone's thoughts. If we think about that dirty dove any further, it might create irreparable damage in the bonds. "What happened earlier? Did you find any information?"

This piques my interest. Brandon went out to be the eyes and ears whilst I recovered this morning. I am very intrigued to see what information he found.

"Nothing," he growls. "Literally nothing. The women are all gone like they never even existed!"

I grit my teeth. "Do you think they are still alive?"

"They must be! I haven't seen any new recruits arrive, and there are no bodies."

"What about any new clubs in the area?" Dags offers. I shake my head. "No, the Dagger Killer operates around here frequently. They wouldn't be stupid enough to stay local. They've probably moved."

"Not too far though, otherwise they lose all their usual customers," Brandon points out. I ponder on that thought. He has a point.

"If only we could pretend to be a prostitute to know where they all are." Dags sighs dramatically before falling onto the sofa. I roll my eyes. "Yes, because the clients want six foot something men with muscles bigger than their future, to be a little sex doll."

Dags stiffens and I instantly feel guilty. Sometimes it's easy to forget everything he went through. The hurt look vanishes before it fully manifests.

"I have a secret," he suddenly blurts. Brandon and I snap our full attention towards him. He pulls his bottom lip between his teeth and I wait impatiently for him to finally speak again.

"The guy that attacked you..." he says slowly. "I recognised him."

My heart drops in my chest. "Oh, Dags—"

"He was much younger then, of course. It was his dad who was the scary one. The one with black eyes—" he freezes and loses himself in his own world. I almost reach out to reassure him, but I can see his emotions slowly building up. His face is hard, and his eyes turn cold. He takes the mask off his face and tosses it to the side. He doesn't need to say anything more for us to understand where he is going with the conversation.

I swallow a lump down in my throat. "I'll look into that."

He doesn't say anything. Instead, he dips his chin downward to let me know he approves. Then, he twists on his heel and storms out of the room.

CHAPTER FORTY-SIX

Rebecca

Behind me, someone stirs. Large arms pull me closer, and I feel the warm breathing against my skin. It makes me tremble. I push back against them. Brandon's oaky scent drifts up my nose, and suddenly, I'm aware of where I am. I try to sit up, but he groans, and pulls me straight back into him. "And where do you think you're going?"

"Brandon!" I squeak. "Shit. I fell asleep. What time is it? Fish will be all alone! He is hungry—"

"Hush, Rebecca. I fed him last night, and he seemed happy enough on your bed, all curled up. I took him for a quick walk too."

"What? Why would you do all that? You could have just woken me up!"

He snorts. "And miss spending the night with you? As if!"

"Brandon," I whine but he makes no effort to move his arms. He presses a kiss against my neck, and reluctantly, I feel my body melt into him. He sighs happily. "Vixen is visiting him this morning to make sure he's fed and walked."

"Why? I'll go back now—" I start but Brandon spins me around to face him. Those dark hungry eyes stare at me intently. "Let us help you."

"You don't need to help me walk my dog!"

"No, Rebecca," he spits. I feel a shiver course down my spine, and it suddenly feels cold in the bed. Dread kicks in.

He frowns at me. "There was a dead squirrel on your doorstep."

Another dead animal!

"Is it Leo? Is he sending you them?"

"No," I lie quickly. A low growl falls out of him. "Rebecca, don't lie to me. We've gone over this. You said I can step in if he contacts you again, and sending dead animals is a fucking threat—"

"Don't do a thing!" I spit.

"Why are you protecting him? Why are you doing this? Let us help you. Say the word, my dear, and he will be gone."

My eyes widen in shock. "Gone?"

He doesn't mean dead, does he?

He recovers quickly. "I mean like out of your life."

"Now who's the liar."

"Christ, Rebecca, we aren't murderers," he rolls his eyes. Something inside of me screams that he is lying but I push it away. *It can't be true.* Surely, the brothers aren't killers, they'd be caught by now. They are terrifying, sure, but killers... *no. No way.*

"Just let us help you."

"I'm dealing with it, Brandon," I whisper, and now I can't even keep eye contact. He tilts my chin upward with a gentle finger.

"Please," his voice is laced with concern. "Let me in, let me help you."

I bite my lower lip. I feel my eyes shimmer with a faint haze of tears. I don't know why I don't let them help me. I don't want to trouble them, make them think I'm pathetic, or that I can't handle it myself. Or maybe it's the nagging of the unknown.

What if they fail? What if Leo bites back twice as hard? If he finds out I have a new partner so soon, who knows what he will do? The spiteful and sinister part in him will punish me. If I find dead animals and threatening calls bad, just wait until he finds out I'm plotting against him or sending other people to do my dirty work.

"Let me," Brandon grinds his jaws together. "You shouldn't do this alone. Let me talk to him. I promise you I will sort this out."

Suddenly, there is a knock at the door. I jolt in the bed and pull the sheets up under my neck. Dags' face peeks around the door. He looks all sheepish and nervous. "Rebecca, can I talk to you?"

"What's up?"

Then, he steps around the door. He holds a book in his hand, and I instantly recognise it as my first novel I ever wrote. My eyes widen.

"What are you doing with that?"

"I want to ask you a favour," he says.

"What favour?"

"Can you read this part to me?" He enters the room without permission and slots himself next to me. I shuffle up to give him space. I can't help but feel the blush which crosses my face as I lay between the two brothers, about to read a book I completed five years ago. *Which humiliating scene will he make me read? Which awful grammar point, or plot will I have to explain?*

"This," he opens the book and points to a small paragraph.

"Why can't you do it?"

"I, er—" he stumbles to silence before sending a nervous glance at Brandon. He swallows hard. "I can't read."

WE SHOULDN'T

"What?" The disbelief hits me. "Surely, you can. Everyone can read!"

"Not me."

"Did you not learn at school?"

"I didn't go to school," he mumbles, an ashamed look coating his face. My eyebrows furrow together, "What do you mean you didn't go to school? Were you home-schooled?"

"Something like that."

I look to Brandon to check his reaction, but he's stiff, and doesn't make eye contact with me. I go to ask another question, but Dags waves the book in front of my face. "So, will you do it? Will you help me with this bit?"

"Yes, of course."

He lights up excitedly and shuffles closer. I am so aware of how close our bodies are, perhaps the closest we've all been in a nonsexual situation.

"Can you read at all?"

"Brandon taught me phonetics a couple of years ago, and I kind of remember it, and like some words I understand but—"

"And you did very well." Brandon interrupts him with a compliment, and Dags blushes profusely, making my heart swell. Gently, I take the book from Dags. "You try, and I will help if you get stuck."

Nodding quickly, he brings his finger up to the line and starts sounding it out. "T-the girl blan-blinked and then he w-was in front of her. He was furry—"

"Furious." Brandon gently corrects him.

"The girl blinked and then he was in front of her. He was furious, with e—"

"Eyes." I help him. He nods and concentrates again. "He was

furious, with eyes as dark as sin. She flin-flinched. Was he going to hit her a-again? Lev- *no*," he fixes his mistake, "Leave bru-bruises?" his pitch changes as he tries to sound out the word. Then, he sighs, and turns to me. "You read from here."

I swallow down the lump in my throat. This section feels so sore, as if it's still raw feelings. I remember writing it after Leo got mad at me for wearing jeans with holes in it to a reader's event where there were men there. He believed that I purposely wore them to get attention. He called me a whore and hit me so hard I saw stars. The bruise took two weeks to fully heal, and shit ton of makeup to cover up.

I clear my throat. "Was he going to leave bruises on her again? How many beatings could she take under the hand of the man she loved? One minute she was standing there, shivering with fear and the next, she was halfway across the room. The wall kissed her with more passion than he ever had. Within moments, he was leering over her, hands fisted into her shirt —" I stumble into silence. I can feel both men staring at me intently, and my bottom lip quivers. My chest feels like It's constricting again, and my breath is shallow.

Dags continues reading for me. "She thou-thought she was going to die. He was really mad this time, more furrier- furious than he ever had been before. Sure-surely, this was it,"

He carries on but his words melt into the background of my mind. All I can do is feel the pain that he left on me after that event. I've never been so sore and battered in my life, and I didn't leave. *Why the fuck didn't I leave? Why did I let him treat me like that for so long?* A choke catches in my throat and I feel Brandon's hand on my leg. He rubs it reassuringly and the movement oddly relieves some of the tension in the back of my throat. My head thumps. Dags get onto the part where the abuser suddenly switches. He is no longer mad at the woman but instead infatuated. He kisses the pain better and she accepts him easily, before the cycle repeats. That's what I thought love was—*full of misery and forgiveness.*

"Why?" Dags voice is low as he turns to face me. "Why did you write this?"

"It's just a story," I whisper.

"No, it's not. This is real life."

My breath catches in my throat. *How much does Dags know about Leo? Did Brandon tell him about my court case? About the dead animal?*

"This is very real," he sounds distant now and it suddenly dawns on me that we are not talking about me anymore. "Love and anger—hand in hand."

His face contorts and I feel sick as the pain ricochets through him. I raise my hand and cup his face. He nuzzles into me, but his eyes are still distant. There is a flicker of something on his face as he remembers something, something I really want to discover.

"Have you ever been in a situation like that?" I hear myself ask. Dags peers up at me sadly. He purses his lips and for a moment, he seems like he's going to ignore me. Then, after a long pause, he nods. It steals the breath from my chest. *Has my beautiful crazy Dags been in an abusive relationship before? Is that why he is the way he is? How much did they take from him?*

Brandon clears his throat gently. "That's enough reading for now."

I nod quickly. Dags is lost in his own world and his lips curl into different shapes as if he's talking to himself, and I'm mesmerised. Brandon slides out of bed next to me and helps me up. But before I can leave, Dags' hand shoots out, forcing me still. The hairs on the back of my neck jump to attention.

Brandon eyes him warily, "Dags."

"Stay." He whispers quietly, and I can't help but melt. I silently tell Brandon that I'll be okay and that I want to. He doesn't look sure, but then, eventually, lets me shuffle closer to Dags. He instantly puts his head on my chest. I stroke his hair slowly and he softly whimpers; It shocks me how sensitive he is, how fragile and easy to break, and yet I'm happy he's sharing this side with me. I press a kiss against the top of his head, and I can almost feel him smiling.

"I need to go to work," Brandon says uncertainly. "Will you guys be okay, here?"

"Yes, brother." Dags answers but Brandon is looking at me for the answer instead. I nod quickly. "I will see you later?"

"Of course," he smiles, placing a light kiss on my lips, and ruffles his brother's hair, before slipping out of the room.

Dags wraps his arms around my waist to hold me still.

"I like your writing," he sounds like he's in a dream-like state.

"You did very well reading it."

"You think?" Hope flickers across his face. "Your new book, I will be able to read all by myself." There is something childish and hopeful in his mannerism and it melts me.

I squeeze his arm. "I look forward to hearing your opinions on it."

"What's it about?"

"It's—" I pause, looking for the right word. "Much happier."

"Good. I want you to be happy."

It takes me by surprise. "I am happy, Dags."

"I want your work to be happy. I want everything around you to be happy."

"Do I seem unhappy?" I hold my breath and wait for his

response. He peers up at me and those dark eyes capture mine. "You're broken."

"I'm not broken," I lie. His lips pull into a straight line. "I am broken."

I frown at this confession. "Why?"

"Many reasons."

"Such as?"

He pauses. "Right now? I'm feeling stressed."

"Why are you stressed?" I gawp at him as he opens up to me a slither. He trails lazy patterns on my stomach with his fingertips.

"My job. My brothers. *You.*"

"Me?" I blink back the shock. "Why do I stress you out?"

"I want you to choose me."

It feels as though I'm winded. The surprise of his statement completely takes me back. "What do you mean? I choose you. I choose all of you."

"No." he doesn't expand further.

"What do you mean, Dags?"

"You haven't chosen any of us yet, but you will this weekend."

My eyebrows furrow together. "Dags, you're speaking in riddles. What are you on about?"

"This weekend you can choose which one of us you want to be yours for good." He sighs happily and nuzzles in closer. "You can decide which one of us is right for you."

"You're all right for me." I feel the panic rise inside my chest. *I knew this would happen.* When they'd be upset about sharing and make me choose one of them. I just didn't think it would be so soon; I thought we'd have more time together, more of a chance to get to know one another.

"Pick me," he whispers. "Pick me and I will fuck you so good you'll never need my brothers again."

"Dags—"

"I can give you everything." He says, twisting to face me more. "I should be the first one you sleep with. I know how to make your dirty fantasies come to life."

"The first one I sleep with?" I am almost disgusted by his choice of words.

"Yeah," he says, completely unaware of the growing anger in my chest. "May the best brother win your pussy first."

"What?" I'm mortified. I push him off me, and he shoots up. Confusion spreads across his face. "What's up? Why did you push me off?"

"Are you kidding me right now, Dags? There is a competition for me?"

"Of course, there is. Look at you. You are the best fucking prize and we'd be idiots not to want you all to ourselves."

"I am not a fucking object, Dags," I squeal. "I am not something you can win!"

He raises an eyebrow. "But you're something we can pass around?"

Fuck. That one hurt. My mouth opens and shuts in despair. I am utterly speechless, there are no words for the emotions that rock through me. I am incredibly offended to be reduced to such labels, but something within me tells me not to be surprised. These are three alpha males, my dream of sharing them all at once was never going to fucking work. *Why did I get my hopes up?*

I push myself off the bed and quickly redress.

"Where are you going?" he calls after me. I race around, grabbing my jumper, and struggling to put my shoes on. "Home."

"This is your home."

"No, this is the fucking game arena." I spit in disgust.

"Why are you so upset? I don't understand. What did I say?"

"What have you said?" I'm delirious. "You have just told me that I am a prize! I am not something you want because you want me, you want bragging rights that you won the girl over your brothers."

His eyes are wide, and he's alarmed. "What? No! No, my little freak, that's not—"

I don't stick around to find out what else he has to say. I charge out of the flat and run to my car before the tears fall down my face in front of them. They don't deserve my tears.

No man ever does.

CHAPTER FORTY-SEVEN

Rebecca

The first thing I did when I returned home was open a bottle of gin. I haven't eaten today, and I don't plan on doing anything but drinking away the sadness bubbling in my chest. All this time, I thought I was special and loved— but no, I was a pawn in their fucked-up ego game— nothing more, nothing less.

I tip my head back and finish yet another glass. The room started spinning about an hour ago, and my eyelids are shutting much slower than I remember last time. I hear the doorbell ring, but I've ignored it three times. Dags can fuck off if he thinks he's coming back in and apologising after he revealed that secret. It rings for a fourth time, and the noise echoes around my head loudly. I wince and try to drown it down. I pour a hefty measurement with a splash of the mixer and gulp it down. The bell goes again—and again.

Finally, my temper snaps. I storm over to the door and throw it open. Vixen stands there, frantically pressing the button. "What the fuck, Rebecca, you left so fast! Dags is in tears and —" he watches me stumble and quickly right myself. "Are you drunk?"

I shove a finger into his chest. "Fuck off."

As I try to shut the door, he pries it open effortlessly. I stumble backwards in shock, before protesting louder. "Get out of my house, Vixen, I don't want to talk to you right now!"

"What happened? Did Dags do something—" he looks furious and it makes my heart skip a beat. His fists curl. "What did he say? How did he upset you?"

"It's all of you! Fucking men! Using me as a prize!"

"What do you mean, Rebecca?" He slams the door behind him and follows me into the living room. I stumble around, grabbing my glass and gulping down my drink.

His eyes harden. "Stop that."

I ignore him and refill my glass, but before I can raise the glass to my lips, he smashes it out of my fingers. I yelp in fright as the glass shatters across the floor. When I turn my gaze back to him, he is seething. "For fuck sake, Rebecca! Speak plainly. Stop drinking!"

"You—" I thrust a finger into his chest. "—trying to fuck me before your brothers. I am nothing but a game to you, and all your egos!"

His eyes almost pop out of his head. "What?"

"You calling me a liar?" I fold my arms angrily across my chest. "You saying that you didn't want to fuck me first, before your brothers?"

"Of course, I want to fuck you, Rebecca. And yes, I wanted to do it before my brothers. But not for an ego thing or whatever—"

"Then why?"

There is a long pause before he glares down at the spilt alcohol, and it's as if the room around him disappears as his pupils dilate and he licks his lips. For a long moment, he's silent as he scans the room for my bottle of gin. When his gaze lands on it, he looks as though he is going to attack me to get a drop. I instinctively take a step backwards to let him have access to it, and he prowls closer to it, reaching out for the bottle. However, before his hand can grab the bottle, he snaps back, suddenly out of his trance. "You got yourself drunk because you were sad about us wanting to fuck you?"

"How dare you," I spit. "It's more than that! You treated me like a game, not a person!"

"No, we each wanted to have you completely and utterly to ourselves, but we knew that it wouldn't work because you liked each of us! This was for you! It's not who fucks you first, but rather who you would choose. You have all the power in this game—this is all for you, Rebecca."

I'm stunned. My mind races faster and faster. I feel sick as the words process slowly. *Is it true? Do I really have a right to be mad in the circumstance?* Surely, I should be thankful that they allowed me to indulge in all of them, but maybe it's my disappointment that I know it will end soon. Nothing this good can last forever—*right?*

My eyes cast out to my garden, and I instinctively look for my stalker. I haven't seen him in ages. *I wonder if he has grown bored of me too?* Or is he just better at hiding? What if he is there right now, watching me and Vixen? Would he be jealous? Mad? Horny?

"What are you looking for?" Vixen asks me with a raised eyebrow.

"Nobody."

"*Nobody*? Don't you mean *nothing*? Is there someone who is usually there, Rebecca?"

A drunken hiccup pulls past me. I bite my lower lip and debate telling him about my stalker. Something in me *knows* that he will be mad, he will want to kill the fucker, but at the same time, I almost want him to be jealous. I like the idea that the brothers have competition without someone else, and in my drunk stupor, I run with the idea.

"I have a stalker," I say with a proud beam.

He stiffens. "You do?"

"I do."

"Who?" He scans me for a reaction intently. I shrug and fix my slumped posture. The world is hazy, and I hiccup again. "Some hot masked man."

"Do you want to fuck him?" The question takes me by surprise. He grinds his teeth together aggressively.

"Yes," I say, trying my hardest to make him jealous. "I want him to fuck me more than I want you to fuck me."

He looks amused and grins with that beautiful lopsided smile of his. "Oh, really now?"

"Yes."

"What does he do that I don't?"

I throw my hands to my hips but it's clumsy. It takes everything in me to try and figure out an answer. *What could I say that would make him mad?* My brain rushes loudly before I finally find something. "He is very dominant."

"And I'm not?"

"He's *more*," I say with a teasing smile. With a low growl, Vixen yanks me close to his chest, and I gasp in shock. My head falls back as I try to maintain his unwavering eye contact.

"Want to make a bet?" He snarls.

"Sure. You're not even half the man he is!"

"Lie."

"Truth." I force as much power into my voice as possible, but he sees through it quickly.

"You're lying to me, dirty little dove. Have you fucked your stalker yet? Spread your legs for him? Has he made you cum? Plunged a toy so deep in your pussy that you cum repeatedly —"

I startle at his words. Then, it hits me. My jaw drops and I scramble out of his hands. "What the fuck?"

Grinning, he holds his hands up proudly before stalking around me in circles, like a lion cornering its prey. He clears his throat and changes his voice into that sinfully sexy accent. "Hello, my dirty little dove."

"Holy shit!" I leap far away from him. The humiliation rocks through me. He *knew*! He was the one watching me all this time, making me do sinful things! "Fuck, Vixen! H-how—"

"I didn't realise it was you until you came to the club that time with Brandon." His eyes darken. "And then I realised that he was touching what was *mine*." He yanks me close like I'm nothing more than a rag doll. "And I was fucking seething."

"You being mad at me and the rudeness—"

"I just couldn't understand why I found the perfect woman and she was too busy being distracted by my brothers." He growls. A range of emotions flicker across his face, and it contorts painfully. "That was when the deal came up to share."

I'm utterly fucking speechless. I want to be angry, I want to drive my fist into his face, but then I want to kiss it better.

"I won't apologise for stalking you, I won't apologise for sharing you with my brothers. It was the only way I could keep you close. I would fucking do *anything* to keep you in my grasp." He is inches from my lips. I want him to ravish me, to prove those feelings, to make me *beg* to be used like I usually do for him. "You are mine, my dirty little dove, and I will not let you go."

"Vixen—"

He slams his lips against mine. A breathless moan falls out but I'm not sure whose mouth it came from. Consuming me, he ravishes me with his tongue as his fingers curl into my shirt, making it tight against my body and the biting pain makes my knickers instantly damp. He is so delicious; my stalker *and* my Vixen.

"When do I have to decide?" I whisper against his lips. "When is the bet up?"

"Three days."

"And what do I have to do?"

"You decide who you want to fuck first. Then, you can walk away with just one of us if you so choose." His voice is low and deep.

I lick my lips. "You're telling me that if I laid here, and *begged* you to fuck me, that you wouldn't do it?"

"Rebecca—" he warns.

My fingers jump to the buttons on my shirt, slowly stripping for him. Enraged, he forces me still. "Stop it."

"But I'm just *so* horny and desperate for your cock. If only there was someone here to satisfy me."

"Rebecca, stop it. Not only do I respect the rules of the game, but you're drunk. I would be taking advantage."

I stare at him through low lashes. "I *want* you to take advantage of me."

"Stop it. You're making this harder than it needs to be."

"Show me how hard," I smirk, but then everything happens so fast. One minute, I was in control, teasing him, gently pulling at his zipper on his jeans, and the next, he's grabbing my whole body and swaddling me in his arms like a fucking baby. I squirm around but it's no use, he effortlessly drags me to my bed and pins me down with his body. I try to move again, to press my ass up against him, but he gives me no room to move.

"Sleep," he growls into my ear.

My body is alive with the sound. "Vixen, please—"

"Don't make me tell you again or I'll leave."

I stiffen in his hold. I really don't want him to leave. It feels empty and lonely in this large house without him watching me.

"Can we at least talk?"

"What about, little dove?"

"Tell me about yourself," I say slowly. "You've stalked me for weeks, you know almost everything about me, but I barely know you. So tell me; who are you Vixen?"

He hesitates, and I hear his breathing become uneasy in my ear. Then, his arms wrap tighter around me. "I am Vixen, I am twenty-nine years old. I've worked with Brandon for over ten years, Dags for eight. I grew up by the coast—"

"That's surface level things." I sigh. "Tell me a secret. Tell me something that you wouldn't tell a stranger."

"Rebecca—"

"Come on, work with me here. Open up a little."

I feel as though I've pushed him too far when he doesn't respond. Then, he presses his lips to my neck gently. It's a soft, endearing movement, but it sends delicious shivers throughout my body. I melt into him.

"I had a drinking problem," he whispers. "Quite a bad one, too. I was in alcoholics anonymous for a couple of years, in recovery. They tried to send me to rehab, but Brandon got me out." He holds on tighter to me as if I'm bringing him strength.

"I've been sober nine years, but I crave a drink every day. It's ridiculous how addictions never leave. They will always be a part of your soul, eating you up."

The breath in my chest hitches.

He continues. "I relented the other night, and I broke my sober streak and it felt so fucking good to get drunk again. I almost punched Brandon in the face for taking the bottle away from me. I could have done serious damage. Nobody understands what an addiction does to you, like, you're not you when you crave something that bad. The thing is, my little dove, I have a very addictive personality."

"You do?" My words are just a squeak, the intrigue taking hold of me.

"I do." He nods. "I will always be addicted to something; I just switch my poison. You are my drug at the moment. I am fucking obsessed with you. I'm always thinking about you, stalking you, fucking you. I can't get enough, and truthfully, I don't think I ever will get bored. You're my one addiction that I don't want to get over and I don't think I ever can."

"Vixen—" I say breathlessly. His words are so heart felt and powerful. They make me feel sheepish inside, like I want the bed to swallow me whole and hide my blush. It's a confession I haven't heard before. That *I* made him obsessed. I should be fucking terrified of him and his words and his promises. After all, he is my stalker and stalker's are crazy and unpredictable— no, he's worse because he makes me feel things I should never feel for someone who spends every waking moment stalking me.

CHAPTER FORTY-EIGHT

Vixen

I left her in the morning as she began writing her book again. She seemed so happy and carefree as she typed away on the laptop. I had really wanted to curl up on her sofa and watch her closely from the comfort of the same room, but duty calls. There is still someone to be tracked down. I can smell this case coming to a close too. Soon I will have the ringleader in my grasp, and he will fucking pay for all the shit he's done.

I'm back at the warehouse. I stalked one of the pimp's I found at shark city back to the warehouse where Dagger recognised that guy he killed. I've been waiting in the shadows for at least an hour now. He is chatting to a young woman, who trembles until his intense gaze. She came in fully dressed, and now he has her down to her underwear. She is trying so hard to please him. It makes me sick.

"Good. Do you remember what you tell the client when he arrives?" The pimp raises his eyebrow. She nods quickly. "I tell him how big he looks, and how he won't fit inside of me. Then I need to protest a bit—"

I hate the fact the pimp is teaching her the tricks of the trade. I have no clue who is arriving soon, but from the sound of things, he likes them reluctant. In other words, he enjoys rape.

WE SHOULDN'T

End of. He deserves to die so I have already reached out to Dagger who will be here soon. I hold my breath as the pimp grabs the girl and shakes her around a little bit. She squeaks and acts that she doesn't enjoy it, but she wears a smile. He strikes her around the face, and she is momentarily stunned.

"You're not supposed to smile."

"But—we are just pretending—"

Another smack around her face, has real fear sinking in. She tenses up and trembles faster and the pimp nods his head approvingly. "Good. Now you are learning."

"Please don't hit—"

He punches her this time and her head flies back. She shrieks in pain and grabs her throbbing cheek, crying out. My fingers curl into fists. I count down the seconds in my mind. I *really* want to interfere, but I don't. Princess's face pops up in my mind, and I cringe. I tried to save her, and I only made it worse. I established that *we* are the bad guys, and the pimps will be the ones who save them.

Reluctantly, I wait for Dagger instead of interfering.

But he strikes her again. I pull out a pebble from my pocket, ready to throw it to cause a distraction, however, just as I go to raise it, I see Dagger slip in through the window. He is clumsy, but somehow, isn't caught. I watch as he creeps around the outside of the room, hiding in the shadows, before finding me on the opposite side. His dagger reflects off the light in the room and I snatch it down to hide us.

In the middle of the room, the pimp strikes the girl again. Dagger lurches forward, but I hold him back quickly, as the door on the opposite side of the warehouse swings open. A dark shadow saunters in and quickly advances towards the young girl who is now splayed out on the floor, terrified. Her eyes are wide, and she stares back at her pimp with a tear-stained face.

"Please, don't make me do this."

"Shut up," he spits. The client's face is revealed under the light and *boy* is he an ugly fucker. Acne clings to his monstrous nose, his eyes are halfway dragged down his face, thin lips and I notice he's missing teeth as he grimaces down at the woman. Beside me, Dagger stops trembling. Instead, he is stiff, and I can no longer hear his breathing as he holds his breath. I pull away from him and dip my hand back into my pocket for pebbles, ready to cause a distraction.

"This the girl?" the client asks the pimp. "You think she's going to make us money?"

The pimp grins, "I know she will."

"I won't! No- I won't. Please, I don't want this—"

The client grabs his cock and readjusts his pants. He is getting turned on by this— *the fucker*! When I turn to Dagger, he is no longer there. I hold my breath and frantically scan the room for him, but he's gone.

Fuck! Fuck! Panic sinks in. In the middle of the room, the girl cowers away. She hides her face and tries to protect herself as the client leers over her. I sink my teeth into my tongue and wait for Dagger to strike wherever the mental fucker is hiding. Then, I see him. His entire body inflates and deflates, curled over as that monster takes over. Within a blink of an eye, he lurches onto the client and begins pummelling him, with a mighty howl.

The girl shrieks and throws herself to her feet, running from the room without another look back. The pimp gives chase, but I get there quicker. I drive into him with my good arm and send him flying to the side. He howls out in pain as I strike him in the face repeatedly with my good fist until he's unconscious. My shoulder throbs as the pain kicks in, and I clutch it as if it will help, before casting my gaze to find Dagger, expecting to see him leering over a dead client.

However, instead, he drags the man out of the room by the hair, completely taking me by surprise.

Leaving the pimp on the floor, I race over to Dagger. "Woah, mate. What's going on? Where are you taking him? You can't move the bodies! It'll come back to—"

"It's him." I barely recognise the growl.

I stiffen. "What?"

"It's the man who gave me this scar."

Below him, the man howls in realisation of who he is dealing with. He struggles, but his age has caught up with him, and now Dagger is the one with all the power. My heart leaps out of my chest, and it feels as though time has slowed down around us. I spring into action, grabbing my phone and calling Brandon.

"What's gone wrong?" he instantly says.

"Brandon, we've found him. We found Perry."

"Perry, as in—"

"Yes. Dagger is currently dragging him out of the warehouse. What do I do?" I stumble to catch up with my brother who seems miles away in his mind. With a growl, he throws his car door open and chucks Perry in as if he weighs nothing more than a rag doll. The breath hitches in my throat as I report back to Brandon.

"He's about to drive."

"Get him back to our place," Brandon barks.

I hang up the phone and race towards Dagger. He doesn't even bother climbing in front of the steering wheel. Instead, he climbs on top of Perry and continues beating the living shit out of him. I dip my hand into his back pocket and retrieve the keys before spinning the car out of the parking lot.

As soon as we pull up outside the club, Brandon greets us. He pulls the door open and yanks Dagger from the groaning man in the back. Then, he strikes him multiple times around the face. "Snap out of it, Dags. What the fuck are you doing? Bringing this shit here? You'll have to kill him now!"

Dagger is vicious in his response. "You think that wasn't the plan?"

Perry groans in the back seat, and tries to leave, but I quickly grab him. With one look around to check the coast is clear, I grab him by the shirt and drag him into the flat. Dagger chases after us, Brandon close on his heels.

As soon as Dagger is in the flat, he jumps back onto Perry with a noise that can only be described as a war cry, and the tears stream down his contorted face. He pummels him over and over, before snatching his dagger, and holding it under Perry's chin.

I go to stop him, knowing that he can't kill a man in our flat, but then I freeze. Dagger has waited eight years to find this cunt, and there is no way I will take that moment from him now. Besides, not even God himself could step in the way of the justice Dagger is about to dispel.

CHAPTER FORTY-NINE

Rebecca

The book is finally done. I scroll through the hundreds of pages with a huge smile on my face. The sense of relief is instant, and I can't help but feel a huge weight has been lifted from my shoulders as I click send on the file. It shoots off to my editor, and a relieved sigh slips from my lips.

I check my phone to see if any of the men have messaged me, but they haven't, and it fills me with a weird sadness. They are most likely giving me my distance after I went psycho on Dags and Vixen yesterday, but I don't want distance. I want their crazy erotic attention on me.

The anger for being a pawn in the game has transformed into something much more deadly: *anticipation*. The evil plan forms in my head as I race to my bedroom to get changed.

I have two days until I decide, but they also have two days to try and *stop* themselves. The grin grows wider and wider across my face as I pull up my slutty bunny outfit and fix the tail on the back. It's a tight leather corset with fish net tights and black arm-length gloves. My breasts spill out of the top and I've put a dark dog collar around my neck to trigger Brandon in particular— *I know how much he loves it when I wear it.* My makeup is dark and smoky with bright red lipstick, because I know how they like it when it smudges down my face. My stomach twists deliciously. I wonder who will be the first to break. *Who will be the first one to fuck me and anger his brothers?* The rivalry only turns me on so much more. *Did they really think I'd let them have all the fun in this game?* They might be moving their pawns toward me at their own pace and in limited moves, but I'm the mother fucking queen piece— I can go wherever I want— and I plan to make them regret ever making that stupid fucking pact. I throw my long trench coat on to hide my outfit from any prying eyes and slip out of the house.

By the time I get to the club, my heart is in my throat. The excitement courses through me. Anticipation makes my pussy wet, and my body tremble. I wipe my clammy hands on my short skirt before taking the stairs to their flat. After a couple of seconds, I take a regulating breath to calm my nerves. Then, I raise my hand to the door ready to knock, but to my surprise, the door is slightly open. With a wide smile, I push the door open and lean seductively in the door frame, ready to surprise them.

However, I'm instantly stunned. A gargled shriek echoes through the flat — pitched and tortured— and it makes the hairs on my arms jump to attention. The noise is followed by cries and pleading and more shrieks of agony. And then, I see it.

Dags, blade in hand, plunging the weapon in and out of a squirming man, blood oozing into the cream carpet. His guts are everywhere—intestine around his neck, his face black and blue, but he is still alive, shrieking bloody murder. Vixen is yanking at Dags but he's barely making a dent— Dags is fucking crazed and in his own world, screaming as he kills the man.

The fucking stench, the screams, the gore— *oh God! I can't take it anymore!*

Before I can help it, a horrified shriek passes my lips. My heart stops in my fucking chest, and my legs almost give out.

WE SHOULDN'T

Everything in me screams to run away. *Escape! Leave! Hide!* But I'm frozen to the floor, unable to tear my gaze away from the scene. Suddenly, Dags head snaps up to face me. Those eyes, once so sinfully attractive, are empty of humanity. He is a fucking animal, hacking away at the victim, with blood splatters stain his skin and matted hair, sticking to his sweaty face. He is pale— *so fucking pale*— he doesn't even look human. Even the way his body is curled looks disfigured and wrong. Another cry leaves my lips and I stumble backwards in fear.

Then, a huge body steps in my way. It takes a couple of seconds to see Brandon's shocked face staring down at me. He says something but it doesn't make sense. The words turn to jelly in my brain. I feel his hand try to take my arm, and now the air finally slams back into my lungs. Mortified, I push back from him. I can't seem to get enough fucking distance between us. My eyes are still fixed on the mutilated body under Dags.

No— not *Dags. Dagger. The Dagger killer. How the fuck did I not put the two together before now?*

"Rebecca. Shit," Vixen's voice rips through the silence. My bottom lip wobbles and the tears burn my eyes. *They are murderers! I have been playing with murderers!* Brandon reaches out for me again, but I smack him away with as much force as I can.

"Don't touch me!" My voice is hoarse and agonising even to my own ears. He visibly recoils, pain stinging across his face. "Becks, please! Wait—"

I don't stick around to find out what the fuck is happening. I tear out of the building as fast as I possibly can. My entire body heaves in fear, and the dull ache in my lungs begins. I choke on the lump on my throat. It's hard to see as my vision goes blurry with tears and my ankles threaten to buckle under my heels, but I keep pushing. Further, *further*. Finally, I get back to my car and it shrieks as it roars to life, shooting out of the parking lot. In my mirror, I see the Vixen charge out of the building after me. He spots me, throws his hands into his hair, panting and frightened, and screams something but I don't hear as I slam my foot all the way down on the accelerator.

The tears stream down my face, and it feels like my heart has snapped in two. The men I adore, the men I lust for they're nothing more than killers! It's as though my entire world is crumbling down around me, and all I can do is sob.

As soon as my car pulls up to my home, I storm inside, leaving the engine running. I don't think, I just *do*. I snatch a rucksack and start stuffing clothes in. Fish bounces around in madness, getting under my feet. A cry of frustration leaves me, and he settles down in a corner, shocked by my outburst. I grab my toothbrush and medicine— everything I will need to run away. *They know where I live.* The murderers know who I am and nearly everything about me. *Hell, who to say they aren't on their way already to finish the job off?* I know too much! I've now seen too much! Surely, they won't keep me ali—

A car door slams outside the house and my heart sinks. I grab the rucksack and bolt to the bathroom, before slamming the door and locking it. Guilt instantly hits me that I've separated myself from Fish but something tells me that they won't harm my dog. *Surely, not.* But then again, do I really know the men I've been playing with?

"Rebecca!" I hear Brandon cry out. "Rebecca, come out!"

"Please, my dear, we're not here to hurt you!" Vixen joins in. Mortified, I pull my knees to my chest and cry. There is nothing else I can do. In my mind, they are no better than Leo anymore. *They are fucking worse—they're killers!*

"Rebecca, please!" he tries again. I hold my breath as I hear footsteps come closer. Then I watch the door handle get tugged at. Miserably, I count down my final minutes, too frightened to do anything to stop the inevitable outcome.

"Rebecca, open the door!" Brandon demands. "Let us talk to

you. We can explain everything."

"You're fucking murderers!" The sound that leaves my throat is unlike anything I've ever heard before. It's so full of agony and despair and hopelessness. The familiar pull of elastic bands around my heart which signal a panic attack tugs at me, and I struggle to grasp the air in my lungs.

"N-no, we're not," Vixen responds. The delirium sinks in.

"Liars! Fucking liars!"

"Let us in!" Brandon barks. "Rebecca, please. Don't make us break the door down."

"Get out! Get out of my house! I am calling the police!"

"Don't you dare." Vixen growls, and it sends shivers through me. My teeth sink into my lower lip, and I choke back the sobs. I reach into my pocket, before the terrifying realisation that my phone has fallen out, sinks in. *Shit!*

Helplessly, I tear my gaze to the window in the corner and a plan quickly forms. *If I stand on the toilet, I might be able to escape and run fast enough into the field to get away, then, I can run away.*

Within seconds, I'm moving. I leave the rucksack behind, and I push the window open as quietly as I can before slipping through. It's a tight fight, but before long, I'm through. I can still hear them begging and pleading for me to listen to them as my feet touch the floor. Then, I'm full-on bolting away from the house. The wind howls in my ears but that's not the scary part. All of the sudden, I can hear another set of footsteps behind me. I race down the garden path and into the cornfield, hoping to lose my stalker. The pieces of corn whip my body and I try as hard as I can to hide my cries of pain. Behind me, it sounds as though a beast is close to my heels. I push faster— farther—*my fucking life depends on it!*

Suddenly, I'm flying to the floor. Strong arms snap around me and they hold me still. I scream in despair, my fists and feet fly repeatedly into my attacker, but I barely make a dent in them.

"Stop resisting," Dags' deep and menacing voice rings through me. My heart sinks. *The worst one has found me.*

I desperately appeal to his reason. "D-Dags, please! Let me go!"

"No can do, darling." I can even hear the way he grins as he spits the words. Another cry for help leaves my lips. It's now no longer an attempt to escape the brothers, but a cry for help for Brandon and Vixen to save me. The madman has his grips on me, and I know that he will not let me go now he has me.

"Stop squirming," he grunts. "Stop!"

"P-please!" I'm full-on sobbing now. I pray the ground will swallow me hole, or at least for a quick death.

"Why are you crying, Rebecca?" he sounds genuinely confused. "Why are you sad? Don't be sad. I'm here now. You're safe."

"Safe!" I scream in despair. "I'm not safe around you! Y-you you killer!"

"You are safe around me."

"Get off me!" I buck back against him. Suddenly, he repositions us so that I'm flat on my back, securing each of my wrists above my head and sitting on me so his weight pins me to the ground. Those dark eyes scan me, desperately trying to get me to look at him and I do everything I can—shut my eyes, shake my head — *anything* to block him out. Another frightened shriek leaves my lips.

"It's okay, my darling," he whispers. There is such a soft tone to it, it makes my heart lurch. "I am not going to kill you. I would never kill you."

"But you're going to hurt me!" I whimper, eyes flying open, as I become pleading.

His head tips to the side and he looks utterly confused. "Why would I do that?"

"Because you're the Dagger killer! Y-you're crazy!"

"Listen." He loses his patience with me, and I slam my lips shut. "The only time I will ever hurt you is to make your body feels pleasure you've never felt before. Got it? I maybe crazy— trust me, I'm reminded enough—but I would never do anything you didn't want me to do. I only want to serve you, my beautiful freak."

Leering over me, I feel his hot breath against my skin, and my traitorous body remembers all the times he had me in positions like this before as I came hard for him. I force them away, and start to yell again but he interrupts me.

"I like you, Rebecca." His face contorts as he tries to find the right words. "I *really* like you. You're fun to be around, and you make my brothers happy, and you make me happy."

"Please, just let me go—"

"I'm not finished," he snaps and I flinch. Even when confessing his fondness of me, he must be in control. "I don't want you to hate us for what we do, for who we are. We do it for a good cause. We try to help people, I promise you."

My bottom lip trembles. "By killing them?"

"By killing the bad guys," he corrects me sternly. "And by *we*, I mean *me*. I'm the only one who kills. So, if you don't like that, please don't take it out on them, take it out on me. I'm the only killer."

I am stunned into silence.

"I am a killer and I am a bad person, and I am a little bit unstable, and I will make many mistakes—like *tons* but I never want to hurt you and if I do make a mistake, I will spend the rest of my life apologising, Rebecca. You can be mad at me, you can avoid the club, you can try and run from me, but I will never let you go. If you want to be free from me, you will have to kill me. I think I am obsessed with you. I was addicted from the first taste."

I'm breathless. "You're crazy."

"I am." His eyes search mine frantically. I feel like I'm losing my fucking mind. The way he looks at me, talks to me, *touches* me—it's clear he is out of his fucking mind, incredibly dangerous, and yet I don't think I want to be away from him. I don't think I'll be able to stay away from any of them. Maybe I'm the crazy one? They are addicted to me, and I am addicted to them, their crazy *and* their ruin. It's like I can only thrive in their sinful world. But can I really deal with *murderers?*

"What do you say? Can you overlook my mistake?"

"Killing people is not a mistake, Dags!" I square.

"What is it then?"

"It's a sin."

"Okay." He ponders on this thought. "Can you overlook my sin?"

It's crazy. It's insane. He is a murderer! He is a very *very* bad person, stealing lives away, and yet something inside of me refuses to push him away. It's like I'm drunk on his sin. "You have a shit ton of explaining to do."

"Scouts honour. I promise I will explain everything," he visibly lights up, and that smile which flickers across his face melts my heart. Then, I feel his grip on me roughen up and the innocent look in his eyes flashes into something hungrier. "Is it bad that you look really fucking hot in this position?"

"No." I'm breathless. My chest rises and falls, and his eyes are fixed on my breasts which spill out. I hate how much I fucking love this, squirming under his intense gaze which rake up and down me. I must be fucking insane.

"I *really* fucking like this outfit."

"I wore it for you. For all of you."

"Mind if I use you first?" his lopsided grin melts me to the core. I feel his knee slide between my legs and his hot breath on my face. He kisses my tears away and runs his tongue all over my face. It feels like an animal asserting his dominance. I can't help but shiver under him. This is so fucking wrong. After what he just confessed, my pussy shouldn't be soaked, and yet I spread my legs further for him.

"Fuck—there you are," Vixen's voice echoes around us. "Bran! They're over here!"

I hear the corn around us get squashed under their feet as they run closer. Then, all three of them look down at me. My cheeks are flushed and I'm sure I look hot and wild and ready. My body responds so fucking well to a single look, and humiliation coats through me.

"Rebecca, are you okay?" Brandon is panicked. He assesses the situation and arches an eyebrow before glaring at Dagger's knee between my legs and chokes on a breath. "What's happening?"

"Can't you see, brother. My beautiful little freak loves being roughed up." Dagger smirks. With a hiss, I push him into his chest, and he rolls off me. Warily, Brandon helps me to my feet and I let him. Reason tells me I should run away, call the police, escape the mad men, but then again, I've never listened to reason. I respond only to sin.

In a blink of an eye, I feel all their hands on me. They brush off the mud and twigs which cling to my skin, and for such an innocent action, I am wildly turned on.

"We can explain—" Vixen starts but I interrupt.

"Dagger has done a good job filling me in so far. We will all sit down and talk about this later, but for now, I need to say something. I am not an object, nor will I choose which one of you I want to fuck me first."

Dagger's eyes flash as dark as sin. "I have a game to help decide who should do it."

This piques my interest. "I'm listening."

"You have two minutes to run and hide. The first person to catch you gets to fuck you first."

Holy fucking shit. The floodgates are open, and my cheeks are a vibrant shade. I look to Brandon and Vixen who are ravenous, and I wait for any refusals of the game. Nobody makes a single noise— I don't even hear a single breath being drawn.

Fear and arousal sink through me as I take a slow step away from them, keeping my gaze on them. And then, I do something fucking crazy... *I run.*

CHAPTER FIFTY

Rebecca

I know I've set off their instincts as soon as I lurch forward. I hear Dagger growl but for at least thirty seconds, I am alone, charging through the cornfield. And then suddenly the sound of the wind against my ears is not the only thing stalking me. I can feel someone on my ankles, so I take a sharp left. I try to stop the crops from smacking into me by holding out my elbows, but it only slows me down. Panicked, I shoot a glance behind me to check how far ahead I am, but I'm completely alone.

To my left, I hear the thuds of the corn smacking into another body, so I steer right and push faster, harder. My lungs scream out and feel cold, but I don't stop running. It's fucking insane but the farther I run, the wetter my pussy gets at the thrill of the hunt.

"Beautiful little freak!" I hear Dags' voice sing out from behind me, sending thrills straight to my humming clit. In the near distance, I see the end of the cornfield and the beginning of the forest, and I aim for that. I risk one more glance over my shoulder to check if I'm being followed, but as soon as I do, I charge straight into something. It wraps his arms around me and holds me still, much to my pounding and frightened heart. My gaze shoots up to find which brother has found me.

Brandon grins. "Gotcha."

"Fuck." I whimper when his grip tightens.

"And now for my reward." He doesn't waste a second before pulling my tits free and my nipples leap out as the cold hits them, much to Brandon's groan of approval. Frantically, he grabs me by the waist and pulls me closer, before his hand snakes down to my pussy. He tears my knickers off and leaves me in my little skirt. Then, plunges two fingers inside of me before I have a chance to register what is happening. I scream in pleasure and shock, deeply humiliated with how wet I am and how much ease it was to slip inside of me.

"That's it, baby. Scream for me. Let my brothers know who is fucking this pussy first." He growls before spinning me around and bending me slightly over, one hand on my ass, and the other on my stomach so he can position me with ease. Then, I feel his hard cock against my wetness. A sharp hiss falls from my lips as he slides the head into me, not wasting a single second. The pleasure is blinding as my walls wrap around his fat cock, and I cry out.

His hands grab my tits, and he squeezes, then thrusts into me all at once, causing a scream to leave me. The pain is so bad but so fucking good at the same time. Instantly, his fingers jump to my clit and he plays with it expertly, until I'm a panting mess. My tits bounce up and down and I struggle for breath, but I wouldn't have it any other way. If this is how I die, then so be it, I'll go out with a smile on my lips.

Skidding to a halt, Vixen and Dags appear in front of me. Vixen's eyes are wide as he watches his brother pound my pussy, and he growls. It only makes Brandon fuck me harder, pulling me flush against his body protectively.

"Well done, brother." Dags smirks. "Fuck her hard for me."

On cue, Brandon starts pounding into me so hard that my eyes roll to the back of my head. Dags lurches forward and clamps my tits between his lips, not able to resist. I feel him take over playing with my clit, and I scream in ecstasy. "Oh, fuck!"

It's all too much and the orgasm smacks into me before I can stop it. I fall forward but Brandon never relents his thrusts. It pushes me off the cliff over and over until my head is dizzy. Then, I feel his hot cum fill me up, followed by his low grunt. As soon as he comes down, I'm spun around, and a new hard cock is forced into me. Vixen's hands grip my hips and I wrap my thighs around him. He plunges into me, forcing me to keep eye contact, and then, I feel Dags behind me. He spits and lubes up his cock. Then, I feel him push it to my asshole. "Oh fuck!"

Then, I feel the tip push into my entrance. I howl as I feel so fucking full.

"That's it, baby. Take both these cocks." Dagger growls and the sound is so hot, that I'm on the edge almost instantly. He thrusts in slowly and then matches Vixen's pace.

Vixen's hand wraps around my throat. "You" *thrust* "are" *thrust* "ours" *thrust*. My tongue falls out of my mouth and my head falls back in bliss. I can't do anything but take their hard fat cocks being plunged in and out of me. Brandon's fingers connect with my clit again. The hot flush shoots through me and my toes curl. "Oh, shit! Right there! Right there! Oh my god, I'm going to cum again!"

I try as hard as I can to hold off, but it's too late. They smack into the right angle, and suddenly the orgasm shoots through me again. I howl out my release and it sets them both off. The night sky is full of grunts and moans as they both shoot their hot loads inside of me. I milk them up greedily, loving how it feels as it squirts inside. Holding me against their hot bodies, they slow down their thrusts, and I can't resist taking a look at the cum leaking out of me, all down my thighs.

It looks so fucking perfect. I don't think I've ever seen a better sight. I run my hand down and I scoop up as much cum as I can before bringing it to my lips. I suck on it hungrily and groan. *It's the most perfect fucking thing.*

"Brothers, look how fucking hot she is with our cum dripping out of her greedy holes." Dagger smirks. His words instantly have me back on edge. I want to take everything they have and more. I never want them to leave me.

"Fuck, my dirty little dove." Vixen's voice is low. "I knew that you were such a whore for us. Do you like being fucked by me and my brother's all at once? Does your greedy pussy hunger for more than one cock? You can never be fully satisfied by one but you don't have too now. You'll never be alone or without cocks. We fucking live to serve you."

The words are so fucking rich and erotic. I can't help the feeling in my heart which brims. "So, does that mean I don't have to choose? I can have you all!"

Brandon looks to his brothers and hesitates. If there is anyone who will forbid this from happening, it's him. I expect him to refuse, drag me off, and close down our reverse harem romance. Instead, he smiles and tips his chin to nod at me, which makes my heart burst with joy.

CHAPTER FIFTY-ONE

Brandon

She listens intently. I expect to see more pain, anger and confusion across her face, but she listens patiently and without judgement. As soon as she found out our motives behind this hunt, she dropped her disgust for Dags's killing. Now, she cuddles into him. His breathing is erratic, and it's been almost impossible to let him describe the situation he was in. Every now and then, he choked up on a sob as he recounted past trauma, but Rebecca was perfect. She stroked his arm gently and gave him his time to explain. *Everything about her is fucking perfect.*

"And that brings us to now," Vixen huffs.

"So, your arm?" Rebecca gawps at Vixen, "It wasn't a bar fight, was it?"

He shakes his head slowly. "No, a bunch of pimps tried to ambush me."

"Emphasis on the tried," Dags grins, making Vixen roll his eyes. He readjusts his position on the sofa and clears his throat. "We are so fucking close to the ringleader I can almost taste him."

Her eyes are wide. "How will you find him?"

"I have no clue. We have culled most of the pimps, but if we can't touch the main guy, we are pretty much screwed. He will just keep finding new men to take advantage of vulnerable women."

"Well then maybe you need a vulnerable woman," she arches an eyebrow suggestively. My heart leaps in my chest as she starts to suggest the most impossible fucking move ever.

"Use me as bait." She says nonchalantly.

"No fucking way." I don't even hesitate. "Don't be fucking stupid, Rebecca. It's dangerous."

Her eyes widen and she grabs my hand, squeezing tightly. "I know it is. That's why I can't help feeling awful for those women. Use me, save them."

"I'd rather burn the whole fucking world down." Vixen snarls. "You're not going. That's that."

"But—"

I cut her off, "No fucking buts."

"I think it's a wonderful idea." Dagger takes me by surprise. My head snaps towards him, mortified. "What the fuck do you mean?"

"They won't see her coming."

"They will also rape her, and that's getting off lightly," I spit. I shake with the fury racing through me. *What the fuck does he think he's doing? Is he that stupid that he can't see the obvious result?*

His lips are thin. "Not at first they won't."

My jaw drops in disbelief. "Are you shitting me, Dags?"

"No, he has a point," Vixen says reluctantly as his face contorts into many different emotions, but finally, it settles on repulsion. "She would have to go through the grooming stages first. They wouldn't touch her until they believed she was infatuated with them. By that time, we will have our ringleader and wipe him out."

"Exactly!" Rebecca smiles brightly. My fingers curl around her tighter. I can't get behind the plan at all and there is no fucking way I'll let her go into that den of wolves.

"I will be there. I am always watching. You know I won't let them hurt her," Vixen tries to reason with me.

I shake my head. "No fucking way."

"It's our only chance."

"We will find another way."

"Brandon, don't be like this." Rebecca's pleading eyes stare up at me. "I want to help so please let me. I will be safe, and worst case, Dags can teach me how to use a weapon so I have some protection!"

Dagger groans at the thought. "Oh, fuck yes, my little freak."

I shake my head. "No."

"Why not?"

"It's too dangerous."

She shakes my arm desperately. "It doesn't have to be!"

"But it fucking is!" I roar. "Look at Dagger, huh? Is that the mindset of someone who protected himself? Look at the size of him— *his power!* If he didn't get out untouched, then there is no fucking way you will either! You're not going, Rebecca. That's fucking final!"

My words are violent and spiteful but fucking true. Out of the corner of my eye, Dagger's lips slam shut. His eyes flutter open and shut a couple of times. I can see the cogs turning in his brain. Guilt consumes me, but I don't do anything about it. I need them to get the message somehow even if that means making my brother cry. His bottom lip quivers a little bit.

"You're horrible," she whispers in disbelief.

I can't help the scoff that rips through me. "For wanting you to be safe? Fucking sue me, Rebecca."

Her eyes widen in disbelief and for a second, a glossy mist flickers across them. My heart lurches from my chest as I realise my poor choice of words, given her situation with Leo. "Oh, Rebecca. I'm sorry, I didn't mean—"

Even when hurt, she consoles Dagger. He snatches her into an embrace and holds her close. I can't hear him sobbing yet, but his deep breathing into her hair tells me everything I need to know. I look to Vixen for some support but even he can't look at me.

The anger rises in my chest. I push myself to my feet. "Whatever. Hate me. Don't talk to me. I don't fucking care. She isn't going. We are not using her as bait."

As I rise to leave the room, Dagger appears in front of me, eyes dark and malicious. The monster is screaming to escape, I can tell. "Do you trust me?"

"Dagger, don't do this—"

"Answer me, Brandon," he hisses. "Do you trust me?"

"Yes, of course I do!"

"Then, trust me, that this plan will work."

My jaw drops. "Are you insane? It's not you I don't trust, or her, or Vixen, for fucks sake! It's those slimy cunts! They will hurt her, Dagger. What part of that do you not understand?"

"Oh, I understand, very well," his voice drops a couple of pitches so the others can't hear. "Trust me."

"What are you planning, Dagger?"

"Nothing, brother," He smiles innocently and puts distance between us. I can't shake the feeling in my gut. He knows something that he isn't sharing, and it's fucking terrifying. Rebecca's small hand takes mine and I reluctantly peer down at her; her large, round eyes look up at me, and it melts my heart. I feel sick just thinking about involving her in our work.

"I can do this." She whispers.

"I know you can, Rebecca—"

"Think about it," she interrupts me. "All I will do is lure them to us, and then you can follow them back to wherever they drive next. Simple!"

"And what if they kidnap you?"

"What if the plan works?" she pushes herself flush against me. "Stop being so negative and see the potential of the plan."

I chew on my lower lip. It's hard to keep my gaze still as it jumps to everybody in the room. "I don't like it."

"You don't have to," she whispers before rising to her tiptoes. She plants a soft kiss against my lips and if anything, it makes me more reluctant to let her go. I'm instantly infatuated by that strawberry scent. My arms curl around her waist and I pull her flush against me. "I don't want to see you get hurt."

"I won't," she promises. My gut screams at me to refuse and stand my ground. I want to wrap her arm in my embrace and coddle her. She is too pure and caring to be exposed to these wicked things. But, at the same time, we are no closer to finding these women and bringing justice to them. It would be so much easier if we had someone on the inside.

She bats her eyelashes at me, "Please?"

"Fine," I grind out. "But Vixen, you will be opposite the street from her in case there is a fight. Me and Dagger will be in the car two streets away, readying ourselves to follow them." I turn back to her. "Under no circumstances are you to get in the car, give him your real name, or get close enough that he can strike or drug you. Got it?"

"Got it." She agrees merrily but I can't find any reason to be happy. She is far too excited for what she is about to experience. *And something tells me this will come back to bite me in the fucking ass.*

CHAPTER FIFTY-TWO

Dagger

"Oh, my beautiful little freak," I sing as I slide into the living room. She's curled up on the sofa, under Vixen's arms and they watch something on the television, but it bores me, so I disregard it. "Up you get!"

"Why?" She arches an eyebrow suspiciously. It only makes my smirk grow wider. I pull my hand from out behind my back, and I show her my dagger.

Her eyes widen, "Oh, my goodness!"

Vixen stiffens, and I know he is anticipating a meltdown. She is looking at the very same dagger that has slaughtered dozens of lives, but I know my little freak—*she will fucking love this.*

"Can I touch it?" She scrambles off Vixen and towards me. Pure amazement and fascination sit on her face, and it makes my cock bob. She is so fucking hot without having a weapon in her fingers. *But with one...*

"Hold it," I say hurriedly, grabbing her hand and forcing it into her grip. It's heavier than she expected, and she almost drops it, but quickly strengthens her grasp. She inspects it slowly and blows out an appreciative breath. "It's beautiful!"

"I know," I watch her instead of the dagger.

"Where did you get it from?"

I stiffen. For a moment, I consider lying to her, to spare her the tragic story, but when I look into those soft eyes, I don't know what comes over me. "Perry. The man who used it on me, on my face."

Shock ripples through her. She stares between me and the weapon in her fingers. A short pause sifts around the room before she takes a small step forward and reaches up for the mask on my face. I flinch and try to pull away from her.

"Let me," she says softly. I freeze and hold my breath as she gently takes it off my face with shaking fingers. I wait for the usual flinch or disgust that usually fills people when they see it. It's disgusting and wiggly, making my eye a different colour to the other one. Mum called it unique—everyone else calls it terrifying. I feel her soft caress against my cheek, and she tilts my face down gently to inspect it better. My heart pounds in my chest. *What is she doing? Why is she not scared?*

Then, she places the lightest kiss to the bottom of my scar before working her way up. Something tingles in my heart and then my cock. I don't know why I react so deliciously to her. A whimper falls from my lips, and I scold myself for sounding so weak, fragile, but that's exactly how I am around her. She removes all the hatred and fear and anger. Or at least, all the *bad* parts of those emotions. She keeps the tasty sin— *and I fucking love her for it.*

"Never hide it from me, again. Got it?" She whispers, pulling back. A stinging sensation in my eyes has me blinking a couple of times to clear the mist. I can't look at her. I don't know what I will do if I see that caring face. She fixes my chin downward and forces me to maintain eye contact. "Say you won't ever hide from me again."

"I-I won't." It's barely a whisper, and I'm surprised she even heard it, but that small smile on her lips tells me she understands. "Thank you."

Then, her gaze flutters down to the knife. "Teach me how to use it."

My cock springs up at the thought of it. All the emotion and distress dissipate from my body. Rolling my shoulders, I put some distance between us to clear my racing thoughts. "First, stand like this."

She copies me by turning her body to the side, knife in her back hand, left foot in front of her, knees slightly bent. She smiles, eagerly waiting for my next instruction. I resist the growl in my chest at how fucking good she looks. I am half tempted to sack off the lesson and fuck her instead. The only thing stopping me is the knowledge that in the morning, she will be up against those assholes, and I need my pretty little freak to win.

"Good. Now when you thrust the knife, take a step forward. You want all your power and strength to come from your body weight."

She does as she's told but holds the knife clumsily. I gently reach forward and correct it. "Again."

She fixes her position before throwing her body forward and stabbing the air. Even a mean little look crosses her face that makes my heart and cock swell. "Beautiful. Well done."

"Yay," she exclaims. "That was easy. What's next?"

Vixen chuckles on the sofa, reminding me I'm not alone with her. He slowly rises to his feet and stands behind her, hands jumping to her hips and I'm instantly jealous, but I know what he's doing. He's helping her with her fight.

He arches an eyebrow up at me. "You ready brother?"

Something inside of me sparks with excitement. I raise my fists and nod my head. "Bring it on, my little freak."

Her eyes are wide and worried. "What? No! He doesn't have a knife, it's an unfair fight."

"Hah! Let me tell you something, my little dove, *no* fight with Dagger is unfair," Vixen scoffs. "Aint that right, brother?"

"It's true." I grin. "The voices in my head mean I'm always at an advantage."

She visibly trembles; it's so fucking delicious. I cock my head to the side. "Give me your best, beautiful. I bet you can't get near me."

She peers around at Vixen as if to ask for permission. He gives her a nod, and she turns back to me, nervously. I advance closer towards her to give her a head start. She lunges, but I easily miss it with a quick dart left. She tries again, and again, staggering around whilst I effortlessly slip past her. "Come on, my little freak. Where's that anger? Where is that drive?"

"How are you so fast? How do you know exactly where—" she drives the knife towards me, but I spin, and clear it. "What? How?"

"Where am I going to go next?" I finished her question. "Come on. *Think*. Which way do I keep turning?"

"Left."

"Good. Drive it left," I tell her. She does as she's told, and I turn right. An exasperated gasp falls from her lips. "Are you kidding me? That's cheating!"

"There are no rules in a fight," I tell her darkly. For a second, she slumps over, but Vixen pushes her back straight and she fixes her position. He whispers something into her ear, and like a wild beast, my head snaps to the side as I try to listen. My tongue darts out and I wet my lips. *What delicious secrets and game plans is he telling my little freak?* My body starts to shake with anticipation. Her eyes sparkle and she nods quickly.

I lunge towards her, but she doesn't react like I had anticipated. Instead, she just watches me with a knowing smile. It makes my heart race. *What is she doing?*

"Fight," I tell her, but she completely ignores me. I advance quickly towards her and push a gentle hand into her shoulder to snap her into action. "Fight!"

As if I never touched her, she doesn't move. Those delicious eyes never leave me, and she continuously scans me for my next move. Vixen puts distance between them, and I start to circle around her like a predator around its prey. She doesn't even fucking flinch. My mind whirls. *What did Vixen tell her? What plan did they conjure up?*

Then, her fingers jump to her shirt. I stiffen. With a small smile, she starts to unbutton her top with slow and sensual movements. All my blood rushes to my cock.

"Stop it," I say reluctantly. "We are training."

"I know," she finally responds as she shrugs out of the shirt. My eyes are instantly on the rise and fall of her breasts straining her lacy black bra. All I need to do is step forward and I can snap it from her body, revealing those beautiful rose buds. I wet my lips again. Everything in me screams to go closer to her, so I do the opposite. I take a reluctant step backwards. She arches an eyebrow and cocks her head to the side. I almost hear her thoughts scream *'game on'*. Then, she unzips her jeans and sinks her thumbs into the belt loops. Slowly, she pulls it down her legs, but doesn't step out of it at her ankles. It traps her. It's so fucking delicious as she knowingly makes herself even more vulnerable for me.

I look at Vixen desperately. He doesn't even entertain my pleas, and instead, rocks back on the sofa, legs spread apart, cock shooting up. He touches himself through his jeans. I growl and switch my attention back to my little freak. "You would do this tomorrow?"

"Only for you."

Fucking hell. She knows how to play me.

"This isn't fighting." I protest.

"Yes, it is."

I stalk around her again, not being able to resist checking out her ass in that little thong. It's so fucking round and peachy. I want to sink my teeth into her soft flesh.

"Do you want me to bend over?" she whispers seductively. My stomach flips in my chest. I eye up the dagger in her fingers suspiciously. I know she is trying to seduce me to attack, but at what point will she attack? Without waiting for my answer, she creeps towards the sofa and bends over. She kisses Vixen passionately, making sure to stick her ass out in the air.

I snap. Lurching towards her, I disarm her from the dagger, chucking it across the room. Then, I spin her around and claim her lips with mine. She yelps out her surprise but responds deliciously. A smirk pulls at me. "Now what, little freak? You've been disarmed, and you're not going to win a physical fight against me."

"No, I wouldn't—" she agrees, before pulling away. Then, suddenly, I feel something sharp at my back and I tense up.

"But she would never fight alone." Brandon's voice rings through the room. Shock and surprise fill me. *How the fuck did he sneak up without me hearing him? How the fuck did they organise that without me knowing?* I drop her legs from around my waist and hold my hands in the air. "Fine, you got me."

She chuckles in delight before throwing herself into Brandon's arms. He drops my dagger to the floor, and I scramble quickly for it. It feels weird seeing anyone else hold it. I slot it into its home which is attached to my belt buckle, before turning around to my little freak with her legs wrapped tightly around my brother's waist. He moves her around, so her clit is pressing up against the bulge in his jeans. Her laughter turns to a breathless moan.

"Shit—" Vixen growls. He no longer lays on the sofa, but now slots himself behind her. I watch my brother's hands roam all over her body. I wait for the jealousy to burn through me, but I'm so fucking turned on. My little freak takes us all so well. It was like she was made for my brothers and me.

"Dagger," she says breathlessly, reaching out for me. It snaps me back into action.

"What do you say, brothers? Should we fuck our dirty little whore until she can't even remember her own name?"

"Fuck yes," Vixen says before ripping at her thong and snatching her bra. She gasps as she is instantly exposed to us. Quickly, she reaches forward and frees Brandon's cock and then does the same for Vixen. I get naked and fist my cock when Vixen runs his cock through her wet folds. Then, he pushes against her asshole, and she squeals in delight. I can't hold off anymore. Within a blink of an eye, she has been repositioned, so she is laying on top of Vixen. He thrusts in and out of her asshole, leaving her in a whimpering mess. I position myself between her legs and sink into her pussy, pushing her legs up. Brandon moves in front of me and smacks his cock against her clit, which makes her cry out in pleasure. Then, I feel his cock against mine as he slides into her pussy too. She is so fucking tight that I don't know how long I can last for.

She squeals in pain. "Oh, *fuck*! I am so full! Holy shit!"

We each move slowly at first, but then quicker when her whimpers turn to desperate moans. "Yes, please! Oh, fuck! Holy shit!"

Brandon grabs her tits, and I snake my arm around to play with her clit. Before long, she tenses up and it's too much. She milks our cocks so beautifully as she sings out her orgasm. Her face contorts beautifully, and I am fucking obsessed with her cumming face.

We each pull out, and as if we are in sync, we all position our cocks over her body. She squeals in delight. "Yes! Please! Drench me in your cum!"

"You're such a whore," the growl falls from my lips before I can help it. She plays with her tits and spreads her legs for us to watch. It sends me over the edge. I snap forward as my cum shoots out and coats her pretty body, and both of my brothers cum shortly after. She screams happily, her tongue shooting out as she tries to catch the drops.

The sight is one that will burn in my mind for the rest of eternity. My beautiful little freak being so fucking good for my brothers and me.

CHAPTER FIFTY-THREE

Rebecca

I'm shaking so hard. I didn't think I'd be this nervous and frightened when I first agreed to do the mission. I'm wearing a flimsy summer dress and chain-smoking this pack of cigarettes, perched on a bench in the middle of nowhere. My hair is unbrushed and my makeup is super light. Vixen purposely dressed me like this because it mirrors the other women who get taken. It makes me feel sick. I know that he's in the shadows somewhere, too. I know that he won't let anything bad happen to me, and I trust those brothers more than anything. It doesn't stop the fear of encountering men who would do these things to women though.

I've been here twenty minutes now. I have no clue how long I'm supposed to sit here. *When will they call it off? What if the pimps don't want me? Was I too arrogant in thinking they'd want me?*

Then, suddenly, a pair of flashing lights pull up the dark street. It's followed by the squealing of brakes. My heart lurches in my chest as the car pulls up beside me, and a thin man with a cigar between his lips rolls his window down. He wears dark shades so I can't see his eyes, but something is terrifying about his demeanour. "You okay, miss? What are you doing out here alone?"

I stick to the script. "Just escaping the house for a while."

"How come? Is your boyfriend roughing you up? Dad?"

I force the bile down. He assumes the worst-case scenario. Brandon told me he'd assess me for my vulnerability at first, he'd see if I'm a weak enough target to attack. I lower my eyes. I should have agreed or said something, but the voice is instantly stolen from me. The lump in my throat worsens and I fear I'm going to choke.

"It's okay, miss. Want me to come to sort him out for you? I don't like abusers," he repeats the script almost line for line. Vixen knew exactly how this was going to go down. It makes me sick at how many people he's encountered like this.

"It's okay. I'm going to find a hotel to spend the night," I peer up at him again. The corner of his mouth twitches up at my response. Then, he glances at his mirrors and scans the surroundings. Reason tells him that this is too easy, but greed makes him persevere. "You can crash at mine?"

"You're a stranger!"

"I won't hurt you. As I said, I'll rough up whichever man put his hands on you wrong. I hate men like that. You can trust me." He reaches his hand out of the window and continues. "It's a large house. There are plenty of girls there. My sisters and my brother's girlfriends. You won't be alone. You'll be safe. I was going to the store but I can take you there instead?"

My heart leaps in my chest. It feels like the world around me starts to fade out. Brandon told me *not* to get into the car. He said if they make any move to get me to go with them, I should run away screaming and let Vixen and Dags take it from there. But something in me stiffens. *How can I refuse the offer to lead them directly to the source?* Something in my gut screams that these women need saving instantly. I know *exactly* what it is like to have a partner like this. Who manipulates your head to goo, and then uses and abuses you.

"You sure I won't be too much trouble? It's just for one night." I bite my lower lip nervously and twiddle with my hair. His face lights up like he's hit the jackpot. "Of course, darling. I'll even give you a lift back here tomorrow morning."

Creating trust bonds— that's what Brandon called it. They'll say and do whatever they need to make you trust them, and then, when you're too far deep into the deceit, they'll start hurting you for real, and asking for forgiveness. Perhaps that's the thing which has me opening the car door and sliding into it. The knowledge that I won't be hurt instantly and that I'd be saving many women who are like the old me. He grins at me before throwing the car into gear and pulling off. He speeds off and it's like a blur, but I don't miss the way Vixen charges out of the shadows last minute. I catch him in the mirror, throwing his arms around violently. My head snaps back toward the man driving, but he's too busy smirking at the road ahead to notice. Nausea instantly hits me when he tears around the left, and then a right corner. He moves so quickly it's hard for me to remember which way we are going, let alone for me to hope and pray Vixen or Dagger or Brandon are after me in case of trouble.

The situation slowly sinks in how dangerous it is. My heart constricts in my chest, and I hold my breath. The panic rips through me.

"It's okay, my dear," he says, patting my hand. "We are only a couple of minutes away."

The rest of the journey I keep my lips sealed and force the directions into memory. I'm doing this for the brothers— *for the victims.* I keep repeating my purpose over and over again, but it doesn't help the sinking feeling in my stomach. Eventually, we pull up on a narrow street with town houses hugging each other for miles ahead. The man casts me a lopsided smile. "We are just going in there."

"Sure," I respond timidly, climbing out of the car. The house he leads me towards looks like every other house on the street, but I can *feel* the evil seeping from this one. It's such a shame because, without these men attached to it, it would be a sweet little two-story place. I'm particularly drawn to the beautiful ivory weaving in and out of the bricks in the wall. They bleed into the cracks and completely take over. I like the fact nature is winning the fight against man.

"Come on, Hunny." I feel the man's hand on the small of my back and I stiffen. He hoards me through the gate on the side and into a small, unkempt garden. I feel like a pig being led into slaughter and it hurts to breathe now. He brushes past me and unlocks the back door before giving me a slight shove forwards. I'm instantly greeted by half a dozen women, each skinnier than the last, curled up on different types of furniture. Some of them are brave enough to cast me a look, others are too lost in their own world. It doesn't take a genius to realise most of them are off their fucking heads on some type of drug. Loose needles and vials are also scattered around the floor. One blonde girl with frazzled hair glances at me. She is hopeful until the door is locked behind me, and her gaze drops miserably. It rings alarm bells. Unconsciously, I take a step backwards. "Actually, I think I might return home—"

"Nonsense. You're here now." The man's rough hand pushes me towards an open spot on the carpeted floor. My heart begins to pound, and the adrenaline sets in. "No, really. I would like to go home."

He starts to answer me, but shuts his mouth when the front door slams somewhere else in the house. Then a malicious smile pulls on his lips. When his gaze falls back on me, I almost choke on the nausea in my chest. "Sit down, Rebecca. I have a guest for you."

Fuck. Shit. How the fuck does he know my name? Dread sinks in. I push him with all my might. "Move out of the way. I'm going home. I mean it—"

He effortlessly holds me still like I'm not struggling against him. "Calm down. We don't want to hurt that pretty little face before the boss gets here."

"Boss?"

He smiles knowingly before casting a look over my shoulder.

Suddenly, the room turns icy cold. The shivers rack through my back and I stiffen. I don't need to turn around to know *exactly* who has walked through the door. I feel it in my bones- *the ache, the pain, the trauma.* And then, the devil himself speaks, "Hello, my dear Becks. Long time, no see."

Leo.

CHAPTER FIFTY-FOUR

Brandon

Everything fucking snaps.

"What do you mean you lost her?" I roar. I can hear Vixens' engine rev as he tears the car around another corner. My heart is in my throat, and it feels like everything is blurring into a mist. I spin the car around another corner, desperately seeking out the silver jaguar. It feels as though time has slowed down, and I can't fucking breathe. Beside me, Dagger is lost in his own world, mumbling to himself. The moment he found out that she was gone, he shut down. The only time I want him to release the fucking beast and he locks him away. He twiddles his dagger in his bloody fingers where he keeps catching himself on the blade. Not once has he winced. He is too far gone to recognise physical pain, lost in the depths of his past.

"I don't know, Brandon! She got in the fucking car! I couldn't stop her in time!" Vixen screams back at me. I know it's not his fault, but my rage is directed at him. I knew this was a stupid fucking plan. I knew that it would end poorly. He convinced me, hence, it's *his* fucking fault.

"I checked south lane, rose avenue, Brighton road— all of them! I thought they would have gone there." He rambles angrily. "I just don't know where they would have gone!"

"You better fucking find her!"

"You think that's not the plan?" he shrieks. "I'm trying, Brandon! They have never come down this area before! I have no fucking clue why they'd be here!"

"Think!"

"I swear to fucking God—" he starts to threaten me, but Dagger finally speaks. "London Avenue."

My gaze tears around to him. There is a blurred look in his eyes, and he seems far away. "What?"

"They will be at London Avenue," he repeats slowly.

I frown. "How do you know that, Dagger?"

"I remember now— where they take you in times of trouble. I couldn't read the street name at the time—" he whispers. "but that's what it said. London Avenue."

I lurch towards the satnav and type it in, hissing when I see the fifteen-minute drive. After telling Vixen the place, I spin the car around and race to find my girl.

It's the longest fucking drive of my life, and I haven't been able to take a normal breath. Dagger is trembling now but I can't tell if he's scared or angry. His gaze is fixed firmly on the street road ahead of us. He gasps when the road sign comes into view: *London Avenue.* I tear the car down the road, frantically scanning the houses. "Which one?"

He doesn't answer. His eyes remain firmly fixed ahead.

The panic consumes me. Now is not the time for one of his crazy episodes. "Which one, Dagger? For fucks sake! Which one?"

I spot Vixen's car tearing around the corner in my rear-view mirror. He pulls the car over and I quickly do the same. As I climb out, I turn to Dagger. Panic consumes me and I force back the bile in my throat. *What would they be doing to her right now?* I can only pray that Vixen is right, and they won't touch her yet. That, or some sick fuckers are going to die today.

"Are you sure this is the right place? The car isn't here."

Vixen joins us quickly. Dagger doesn't hear me. He is as stiff as a rock. I follow his gaze to a house opposite us with a little yellow and red swing set and a green seesaw on the small piece of lawn. The look in Dagger's heart destroys me. He remembers something— I can see it through the painful contorting on his face.

"Do you think it's that one?" I start. "Dagger, do you recognise this house?"

He looks deflated. "It's familiar, but it's not the right one—"

"What? How do you kno—"

Suddenly, a scream echoes down the street.

My Rebecca.

I've never run so fucking fast in my life to save her, my brothers close on my heel.

CHAPTER FIFTY-FIVE

Rebecca

Time screeches to a halt. I can't even get myself to turn around and face him. The tears pool instantly in my eyes as all the unwanted memories flood back into me. Almost immediately, I feel like the weaker, trembling version of myself he created.

"Please—" it's no more than a whisper. Wide-eyed, I try to reason with the man who brought me here. "Please, don't let him near me."

"Sorry, sweetie. No can do—" he steps around me. I violently snatch him by the arm as the anger pours through me, and I desperately clutch at straws. "You said you'd protect me. You said you don't like men who beat women. You're a liar."

He feigns shock and grabs his heart. "Me? A liar? No! How did you ever guess the stranger you met twenty minutes ago wouldn't keep a promise?" his gaze turns cold. "Grow up."

Then, with that, he grabs me by the hair. I scream and throw my body around violently and one foot connects with his stomach, but it's short lived. I smell the cigar smoke wrap around my chest, followed by Leo's rough grip on my arm. He squeezes it so tight It feels as though it will pop. Then, he yanks me into him. I scream as loud as I can as pure terror sinks in.

Around us, the women scatter away. Whimpers fall from their lips, and they all shield themselves in horror, anticipating that they are next. My voice cracks as I scream again and again. I feel like I'm twenty-three again, crying out for the neighbours to save me. *They never succeeded.* Leo had the police force in his back pocket with bribes and concert tickets. His rough hands jump up my dress and I scream out in fear as he secures my knife. Then, he pulls it out and eyes it suspiciously. "And what were you going to do with this?"

Helplessly, I watch as he passes it to another pimp who has entered the room, putting it away in his back pocket and moving it out of sight. I choke on a sob. *Fuck. He has me*— he has me *again. This is all my fault! I should never have come! Now I'm going to die! I'm weak, defenceless, helpless—*

"Oh, baby," he pretends to care as he wipes a tear from my cheek. "Don't cry. Not yet. You hear me? I hear you're much stronger than when I left you. I mean, look at you! You had a knife! Shall we put your strength to the test?"

"P-please! Let me go, Leo! Don't do this—"

His whole demeanour changes, "Shut the fuck up. I tried to reason with you. This is your fault, baby. Do you hear me? *All— your— fault!* You should have just signed the fucking contract, but no—"

"Please! I'll sign it! I'll sign it! Just let me go."

He softens and it's far scarier than his rage. "Oh, no, baby. We can't now. The damage is done."

"Please, Leo—" my begging is futile. It only makes him smile, and his horrifying eyes sparkle joyously. "Whose fault is this? Tell me."

I shake my head and resist against his hold again. It tightens. Then suddenly, that fucking ringtone starts playing, the one that tortured me for three endless years. A shriek louder than I've ever made before escapes my lips. Suddenly, his hand strikes me across the face. *Once. Twice.* Then, his violent grip snatches me by the chin. He admires the dark red mark on my skin and licks his lips. "So, fucking beautiful. Oh, why did you have to leave? We had so much fun."

"Let me go, Leo. I swear—people will notice I'm missing. They'll find me."

"Oh yeah?" he raises an amused eyebrow. "Like whom?"

"Sara! My Dad!"

He frowns. "Oh, not Dagger, Brandon and Vixen then?"

My heart sinks in my chest. It's like someone has stabbed it multiple times until it's deflated.

"Oh yes, baby, I know about them. But no, I'm not worried. They haven't been able to find me for years because I'm quicker than them. *Smarter*. We move constantly, keep everything low key. They won't find us."

"They will," I spit. I don't know if it's because I fully believe in it, or because I desperately need something to hope for, but I stand confident in my words. "They have something to find now. They will find me!"

"Perhaps." He ponders on this thought. "Yeah, I guess that you're right. They will go to the ends of the earth to find you, so I'm told by my sources. It wouldn't be right not to give them closure. So, maybe that's what I'll do—" his face lights up. "—yes, *that's* what I'll do. I will leave them your body, and whilst they're mourning over it, I'll disappear."

Tears brim in my eyes. "They will find out you did it!"

"Will they? They haven't linked this organisation to me yet."

"They will notice the patterns are different if I don't go home. They will make the link!"

"Perhaps, but it'll be far too late then, won't it, my love?" He wipes a hair away which was stuck to my tear-stricken face. Then, he lowers his lips to the same spot and kisses me. It makes my stomach flip violently. Again, I resist in his hold, but he is much stronger than he used to be. "Let me go!"

"There it is," he grins. "The desperation. Yes, fight me, Becks. I've missed it so fucking much."

"You're sick in the head!"

"That's not very kind," his lips thin. Then, he punches me in the face. Instantly, the blood gushes out of my nose and I fall to the floor, gripping it, whimpering in pain. He broke it a couple of times before, and it never recovered the same since. It snaps like a twig nowadays and hurts worse each time. I scramble backwards, pulling my legs to my chest and readying myself to kick him if he comes much closer. He anticipates my response and belly laughs.

"They will kill you!" I cry out. He beats me again and again until the world feels hazy. That awfully familiar ringing noise calls out in my head, and I feel my heartbeat in my ears. My nose throbs unhappily, and my body aches from trying to shield myself. Soon, he tires and gives me a moment to recuperate. I take the risk of peeking up at him.

"Tell me," he hisses, snatching me by the shirt and pulling me close to him. "Whose fault is this?"

I glare at him with all my might through half-closed eyes. "You won't break me."

"Oh, baby, I thought you'd never challenge me!"

"Fuck you, Leo."

"Is that another challenge?" He smirks. My heart sinks as I realise what he means. Suddenly, he flips me back against him and grinds his growing erection into my ass. I scream loudly like my life depends on it. It distracts him enough to slam his hand over my mouth but it's better than travelling along my body.

"Shut the fuck up, bitch," he barks, and it sends awful shivers down me. The tears stream down my face and I helplessly look around at all the women in the room who pretend that nothing is happening. I cry out for them to help me, but of course, they don't. Part of me doesn't blame them either.

"Let's see what those cunts taught you then." I feel his horrible breath on my cheek. His hands try to tear my dress away but it's clumsy. I count down the moments and pray for the ground to swallow me whole. Everything in my life has led up to this moment— *the monster has me again.* Through tear-stained eyes, I stare out of the window to the garden, and I almost relax. I almost give up. It would be so easy to stop resisting and get it over and done with. There is no hope. Not against Leo. Maybe he was right all along— he will always win.

But then, something in my chest screams out for a fight. It's like I won't give up on myself. I channel my inner Dagger and force all the anger and rage to the surface. My elbow flies backwards, winding Leo before he can pull my dress up any higher. Then, I spin around and kick my foot into his stomach as he's still staggering away. He grunts but is much quicker, and charges at me. However, just as his fist connects with my face, the sound of shattering glass rings through the room, followed by terrified shrieks from the women.

My head snaps left and that's when I see them. *My lovers. My heroes.* Hope brims in my chest and I cry again but from relief. Leo startles and pulls away from me. He desperately tries to figure out the situation. Brandon snaps into action, he starts ushering the women out of the house, and they all gladly escape as fast as they can. Their whimpers slowly die out, and now, all I can hear is my pounding heart and Leo's heavy breathing. Leo takes a slow step backwards and for a moment, he considers running, but Dagger's head cocks to the side. His eyes are dead, and his nose wrinkles as if he is smelling fear. I can't help but smile at that beautiful crazy man.

"I told you they would come for me." I spit, feeling far braver. I fix my dress quickly to regain some composure. Then, I look back at the man who ruined my life. "Run. I dare you."

He does. The stupid fucking idiot thinks he's faster than Dagger. Within seconds, Dagger lurches out of the door after Leo. The man who brought me here pulls out the knife Dagger

WE SHOULDN'T

gave me and tries to attack Vixen, but my Vixen is much stronger and quicker. His hand shoots out and he grabs the man's neck before squeezing. The squelching and popping noise ring around the room. I expect myself to be disgusted, but I can't. Vixen snarls before snapping the man's neck in half— killing him instantly. More pimps flood into the room, taking me by surprise.

"Get out of here!" Vixen yells at me. My heart drops as five men carrying large knives start to circle around Vixen. I catch the nervous look in his eye. He rolls his shoulder as if to test if he's good enough to fight again, but winces, not fully recovered from the injury. There is no fucking doubt in my mind. I am *not* leaving him here to fight alone. I leap for a knife, and I throw myself onto the huge man closest to me. I wrap my legs around his back and sink my knife into his neck multiple times. He howls out in rage.

"No! Fuck!" Vixen hisses when he sees me. He moves so fucking fast, but so does the man I've stabbed. He throws me off him as if I weigh nothing and my back slams into the wall behind me and I cry out as the pain smacks me when I fall to the floor. My vision is dizzy for a moment. I desperately try to find the man I'm fighting, but he appears too fucking fast in front of my face. I roll over and shoot my legs out to keep him at some distance. He slashes the knife in front of my face, missing me by centimetres. I cry out in fear and look to Vixen helplessly, but he's too busy taking on three of them at once. He notices me and tries desperately to get to me, but they keep us apart.

My legs tremble under the man's weight. He flashes his disgusting teeth at me in an awful smile and leans more on me. He is so fucking heavy. *Too* heavy. I beg my body to keep pushing, but I'm exhausted. It just won't keep him up anymore. Just as my legs go to give out, a knife shoots through the man's chest. I scream as the man's eyes grow large and he frantically grabs at his chest which now the knife has been pulled from. I scramble away as the large man collapses in a heap where I just was. Mortified, I stare up at Brandon who clutches the knife that killed my attacker. His eyes are so fucking dark, and he is murderous. He scans me quickly, checking for any wounds, before quickly turning to help Vixen in the fight. Another three pimps file in, and I keep my distance this time, so as not to distract the men. The pimps have no fucking chance against the men I love, and they are quickly all defeated.

Soon, Brandon's arms are wrapped around my chest. He yanks me close to him and tries to pull me out of the building.

"Wait! What about Dagger?" I cry out. Brandon huffs and throws me over his shoulder. "He'll follow."

"Go!" Vixen pushes us out, holding his knife up to some more men who have filed in. Brandon races away and quickly throws me in the car. Vixen is close behind us and slides in too. Mortified, I stare out of the window, and I spot a pile of dead bodies. Then, I see a face I recognise. *Leo.* He is under a pile of three men, but his face is perfectly positioned in my direction. Blood trails out of his mouth, and he struggles to breathe. He chokes a couple of times, spluttering blood all down another man's back. I wait for the horror to sink in. For regret and agony to hit me— all the self-aggressive thoughts he taught me to have, but nothing comes. If anything, I feel myself smiling. It's incredibly fucked up, but I can't help myself. A laugh falls from my lips. It's one of relief and hope, that my nightmare has finally ended.

In the distance, I hear the wail of sirens. Then, the car door slams. My heart leaps out of my chest and I twist around, expecting to see an attacker. Instead, Dagger slides, and throws his seatbelt on. He grins and licks at the blood splattered across his face. His eyes are still dark and dangerous, but he looks different. *Feels* different.

Brandon starts the car and races down the road. He reaches back and grabs some wipes before throwing them at Dagger.

WE SHOULDN'T

"Wipe yourself down. The police can't see you like this."

Dagger roars with laughter as he yanks out multiple wipes. He is almost unrecognisable in his laugh. It's so full of light and love, and even his eyes seem brighter. He runs the wipe down his face, stares at the blood which smudges onto the wipe, and howls out another laugh.

It's Vixen who checks on him. "You good, brother?"

"Am I good? I am fucking amazing!" he roars. "Do you know how good it feels to kill bad people?"

I choke on the breath in my chest. He says it with such enthusiasm. "Do you know how good it is to slaughter the man who has hurt my little freak?"

Vixen ruffles Dagger's head that now falls on him happily. The sound of Dagger's happiness fills the car, and I even catch a ghost of a smile on Brandon's lips as he watches his brother in the rear review mirror. I reach out and squeeze his leg. He turns to me, but the joy vanishes. I can feel him inspecting the bruises and marks on me.

"I'm fine," I tell him.

His jaw is tense. "You got in the car— you disobeyed me, and you got hurt."

"But I'm fine now."

"But you might not have been." He is *so* fucking angry at me. My stomach flips and I feel guilty, like a scolded child.

"You disobeyed me, Rebecca." His eyes harden. "You shouldn't have fucking done that. You put yourself at risk. You went to an unknown place. You purposely ignored our instructions. Do you know how fucking stupid that was?"

I hold my breath and keep my head low.

He pauses for a second before releasing a long sigh. "But you also saved dozens of women who are now with the police. And you helped us solve this shitty case. So, thank you."

My head snaps towards him suddenly. He is already looking at me intently. "But if you ever do that again—"

"I won't!" I yelp a little too quickly. "I promise you!"

He bites his tongue before reaching out and gripping my thigh. It's dominant and reassuring all at once. My heart flips in my chest.

When we get back to their flat, the mood instantly changes from hysterical to something much more intense.

"Strip," Brandon barks, circling me like a beast around the prey. With a gulp, I quickly obey him. I shy away when they spot the marks and bruises on my body, but Vixen holds my hands back to stop me. I feel his hot breath against my cheek, and I melt into him. "We are going to kiss every part of you that he touched. Do you understand? You are ours. No other man has the right to touch our property."

My body is instantly alight at the thought. I nod quickly and it takes everything in me not to scream *'yes please'*.

Dagger drops to his knees, and he starts on the red mark on my thigh. I tremble when his tongue darts out and tastes the slow-forming bruise. Then, I feel Vixen's lips on my neck and in my hair. I melt back into him. Brandon kisses my arms, and soon my body is screaming for more. I frantically try to undress them each, much to their amusement. They smirk and do it for me and I gawp at their large cocks that promise me so much pleasure. I feel them attack my body with their kisses and tongues, and soon, I'm shaking so fucking much. Every inch has been replaced with their touch— a*nd I've never been so fucking thankful.*

There is no time for foreplay. We each need each other instantly, as though to fuck out the anger and the fear of almost losing one another.

Dagger gently pushes me onto my hands and knees, and Brandon slides between me. He positions in line with my pussy, and Dagger pushes into my ass. The pain is instantly replaced with unimaginable pleasure when their fingers jump to my clit. I slowly ride up and down, earning delicious groans. Then, I reach out to Vixen. Never removing my eyes from his, I bring his cock to my lips and wrap my tongue around it. His delicious pre-cum sweeps through me and I tighten around the cocks below me. Vixen holds me still and starts thrusting in time with Brandon. I hollow out my cheeks and suck faster on Vixen's cock, and his low growls only spur me on.

"That's it, you dirty little whore, show my brothers how well you can cum for us." Vixen growls. It sends me over the edge, and before I know it, I'm screaming my release. Brandon's hot cum shoots into my pussy, and it slams another wave of orgasms through me. I fall forward, and Vixen's cock slams the back of my throat. He cums instantly and I desperately lick it all up. At the same time, Dagger roars his orgasm and fills my ass up with his hot seed. I push back on him, milking everything he has to give me. The pleasure rocks through my body and I can't help smiling madly.

It's so wrong to fuck my dad's best friend, my stalker, and a murderer; but how can it be sinful when they fill me up so fucking perfectly?

EPILOGUE

Rebecca

One month later.

I smother my pink dress down with my clammy hands. The excitement races through me, and I can't stop smiling. At the front of the altar, Brandon stands in his dark suit, hands behind his back. He stands next to my dad, and they are lost in happy chatter. They both look so carefree and joyous. My dad looks so handsome in his navy-blue wedding suit, and he rocks back and forth on his feet nervously. Brandon casts me a small smile over his shoulder and I can't help the huge smile on my lips.

The music starts and we all stand. On the other side of the aisle, Sara is clutching Andrew. She blubbers just as pathetically as me at the sweet sight. The way she is standing makes her swollen belly protrude. Joy and happiness consume me as everything falls perfectly into place.

When I turn to face Cheryl slowly walking down the aisle, I can't help but sniffle up tears. She looks so beautiful, clutching onto her elderly father's arm. When she sees me, she smiles, and it sets the tears that I've been desperately fighting for a solid minute.

Gently, Dagger's hand slips into mine and he tries to reassure me. In his other hand, he clutches a signed copy of my most recent novel that he hasn't let go of since I gifted it to him this morning. That beautiful, crazy smile hasn't left either— he even tried to convince me to leave the ceremony early to listen to him read. My heart swelled with joy; I promised him that we would do it tonight. I also feel Vixen's hand on my lower back. I keep both men close and try to control my ridiculous surges of joy.

Soon, Cheryl joins my dad at the front of the ceremony. When he sees her, he explodes into tears which only pushes me over the edge again. They read their vows, staring lovingly into one another's eyes. My dad smiles brighter than he's done in years, and it's at this moment, that I realise everything is going to be alright. My dad has found happiness. My best friend is starting a family. And I have three perfect brothers wrapped around me for now and eternity.

THE END

BOOKS BY THIS AUTHOR

Please Don't Make Me Kill Him

I fell in love with the man I was supposed to kill, and the man who wants to kill me. Both relationships are forbidden, but I've always craved sin. Must I choose only one, or can I have both?

Isla
Being a killer is scorched into my DNA. I infiltrate my target's lives to gain information about them before I make my fatal hit, all in the name of profit. For twenty years, I never made an error. And then Lucius's name appeared on my hit list. I never anticipated that he would teach me that life without sin is incredibly delicious. And now I must choose between his love and my mission.

Titan
Isla Morris is as good as dead. One day, I will crush that pretty little monster, and I will give my murdered family the justice they deserve. She will regret the day she ever missed my name from her hit list. But first, I want to play with her as much as she played with my family. Her dark love is tasty, but I hunger for her ruin even more.

Illegal Activities

After Maya is freed from the Russian Mafia prison, she falls into the arms of another Mafia boss- Alessio Morisso. She swore that she would never become a prisoner again, but after stirring up a war with her feisty and sarcastic attitude, she is no longer safe to return home. The only way to ensure her survival is to marry Alessio.

However, beautiful and bold Maya will not be an obedient little housewife. On the contrary, she wishes for control and to escape. But when the lines blur between wanting to escape and desiring her new husband, Maya finds herself doubting everything she knew about herself.
Could she really resist his charms or must she join forces with him to take revenge against the Russians?

Mr Anderson

It is scandalous. It is forbidden. And yet it feels so right!

When Willow is forced to return to University after a tragic incident, the school assigns her a tutor to get her back on track. This tutor, Mr. Anderson, is everything Willow tries so desperately to avoid: dangerous, unpredictable and completely irresistible.
Despite the risks, Willow finds herself head over heels for the gorgeous man with the mysterious past, and very quickly learns that nothing is as it seems.
As she battles her intense attraction for her tutor and the chaotic life events unravelling around her, she is forced to solve the one question she cannot answer no matter how hard she tries: who really is Mr. Anderson?

Delphi Deceived

I am cursed for eternity.
He is using me for his personal gain.
There should be nothing erotic between enemies. And yet there is.

Roughly six centuries ago, a war wrecked chaos in the kingdom of Heaven and Hell. Laws were written in the blood of those fallen in a desperate cry for peace. Restrict the Original Beings, force them into submission, and no more war or suffering would occur.

Ideal on paper. A death sentence for Delphi, the High Priestess of time and fortune.

And then things got worse for her.

Kidnapped by Power, the God of strength and power, she is forced to help him on a dangerous mission he refuses to disclose. Power is an allusive, mysterious, and ruthless Original Being, and nothing will get in the way of what he wants.
Even if that includes Delphi herself.

Printed in Poland
by Amazon Fulfillment
Poland Sp. z o.o., Wrocław